MICHAEL J. MCLAUGHLIN

EXTINCTION

This novel is a work of fiction. Names, characters, corporations, institutions, organizations, places, and incidents are products of the author's imagination, or, if real, are used fictitiously without any intent to describe the actual conduct of any entity or individual.

Cover illustrations designed by Taylor Cotton.

To Kristin, for far too much to list.

TABLE OF CONTENTS

EXTINCTION

PROLOGUE

“We are in search of the pivot point that converts thriving to dying and initiates the series of events leading to extinction.”

– Mark Brozine, PhD

1

TAIMYR PENINSULA, SIBERIA
13,000 BC

The initial approach of the beast was imperceptible.

The Northern Lights twisted eerie purple and green hues across the Arctic sky. Rivers arising from the mouths of glaciers intersected, partitioning the tundra into boggy fragments. The sea bordering the peninsula, now swelling from the melting polar ice cap, swallowed the shoreline.

The first ripple emerged. It released the shore, cut across the liquid onyx, and fused with the night. Another followed. One was accompanied by a vibration along the riverbank, and the next by the dull thunder of flesh against frozen ground.

Fragments of ice and dirt shook loose from the riverbanks and sank through a web of channels until joining the subterranean pockets of chocolate slush that gnawed at the overlying surface.

Grass crunched under massive legs. Icicles rattled in a mesh of entangled hair.

They once dominated this region, spreading out as far west as modern-day Ireland and as far east as the United States. Four million years of evolution enabled them to conquer this inhospitable environment. A few thousand years of destruction would leave them extinct.

EXTINCTION

The mammoth stood at the edge of a thin crust of ground overlying a sinkhole.

Mud lapped at the walls of the cavern just a few feet below, slurping and belching, eager to claim its prey. The next step cracked the frozen crust. The surface splintered. The ground cascaded down into the frosty cauldron. Front legs slid forward. Hind legs buckled beneath five tons of weight. Disoriented and off balance, groaning in pain, the creature crashed through the earth.

The mammoth thrashed through the muddy slush for a nonexistent foothold. Titanic tusks slammed against the slippery walls of the sinkhole. The mud latched onto the beast and began to drag it down. Legs and body submerged. The head followed. Groans dampened into gurgles within the incessant churning of the cauldron. A rush of air bubbled up between the tusks. Majestic ivory spirals corkscrewed into the muddy slush.

Within a few minutes there was no remaining evidence that the mammoth ever existed. The creature would lie there, frozen and preserved, untouched for fifteen thousand years.

2

TAIMYR PENINSULA, SIBERIA
2002 AD

The pain penetrated Mark Brozine's legs like a chainsaw. His right knee. His left hip. Just about everywhere else in between.

He was trying to walk from his bunk to the shower. That's all. He hoped that the warmth of the water might relieve the agony in his legs, but now he questioned whether he could even reach the shower. The sleeping quarters in the mammoth research station were small. Normally just a few steps would traverse the room, but not now.

Every step seemed to take minutes as he recruited the strength and courage to continue. His body wanted to go back and lie down – anything to ease the suffering. But he was determined not to let the project down. This expedition was a once in a lifetime event for a comparative zoologist. Nothing was going to come between him and this opportunity, no matter how much it hurt.

He looked down at his legs in search of an explanation. There was nothing to see. No bruises. No swelling. He almost wanted to see something. They were still the same muscular legs that had carried him through triathlons back home, at least on the outside. On the inside something was wrong. Horribly wrong.

A jump rope was draped over his bedpost. Cross-country skis and poles were wedged beneath his bed. The photograph of

Nancy in her red Christmas sweater was the only color in the windowless room.

What happened? The first three months in Siberia were fine. Then the pain just started without any apparent reason. It felt like something was eating away at his bones. Within just three days the pain crippled him.

The impact of the pain, the metallic taste of fear, and the smell of disinfectant – the Lysol that they used on Solnorov's mattress after the body was removed – all combined in a wave of nausea that rose up within him. He swallowed hard and took a deep breath.

He was going to get better, had to get better. Could he feel any worse? But he did feel worse, day after day. Yesterday was nothing compared to this. Today land mines were detonating frequently, almost simultaneously, in his bones.

What was happening to him? Was there any way to stop this?

He heard the soft crackling noise of someone stepping on corn flakes, or else he felt it inside.

He was frozen in the middle of the room, trembling. Every direction looked like a distant shore to a drowning man. Should he go back toward his bed? Should he push forward? Either way, he might have to crawl. Sweat poured down his face and dripped onto the floor. His right knee started to buckle, about to collapse. The support was completely gone.

Suddenly, the bones in his right lower leg shattered like a vase dropped on a marble floor. He heard a slurp, a crunch, and a rip. Denial that such a noise could actually be coming from a human being's legs, let alone his own legs, registered in his mind a millisecond before the sensation accompanying the sound. The lower portion of the bone tented up the overlying flesh, stabbed through the skin, and tore open his pants. He didn't have to look to know what had happened.

Blood sprayed the wall.

Mark's body twisted instinctively in search of support but found none. His entire weight crashed across the defective remnants of his legs, which jutted out at distorted angles. Something in his back snapped loudly as his limp form plummeted to the floor.

The pain mercifully rendered him unconscious, unaware of the number of fractures that were occurring simultaneously throughout his body.

Mark Brozine would never wake up.

PART 1.
CHANGE IN ENVIRONMENT

"Even a seemingly imperceptible change in the environment can have a profound impact on a species, from the most simple to the most complex. The effects intensify exponentially with greater degrees of change."

– Aniello Bonacci, PhD

3

MANHATTAN MEMORIAL HOSPITAL
NEW YORK CITY

"Is he conscious?"

The words passed through the recesses of Drew Chambers' brain. They slid into the mental storage area between awareness and memory, the place where the last few words of a dream lodged after a sudden awakening from an alarm clock. Just close enough to sense, but too far to grasp, too far to interact.

He was unable to speak. He couldn't move, couldn't feel anything. That was it, more than anything. He couldn't feel. It was as though an acrylic shell was lining his entire body, separating him from the rest of the world.

The smell was so familiar.

"Doctor Chambers?"

"Can you hear me?"

"Are you all right?"

"Doctor Chambers?"

Drew waited for the boy to appear again. The boy with broken arms and legs. No face, just broken arms and legs. It wasn't for lack of trying that Drew never saw a face.

It was pine needles that he smelled.

There he was. This time his arms were wrapped in splints. His left leg was covered in a cast, and his right leg was encircled by an external fixator consisting of metal bars and screws. There was no face, not even a torso. Just four broken limbs crisscrossing in the center.

The boy was about seven years old. There was no way to tell from what was visible, but Drew knew. He stared at the center, looking for a face.

The acrylic shell was coming from inside his head. The boy was inside his head. They were nothing more than products of his imagination. But he wasn't going crazy. If he were crazy, he wouldn't be able to tell the difference between reality and his imagination. There was no question that this was not reality. He knew that, so he wasn't going crazy.

Someone held his arm.

"He seems like he can hear us now," a voice said from somewhere between where he was and where he was going.

He wanted to speak to the boy, but time was running out. The broken limbs were dissolving.

Drew smelled the faint burning scent of the electrocautery. The bright lights and blue drapes of the operating room were coming into focus. He was standing at the operating room table near the lower thigh incision. The broken femur was visible at the base of the leg wound. The orthopedic resident was holding the metal rod, standing at attention and waiting for direction.

"Daddy," The boy's voice was somewhere on the other side, somewhere out of reach. "Stay with me, Daddy."

Drew looked across the patient at the scrub nurse. One eyebrow was raised in shock, and the other was twisted with a pained expression. She had pulled the instrument tray back from the operating table and was resting her arms across it as though she would fight anyone who tried to resume the operation.

A hand came around Drew's face and wiped the sweat from his forehead with a gauze pad. The air felt cool on his skin. The shell was gone.

"Are you all right?" one of the nurses whispered in his ear.

Drew wasn't sure if he could speak, so he gave several rapid but abbreviated nods. He stretched his fingers and then made a fist a few times, as though restoring the circulation after being in the cold.

He looked up at the clock. How much time had passed?

4

GLOBAL INVESTORS HEADQUARTERS
NEW YORK CITY

Thorton Grovely was sorting through his mental catalogue of lies.

He checked his Rolex, not for the time, which was only a minute later than the last time he looked, but for something to do while he waited. The pill in his stomach was bouncing like a pinball. He ran a soft fingertip along his forehead, intercepting a bead of sweat dangling below his razor-precise, blonde, Caesaresque locks. Gaines still had his back to him.

Troy Gaines, CEO of Global Investors, stood before a full-length window, his hands cinched down against his hips. The sun seemed to radiate from the periphery of his chiseled features like the outlines of a saint in a Venetian painting. Even the occasional speckle of gray hair that heralded the end of his thirties was the result of artistic strokes, rather than a flaw of the aging process.

These were only a few of the reasons why Grovely hated his boss more every day. But today he was going to play Gaines ... iolin.

... view of Central Park was always impressive from ... n the top floor of the Steinway, but the morning ... e fall foliage today in a way that was particularly ... hen faced the autumn spectacular, but neither focused on the view. Gaines was listening patiently to his wire-thin phone headset, and Grovely was imagining digging a curved, jewel emblazoned dagger into Gaines' back.

Grovely's crisis was about to take center stage. There was no other reason why Wonderboy would have called him into his office. He must have heard about Siberia.

Grovely tried to pace the room without looking like he was pacing, without revealing his anxiety over the matter at hand and his frustration over having to wait. He stopped momentarily in front of Gaines' diploma wall, the framed crimson and white wallpaper that made up the "shrine to me." The undergraduate diploma was from Harvard. The MBA was from Harvard. Even a plaque recognizing "Ecologically Sound Business Practices" was emblazoned with the Veritas shield and laurels. It must be nice getting handed the business world on a crimson platter.

Play him like a violin, Grovely told himself.

Grovely enjoyed any opportunity to get the best of Gaines. Global wouldn't be anywhere without Grovely's management of the scientific technology sector, and that was just the information that appeared in the stockholders' annual reports. If Gaines knew even a fraction of what Grovely had going on, he'd fall over backwards. It was so easy if you knew what you were doing. All it took was some street smarts, something you couldn't read in an Ivy League textbook. Mr. Clean would never have a clue.

Gaines was still silent on the phone. Typical. He would listen as though your comments were born of divine inspiration, but then when it was his turn to speak, the conversation would last less than a minute. Almost every sentence would begin with the word "I." Didn't anyone else notice that? Why didn't he get under everyone else's skin? All the PR people, all the business journalists, all the idiots voting for the awards. Apparently not.

Gaines would be succinct and convincing, and he would close the deal. Every time.

There was a squawk from the corner of the room. It was Gaines' African Grey Parrot – one of the most intelligent species in the world, capable of learning 1,000 vocabulary words. Gaines wouldn't settle for anything less. A genius bird. But you only speak 250 words, don't you? Stupid bird. Grovely walked toward the cage; maybe he would have some amusement today after all.

The bird cocked its head. It had to hate Grovely as much as he hated it, as much as he hated almost everything.

Grovely made soft kissing noises as he pulled a rubber band from his pocket. Here birdie birdie birdie. His lip curled at the corner. He reached to the edge of the cage and grabbed a seed. The bird squawked again and took a stab at Grovely with its beak, causing him to lurch back.

A glance at Gaines. Still on the phone. He hadn't heard.

"I think you raise excellent points, Karl," Gaines said, "but I see the situation a little differently."

Grovely moved in closer to the bird while listening to Gaines begin his minute-long acquisition. He spread the rubber band with a thumb and index finger and drew it back with the seed inside. He aimed the seed at the bird. Then he transferred some of the tension he was experiencing into the rubber band. The bird tilted its head again as the rubber band twanged free and the seed propelled forward.

The seed struck the bird so hard in the head that it reeled back off its perch. Grovely's satisfaction was tempered initially by the fear that he had actually killed his boss' prize possession. The bird stood up, still dazed. Grovely leaned his face in close enough to line up each eye between pairs of cage bars and smiled his only genuine smile of the day.

Grovely thought through his explanation of the last days' events in preparation for his impending conversation with Gaines. He would go with the "We have a problem" approach – brief, to the point. If he caught Gaines off-guard, he could steer the conversation. He had learned from past mistakes. If Gaines could steal the glory of Global's financial victories, he would also have to take the fall for the disaster developing in Siberia.

Play him like a violin.

Grovely sank into one of the leather chairs beside a jade and ivory inlaid coffee table. As always, a platter of pastries from Giordano's Bakery sat in the center. Gaines never ate pastries. He had never been seen eating anything. The pastries were for visiting clients and were replaced by a fresh platter every few hours.

There was a jelly thumbprint on the pastry platter.

He looked away, across the office, which seemed even smaller from a seated position. A fifteenth century Italian armored helmet called for battle from within its glass case. A Samurai sword hung on the wall over the entrance to the room. Each represented an acquisition abroad.

The smell of pastry fillings nauseated Grovely. The jellies and cinnamon weren't so bad, but the creams and cheeses were intolerable. How many hands had already touched them? How long had they been sitting out? He could see the bacteria oozing out in a stream of blueberry filling. He could smell it spoiling the vanilla cream. His saliva evaporated. The sides of his throat stuck together. He tapped the manicured nails of his left index finger and thumb together ten times, and then did the same with his right hand. The feeling in his throat improved.

Grovely tried not to focus on the pastries. Instead, he looked at a New York Magazine cover framed on the wall. Gaines was on the cover holding a globe in one hand and a red apple in the other. His tie knot should have been more symmetrical, and his black prep school hair should have been parted more evenly. Wasn't he embarrassed to be photographed like that?

Gaines turned momentarily, covered the telephone mouthpiece with one hand, and gestured for Grovely to have a pastry. Grovely's eyes followed the hand motion. Mold was growing as thick as a moss on the surface of an éclair. He mustered a "no thanks" wave to Gaines, who shrugged and turned back toward the window. He tapped the index finger and thumb nails together ten times with both hands simultaneously, but he didn't feel any better.

Grovely struggled to his feet and backed up toward the doorway. The giant silver Samurai sword hung menacingly over his head. Curvilinear etchings along the handle depicted dragons among diminutive but threatening images of warriors. The etchings were worn from use, and the blade was tainted with a crimson hue that matched the diplomas on the adjacent wall.

Gaines removed the telephone headpiece. His back was still toward Grovely.

Grovely swallowed repeatedly, even audibly once or twice, against the feeling of cement hardening in his throat. He opened his mouth to deliver the "We have a problem" speech.

Like a violin.

Gaines spoke without turning around from the window. "Grovely, we have a problem."

5

MANHATTAN MEMORIAL HOSPITAL
NEW YORK CITY

"It happened in the O.R. this time."

Drew Chambers sat in the office of his department chairman and longtime friend, Doctor Reed Watley, like a confessed killer waiting for sentencing.

Drew had bags under his eyes and a fresh indentation left by the surgical cap on his forehead. Rubbing the indentation, he remembered that his hair must still be sticking out in several directions like black patches of crab grass. He patted the top – worse than he thought. It was hard to convince yourself, let alone those around you, that you really weren't going crazy when you so perfectly looked the part.

"I heard," Watley said. He looked at Drew from head to foot, squinting a few times. "What happened?"

"Same as before," Drew said. "I saw him. I saw Matty."

Watley winced. He was the same age as Drew, but his hairline was receded. His chest expanded with a deep breath as he searched for something to say. He avoided making eye contact with his friend. He fumbled with the items on his desk instead.

"It wasn't exactly like him," Drew said. "It was more like a Picasso painting of his arms and legs."

Watley fidgeted in his chair while running a finger along the top of a picture frame on his desk. When the two of them gazed simultaneously toward the frame, Watley pulled his hand back as though he had received a shock.

Drew looked around, as though expecting to see the boy right there. "It's almost impossible to describe the experience to you. It's like I'm in two places at once. One is real. The other isn't. But I keep choosing to look at the one that's not real."

Drew was still looking at the back of the picture frame. All of the photographs on the desk were turned away from him. He was pretty sure that they were usually turned the other way, and that a few of them were missing. Watley must have known that he was on his way over and didn't want to provide any reminders.

"I lose the feeling in my body when it happens," Drew said.

"Maybe you should be reevaluated by the neurologist if you're experiencing numbness," Watley said.

"It's not numbness like that," Drew said. "The sensation is there. It's just turned off somewhere in my head. It's as though my brain is choosing not to feel anything."

Watley frowned. He was trying to understand.

"I heard his voice this time," Drew said. He wondered what he would think if he was on the other side of the desk, hearing a friend talk about hearing voices.

"What..." Watley started. He seemed as though he was about to ask what Matty said, but he stopped short. He lowered his eyes and swallowed.

"Anyway, I think we both know what this means," Drew said. "It's not safe for me to be in the operating room anymore. I'm withdrawing from my surgery privileges at the hospital. I've been spending about 80% of my time in the laboratory anyway. Now I'll just do my research fulltime, and maybe put more effort into launching the foundation."

"There must be other options," Watley said. "What about going back to the psychiatrist?"

Drew shook his head. "Been there done that. What are they going to say this time, Reed? They can label it whatever they want, but they're not going to get him out of my head."

"You shouldn't get him out of your head," Watley said. "But you need to get rid of this Picasso painting, as you called it."

"I can't," Drew said. "I've tried, believe me, but I can't. I have to stop operating. I'm not safe like this."

Watley leaned back, folded his hands together as though praying, and tapped his index fingers against his lips. He shook his head, then nodded, as though losing an argument to himself.

"Listen Drew," he said, leaning forward again, resting his forearms on the desk. "We went to medical school together. We did our residencies together." He paused but seemed obligated to proceed. "Our families were like one family, for Chrissakes."

"Then say what you need to say, Reed," Drew said.

Watley delivered the blow with a pained expression. "I've been through this with the administration a thousand times. I know what they're going to say. They don't care that you were once the department's rising star. They don't get the potential of your work. The bottom line is your research isn't bringing in enough funding on its own to support your position in the department. If you lose even the few surgical cases that you've been doing recently, there's no way they're going to let you stay on board."

"I understand," Drew said. "I know this isn't your decision. I've been a lead weight in the department ever since Linda left."

Drew tried to think back to Linda, their lives together with Matty, their dreams for the future, but he never made it back that far; there was just too much in the way. Instead, his memory veered off course, following his downward spiral, flashing snapshots of his subconscious escape into the laboratory, his inability to invest energy in any form of social interaction, and his resolution to pay penance for experiencing life beyond that point. All of the psychobabble that proved correct the more he thought about it. The guilt of outliving his son pulsed through his bloodstream and ate away at his world, eventually driving his wife away and dismantling his career.

"Actually, it is my decision," Watley said. "That's what's killing me. In the end it has to be my decision. But my hands are tied here. Between the board of directors and the dean's office..."

"What if I could get more research funding?" Drew asked.

"I don't think I could stall the administration long enough," Watley said. "We played that card when you were getting started on the surface protein receptor project."

"And it paid dividends to the hospital," Drew said.

"Of course, it did," Watley said. "They got great PR from your surface protein and genetic engineering work. And someday the research might pave the way to curing otherwise untreatable bone diseases. But the administration has a 'what have you done for me lately' attitude. There's no way around that."

The smell of burned popcorn came from outside in the hall. Watley's nose twitched. Normally one of them would have made a joke about the smell. But Drew was out of jokes and small talk, and Watley knew better.

"I appreciate your efforts," Drew said. "I can only imagine what you've gone through on my behalf." He shook his head with conviction. "But there's no way I'm going back into the operating room. I'm just not going to place my patients at risk."

Drew stood up and shook Watley's hand.

"But what are you going to do?" Watley asked, not releasing his grip.

"Find a way to survive," Drew said.

6

EMPIRE STATE BUILDING
NEW YORK CITY

From this spot he could see all of Manhattan. From this spot he owned Manhattan.

Thorton Grovely stood just inside the observation deck of the Empire State Building. The vantage point from the eighty-sixth floor left the surrounding buildings dwarfed. The filthy vagrants and honking cars and urine stenches were somewhere far below, out of sight, sound, and smell.

He waved his hand out across the top of the city and then curled his fingers closed, one after another, into a tight fist. He imagined grasping everything before him in his hand.

He took his cellular phone out; it was time to make his call.

He stopped short when he spotted his reflection in the glass boundary that kept suicidal and homicidal lunatics from succeeding. Rising up above the city, floating in the sky before him was a well-tailored refined display of perfection. The suit was crisp. The tie was held securely into a perfectly centered position with a gold chain. A slight turn of the chain eliminated a kink and made for a smoother arc. The blonde ringlets curving down along his forehead were of equal thickness and evenly aligned.

The wind rushed against the observation window. Grovely closed his eyes and absorbed the power of everything around him.

It was the Grovely equivalent of skiing down a vertical slope, or bungee jumping from a bridge. He was surging, filled with power, but power balanced with control. He had come up here to restore the control in his life. This was the perfect escape from his torments below.

"Beautiful, isn't it." The voice came from somewhere behind him.

Grovely turned toward the direction of the intrusion and saw an old woman. She was smiling at him and squinting from the sun.

"I love the view of New York from up here," she said. Crevasses recessed into the shadows under the pull of her facial expression. Meaty fingers clutched the tan shawl wrapped around her neck.

At first Grovely ignored her. Then, when it was obvious that she would not leave without an answer from him, he cleared his throat. "Please get away from me," he said.

Disappointed, she made her way through the doorway out onto the observatory.

Grovely looked out the window again, but the view was lacking something that was there just a few moments earlier. He pressed the redial button on his phone.

The same idiot woman answered. "Manhattan Memorial Hospital, Department of Orthopedics."

"Hello," Grovely said with strained civility. "Is Doctor Chambers in?"

"No, he's not. Is this Mister Grovel-lee again?" She rhymed the first part of his name with the word 'novel.' Her mispronunciation might have been intentional and annoyed the hell out of him. "I left your other messages for him."

He patted down the area at the back of his head where his hair was thinning ever so slightly, unknown to everyone but him.

"It's pronounced Grovely, as in orange grove," he said. He turned slightly to view his hair in the reflecting glass. It was perfect.

"I'll leave him another message," she said. She obviously didn't care about the pronunciation of his name, and she probably didn't care much for him. "He may be in the operating room, but I can page him if you like."

"Just leave a message and let him know it's important," he said. He took pleasure in the audible click that killed her voice, mid-sentence, as he ended the call.

The city was gray. Traffic slithered through the streets below like a thousand hungry snakes. Grovely sensed his troubles rising up along the drab stone buildings and mingling with the foul stench in the air as the gusts of wind died down.

7

MANHATTAN MEMORIAL HOSPITAL
NEW YORK CITY

Why were they so interested in him all of a sudden?

Drew Chambers was tilted back in his chair with five pink telephone message slips fanned out in his hand like playing cards. Thorton Grovely's name was on each one. Five of a kind.

His feet rested on a mountain of paperwork – the trails of bills, the marble laboratory notebooks, and partially completed grant applications – concealing a desk somewhere below. The landslide reached the floor, covering years of root beer stains and embedded pretzel crumbs.

A data sheet on the computer screen flashed before transforming into a screensaver image. Old Faithful shot steam one hundred feet into a blue sky. Snow rested on the branches of pine trees in the background.

Outside the crusted windows of the orthopedics laboratory, fifteen stories down, a siren overrode the white noise of traffic and car horns surrounding Manhattan Memorial Hospital.

A knock on the door nearly sent Drew toppling backwards. He grasped the bookcase behind him and righted his chair.

He crumbled the pink slips and threw them on top of an overstuffed trashcan, where they dangled precariously. He was in no mood to speak to Mr. Grovely today.

Cathy Patterson, the director of the "Matty's Hope" foundation, stuck her head in. A strand of sunlight found the edges of her jack-o-lantern broach and reflected against one of her red curls. She smiled and held her hand up in a stationary wave.

Cathy's eyes slid down the paper cascade and then scanned the room. She gradually turned 360 degrees, looking from floor to ceiling, taking in the surroundings – the chipped black countertops, the blood-stained rat dissection mats, and the rows of incubators. Her nose twitched. Her eyes widened. She wrapped herself in her arms as though suppressing a shudder. She could just as easily have stumbled into the lair of the Phantom of the Opera. *So, this is where he lives. This is where he hides from the daylight.*

"If there was good news from Empire State Bank, I bet you would have yelled it all the way down the hall," he asked.

She bit on the corner of her lip. "Well, yes," she started. "That news came first thing this morning. They seem to be interested in the foundation, they really do, but they're not ready to make a commitment, at least not through next year."

The loss of a financial commitment from Empire State Bank eliminated any possible future for Matty's Hope, but Cathy was still thinking a year ahead.

"Five years of working together and your optimism still never ceases to amaze me," he said.

Cathy didn't answer. Her gaze was transfixed on the photograph of Drew and Matty on the desk.

The frame was shining silver, the only object in the room that wasn't embedded in dust. The photograph captured all of the color of spring. The Drew Chambers in the photograph was a little chubby. There were no gray hairs sticking out from beneath his Yankees cap, no frown lines.

The boy in the photograph was laughing hard enough that you could hear it. He sat on the steps of a brownstone building.

Lump-laden attenuated legs connected the dots from his shorts to his sneakers. White plastic splints contributed most of the substance to his arms. He pointed at his Mets hat while Drew feigned an attempt to conceal the emblem with his hand.

Cathy dragged her stare away from the photograph. She seemed to be breathing a little faster.

"That's not the only reason you're here, is it?" Drew asked.

She shook her head, avoiding eye contact.

"You want to know if the rumors are true," he said.

She looked up at him. "I heard what happened in the operating room." If a facial expression could wipe away pain and erase loss, this one had a chance.

"I can't believe I did that to a patient," he said.

"The patient is fine," she said.

"That's not the point," he said. He reached up and grabbed a handful of his hair, suspending his arm by it. "This patient ended up being all right. But what about the next, or the one after that?"

She took a step closer. She stopped. Her mouth opened and then closed again.

"I can't operate anymore," he said. He looked up at the ceiling, exhaling slowly through pursed lips.

"For now," she said.

Forever, he thought. Instead, he said, "The rumors you've probably heard about the laboratory are true." He recounted his conversation with Watley.

"How could they do that to you?" she asked.

He shrugged and said, "They are. Listen, I want to speak with you about the foundation. I have to admit that I don't see how we will ever get the project off the ground. The Empire State Bank partnership was our last shot. We barely have enough left to pay you a salary for the next few months, and then there won't be anything left. Now that I'm losing my hospital privileges and laboratory, our office is soon to follow."

"I can take a temporary pay cut," she said. "I've got the rent and the tuition covered for a while."

"You can't do that again," he said. "You've taken care of my family. And all those other families. Now you have your own daughter to think about. I know this comes as a huge blow for you. In a lot of ways, the foundation is a part of you."

She was one of Matty's ICU nurses at the end. She stayed with him, stayed with Drew and Linda, long after others in the ICU drifted away, after they began averting their gaze from the dehumanized collection of tubes and machinery while passing by.

It was Cathy who had convinced Drew to start Matty's Hope, a foundation devoted to bone research and funding for families of children with incurable bone diseases. Cathy then convinced the hospital administration to provide the initial financial support. She resigned from her ICU position to manage the foundation's PR and fundraising efforts full time.

"I appreciate all the effort you've put into the foundation," he said. "I know how much you love this project, and how much you believe in it. It's hard to give up something you love so much." He paused. He hadn't meant to put it that way.

"It's your passion," she said. "Don't give up on it."

"Sometimes I wonder if the wrong passion is guiding me. Maybe it's just all revenge. Like it's not a love for the foundation, but a need to avenge Matty's death." He paused, waiting for her to disagree with him, to set him straight. She was silent. "A project born out of hatred, no matter how lofty the goal, is doomed to fail."

He watched the acceptance of defeat appear in her eyes. The expression was unmistakable to him. He saw it in the mirror every morning when he shaved. It was captured in the photograph on his hospital ID badge.

"I can go back to nursing," she said. "They can take me back into the ICU. They've been calling me for a while. Believe me, if there was a way..."

"I know," he said. "I know," he repeated more softly.

Cathy was on the verge of speaking several times but struggled to find the right words. She opened her eyes widely and tilted her head back to prevent the tears along her lower lids from running down. She swallowed hard, nodded a goodbye, and left.

The door shut. Light from the window faded as a cloud eased in front of the sun. Drew felt the emptiness seal him in.

He stood, side-stepped the framed diplomas and certificates stacked behind the desk, and leaned against a bookshelf that sagged in the center under the weight of medical journals. Post-its protruded from unread articles in the Journal of Bone and Joint Disease and the Journal of Orthopedic Research, which leaned hard against a plastic knee joint bookend.

One of the crumbled pink pieces of paper was lying on the floor next to the garbage can. He grabbed the paper, intending to return it to the top of the garbage pile. Instead, he unfolded the message slip and flattened it against the desk surface.

He read the message, "Call from Thorton Grovely. Global Investors. Urgent."

He hadn't spoken to anyone from Global in three years. He had never spoken to Grovely directly. Now the man behind the scenes was calling him.

The computer screensaver clicked to another colorful image of Yellowstone National Park – Emerald Pool. A radiant stone casing shone below the water, which looked inviting. A puff of steam was the only indication of the two-hundred-degree temperatures waiting beyond the tranquil surface.

"Urgent," he read again from the message slip, and reached for the telephone.

8

DERRINGER'S CHOPHOUSE, NEW YORK CITY

Orchestrating the perfect dinner meeting could be so time-consuming.

Thorton Grovely arrived at Derringer's half an hour before his meeting time with Doctor Chambers in order to make sure that everything was arranged properly. He wouldn't be eating anything, not at his current level of affliction, but appearances would be important. They always were.

The waiter smiled cordially. "Mr. Grovely, it's wonderful to have you dining with us tonight." He wiped what appeared to be a spotless menu with a fresh white napkin and handed it to Grovely. "I hope everything is to your liking."

Grovely took the menu and leafed through it as a formality. As he turned each page, he saw broken bones – in the appetizers – in the entrees – in the desserts. Yesterday was not a good day. This was not a good week. And it was only Tuesday.

The chocolate velvet cake on the menu caught his attention and lured his mind back from Acapulco. Velvet cake. Cake like velvet. He locked onto the splendid image. Smoothness and richness were qualities as appealing in food as they were enviable in life.

The waiter returned with an unopened bottle of Perrier and three glasses on a tray. He placed the bottle on the table, handed

Grovely the first glass, and stood at attention with the tray pressed against his chest.

Grovely inspected the glass. Light played off the crystal as he rotated it between the tips of his thumb and index finger. He reached a finger over the brim and scratched at the inside with the back of his nail. Disappointing. Before he could comment to the waiter, a new glass appeared in his hand. After a similar inspection, Grovely nodded and thanked him.

Grovely hated beef. Trichinosis lurked in pork. Salmonella ran rampant through chicken. But beef? Ugh. Beef was a bacterial and parasitic playground. A Trojan Horse loaded with *E. coli* exuding deadly toxin. *E. coli* toxin could withstand freezing. It could give you everything from diarrhea to kidney failure. It could kill you by rotting a hole through your heart.

Whenever the visions of *E. coli* danced through Grovely's head, Mad Cow Disease invariably cut in. Bovine spongiform encephalopathy. BSE for short. Swiss cheese holes in your brain. All from a prion, a small protein, not even a living organism. Nothing you could see. Nothing you could kill. No way to fight back. Swiss cheese.

In researching the subject, Grovely once came up with a list of bacteria and parasites that lived in cattle. The list far exceeded what he ever wanted to imagine – actinomyces, anthrax, brucella, campylobacter, cowpox, cryptosporidia, foot and mouth disease, giardia, leptosporidia, mycolosteria, pseudocowpox, Q fever, rabies, salmonella, streptococcus, Taenia, Yersinia – just to name a few.

So, beef was out.

Grovely's intellect told him that Derringer's was a safe place to eat, probably more so than the vast majority of restaurants in the city. But the affliction told him that all of that didn't matter. He generally only ate food that he opened and prepared himself.

This way he didn't have to worry about *E. coli* and BSE and the other goodies.

A steak was a prop with which to do business, rather than something to eat. Big deals didn't happen in health food restaurants in Grovely's world. They were conceived with cigars and nourished with steak sauce, the same as always. As long as he didn't have to eat any food, everything was dandy.

Grovely tightened the tablecloth down against the edges of the table like a cadet working on the sheets of a military bunk. A particular fold in the tablecloth disturbed him, mainly because it wasn't centered along the table. He readjusted the tablecloth position several times but couldn't set the crease in the center without leaving an edge of the table bare. The irregularity annoyed him immensely. He checked his watch. Only ten minutes until Chambers was scheduled to arrive, and he had wasted four minutes obsessing over a tablecloth crease.

Grovely stood up, pretending to be looking for someone. He tried to stop hyperventilating and searched for anything to divert his attention from the tablecloth.

There was a ring of empty tables around him, by request. Just beyond this comfort zone, a man sat with two young children. The boy was chewing loudly on a wad of purple bubble gum, stretching the spit-covered wad out in front of his face periodically and then sticking it back in his mouth. The girl was idly chewing on her necklace. She ran the beads along her teeth, making a series of clicking sounds.

Grovely closed his eyes and turned back to his table. The stereo effect of gum-chewing and bead-clicking became deafening. He needed some release – to reach down inside of himself and exorcise a few of the demons with a blood-curdling howl.

The waiter returned carrying a tray with several plates of food. Grovely sat and poured himself a few ounces of his Perrier, enough to wet his throat, but not so much that he would have to use the men's room at the restaurant. He turned away as the waiter placed the food on the table.

The largest plate contained a one-ounce sliver of filet. *E. coli* was probably dancing across the top of the cow muscle. The second plate contained a single spoonful of creamed spinach, which Grovely scooped up and smeared across the steak plate, wondering how much Staphylococcus it contained. He added the contents of the third plate, a single spoonful of mushrooms, one of Derringer's specials – big blobs of fungus. Now he had what appeared to be a mostly eaten plate of food.

He checked his watch again – five minutes before the scheduled meeting. He strategically placed an envelope displaying Chambers' name over the crease in the tablecloth, concealing the imperfection.

He was ready for the meeting with the doctor. Hopefully his time in this white-collar slaughterhouse would be brief.

9

DERRINGER'S CHOPHOUSE, NEW YORK CITY

It would be hard to resist sinking his teeth into a big fat juicy Porterhouse.

"I'm meeting someone for dinner. A Mr. Grovely. He may be here already." Drew looked around the restaurant.

"Of course, Dr. Chambers," The maître de said. "He's at his usual table." He motioned with an elongated bony finger for Drew to follow.

It had been five years of cholesterol-conscious dining since Drew had been to a steakhouse. Linda had imposed strict dietary changes. Despite his divorce two years ago, Drew continued to watch his cholesterol consumption, mainly as proof to himself that it was his decision all along to alter his diet, rather than pressure from an ex-wife.

His senses were now overwhelmed by the dense aroma of beef. Filet mignon. Rib eye. NY strip. Porterhouse. He sliced through the air with his nose to reach the tables. An instinctive carnivorous appetite ignored years of forced abstinence. He wiped his mouth to check for saliva as caveman portions of beef floated by on platters and swept by on carts. He momentarily lost track of the maître de gliding deftly through tables of investment bankers and lawyers. Jackets were still on and ties were still tightened to the collar; the Manhattan dinner crowd was just getting started.

They walked up the stairs and back toward the corner of the restaurant. The lighting and the décor darkened as they ascended. A thirty-something year-old man was sitting alone at a table for six. His blonde hair looked as though it had just been removed from a mold. A ring of empty tables surrounded his in the otherwise crowded restaurant. On the wall behind him was a painting, a darkly colored series of brownish red swirls.

Drew knew about Grovely's affinity for making business deals in Derringer's. He wasn't sure what Grovely actually did, or what Global Investors Corporation did, for that matter. They seemed to have their hands in everything, at least from what he read in the Journal and the Times. They made money from money. Troy Gaines, the CEO, was a relatively young but nonetheless established star in the New York business scene. Grovely apparently shared in some of the wealth that trickled down from his younger mentor, but not in any of the accolades of the press.

Grovely had business interests in biotechnology, although he lacked any formal scientific training. He was the one that led Global to Manhattan Memorial Hospital several years earlier to discuss investing in ReStructure, Drew's cartilage-producing cells produced through genetic engineering. Global eventually lost interest in the project but kept an eye on his subsequent research progress. About two years ago they inquired about the genetic sequencing work that Drew was doing on bone cell surface proteins. They went as far as to sign a confidentiality agreement and review his laboratory records.

Drew was never really sure why Grovely backed out, since all of their communication was through "his people." He had wanted the opportunity to discuss the research with Grovely directly. Perhaps he was about to get the chance.

Grovely looked up from his Fortune Magazine, spotted Drew, and waved him over to the table with a bottle of steak sauce.

"Ah, the good doctor. What a pleasure. Finally, we meet." He reached out and shook Drew's hand.

Drew grasped Grovely's hand, aware of the soft texture and well-manicured nails – not the hands he would picture jamming a fork into a 16-ounce Porterhouse in Derringer's.

"Well, our telephone conversation left me intrigued," Drew said. They sat down. "Though I'm still in the dark on the details."

"In the dark," Grovely repeated. He seemed amused by the word choice. "Yes. The details. And to think I often pride myself on being a true details man." Grovely smiled with whitened teeth. His tie was pinned perfectly into position. His shirt collar was starched into submission. Symmetry defined.

Drew smiled politely. He wanted to hear the details of Global's offer right away. But he would have to wait a little longer.

The painting behind Grovely was in better view. The brown swirls around the periphery were dogs – hunting hounds. They were in a frenzy, their teeth and gums showing, the hair on their backs jutting out. They were attacking a fox, which made up the brown and red swirl at the center of the painting. One dog was twisting its neck, and another was ripping into its thigh. The fox's eyes were thrust wide open, threatening to fall from their sockets.

Drew noticed a nearly finished plate in front of Grovely, with just a sliver of filet and some other remnants remaining.

"Oh," Grovely said. "Forgive me for having eaten already. I've had three meetings in a row here. The food is excellent, so enjoy your meal. I'll need to do most of the talking this time anyway." Another white smile. "I can highly recommend the filet or the Porterhouse, depending on your appetite." He rested his hand on a manila envelope.

A man a couple of tables away was trying to get two young children to eat their onion loaf appetizers. The kids seemed out of place in the Manhattan steakhouse. They looked as though they were spending their Tuesday night with their weekend dad.

Drew was struck by a memory – a snapshot of surf-fishing with Matty on Long Island. That was before Linda divorced him. Back when Matty wasn't very sick.

A woman in a business suit joined the nearby table and hugged her children. Her greeting to her husband made it obvious that they were still very much together.

"Doctor Chambers," Grovely said. "I've been impressed by your work since the ReStructure project. It's rare to find someone with such dedication and potential, but when they do appear, there's no mistaking them. It was disappointing when the decision was made not to pursue that project." He sighed and shook his head, suggesting that he had done everything he could do, but to no avail.

"Your current work on osteoblast and osteoclast surface proteins is very exciting," Grovely continued. He said the words "osteoclast" and "osteoblast" slowly and deliberately as though speaking them for the first time. "The impact this work can have on future treatments for bone disorders is significant. As we informed you two years ago, however, the FDA backlog in this country extends the time required to complete such a project beyond the patience of a company like Global Investors."

Why did this man ask him to come here? Grovely became distracted by a fold in the tablecloth, repeatedly pressing down on it lightly with his hand, and then letting it spring back up in a straight line. Drew waited for him to refocus on the matter at hand.

"Under normal circumstances, that is," Grovely said, still looking down at the tablecloth.

Under normal circumstances?

Grovely looked up with a slanted grin. "Every now and then, we find ourselves in unusual circumstances. And every now and then, one has to trade a favor for a favor."

The waiter wheeled a cart with two trays up against their table. The first tray was covered with a stack of cellophane-wrapped meats and a lobster the size of a small dog. The other tray contained oversized vegetables resembling a state fair awards display. The waiter used the display as a three-dimensional menu, describing how each item could be prepared.

Drew cleared his throat, leaned in close to the waiter and softly said, "I'd like the swordfish."

"The swordfish with the Béarnaise sauce?" the waiter asked in a tone that asked why he just wasted his time going through the entire selection of steaks.

"On the side," Drew said.

Grovely writhed in his chair and looked about, as though wondering if anyone had heard his dining guest order fish at a steakhouse. "No steak? At Derringer's?" He gave an incredulous look to the waiter, who shrugged.

Drew shook his head. He was committing a business dinner *faux pas*. The waiter hadn't left; he was hovering over Drew, certain that he would change his mind.

"Oh, yes," Drew said, deciding to make a compromise. "And I would like the beefsteak tomato with the purple onion and blue cheese dressing."

The waiter nodded and rolled his cart away. They watched him disappear into the kitchen.

"Blue cheese, "Grovely said with a peculiar expression that Drew couldn't decipher. "That's made with some type of bacteria, isn't it?"

"It's mold, actually," Drew said. "The best tasting mold on the planet."

Grovely nodded silently. The left corner of his mouth curled upward. He strayed ever so slightly from his usual perfect posture, leaning about an inch to his left. From Drew's angle, Grovely was centered directly under the painting on the wall. Droplets of fox blood dangled over his impeccable hair.

"You were saying something about abnormal circumstances," Drew said.

Grovely was symmetrically realigned in an instant. "Well, as you know, we're involved in projects around the world, including some pretty remote places. I've taken a personal interest in pursuing these types of projects. Projects that other companies wouldn't dare touch, wouldn't even know what to do with." Grovely paused as though momentarily overwhelmed by his self-worth. "This has allowed us to expand our business exponentially, especially over the last decade or so while I've been with the company. Unfortunately, we've also found that a small problem over a great distance can mushroom into a huge headache." He tapped a fork against one of the mushrooms in front of him, and then let the fork drop onto the plate. "That's basically what we're dealing with now: a small problem that's a big headache."

"What's the problem?" Drew asked.

"Fractures," Grovely said in a reassuring tone. "Right up your alley,"

"How many fractures?" Drew asked. "There are three people injured. What we need is someone to go there and treat them," Grovely said.

"Why not just fly them out for treatment?" Drew asked.

"I wish it were that easy, believe me," Grovely said. "Unfortunately, the red tape involved is unbelievable, and we'd lose three people crucial to the project. Not to mention the negative PR we'd get. I'm sure that you understand that Global isn't about negative PR. We would go to almost any length to avoid that. Like

I said, I have a vested interest in these projects. What we need is to have these people treated on site."

The waiter returned with the tomatoes. They were nearly half a foot in diameter, covered with an equally gargantuan onion slice, and smothered in blue cheese chunks and dressing. The dish could have served as an entree.

Drew cut a portion of the appetizer and raised it to his mouth. Before eating it, he rotated his fork to look at the pale blue speckles peeking out from the cut edges of the cheese. He plunged the wedge into his mouth as a small drop of dressing fell to the table. The taste of cholesterol was worth the five-year wait.

Drew's dining partner was atypically silent for a moment.

"Where are they?" Drew asked.

"In Siberia," Grovely said.

"Siberia? What are they doing in Siberia?" Drew asked.

"In due time, doctor." Grovely said.

"I can't go to Siberia." Drew said.

Grovely slid the manila envelope across the table, patted it twice, and smiled. "Take this home," he said. "Have a look at our offer. Then call me so that we can get started."

10

5TH AVENUE, NEW YORK CITY

Smooth as velvet.

Grovely was itching as they left Derringer's. At first it was just his arms.

He ditched Chambers by saying that he was running late, although he really had nowhere to go. He sent the doctor off in a limousine, and then scurried through the fallen leaves along the sidewalk.

Where to go? Where to go? Slipping into the comforting anonymity of midtown Manhattan seemed ideal at times like this. He needed the mental distraction of an open space.

A typical day found him hard at work or secluded in his condominium on the Upper East Side. Neither place seemed appropriate right now. Neither place suited his current state of mind. Right now, all Grovely wanted was to get his mind off of Taimyr.

Red blotches were forming on his forearms, and now the itching seemed to be all over.

"Velvet," he thought.

His waking nightmare replayed in his head in scrambled fragments. What went wrong up in Siberia? Was it what he thought? Maybe there was some other explanation, but right now he couldn't think of any. Was there anything he could do? And, with Gaines now watching the company accounting through a microscope, how could Grovely come up with the finances he'd need to find a solution?

Grovely's neatly filed and precisely orchestrated world was tainted and twisted, a world of uncertainty, of endless questions.

What about Chambers? The doctor was going to say yes. But then what? Why send him there? Would he be able to figure out what was happening? Could he do anything about it? There was no way Chambers would ever make it out of Siberia alive. No way. But what other choice did he have? It was Chambers or else.

He could see the red areas on his arms rising into welts. His eyes and throat were burning.

"Like velvet." Grovely said it out loud this time. He had been smooth as velvet in the face of disaster. If he repeated it to himself enough, he would start to believe it. He forced a smile. When the left corner of his upper lip rolled awkwardly and stuck along the arid surface of his canine, he had to free it with his tongue.

"Like velvet." He was skillfully managing an extremely messed up situation. And he hadn't started the problem. It wasn't his idea to send them up there. They had Gaines to thank for that. And Grovely had no control over the events that followed. Their blood wouldn't be on his hands.

11

CHAMBERS' APARTMENT, NEW YORK CITY

Have a look at our offer. Then call so we can get started.

Drew dragged a box out from under his bed, causing a snow-plowing effect on the advancing line of dust along the floor. The words "medical school" were scribbled in black magic marker across the top. He straddled the box while dragging it into the center of the living room. The dry brittle tape cracked open with a rap of his knuckle. He yanked open the cardboard lids and stared into a time capsule of his life.

An assortment of papers wedged into a large envelope was lying on the top. This wasn't what he was searching for, but he couldn't resist leafing through the papers. He spotted his acceptance letter from medical school. The gold crown of the Columbia College of Physicians and Surgeons crest was shining as though the letter had been sent yesterday.

He found a reprint from his first medical journal publication entitled "Porcine Joint Transplantation into Humans." He presented the research results at a student symposium in the Bronstein Research Building auditorium. The night before the presentation he practiced it at least thirty times with Linda as the audience. He could still see her sitting there, attentively listening to each practice run and nodding as though she was hearing the presentation for the first time, as though there was nothing of greater interest to her than pig joints.

During their last year together, Linda would listen to him only through her lawyer at a cost of $400 an hour.

Drew sorted through the other contents of the box, finding the object of his search: his doctor's bag. Dust lined the black leather seams. The monogrammed buckle was tarnished. Sitting on the floor, he rested the bag on his lap and wiped it with his sleeve.

The doctor's bag was a medical school graduation gift from his parents. He never used the bag as it was intended. He never did a house call. The bag once decorated the center of his bookshelf and served as supply storage during his residency. Now it was pressed down under the weight of paraphernalia in a box. His parents were still living in New York then. A lot had happened since they retired and moved to Arizona. A lot had changed. They were better off so far away.

He dumped the contents of the bag on the floor. The otoscope and ophthalmoscope skidded out first. Ears and eyes. Not exactly the tools of the orthopedic trade. The bone doctor. The stethoscope and the reflex hammer followed. He smiled. He hadn't used a hammer to elicit reflexes since medical school; in residency he used the knuckle of his middle finger. A knuckle worked just as well as a hammer and weighed less. A steady flow of gauze packages, tongue depressors, culture swabs, suture removal kits, and antibiotic packets tumbled out of the bag. Drew sifted through the items, threw the majority of them into the garbage, and then replaced the rest.

He brought the bag into the kitchen. The manila envelope from Global beckoned again from the kitchen table. He sat down and looked at the clock. It had been less than thirty minutes since he last looked at the paperwork. He had spent the last two hours reviewing the contents of the envelope and rereading the check.

He lifted up the airline ticket to Oslo, Norway. The information hadn't changed; the flight left in just eight hours. The new passport with his photograph was tucked into the back of the ticket jacket. The check was now visible on the table. He couldn't resist looking at it again. It was as though he needed to keep reassuring himself that the check was really there, and that he was reading it correctly. Was one of the zeroes a mistake? Was the comma in the wrong place? He wondered whether there was a limit on the dollar amount that you could put on a check.

The check rested almost imperceptibly in his palm. Lowering his hand quickly, he watched the paper float back into his grasp. So much money, and a light breeze could carry it away.

When he first opened the envelope, which was about ten seconds after returning from Derringer's, he considered ripping the check into pieces. The whole deal made him nervous. Hell, he was terrified. Grovely was less than trustworthy, and the Siberia project remained a mystery. A confidentiality agreement in the paperwork claimed that the benefits of the "research" in Siberia would be in jeopardy if unauthorized information were disseminated. In Oslo, the nature of the research and the information about the injuries would be revealed to him.

If Drew didn't respond by 8AM, just six hours from now, the offer would be rescinded. If he decided to back out after his briefing in Oslo, the check was still his to keep. The rest of the promised sums, however, would be lost.

The rest of the sums.

The check was for $250,000. But that was just a fraction of the total sum. The financial agreement in the package promised another $250,000 to him at the end of his three months in Siberia. But most importantly, it also promised $1,000,000 to the Matty's Hope Foundation to support the continuation of his research. One million dollars. That kind of money would cover the project launch and support an additional five years of research.

Global had thought of everything. They provided an itemized list of arrangements that would be made in his absence, everything from paying his bills to maintaining his medical association memberships and journal subscriptions. Drew tried to think of things that they had forgotten, only to find them somewhere on the list. They had also made arrangements for everything that he would need for the trip. His only responsibility was the paperwork from the envelope and the clothing on his back. They had made it difficult to say “no.”

The offer seemed ludicrous in many ways, but he had nothing to lose. His days at Manhattan Memorial were numbered. Matty’s Hope was stalled on the launching pad. The money from Global would help get his life back on track. He was certain of one thing; if he turned them down now, the opportunity would never come his way again.

He found that there was something about a check for $250,000 that made it tear-resistant, perhaps some indestructible power embedded in all the zeroes. He signed his name on the back. Then he added “for deposit only” beneath the signature, as though there was a snowball’s chance in hell that he might lose the check on the way to the bank. He tucked the thin blue piece of paper into his wallet.

Doctor Chambers wondered about the long-distance house call that he was about to make. And then he worried. And then he picked up the phone and dialed Thorton Grovely’s number.

12

5TH AVENUE, NEW YORK CITY

Hives the size of cockroaches covered the skin on his arms and crawled up under his sleeves.

Grovely scratched while crossing at 50th and 5th in a steady pedestrian flow. The human mass widened and slowed near St. Patrick's Cathedral, even on a random Tuesday evening.

A preacher's voice rose from the square by the cathedral.

"I will send a pestilence down upon the people, one of grand proportions. I have warned you, and now the prophecy will be fulfilled. The earth will be purged of hatred and violence, greed and jealousy, lust and sloth that poison your souls."

The pedestrian stream curved away from the voice. Grovely peered through the crowd and glimpsed the disheveled man with a bible in his hand delivering a street oration. Another street prophet. Gaines had once used the expression. Grovely generally tried not to quote Wonderboy, but he liked this one. It amused him to think that if the Second Coming of Christ had the ill fate to occur in Manhattan, the competition for oration would be steep, and the Son of God would be placed on Prozac long before being placed on a cross.

The crowd regurgitated Grovely and forced him toward the stairs leading up to the cathedral square. His arms and face felt like they were on fire. He wanted to squelch them with ice cubes.

Three teenagers adorned in loose black clothes and countless body pierces stopped talking and looked at him from the stairs. Grovely stopped short in front of them, searching for a safe passage. Their disdainful facial expressions bore holes in him. Another outburst from the street prophet caused the crowd to sway in unison, sending waves of nausea through Grovely.

"Will you stand by, ridden with sin, filled with greed and devoid of remorse, making demands on the Lord when you should be penitent on your knees, casting his message aside when it is your one remaining hope at salvation? These are your choices, choices of a stray flock."

A married couple was arguing next to Grovely. The husband, with his Big Apple hat and his Statue of Liberty shirt, looked like a poster child for the New York City department of tourism. He tried to snap a photograph of the teenagers while his wife swung overloaded FAO Schwartz bags at the camera.

"Don't make a scene," she kept telling him.

"This is a scene," he yelled back. He was greeted by three sets of middle fingers as the flash went off.

Grovely ducked out of the photograph, only to have the crowd wedge him closer to the street prophet. The upper half of the man's red bathrobe was messiah-worthy. The lower half was shredded, exposing an American flag Speedo, the only clothing beneath the robe. Days of beard growth concealed his face. His eyes clenched shut from the force of God surging through him.

"The Lord said to Moses and Aaron, 'Take handfuls of soot from a furnace and have Moses toss it into the air in the presence of Pharaoh. It will become fine dust over the whole land of Egypt, and festering boils will break out on men and animals throughout the land.'"

Boils.

The street prophet was loomed directly over Grovely's head, howling through the passages of the bible in his hands. Saliva and lice swirled through the air and found their way into the pollution comprising Grovely's mind.

Grovely's condominium was just fifteen blocks uptown, but it seemed more like fifteen miles right now. He undid his shirt collar button with trembling fingertips and loosened his tie.

"You can avoid the correct choices in life, but you cannot avoid God. God walks amongst us. He is the man or woman next to you. He gives you the option to make the right choices, and he is watching closely. God is angry with your sins. His next plague will spare no person. No man. No woman. No child. A pestilence will cleanse the world of the disease of hatred."

"Like velvet?"

Plague. Pestilence. Disease.

Palpitations thumped in Grovely's chest. The hives were growing like sponges absorbing water. His throat felt tight.

Everyone was pressing in at the same time, rubbing against him, breathing on him. The intrusion was unbearable. He felt trapped. A child in a stroller shot a sneeze directly at him. Grovely watched the sneeze droplets spray into the air that he was breathing, felt them being sucked down into his lungs with every gasp for air. He looked down in horror at the line of pale yellow mucous linking the child's nose and mouth.

The nausea worsened. Lights flashed. The thumping in his chest accelerated as though his heart was tumbling downhill. *Oh no,* he thought, *not again, not here.* He had to escape. He pushed the baby stroller aside and broke through the crowd into the street. He stood between lanes on 5th Avenue, unaware of where he was.

Yellow flashes roared beside him. Horns blared.

He waited for his vision and sense of balance to return.

13

AIRPLANE, OVER SIBERIA

There were no lights visible on the ground since takeoff more than three hours ago.

The plane rumbled through the darkness over Siberia. Drew was the only passenger in the small plane. He hadn't slept in nearly 24 hours, but he was wide-awake. Too much was happening too fast. Three days earlier he was working in his laboratory in New York. Now he was headed up to a woolly mammoth research facility in Siberia.

He would have been excited about becoming a part of a woolly mammoth expedition if he hadn't seen the photographs of the injured researchers.

The sound in the plane was brain-numbing, and the vibration was threatening to liquefy Drew's internal organs. Apparently, this was the price one paid to fly in a plane with pontoons capable of landing on ice. The pilots were eager to tell him about the plane when he asked. They were eager to talk in general, despite the need to shout over the noise.

The pilots were a married couple topped with gray hair, coated in thick skin, and still rugged enough to win barroom brawls on a nightly basis. The man was born with a consonant-laden name with a lot of K sounds that Drew gave up on pronouncing after the third attempt. After retiring from his career as a Soviet military pilot and his life as a bachelor, he moved to Chicago for an arranged marriage at the age of fifty.

The temptations of the Windy City ended up being too much for someone devoid of self-control, however, and he found himself running away from his new wife, loan sharks, and the local police within a matter of weeks. In a series of encouraged moves he made his way toward the northwest, and didn't stop until he reached Peterson, Alaska. Somewhere along the way, he permanently borrowed two hundred dollars and the name of Brendan Connolly from the owner of a pub that he frequented.

"I wasn't running from anyone," Brendan told Drew in his thick Russian accent.

"You should have been," his female co-pilot added with a cigarette-thickened voice.

In Peterson Brendan had temporarily outrun his past. There, it seemed, everyone had some interesting story for how they or some ancestor got to Alaska. As a result, people were less inclined to judge their neighbors. It was in Peterson that he met his wife and co-pilot, AC, short for Antoinette Cleopatra.

AC was born in Alaska. Her mother died during childbirth, leaving her to be named and then raised by her father, a manic glacier pilot. While growing up, AC learned to fly by helping her father through the most harrowing of conditions, usually to rescue injured or stranded adventurers from the glacier-topped peaks of megaliths with such imposing names as Devil's Thumb.

Brendan and AC lacked the ability or desire to stay still for any significant length of time yet, somehow, they remained together for the last ten years while puddle-jumping the outskirts of the planet. Now they were working in Siberia, making specialty flights such as this one.

"I missed beauty of Russia," Brendan told Drew.

"He missed alimony payments to his ex-wife," AC corrected, hitting him with an elbow that sent the plane angling starboard.

The intermittent conversation distracted Drew from the memory of the injury photographs. He feared whatever awaited him when they landed. From what he could tell, his pilots didn't know very much about the activities of Global Investors in Siberia. They probably preferred it that way. They seemed satisfied to be getting paid to fly, and if Global was going to be paying this month's bills, that was just fine with them.

It was still dark outside. Drew checked his watch. "What time is it?" he yelled, tapping the side of the watch to make sure it was running properly.

"Three in the afternoon," Brendan yelled over his shoulder.

Afternoon? Drew looked outside again. Behind them was a faint orange strip along the horizon that must have been connected to the sun. The remainder of the sky was black. "Haven't they heard of daylight savings time?"

AC yelled this time, "If there was any daylight in the winter in northern Siberia, we'd definitely save it. If I were you, I'd get my money back from my travel agent."

Drew took a deep breath to yell again. "Where are we?"

"Western Siberia," Brendan said. "Taimyr Peninsula."

Drew shrugged.

"Fifteen hundred kilometers north of the Arctic Circle," AC said.

"What's that in miles?" Drew asked.

"A long way," AC yelled.

"What's the closest town?" Drew asked.

AC unbuckled her seat belt harness and stood. Brendan tried to pull her closer by her arm, but she broke his grip. She waved him off with an "ah, shut up" motion. He looked upward as though appealing to some greater force. AC turned to face Drew. She used both hands to pull her jeans up by the oversized bald eagle belt buckle in the front. Crouching slightly beneath the low clearance of the ceiling, she leaned in closer to Drew.

"If you take a look out of the left side of the aircraft," she said, gesturing with a waving palm to mimic an airline stewardess, "you'll see nothing." Drew followed her gesture and looked down into the blackness below. Nothing. When he looked up AC was displaying a television commercial smile. She then gestured in mirrored fashion with her left hand. "In just a few moments, if you look out to the right, you'll be able to see that we'll be passing over nothing." She laughed herself into a hoarse coughing spell. Brendan had his back to them and was still slowly shaking his head. Drew leaned across and looked down into the blackness on the opposite side of the plane. Nothing.

AC cleared her throat several times to gain control of her cough. "The Kara Sea is eighty kilometers north of us," she said. "It's not on the tourist maps, but at least it has a name, which distinguishes it from most of Siberia. Dudinka is the capital, the crown jewel, if you will, of Taimyr."

"How far away is Dudinka?" Drew asked.

"About 1200 kilometers," she said. "It's a lovely walk, if you're a Doolgan reindeer herder."

"How do they get electricity up here?" Drew asked.

Both pilots laughed.

"No way to run cables up here," AC said. "Just gas-powered generators. We fly in fuel for Global every month or so."

Unexpected turbulence rocked the plane. AC tried to brace herself. Brendan's arms flexed to stabilize the controls as AC scrambled back to her seat. He shot her a reprimanding look.

When the plane was level again AC turned back to Drew. "Phones and computers go through satellite dishes," she said. "Access varies at this latitude. Getting the right angle is difficult."

"My wife is rocket scientist," Brendan said.

Another jolt of turbulence made Brendan and AC focus on their flying for a while. Drew's thoughts returned to the photograph of the broken leg. He removed the manila folder from his duffle bag and flipped it open. There was very little information on each researcher – just a photograph or two, their initials, and a brief description of the injury.

MB was first. The quality of the digital photograph was poor, but there was no mistaking the segments of tibia sticking out through the lower leg. The bone had to be broken in at least three places. It was the kind of injury you might see after a high-speed motor vehicle accident, or maybe a bomb blast. How such an injury could occur in a healthy young scientist at the woolly mammoth research station was mind-boggling.

MB was the first person to develop fractures. He slipped and fell in his sleeping quarters. *Slipped and fell.* Drew closed his eyes but still saw the protruding shards of bone. What had been done for the man in the two weeks since the injury? An open fracture like that could be disastrous, even under the best of circumstances. But in the Arctic? He could only imagine.

The other two fractures were equally puzzling, and equally disturbing. SC, another healthy young man, injured himself when a cart of supplies that he was pushing jammed against a doorway. Drew shuffled one more time through the photographs and papers, checking the information to make sure that the photo was correctly matched with the other information. The grotesquely deformed arm in the photograph was collapsed like an accordion – another injury more consistent with a high velocity, high impact trauma case, rather than with the injury described.

The third case was the one that made Drew reconsider the trip when he first saw the photos in Oslo. HB began to experience pain while chewing. Within two days her face changed into the deformity in the photograph. The sight was frightening – the crooked, swollen chin, the twisted jaw line. It looked as though someone held the upper half of the face still and rotated the lower half in a clockwise direction.

What was happening to these people? None of it made sense. It was obvious that they were in desperate need of help. Drew wasn't sure what he could accomplish all the way up there, but he knew that he had to follow through on his plans to go. He would evaluate them and convince Grovely to fly them out, regardless of the red tape and expense.

"We're landing." Brendan yelled. "Get ready."

Lights flickered in the cockpit. Drew reached to open the blind in front of the window, only to realize that it was already open. The plane was landing somewhere in the blackness below. The thin orange strip along the horizon, the promise of another day, was gone. An unnatural and eerie purple hue twisted through the blackness above their little plane.

"What are we doing here?" Drew said, looking out.

"We," AC paused, gesturing to Brendan, "are dropping you off and getting out before the next storm hits. I don't know what you're doing, though. Somebody must want you here pretty bad."

Drew felt the tail end of the plane swinging out from under them, tossed like paper in the wind. He tightened his seat belt across his lap as they descended.

"A storm passed through here yesterday, and another one's on the way," AC yelled. "We have just enough time to get you down and head out. You're lucky we made it in when we did. This runway might not be passable for a while after today."

There still wasn't any runway visible, at least what Drew considered to be a runway – lights, a control tower. There was no sign of life at all. He squinted to determine their altitude.

The plane banged against the surface below and lurched forward. His nose knotted against the window as a puff of powder blew past. Falling forward, he struck his forehead on the empty seat in front of him. They must be crashing.

"Hold on," Brendan yelled. The plane creaked as though it would snap in half at any moment, and then they ascended again.

"Better try that one again," AC yelled.

They tried two more times to land the plane, each time crunching at odd angles against the surface below. On the fourth descent, the plane skidded along the ground and came to a stop. Brendan had brought them down safely.

The decreasing noise from the plane was soon replaced by a powerful howling sound. Gusts of wind slapped snow and ice pellets against the window. Drew sank deeper against his seat, afraid that the window might splinter from the pressure. *Between storms? Where the hell were they?*

AC turned and smiled. "Welcome to Siberia. Enjoy your stay. We appreciate the privilege of flying with you. Think of us in the future whenever your travel plans include the Arctic Circle."

Drew was relieved to have survived the landing. If it was this difficult to get here, how bad would it be to get out?

14

GROVELY'S CONDOMINIUM, NEW YORK CITY

He was safe in his condominium. The way things were going, he might not be safe anywhere else.

Grovely still wasn't exactly sure what happened in front of St. Patrick's, but he wasn't taking any chances. Part of him wanted out of it all. To get into a limousine, ride to Kennedy Airport, throw a dart at a departure board, and disappear somewhere. He had more than enough money to do it. So why was he staying? He had no family, no pets, not even a plant.

Was it Claire? Did she mean that much to him? Did she mean anything to him? He couldn't decide. Anyway, their relationship had no geographic boundaries, at least as it existed now. And there wasn't any possibility for a change. Was there? No, it wasn't Claire.

He enjoyed the power of working at Global. He enjoyed the money, but he enjoyed the power that the money could buy even more. And there was lots of money. He could never make enough of it, and now he couldn't live without it.

For a while the salary and bonuses were enough, but over time Grovely found the need to "improvise." Now he was living in a 5,000 square-foot condominium in one of the most desirable buildings on Fifth Avenue. It wasn't a penthouse suite, but he could live with that – for now. With the money he was making, it was just a matter of time before he moved into the suite upstairs. Everyone who thought that it was Gaines who had the power should come here and take a look around. But they weren't invited.

Gaines' head would explode if he had any idea what Grovely had been up to at Global. Grovely would almost give all the money back to see the look on his face. Almost.

Yes, he was starting to get his strength back. He had no idea what set off his affliction earlier two nights ago. The attacks were getting more frequent. They were getting more severe. The monthly prescriptions were running out faster every time; he was almost finished with the current bottle after only two weeks. Maybe the dosage had to be increased. Or maybe he needed a new medication altogether.

Maybe he should remind Dr. Feeley's answering service to place him on tomorrow morning's add-on schedule as early in the day as possible. He hit the speed dial on the phone.

The same whining screeching hag answered the phone. He barely got his name in before she interrupted. "Mister Grovely, as I told you the other times," she said, "I will give your message to the doctor when he arrives in the morning. If you are feeling suicidal or homicidal, please go directly to an emergency room or call 911." Screech screech freaking screech.

"I wasn't feeling homicidal," he said, pivoting the phone so that he could get a level of satisfaction second only to yelling directly into her face. "But you're making me reconsider my options." He hung up with a definitive tap on the button.

He needed another shower.

He shuffled into the bathroom, avoiding the mirror. Three towels hung evenly on the rack, but they were all still wet from earlier in the day. He removed another towel from one of the color-coordinated stacks in the closet, hung it on the shower door, and stepped inside. He grabbed the customized filter on the showerhead to make sure that it was secure, and then turned on the water. The spray purged his body. He was one step closer to cleansing his mind, to restoring the order that his life required. He loved being in the shower; he found peace there.

After an hour-long shower, Grovely returned to the computer to check for messages from Claire. He bent over his ergonomic chair and saw that he had new emails waiting. He slid his legs between the kneeler and thigh pad, and then eased against the lower back support. Mental balance started with spinal alignment.

Before he could check his emails, an Instant Message from Claire appeared on the screen. "Welcome back."

A series of physical changes occurred inside him. Every interaction with Claire now had that effect. She had dismantled the psychological armor that separated him from the rest of the world. She captivated him. Love wasn't the right word. He couldn't imagine ever being in love with anyone. He was addicted to Claire.

"How could I resist?" he typed.

"I missed you," the screen read.

"I'm with you now," he typed.

Grovely had seen Claire in person only three times, most recently two months ago. She was an accountant at a large midtown firm at the time. Successful accountants, in Grovely's experience, required the mathematical, analytical mind of a man. He even tried to reschedule with another accountant when he learned that Mr. Meestak was actually Ms. Meestak. But then he met Ms. Claire Meestak.

The first dose of Claire stimulated feelings so uncharacteristic that they frightened him. She was in a charcoal gray Brooks Brothers business suit. Precisely tailored. Carefully pressed. Not enough skin showing to entice the average man. Not any skin showing, in fact, except her face and upper neck. But

Grovely took in the long crisp lines of the outfit, the perfectly symmetrical outline of her contour, the confident flow of her motion, and was hooked.

"Are you busy working, or do you have some free time?" he typed.

"What did you have in mind?" the screen read.

Claire suffered from agoraphobia, a condition that limited her ability to function in social settings. When she lost her job due to repeated absence from work, she started an internet-based accounting service. She became more efficient and productive in the comfort of her own home, away from the pressures of social interaction. Over time her decreased need to leave her home fueled her increasing desire for isolation.

Grovely tracked down Claire's electronic business and encountered her electronic persona. He found that her Internet base allowed more frequent communication, albeit through cables and monitors. He found reasons to contact her as often as possible. At times he made small tax-deductible donations as an excuse to email her.

"Have you thought about my offer?" the screen read.

She still wanted him to come over for dinner. He hoped that she had forgotten, or that she would at least let the subject drop.

"Which offer?" he typed. His fingers trembled lightly, causing his nails to rattle against the keyboard.

For weeks he had hidden his feelings for Claire. He wasn't afraid of rejection. He was afraid of tarnishing his perfect image of her. Only distance could maintain this safe and enduring relationship. Physical contact promised either of two dire consequences. Rejection by Claire would end everything. Attraction would be even worse.

Intimacy with a woman had always seemed impossible. No woman could adapt to his habits, his attention to detail. And forget about the hazards of physical contact. The exchange of body fluids. The infections. It was all so unclean.

"Do you want to have dinner together sometime?" the screen read.

"I'm thinking about it," he typed.

He was thinking about it. He was thinking about physical contact with Claire. He couldn't stop thinking about it. He wiped his forehead with a monogrammed handkerchief.

Claire's image was burned into his memory. The way that her hair curved so smoothly up into a bun in the back of her head. The way the muscles in the sides of her neck ran in perpendicular lines to this curve. Refined tone. Perfect lines.

Visions of her had carried him through the darkest moments of the last few days. But the potential of having her was as terrifying as the risk of losing her.

He needed another shower.

15

LANDING STRIP, SIBERIA

Pontoons dug into the ground as Brendan maneuvered the plane through a turn at the end of the landing strip. The plane resisted the tight circumference, fighting against the snow and ice accumulating along the pontoons and torqueing the controls against Brendan's grasp. The metal creaked with relief as Brendan finished the turnaround and steered back into the path etched along the runway from their landing.

Brendan walked through the plane, bending over to peer out through the windows. Without a word spoken, AC slid across to take her husband's position at the controls.

Drew put on his gear – a hooded Gore-Tex coat, wool gloves, Gore-Tex mittens, tinted goggles, and fur-lined boots. His mobility decreased as each garment was added, but he felt well-insulated, at least inside the plane. Every layer compounded his sense of isolation from the rest of the world.

Brendan held a container of petroleum jelly toward him. "Put on your face," he said.

"Why?" Drew asked.

"So you can keep it," Brendan said.

"The petroleum jelly?" Drew asked.

"No, you're face," Brendan said.

Drew waited for a smile that never came. “How long am I going to be outside?” he asked.

“Probably not long,” Brendan said, tossing the container to him.

Drew slowly removed the lid, reluctant to cover his face with the greasy contents. He pulled off his gloves, dipped an index fingertip into the container, and applied a thin layer to his nose and cheeks. He looked up to see Brendan frowning at him.

“Here,” Brendan said. He dipped his whole hand into the container, scooped up a handful of the petroleum jelly, and covered Chamber’s face in three heavy swipes. “Taimyr is not place to be pretty,” he said when he was finished. Drew’s eyes closed instinctively, despite being protected by the goggles. When he looked again, there was a small clump of the petroleum jelly on the right side of his goggles that partially obscured his vision. He patted at the area awkwardly until most of the clump was transferred from the goggles to the gloves.

Brendan wiped his hand on his pants, slid his gloves on, and turned toward the door. His movements were rushed. The ease with which he had navigated through the sky had evaporated. Without any further discussion, he flipped his goggles down over his eyes and leaned down against the door latch. As the latch yielded and the door pealed open like the lid of a hermetically sealed jar, a gust of frigid air invaded the plane.

Brendan had the two overstuffed duffel bags out onto the ground in an instant. Drew followed him as far as the doorway. Looking outside goggles-first, he clung to the doorframe with both hands to keep from blowing back across the plane. Brendan was at the foot of the stairs, shining a spotlight along the tundra.

The dimly lit circle around the plane resembled footage from a lunar landing. Shades of gray. No evidence of life. No plants. No animals. No people. Nothing was visible in the endless darkness that surrounded them. Where was the research station? And where were the people who were supposed to meet him?

"Not much of a welcoming committee," Drew said.

"They'll be here soon," Brendan said. "They must have heard us pass over." Through layers of Gore-Tex and the Vaseline, within the mid-day shroud of the Arctic, Brendan looked uneasy. His eyes quickly shifted over the surrounding terrain, looking more into the darkness than along the course of the light beam that he was directing. He shook his head intermittently.

A terrible image was forming in Drew's head. All of the researchers lying dead in the mammoth station. Their bodies were frozen. He was walking through the station, clinging to the hope that there would be at least one survivor, but there were none to be found. He shook their shoulders, encountering the solid resistance of rigor mortis and ice.

As Drew descended from the plane, he remembered Neil Armstrong taking the first steps on the moon. He shivered, more from fright than from the cold. He walked toward the edge of the dim hue cast by the plane lights and looked out into the frozen void. Suddenly a brief flash and a cracking sound pierced the darkness ahead, followed instantly by the sound of metal striking metal behind him. He knew immediately what had happened, although he convinced himself that it couldn't be true. There was no way. It just didn't make any sense. In a moment of denial, he squinted into the area where the flash had arisen in order to assure himself that everything was all right.

The plane door slammed shut behind him. The motor revved. Ice particles spat out from under the pontoons. The sequence of events registered in Drew's mind in time-lapse fashion, and moments too late.

Someone was shooting at them.

A second shot flashed from several feet closer. Drew heard it buzz past him. He might have felt it go by. His mind instructed his body to turn and run back to the plane in one motion, but shock and terror knocked him backwards into the snow instead.

Shadows ahead were coalescing into three silhouettes. The silhouettes were getting larger. They were running toward him. He was going to die. But why?

Phantasms were running toward the plane, which was now accelerating along the runway. The pontoons scraped along the icy strip. Several more shots rang out, but the plane was pulling away. The plane lifted off the ground, dipped downward momentarily, and then rose into the sky. The plane's lights immediately extinguished, disappearing into the darkness like a shooting star. The rumbling of the plane was the only remaining sign that somewhere in the night Brendan and AC were escaping from the gunfire.

Drew managed to stand. Most of his body remained warm, layered in wool and synthetic materials and wrapped with a protective outer layer of Gore-Tex. His face was sprayed intermittently with gusts of ice particles. He watched spray hit his goggles, heard it ricochet off his coat, but no longer felt it on his face. His nose and cheeks were already numb. The nerve endings were dead. It wouldn't take long for the exposure at these temperatures to cause permanent damage. Maybe just a few minutes. He raised his gloves to shield his face.

His eyes had enough time to adjust to the darkness, but he still could see nothing. The cloud cover was enough to conceal the stars, and there were no lights along the horizon in any direction. He needed to get away from where he was standing, because whomever shot at the plane knew where he was. But which direction should he choose?

Twelve hundred kilometers to Dudinka.

He walked away from the fading rumble of the plane. The ground crunched under his footsteps mingling with the thumping sound of his own arteries pumping under the goggle straps along his temples. Could they hear him through the wind? He tried to change the angle of his feet to reduce the noise, but the crunching continued. The frequency of the sound in his temples increased.

He thought he heard similar crunching on the ground behind him. He walked faster with no idea where he was headed. The crunching was getting closer. The awkwardness and weight of his gear hindered his progress. He was moving in slow motion. Labored breathing now surrounded him.

Sets of gloves seized Drew's arms and spun him around. He expected to be shot or beaten to death. Instead, a searchlight beam pierced his eyes. Somewhere behind the light, like partially detailed and intermingling fragments of a nightmare, three faceless figures stood before him. Frozen breath billowed out of the cinched circular openings of their hoods, further distorting their form.

Certain of his impending death, Drew thought of Cerberus, the mythological three-headed beast that guards the gates of hell.

PART 2.
DISEASE THEORY

"We have seen the catastrophic effects of disease on mankind, the plagues that have afflicted us throughout our short history on earth, and yet we make the mistake of overlooking such causes of extinction among other animal species."

– Aniello Bonacci, PhD

16

OOUÉ-IVINDO PROVINCE, GABON

Sweat ran in streams down Joseph McIntyre's forehead and burned his eyes. He felt it running down the small of his back. The sun streaked past the brim of his straw hat, penetrated past the sunscreen that he applied almost hourly, and reddened the rolls of skin on his neck and face.

"It seems even hotter than the last time I was here," McIntyre said to Quinn, the journalist pressing behind him with pen and pad in hand. "I didn't think that was possible."

He could come here a hundred times and still forget what it was really like once he returned to the United States. The heat was the least of it. He would forget the way the fear and adrenaline tag-teamed their way through his body, the way he would die if he didn't win the battle against them. If he didn't forget all of these feelings after each visit, he would probably never return.

"This is my sixth trip to Africa since joining the CDC," McIntyre said.

Quinn, the National Geographic journalist, didn't have to write the last comment down. He was certain that he had it in his notes at least three times already. This was McIntyre's third visit to Gabon and the second trip that he was leading. Instead, he wrote down the words "Ebola = archenemy."

McIntyre's team from the Centers for Disease Control and Prevention was investigating an Ebola outbreak. This time the virus had taken eight lives. All victims were from the same village, five from the same family. Three more villagers were spiraling downward as the virus took over their bodies. They would be dead within hours. Hopefully those would be the last, this time.

McIntyre lectured as they pushed forward through the underbrush. "Ebola is a deadly virus with no known cure, making it what we refer to as a grade four. The Zaire strain, which is probably what we're dealing with here, kills nearly 90% of its victims. It's deadlier than Ebola Sudan. It's far more dangerous than Hanta or Marburg. Hell, it makes *Yersinia pestis*, the good old-fashioned plague, look like the common cold."

"This is why I took the job at the CDC," McIntyre said, swatting another mosquito on his neck. He removed his hand and looked at the pool of his own blood surrounding the flattened bug in his palm. "This is why all my colleagues are doing what they're doing. This is what we live for." He spoke loudly between short breaths, hoping that his words would find their way into Quinn's upcoming book. But he meant every word of it. To McIntyre, you weren't a true field agent until you faced the deadliest of all killers and returned to tell your story. His pulse raced with excitement.

They broke through a thick mesh of branches and vines into the village clearing. McIntyre and their local guide stopped short, almost causing the others to ram into them. As the other two CDC members entered the clearing, the sound of rustling branches stopped. The sudden absence of sound was unnerving.

McIntyre broke the silence. He hated silence. "Chances are we're too late to help anyone here," he said. "Ebola kills so efficiently that its epidemics usually burn themselves out. In some ways, Ebola is too deadly for its own good."

Across the rows of straw huts no one was visible.

"Where is everyone?" the photographer asked. He wanted to ask if they were all dead, but the question got stuck in his throat.

McIntyre spoke a Boston tainted local dialect to the elderly villager who had come to meet them at their Jeep. The others were happy to rest and wait for McIntyre to translate the man's response. They stared out at the ghost town, wondering how something so small could cause so much damage.

"He says many of the villagers have fled, and the rest are closed up in their homes trying to escape the fate of their neighbors and family members." McIntyre looked along the row of huts. "Some of them think we're here to carry them across to the afterworld. Like a band of grim reapers. They'll probably hide as long as we are here. They won't be happy when we examine them to make sure that the epidemic is over."

"But that's in due time," he said, detaining the silence. He pointed toward one of the huts, where flies were concentrated along the entrance. "The infected people are in the hut over there. They've been brought inside and left to die."

The sound of groaning arose from the hut, as though emitted from the depths of hell. Quinn's arms fell limp to his sides. The photographer somehow snapped a photograph through a trance-like state. The shutter snap seemed deafening. He turned to Quinn, exhaled slowly, and shook his head.

The medical team walked to the hut and placed their equipment and backpacks in the dirt. Their activity aroused the flies along the hut. Quinn nearly dove down to the ground as a fly buzzed past them. The CDC team began to don rubber gloves, paper gowns, and surgical masks. The other Americans followed their example as their sun-drenched guide looked on.

"Simple sanitary measures prevent the spread of the virus," McIntyre said. He paused for emphasis, and then continued, "assuming, of course, that we're actually dealing with Ebola."

One of the other CDC field agents spoke. “Ebola Zaire is spread by contact with infected human fecal matter. There is some evidence that Ebola Reston, another strain found several years ago in monkeys in Virginia, might be spread by an airborne route.”

“The evidence seems clear to me,” McIntyre said, “but the issue is still hotly debated. The medical community isn’t ready to accept the possibility that a virus as deadly as Ebola might spread so easily. Imagine the panic that would result.” He paused to let Quinn’s pen catch up. “But we have to admit that these viruses are smart buggers, or else they wouldn’t have survived for billions of years. Just when we think we’ve figured them out, they change. One day they don’t infect humans. The next they do. One day they can’t spread through the air, the next, well, you get the picture.”

McIntyre sprayed pungent brown liquid into his mask to counteract some of the overwhelming stench that awaited. The rest of the CDC team followed his lead. Quinn and the photographer hesitated, perhaps trying to decide whether to go inside, or else whether they should have come along in the first place.

McIntyre swallowed hard and tried to prepare himself for the sight inside the hut. No matter how many times he encountered Ebola, he would never be truly prepared for the human destruction, the bodily disintegration that occurred from these infections. The way the virus eroded almost every bodily tissue. The way it interfered with clotting, causing bleeding from every orifice. The way the last few reminders of humanity disappeared as patients bled to death through their bowels. It was the worst death imaginable, and then some.

McIntyre pulled open the flap of the hut entrance and looked inside while the others waited. He pulled his head out again and told the others, “It’s Ebola.” His face was puckered, and his jaw was clenched tightly. “There’s no doubt about it.”

He reopened the flap. Three people dying inside.

17

LANDING STRIP, SIBERIA

Drew Chambers was preparing to die.

The three hooded captors led him by the arms, pulling him forward, holding him up. They were headed toward a mound of snow at the corner of the airstrip.

Drew went reluctantly, more afraid of the alternative; there was no question in his mind that he would die if left there alone. If he was going to die, he wanted it to go by fast, not by freezing to death in the snow.

No explanations or apologies were offered for what was happening. Drew was surprised to be alive, so he remained quiet.

They reached the mound, which was actually two monstrous snowmobiles shrouded in a white cloth and a thin layer of snow.

The tallest man sat on one of the machines, grunted something that sounded like a Scandinavian language, and gestured for him to follow. Drew obeyed, lifting a leg over the wide ski jutting out from the front corner of the machine. His movement in the large boots was awkward, and he stumbled across the seat, nearly striking his head on a bar crossing the back of the snowmobile. Frozen snickers escaped the Gore-Tex hoods as the other men straddled their snowmobile.

Twin engines revved frozen steam into the air. Large, tinted domes came down over their heads, covering the snowmobiles from the front hood to the back bar and providing a partial escape from the surrounding elements. Drew held on tightly as they pulled away, each machine ripping two wide tracks into the snow behind them.

Despite their size, the snowmobiles moved with surprising agility and impressive speed across the rugged tundra surface. Drew watched as the wide skis found their way through the ice and flattened the mounds of snow beneath the front of the machine.

Lights on the control panel glowed brightly and rose in waves with each gear change. The combined headlight beams from the snowmobiles reflected off the endless stream of minute ice pellets rushing toward them. There was no obvious destination in sight. Drew clung to the stranger in front of him, a faceless man who shot at the plane a short time ago.

After an hour-long drive the snowmobiles crested a small hill.

Up ahead, maybe a quarter mile through the glimmering swirl, a glow appeared along the invisible horizon like a fallen moon along the snow. The snowmobiles thundered forward. The light intensity grew. This must be the mammoth research center, Drew thought, leaning to look past the driver's head. He had started to wonder whether the research station actually existed at all. But there it was, glowing prominently like the Emerald City from the Wizard of Oz. Now what? He wasn't in New York City anymore. There's no place like home, he thought.

Visibility was still obscured through the snowmobile dome, limiting Drew's ability to make out the details of the research station until they were just a short distance away. The glow was coming from a rim of floodlights lining the edges of a white windowless building.

A wall made from metal slab sheets marked the perimeter of the compound and concealed all but the top of the building within. Portions of the metal wall were dented inward, as though they had been struck with a battering ram. Several areas swayed slightly as gusts of ice fragments rushed against it. The upper rim showed the scars of the Arctic conditions. The light rising from the center was the only evidence that anyone was inside.

The other snowmobile riders jumped off and plodded toward the wall. They struggled together, pulling on a bar stretching between two of the metal panels. Glistening layers of ice encased the metal. One of the men raised a large stone over his head and struck the bar until it shifted downward, causing the panel on the left to lean open and wave in the wind. Light escaped through the opening.

The snowmobiles roared louder as they passed through the gate in the outer wall and entered the compound. The plain white box of a building resembled a giant white tomb, waiting to be lowered into the ground, researchers and all, and covered with frozen earth with the mammoth for another fifteen thousand years.

The snowmobiles stopped beneath an overhang along the inner side of the wall. The roar stopped abruptly and was simultaneously replaced by the sound of ice pellets striking the snowmobile dome. The temperature inside plummeted. The driver lifted the dome open without any notice, and the ice now struck Drew's Gore-Tex hood with the cadence of machine gun fire.

They walked up a ramp leading to the entrance of the research center, which was elevated several feet above the drifts of snow flanking the building. The Scandinavian man opened the door with a loud creak of metal against metal. Only a white space the size of a closet was visible. When they were all inside, one man forced the door closed while another pressed down a latch.

Drew's ears popped from the change in pressure. They were now all sardined into the tiny space. Someone must have released the seal on the inner door at the opposite side of the space, creating the sound of a Bell jar lid being opened.

Standing in the open doorway was a tall olive-skinned man with a single streak of gray hair along his left temple. He wore an expectant expression and kneaded his hands together.

One of the men threw back his hood to reveal a nest of black hair and a matching beard. He spoke in what was distinctively Italian.

The olive-skinned man listened intently. He cringed at the news. His composure deflated. He turned away, closing his eyes tightly and pinching the bridge of his nose between a thumb and index finger. He muttered to himself in Italian while shaking his head several times. Then he spoke fluently to the other man in the Scandinavian language. The tall slender man with ruddy cheeks and feminine cheekbones nodded vigorously and ducked through the inner entrance into the main section of the research station.

The olive-skinned man turned back to Drew, sizing him up. "You must be Doctor Chambers. My name is Aniello Bonacci." His English was devoid of any accent, but a certain finesse in the intonation hinted at Italian. He held an outstretched hand to Drew.

Drew removed his glove and held out a hand with three white frostbitten fingers. He watched the handshake but couldn't feel it. This time the numbness was real.

"I am in charge of this research station," Bonacci continued. "Those of us who are still alive are in danger. Come with me. We have a lot to discuss."

18

APARTMENT, ATLANTA

The mogul that sent him end over end last time was coming up next.

Jonathan Abrams accidentally lifted his right ski, causing a weight shift and an interruption of his rhythm. He was dragged downward to his right and had to compensate by pivoting back hard to his left. The gates were nowhere in sight, and he was accelerating down the steepest part of the slope. A giant spruce tree with snow-laden branches stood directly in his path.

Jonathan pressed the pause button on the video game and dropped the joystick on top of the fully made bed.

He checked his watch – 6:30AM already. Sleep was overrated; being awake opened the door for productivity. Poets use the extra time to write epics, politicians to resolve world conflict. Jonathan's preference was to feign attempts at online research before succumbing to his computer game addiction. We all have our vices, he thought. Isn't that what McIntyre once told him?

What time was it in Gabon, anyway? McIntyre would probably be calling soon. He'd be hot and hungry, sunburned and cranky, and he'd be up to his elbows in Ebola blood.

One of his cell phones started beeping the theme to Star Wars. Jonathan tried three phones before finding the right one.

Susan Mitchell's voice broke through the line before he could say hello. "Jonathan, where are you?"

"In bed, Susan," Jonathan said. "And doesn't anyone ever say 'hello' anymore? I'll check my latest edition of Emily Post."

"Listen," Susan said. "I've got McIntyre on the line, and he's got an Anopheles mosquito up his ass. You were supposed to be here already."

"Is it Ebola?" Jonathan asked.

He was expecting to hear another false alarm story. They seemed to be coming in on a monthly basis; Ebola was all the rage. There had been only one actual outbreak of the real thing during the three years that he'd been with the CDC.

"He's certain that it is," Susan said, as though equally surprised to hear the words come out of her mouth. "I'm going to get you on a conference line with him right now. I'll call you right back at this number."

Abrams hung up the phone. He hit the mute button on the video game and resumed playing. With a quick flick of his wrist on the control panel, he dodged the oncoming tree and spotted the blue gates along the right side of the screen.

When the phone rang again, he scooped it up and tucked it under his shoulder without missing a beat on the video game. "Hello, how may I help you?" he said.

"Abrams," McIntyre's voice crackled across a static filled line. "I hope I didn't wake you."

"No, sir," Abrams said. "But we seem to have a bad connection. Like you're five thousand miles away in the middle of the jungle."

McIntyre didn't laugh – not now, not ever. "Well then I'd better make this quick. This one's the real thing. Eight people are dead. Three more are on their way. Cultures and blood samples are en route to Atlanta."

Abrams sat up straight on the bed. The image on the screen skied off a cliff. "Any animal samples yet?" He asked.

He heard McIntyre's muffled voice. "One of the major challenges in dealing with Ebola epidemics is that the reservoir for the disease, the animals that carried Ebola between outbreaks in humans, is still unknown."

"I know that, but…" Abrams said.

McIntyre continued without hesitation. "No infected animals had ever been identified at an epidemic site in Africa. As a result, the virus lies in hiding, waiting to be inflicted upon human beings without any warning."

"McIntyre?" Abrams said.

"Yes, Abrams. I'm still here," McIntyre said. "I'm just explaining a few things to our friends from National Geographic. Abrams, the local officials are helping us set up traps and arrange hunts. They've got everything here – rats, bats, monkeys, snakes, birds, insects – maybe this time we'll identify the reservoir."

"They're setting up in a half-mile radius around the village," Susan said. "We can expect to see several hundred samples within the next week. We're going to need to pull technicians from other divisions in for this one."

"Well, I'll start pulling them together," Jonathan said.

Silence on the line.

"You still there?" Jonathan asked.

"Listen, Abrams," McIntyre said. "I'm going to let Mitchell run this one from the shop until I get back. She'll need you to help as all these samples start rolling in. Until then I've got two other projects that I need your help on."

What was McIntyre doing? Jonathan had been at the center for five years working his tail off. He was accelerated to level four in the center laboratories faster than anyone he knew there. But that's where it stopped. He had never been sent into the field, not even on a false alarm. He was assigned the title of Assistant Communications Director, which limited his power to running the communication through the CDC Website and posting information on the Hoax information board. Now he finally had an opportunity to get more level four experience, but it was going to be wasted.

Jonathan looked at the computer screen, where the skier was repeatedly slamming face-first against a large pole supporting the chair lift. Stars spun across the screen.

"What are the other projects?" Abrams asked. He picked up a pad and pen.

"First, I'm putting you in charge of dealing with all of the incoming questions concerning this epidemic," McIntyre said. "Everyone and their mother is going to want to know what's going on down here. Get in touch with the folks in public relations and make sure they can make a statement that reflects some degree of scientific knowledge. Then work with the IT boys to get something on the Website that will appease the rubberneckers looking for information on this epidemic. You're good at that kind of thing. I don't want them waiting on my doorstep when I get back there."

"No problem," Jonathan said. If that was to be his top priority, he wondered what the second project might be. Maybe he was going to be in charge of having mugs of hot coffee waiting for them at the airport. "You mentioned two projects," he said.

"I need you to take care of an inquiry from last week." McIntyre's voice was now fading in and out through the static. The signal was almost completely lost. Then he came through clear again. "I forwarded you an email a few minutes ago. It was from someone claiming to be in Siberia at a research center of some kind. He wanted us to help figure out a problem they're having."

"What kind of problem?" Jonathan asked.

"Something about fractures," McIntyre said.

Jonathan regretted having answered the phone. It wasn't taking hot coffee to the airport after all. McIntyre needed a cyberspace operator to answer his prank emails.

McIntyre said, "Take a look at the email, but I can't imagine that we could help this guy. I've tried to send a response, but the emails won't go through. See what the research department can find out so we can give this guy something. Then find a way to get back in touch with him."

Jonathan's fingers flew across the keyboard. Within seconds he was looking at his work emails.

Susan said, "I can speak with Seth Winters. He was at the NIH for several years researching bone mineralization."

"That's okay," Jonathan said. He was in a hurry to be done with this conversation. "I can get started on this one. You'll have your hands full with the Ebola project. Sounds like you're fading, McIntyre. Can you still hear us?"

"I can," McIntyre said, "but I have to get going. There's a lot to do here. I'll be in touch as we learn more."

There was a click on the line, and then Susan said, "Jonathan, are you still..."

Abrams hung up the phone and then opened the email message sent by McIntyre. "Aniello Bonacci," he read out loud.

19

PSYCHIATRIST'S OFFICE, NEW YORK CITY

One day his mother was there, and the next he was saying goodbye to a closed casket.

Grovely wiped his forehead with a handkerchief again; the psychiatrist's waiting room seemed particularly warm today. It was 2:30, and he was the last scheduled patient of the day. Imagine what Feely could be making if he put in an honest day's work.

Grovely was starting to feel better about having to wait until the end of the day to see the doctor. At least this way he could avoid being pressed into the premium Park Avenue office space with god-knows-who – all those incompetent psychotics staring and wondering what was wrong with him – as though they didn't have enough problems of their own. A businessman of his stature reduced to psychiatric treatment became a spectacle for the rabble.

The last year was a battle between the affliction and Grovely's stronger constitution. Still, he was no closer toward understanding or accepting this lack of control. Each time he tried to assess the situation objectively, he was left feeling that his reliance upon psychiatric medication was a failure.

Grovely ran through the routine in his head for one last time – how his mother committed suicide when he was six, how the event came without warning. One day his mother was there, and the next he was saying goodbye to a closed casket. He would pause then for effect. The conversation should then turn toward his father, how he provided no solace, how he said that she was better off now, that they were all better off.

What would Clive Grovely think about his son going to a psychiatrist? Heavy drinking and family beatings were signs of strength, but letting a stranger get involved in your personal life was unforgivable. No, Clive Grovely wouldn't have been caught dead in a psychiatrist's office. He was too proud for that.

Grovely spoke about his parents only when he was in Dr. Feely's office, and only when he was convinced that the discussion would yield prescription medication. Still, the rehearsal in the waiting room forced him into reminiscence and introspection. He pictured his father's cirrhotic liver, shriveled to the size of a walnut, killing him at the age of 42, a new family survival record. Grovely was just entering high school when his father died jaundiced and withered but full of pride. It was fitting that a man full of toxins would rot from the inside out.

Grovely leafed through the innocuous, psychiatry-friendly magazines displayed on the mahogany end table. Better Homes and Gardens. Condé Nast Traveler. Nothing with any political discussion or world events. Nothing that would invoke anger or anxiety. Nothing that would evoke any emotion at all. Just benign photographs shot through soft lenses. Smiling people in beautiful places. Grovely glanced across the magazines, oblivious to the words, trying to tranquilize himself with the inoffensive primary colors and pastels.

He awoke today with a jackhammer pounding in his head and a mild tremble in his fingertips. He only had three more of the green pills left, and only two purple ones in his backup supply. Doubling the prescribed dose had seemed like such a good idea while the pills lasted, but now he was in trouble. He couldn't afford to lose another psychiatrist. Not right now.

Grovely felt like a trapped rat in the psychiatrist's waiting room. He felt small and insignificant enough to crawl up the decorative molding lining the room and run along the top of the ceiling fan in exchange for the gratification of his medication. Empty rooms were safe, but they also gave him time to think.

He dialed the number to the office and waited for Lily to answer the phone. "Helloglobal," chimed the singing telegram voice at the other end of the line.

"Hi Lily," Grovely said. He was allergic to lily the flower and had an equivalent level of tolerance for Lily Fields the woman.

"Missstergroooovely" she said. "Still in a client meeting, are we?"

He hated being considered a part of her "we."

"We are," Grovely said. "We'll be in later this afternoon."

"We're running out of afternoon," she said.

"I'm running out of patience," he said.

He walked to the window and peeked through the blinds. The window was the ultimate test of psychiatric disorders among the patients. The acrophobics avoided the harrowing high floor view by sitting in the far corner of the room, and the claustrophobic had an affinity for the window and doors. There were days when patients huddled in the corner, everyone but the agoraphobics. Grovely rubbed an index finger along the blinds, knowing that his fingertip would not accumulate dust. He chose his doctors carefully through a unique but reliable set of criteria.

"Have I gotten any calls?" he asked. "There were none on my voice mail, but I thought…"

"Two calls," she said. "Both from a Brendan Connolly. Airplane pilot. Weird accent for an Irishman. My guess is he's Northern Irish. He said it was urgent, but it sounded like a wrong number if you ask me. Even Mister Gaines said …"

"Gaines didn't speak to him, did he?" he asked.

"Oh, no. I just mentioned the accent, because I was telling him about my sister's old English teacher, who was actually English, I mean, that's ideal, I suppose, but, anyway, Mister Gaines kept dialing the front desk, looking for you, and…"

Grovely was startled away from the conversation when the front door to the waiting room opened.

A woman entered with a boy about ten years old. He was overweight, and his head hung low over a handful of baseball cards that he sorted incessantly. He had greasy hair and acne. The woman intrigued Grovely. He studied her presentation, making comparisons to Claire, feature by feature. Perfectly aligned pleats on her skirt. Sloping nose. Degree of attachment of her earlobes. Muscle tone of her neck. So many similarities. He had never seen anyone whose linear symmetry even approached Claire's.

An unaccustomed sensation of guilt came over him for making these comparisons, but he couldn't stop. He searched for a flaw but saw none.

"Missstergroooovely. Missstergroooovely," the voice on the cellular phone sang out.

The woman smiled politely to Grovely, a symmetrical smile, not overly stretched, not too gummy. She had a dimple on the left cheek. He waited for a similar dimple to appear on the right cheek, but there was none. What a shame. How embarrassing that he had been comparing this woman to Claire. There was no comparison. He wondered if Claire had emailed him at home.

The doctor's office door finally opened, and Dr. Gerald Feely's neatly buttoned cardigan emerged. "Thorton, so nice to see you," he said, exuding comfort. "Why don't you come inside?"

"Thank you," Grovely said with a smile while tucking his phone back into his shirt pocket.

As they neared the end of the consultation, Dr. Feely began to write the two prescriptions that had lured Grovely to the office in the first place. Grovely was relieved. He had performed well for the doctor today. The trick was to convey a level of affliction enough to get medication, but not enough to land in the hospital.

"Have you felt like hurting yourself, like committing suicide?" the doctor asked while his Mont Blanc pen hovered over the half-written prescription.

"No," Grovely said, thinking back to his interaction with the answering service. While waiting for Feely's next question in the sequence, he imagined strangling the operator.

"Have you felt like hurting anyone else?" Feely asked.

Answering too quickly would suggest he had memorized the routine, but waiting too long would suggest he was struggling to answer. "No," he said. Then, smiling on the outside but clawing on the lining of his skull on the inside, he added, "Should I?"

Doctor Feely didn't smile. He never took Grovely's humorous answers to the suicidal/homicidal ideation questions lightly. "When someone feels trapped, sometimes such impulses become more difficult to control. You seem to be feeling trapped by fears of contamination." Feely leaned forward and placed his chin down against his pen, as though supporting the entire weight of his head on the cap. This indicated Feeley was continuing a thought. "I've seen claustrophobics maul people in an elevator like cornered dogs. The feeling of being trapped can be paralyzing or stimulating, depending on the individual."

All of Grovely's focus was on the doctor's hands, and the stillness of the pen.

Dr. Feely continued, "You're trapping yourself within these fears and obsessions. You are your only true means of escape." He removed the pen from his chin, satisfied that he had ended the session on a profound note. He resumed writing the prescriptions, and Grovely was able to breathe again.

20

RESEARCH STATION, SIBERIA

There were too many questions to ask.

Drew looked down at his hands. The thumbs and index fingers of both hands and the left little finger looked the worst. A clear demarcation from pink to white ran along a point just beyond the knuckles. He rubbed the area of demarcation, trying to encourage the blood flow to return to the tips, but the blanched skin remained unchanged.

"It helps not to look at them," Bonacci said. "The pain will pass faster that way."

The expedition leader was missing part of his left ring finger, which didn't offer any piece of mind. Drew dipped his hands in the warm water, trying not to pay attention to them anymore.

"Why were those men shooting at me?" Drew asked.

"Because they want to live," Bonacci answered. He plopped down into a foldout backpacker chair and prepared to explain the recent events of the research station.

"I want to live too," Drew said. He spoke more easily as the sensation and movement returned to his cheeks.

Bonacci nodded slowly. The contortion of his brow belied terrible news, although his rugged stoicism prohibited him from complaining or panicking.

Right now, Drew was too impatient to let the expedition leader ease him into the reality of the situation.

"Listen, what's going on up here?" Drew asked. "I've seen photographs of people with horrible fractures."

"Who did you see?" Bonacci asked.

"The three people with fractures," Drew said. He clenched and unclenched his fists in the warm water. The demarcation line on the fingers had moved further toward the tips on two fingers and disappeared completely on the other three. The areas where blood flow had been restored were now crimson and throbbing.

"Which three?" Bonacci asked.

Which three? How many were there?

"Someone with a comminuted tibia fracture." Drew remembered the photographs- the deformed thigh, the bone jutting out. "Someone with the initials MB."

"Mark Brozine."

"I guess so," Drew said. "And another with the initials SC."

"Stuart Crinley."

"What's happening with them now?" Drew asked.

"Nothing," Bonacci said.

"But those fractures were severe," Drew said.

"They're dead, doctor," Bonacci said.

Drew forgot about the searing pain pulsing through his fingers. He looked up at Bonacci, who was biting on one of the knuckles of his folded hands. He looked as though he was praying for a way out of this situation.

Bonacci released his bite-hold on his knuckle and said, "They were the first to die."

Drew's eyes widened. "How many others have died?"

"Five others," Bonacci said, "so far."

"What happened to them?" Drew asked.

Bonacci lowered his hands and leaned in closer to Drew. "One died from a heart attack. Victor Solnorov. He was the lucky one. He died before all the fractures started, before all this torture. The rest all developed fractures. Fractures with no apparent cause. I've seen my share of injuries on expeditions. The terrain and environment that we deal with can be fairly hazardous at times, but there's always a reason for the injuries that occur. Always some form of explanation. But there's none here. Not with any of them."

"How many others have fractures?" Drew asked.

"Almost everyone here," Bonacci said. "Fourteen out of nineteen, at last count. It's changing almost hourly."

The situation played through Drew's head like an endless loop. *Seven people dead. Twenty fractures out of the nowhere.* It seemed impossible.

"How bad are the fractures?" Drew asked. There was no way they could be as bad as the others.

"They're all pretty severe," Bonacci said. "It's like their bones are disintegrating."

Disintegrating bones. Fractures without trauma – atraumatic pathologic fractures. Drew thought through the catalogue of possible causes – metabolic diseases like osteoporosis, bone tumors and metastatic cancers, environmental exposures, and nutritional deficiencies.

"This sounds like an epidemic of pathologic fractures," Drew thought out loud.

None of the possible explanations made any sense, and Drew mentally discarded them almost as quickly as they appeared. A tumor might explain one such person, maybe two, but fractures in this many people eliminated tumors from the list of possibilities. Widespread osteoporosis was equally unlikely, even if there was a severe calcium or vitamin D deficiency in their diets. What was left? Some bizarre nutritional problem, or environmental exposure to some kind of chemical?

"I've been working with Dr. Yurov, the team physician, trying to figure out what's going on," Bonacci said. "We considered a nutritional cause, but our diets have been so carefully planned. It seems unlikely that such a problem could develop so quickly. Nobody's been here more than three months."

"Have you considered radiation, or some chemical exposure?" Drew asked.

"Radiation was a consideration," Bonacci said. "There are stories of Russian nuclear weapons being buried in the outskirts of Siberia. But we have radiation detection badges and Geiger counters for that reason, and we haven't seen any significant radiation levels since we arrived." He pulled a small white badge out of a desk drawer and tossed it down onto an empty chair. "Chemical exposure seems unlikely due to the absence of other symptoms. We haven't seen any rashes, hair loss, or gastrointestinal problems. In fact, nothing else happened – just these nightmarish fractures."

Drew couldn't explain what he was hearing. Something bizarre was happening to the people there. He agreed with Bonacci's earlier statement. *Everyone here who was still alive was in danger. He was also in danger.*

They all had to get out of Siberia and back to civilization, no matter what it took. He sat up straight, lifting his throbbing hands out of the water to point at Bonacci.

He said, "Those men were shooting at the plane because..."

"Because getting control of the plane was our only chance out of here," Bonacci said.

"We have to convince Global to fly us out," Drew said.

Bonacci stared at Drew, reading him. The research leader was obviously still trying to decide how much he could trust the new arrival. Trust had already failed in this expedition, but only trust could restore any chance of surviving.

"Global's not going to be flying anybody out," Bonacci finally said. "Global's stranded us. I told Thorton Grovely for a week that there was an emergency here. He told me to be patient. Can you believe that? Be patient when your friends are dying. Then our communication satellite went down, and then our monthly supplies never showed up. We're trapped here, completely isolated from the rest of civilization. That plane was our only chance of surviving."

Bonacci's words hung in the air like daggers.

"Are you running out of food?" Drew asked.

"Yes, but we're running out of fuel even faster," Bonacci said. "We've been conserving as much as possible, but soon we won't have any left to run our generators."

Drew looked down at his frostbitten hands again. The fingers were crimson with the restored blood flow. The pain pounded his fingertips. How fast would the temperature drop in the station after the fuel ran out? How long could they survive?

"I need to see the people with fractures," Drew said. "And I need to speak with Dr. Yurov." He stood up, tucking his hands against his stomach beneath his shirt.

21

HIGHWAY, ATLANTA

It was just out of his grasp.

Jonathan Abrams was stopped in traffic on the Freedom Highway, as usual, but making good use of the web of multimedia wires crisscrossing the inside of his VW Bug.

"I guess I have nothing better to do. I've just been sitting on a woodpile." Ester Mayfield's voice twanged through Jonathan's earphones. Most of the words in the sentence tripped an extra syllable off her tongue, as though there was a two-for-one sale on syllables.

Jonathan had no idea what she was talking about, but he liked the sound of it. "What's a wood pal?" he asked. "Is it like anything like a woodchuck? You make pies out of that down here, don't you?"

"I'm gonna make a pie out of you," she said.

Jonathan's right hand searched the car while his left did the driving. Everything he needed was within his grasp – everything except the watermelon flavored Charms blow pop that fell down between the seats. He could just about touch it, but he couldn't get his fingers around it.

He grabbed one of the large orange Circus Peanut candies out of the bag resting on the passenger seat. When it disappeared in an instant, he placed another in his mouth, and another, and another. The pistachio latte was still too hot to wash the candy down with a single big gulp, so he sipped the foam off the top. He rolled the car another three or four feet forward and then hit the brake again, causing the latte to slap against his upper lip.

"Well?" Ester said, sounding more like *way-yill.* "Is this one headed for the 'weak and dizzies' file?"

Ester was the best research librarian at the CDC. If there were anything to these fractures up in Siberia, she'd be the one to find it. McIntyre would be steamed if he knew Ester was wasting her time with this one, but she was one of Jonathan's many friends at the CDC who were willing to do favors for him on a second's notice.

The "weak and dizzies" term was a carryover from Jonathan's clinical chemistry laboratory days at "Windy City General" in Chicago. They were the stray patients who wandered in at 3AM complaining of being weak and dizzy. The symptoms were usually present for several months but tended to peak under a full moon.

The CDC's version of the weak and dizzies were the people who wrote or called in with reports of cold epidemics or concerns about the sanitary practices of their local grocery store. With its obligation to look into such reports but limited time and resources to devote to such matters, the CDC could only react to such an influx of correspondence by creating positions like the Assistant Director of Communications.

"It'll probably end up in the 'weak and dizzies' file," Jonathan said.

"Actually, I have a new file name for your requests," she said. The Marfa file."

"What's that one?" Jonathan asked.

"Marfa's the town where my baby sister lives in western Texas," she said.

"How many baby sisters do you have?" Jonathan asked. "There's one for every story."

"I have more stories than sisters, believe you me," she said. "Anyway, in Marfa there are these lights that bob and dance in the sky at night. The locals think they're extraterrestrials, but scientists say the Marfa Lights are from car headlights on a nearby highway."

"Are you saying my requests are crazy?" Jonathan asked.

Somehow, she spoke even slower than usual. "All I'm saying is, sometimes you come in here like gangbusters talking extraterrestrials, and all I find is headlights on a highway."

Jonathan wasn't sure if he saw the difference.

The brake lights turn off momentarily on the car in front of him. Jonathan prepared to jockey for position as the stationary lanes of traffic hinted at merging.

"My guess is that there's something going on up there," he said. "I just don't see how it can be explained by anything that should involve the CDC. I do appreciate your help with this, by the way."

"It's going on your tab," Ester said.

"What's that tab up to anyway?" Jonathan asked, reaching down between the seats again.

"You don't want to know, sugar," Ester said.

"I'll take your word for it," Jonathan said. "I also need to find out what companies are involved in research in Siberia. Maybe start with Italian companies and U.S. companies. The one I'm looking for has someone named Bonacci leading the research."

"Slow down, double-o-seven. This sounds more like a spy mission than a medical information search," Ester said.

"But I thought you wanted some intrigue in your life," Jonathan said.

"I might have said I could use a man in my life," Ester said. "Another man, to be exact. But the intrigue I could do without."

"I told you I was running up my tab," he said.

"I'll see what I can do on that one. Now, where do you want me to start on this fracture search?" Ester asked.

"Why don't you start with 'fracture' and 'bone' and…"

"Anything else?" she asked. "Maybe I could throw in 'kitchen sink,' or 'kit and caboodle."

"Maybe," Jonathan said. "What would you suggest?"

A young couple passed by Abrams' stationary car as he sat in the traffic jam. The woman was jogging at a good clip. She looked fit and was decked out in full running apparel. The man, who must have dragged the woman to the altar at gunpoint, was riding a bike next to her. A sun-drenched devil's head tattoo snarled menacingly on his shoulder. The dregs of a cigarette dangled from his lip. The bike swayed as knotty knees swung out lazily with each pedal rotation.

"Let's go with 'fracture epidemic,'" Ester said.

"And what will you do two seconds later, when you're looking at a blank screen?" Jonathan asked.

He watched the biking man hand the jogging woman a water bottle and take a deep drag off the cigarette as they disappeared around the corner.

"We'll see, Mister Assistant what is it again?" Ester said.

"Assistant Director of Communications," Jonathan said. "Although if we break this case wide open, they might move me up to Director of Communications."

"I don't know," Ester said. "Who's the director now?"

"Nobody. The position doesn't exist," Jonathan said.

"Then you do have a chance," Ester said, "unless you want to keep gabbing on the phone."

"Thanks, Ester," Jonathan said. "End call," he added distinctly, and the phone responded.

Traffic wasn't budging, and the temperature was rising in the car. The Bug's air conditioner hadn't been working since late August. It was October now, but it was still hot, compared to Chicago. Driving with all of the windows down worked well enough when the car was moving, which seemed to occur less each day. He was still holding off on replacing the air conditioner, convinced that the old VW wouldn't survive until the next summer. The last thing he needed was to send the car to the junkyard with a spanking new air conditioner. He needed the money for home repairs anyway. Now, he was the only person in Atlanta frustrated at the prospect of another Indian summer.

"Call Chip Williams," Jonathan said, and the phone dialed.

A squeaky male voice answered. "C.D.C.I.T."

"Chip, this is Jonathan. Did you get the hoax articles I sent for the Website?"

"Affirmative," Chip said. "I was relieved to learn that those rumors about underarm antiperspirants causing blood clots were unfounded."

"Everyone at work was relieved," Jonathan said. "Now you can go back to using antiperspirant again."

"Negative," Chip said. "Why? Were you considering actually showing up at work someday?"

"Maybe, eventually," Jonathan said, honking at a motorcyclist threading between the rows of traffic. "Why don't you place the underarm antiperspirant rumor between the one about hantavirus being spread through soda cans and the one about unused feminine sanitary pads containing asbestos?"

"No prob. Coca Cola and Kotex will be relieved to hear the news," Chip said.

Jonathan lifted a sheet of paper off his passenger seat. He glanced down the printed email message with the subject “Many Fractures” and found the email address of the sender. He had already tried to respond twice and had the messages bounce back, as McIntyre had already experienced.

“Listen, can you do me another favor?” Jonathan asked. “I need help tracking down this email address.” He read the address from the bottom of the email printout. He explained the situation with the fractures and the difficulty in reaching the sender. “I need to know how to get back in touch with this Bonacci guy. If not, I’d at least like to track where it came from. He says he’s somewhere in Siberia, but with my luck it’s some high school kid in Cleveland.”

“May have to log in some O.T. for that one,” Chip said. “You’re looking for giga-info on a nano-budget.”

“But can you do it?” Jonathan asked. He threw another Circus Peanut into his mouth and pushed it against the inside of his cheek like a wad of tobacco.

“No prob,” Chip said. “Did you say Siberia?”

22

RESEARCH STATION, SIBERIA

The continuous hum of a machine was coming from somewhere down the narrow corridor. It rose above the perpetual whistle of the wind that reaches every corner of the building.

"Under different circumstances I would start the tour through the laboratory," Doctor Vladimir Yurov said as they walked through the brightly colored but otherwise barren halls of the research station. Yurov walked slightly in front, navigating the narrow corridors with a limp characteristic of a right ankle injury.

Drew was surprised by the relatively large size of the research station. The logistics of building such a facility in this remote location and under such environmental conditions were mind-boggling. The dimensions of each individual area had to be confined, however, in order to maximally utilize the space.

Drew leaned forward to hear Yurov as they walked through the bright green hallway. The humming was louder now.

"The technology of the station here is awe-inspiring to anyone with scientific interests," Yurov said. "I understand that you have been selected to come here because of your clinical ability, but I have also read enough of your work on bone surface markers to know that you have varied talents."

Somehow Drew doubted that his clinical ability was what had brought him all the way up here.

All Drew knew about Yurov was what Bonacci told him. He was a science prodigy who left his home in a small Russian town at age thirteen to attend a national school for boys, and then studied medicine at the University of St. Petersburg. Afterwards, he returned home to join his father's medical practice. He became a world expert on wilderness medicine and published extensively, authoring an internationally regarded text on the subject.

Yurov's decision to devote his time to this unusual project was intriguing. Drew had many questions for the Russian doctor but knew that there were more pressing matters at hand.

The humming sound rose to a peak as they passed an aqua door marked "Genetics Laboratory" in bright purple letters. Drew tried to imagine the laboratory on the other side of the door, wondering how large it could possibly be in the miniaturized world of the research station. On the opposite side of the hall was an orange door marked "Microbiology Laboratory" in blue lettering. Yurov was right; they seemed to have all the science covered. The only thing Drew hadn't seen was the woolly mammoth.

Motion-sensor lights illuminated and dimmed as they progressed through the hall. Their actions seemed to be monitored by the building itself. Drew squinted to look through the dim corridor ahead, toward a spot where one of the lights was already on. His eyes were irritated from lack of sleep and the effects of the wind, and the changes in light intensity accentuated the problem. He raised his hands to rub his eyes, only to be reminded that he was wearing battery-operated warmers resembling oven mitts.

The throbbing sensation in his hands was slow to abate, and he had occasional chills whenever a draft came through. The research station was kept at a cool temperature, maybe 50 degrees. He wondered if he would ever feel warm again.

"This is the area that we have designated as the sick bay clinic," Bonacci said as they turned another corner of the narrow labyrinth. The green color of the hallway wall made an abrupt transition to a bluish-purple that reminded Drew of veins.

Four people were lying in makeshift hospital beds crammed into the room. Drew was relieved to see so few people in the room. Maybe the injuries weren't as severe as he had feared.

"They are the most critically ill," Bonacci said softly.

"The others are brought here from their rooms intermittently for their wound or fracture care," Yurov added. "Many of them have open fractures."

Open fractures could range from a small puncture wound to more severe damage with persistent exposed bone. Infection was one of the biggest concerns in such patients, especially when the treatment options were limited. Such injuries normally required surgical intervention and cleansing of the wound, usually with antibiotic solutions pumped through irrigation systems. Most of them required stabilization and mechanical fixation with combinations of plates, screws, or rods.

Open fractures were hard to manage in ideal circumstances. They often required prolonged hospitalization and extensive resources, both for the initial injury and the secondary complications that arise. Without adequate surgical treatment, however, the risk of these complications rises astronomically.

It came as no surprise to Drew that such injuries at a remote location had led to disastrous outcomes. Nonunion, a failure of the fracture to heal, would be common in such situations, but could be managed until appropriate care could be administered. Osteomyelitis, an infection of the bone, could cause significant destruction. Untreated infections could spread through the bloodstream and then reach the heart, brain, and other major organs, resulting in death from sepsis and multisystem failure.

"Have the deaths been from sepsis?" Drew asked.

"Three of them were," Yurov said. "Another died from broken vertebrae in his neck, and another bled to death from an arterial injury after a femur fracture."

Drew looked across the room. It must have been an incredible struggle to keep these people alive with limited resources. How would they deal with whatever was lying ahead?

The "clinic" was far undersized for the functions that it was now serving. The room was originally planned for a healthy group of young researchers. A minute cabinet probably originally intended for a tube of antibiotic ointment, a bottle of Tylenol, and a box of Band-Aids now revealed dressing supplies such as gauze, Ace wraps, and plaster cast rolls. Empty boxes that once held more supplies were lying on the floor.

The men zigzagged around the obstacles in the room. In the first bed was a man about Drew's age, his jaw distorted and twisted. He looked as though he had been struck in the face with a sledgehammer. Intravenous lines were dripping clear solutions at a rapid rate into his arms as he slept.

"Global flew in one round of medical supplies when the first few people were injured," Yurov said. He gestured to the empty boxes. "Those are almost gone now. We've tried to ration the supplies as well as possible, but there's only so much we could do. We're on our last few bags of intravenous fluids now."

"Do you have any antibiotics?" Drew asked.

"They ran out a few days ago," Yurov said.

The woman in the next bed managed a smile as they walked past. Her legs were each wrapped in gauze from the toes to the thighs and supported by plaster splints.

"Helene woke up with severe pain in both legs one morning last week," Yurov said. "By the next day she had an open fracture of the left tibia and a comminuted unstable fracture on the right."

"How many of are open fractures?" Drew asked.

"Too many," Yurov said.

"About half of them are open," Bonacci added. His expression revealed that he was well aware of the fact that the ones with open fractures had almost no chance of surviving.

They walked past a human form covered from head to toe in blankets. The chest undulated in shallow rapid movements.

Drew looked wondered how severe the man's condition was. Yurov lowered his head and exhaled through pursed lips.

The man in the fourth bed began to moan and writhe, running a hand along the gauze on his left thigh. Drew, worried that the man might injure himself further, stripped off his own hand warmers and reached down to restrain the man. Electric shock sensations ran up from his frostbitten fingers as he braced the man's shoulders and eased him back into bed.

Yurov reached into a cabinet and pulled down a syringe and needle. He unwrapped the packages and screwed the needle into the tip of the syringe as the injured man tore at his dressings.

The injured man was now lying flat, panting in pain, sweat beading on his face. As the outer portion of the man's dressing unraveled, Drew became aware of the extent of the underlying wounds and the unmistakable pungent odor of an infection.

"I'm giving him some morphine," Yurov said, drawing the clear fluid out of the medicine bottle into the syringe. He held up the filled syringe and grabbed for the intravenous line. "He'll be more comfortable in a few seconds."

Before Yurov could inject the morphine into the line, the man lurched forward in his delirious stupor and punched wildly, striking the Russian doctor's hip. The strike was punctuated by a cracking sound so loud that everyone in the room stopped moving.

Matching the horrific quality of the noise was the sight of the man's forearm, which was now bent outward at a seventy-degree angle from its normal position.

23

PSYCHIATRIST'S OFFICE, NEW YORK CITY

The office visit was over.

Grovely put up with the doctor long enough, had enough of his crap with the long discussion and the considerations and the changes of his mind and the recommendations for group sessions and the "how does that make you feel" nonsense and the "do you want to harm yourself" and "do you want to harm anyone else" questions and the other delay tactics, and wasn't that what really pissed him off about Feely, the delay tactics, as though neither one knew that the reason he was there was to make it to the end of the session and get his fingers wrapped around the damn prescriptions.

Finally, Grovely walked out of Dr. Feely's office, finally, with the two prescriptions grasped tightly in his palm, finally.

The doorman waved at Grovely as he passed, the fat doorman with the dent in the brim of his hat and the dirty shoes, the ignorant doorman who held him up at the front desk when he showed up without an appointment slip as though he didn't recognize him from all of his other office visits with Feely, as though there was any way that he could have a pathetic little slip of paper for an appointment that was made over the weekend, as though there was anything the slob could do if Grovely decided to blow right past him, and now he was waving, the idiot, like they were best friends, or college roommates, or brothers for chrissakes, and he could go to hell.

The pharmacy, restoration of normalcy, was just a cab ride away. And there was a cab, right on schedule. No passengers. The "on duty" light was on. He'd wave him down. He'd even step out onto the street to make himself more visible. But the cab kept going, would have plowed through him if he hadn't hopped backwards onto the curb just in time.

Grovely's pants began buzzing. He cursed and fumbled through his pocket for his cellular phone, nearly dropping it in the street. He looked at the caller ID display, which read "unknown." He flipped the front open.

An electronic voice said, "The Mamba's bite is venomous."

God, not now, Grovely thought. He'd have his medicine in a few minutes; then he could deal with this. But not now.

"Never test the Mamba," Grovely responded. He looked around. Somebody might be watching, maybe even the caller. There was no way to tell. The calls came in via satellite, and the voice was electronically altered. It could have been anyone.

"Be ready for my call in one hour," the voice said.

"What do you want?" Grovely asked, but the connection was already lost.

There were several people walking in the area. None appeared particularly suspicious, but Grovely began to suspect them all. Another empty cab sped by. He waved his arms toward the yellow flash but went unnoticed. He kicked a telephone pole.

Grovely began running in the direction of the pharmacy eight blocks away, keeping an eye open for empty cabs. He had to be alone to receive the call, but first he had to get to the office and show his face so Lily could spread the word that she saw him before Gaines put a price on his head. There was no way he was going to face the call or the office without his medication.

Nearly everyone Grovely past along his way stared at him, lending credence to his fear that he was being watched. They were staring at the odd man in a business suit running, shoes slipping, arms flailing, two pieces of paper tightly clutched in one hand and a briefcase in the other. He brushed past some, bumped into others, and registered every curse and stare.

An empty cab pulled closer to him as he ran, like a pace car in a marathon, slowing to just a few miles an hour. Grovely dodged an old Hispanic woman walking two small children as he watched the window roll down. Irregular clumps of hair blew across an otherwise balding head as the cabby asked Grovely if he needed a ride. Grovely looked up at the approaching street sign, realizing that he was within two blocks of the pharmacy. He maneuvered his suitcase to hold his middle finger up to the cabby, who instinctively returned the gesture before driving away.

Grovely didn't stop running until he was in line at the pharmacy. The delay before he could gulp down the first pill seemed like a lifetime. Everyone was a potential threat, a Mamba, hissing and loaded with venom. He tried not to think of all of the infections that all of the customers coming in all day were lathering onto all the money that they handed to the pharmacist, the pharmacist who probably fondled and licked the pills that he would soon be swallowing. He convinced himself that none of these intrusive thoughts mattered because each of the pills contained what he needed back – a little piece of his sanity.

The pharmacist leaned down over the counter and read the names of the medications loud enough to humiliate him in front of everyone there, but that didn't matter because he was now only minutes away from swallowing the first pill.

Grovely walked out of the pharmacy with two new prescription bottles in a white paper bag. His hands trembled while prying the childproof cap off the first bottle. The lid fell off, exposing a pile of blue heaven. Restorer of emotional balance in small doses, cure for whatever ails you when taken to excess. He took a pill out, rolling it in his fingers. The surface was perfectly smooth; the inner contents would make him smooth as velvet.

Grovely ran his tongue along the arid surface of the roof of his mouth, trying to generate enough saliva to lubricate the pill. He threw two pills in his mouth, swallowing as many times as necessary to get them down into his stomach. Then he opened the bottle of purple pills. Feeley had stressed that the purple ones were only to be used at night to help him sleep, and never to be combined with the blue ones. Grovely was tempted to take one of the purple pills right now, but he resisted. He could survive without it, for now. He felt at ease by the mere thought that at any moment he could reach for either medication.

Grovely calmly dabbed his forehead with a handkerchief, uplifted by his newfound pharmaceutical power. He wiped his face and neck. He imagined the little blue pills dissolving in his stomach and being absorbed into his bloodstream, calming his heart, numbing his brain. Thank you Doctor Feeley. What a savior he had been during the last year, for listening, for understanding, and, most importantly, for prescribing.

As the medication coated his nerves, Thorton Grovely easily found a waiting cab. The ride across Central Park to the Steinway building was more scenic than usual. The wait for the elevator was acceptable. He even leaned his hand down against the smudged metal bar running around the inside of the elevator, briefly. He checked his watch. Thirty minutes until the call. He would have to hurry.

Lily's striking but artificially colored green eyes shot open as Grovely entered Global Investors. "Misssstergroooovely, there are telephone messages." she let her voice trail off as though she was expecting him to be gone already. She scrambled for a pile of papers behind her desk. Grovely stood there silently, and when she turned around to see him still there, she startled.

"Thank you, Lily," he said, taking the sheets of paper toward his office. "I'll only be here for a few minutes. I have to get back out to a meeting. How have you been?"

Lily looked at him as though she didn't know who he was. "Fine," she said.

Grovely walked to his office, a third of the size of Gaines', but much better organized. Another buzz of the cellular phone startled him. It was too soon. He looked at the caller ID display. The number came as a disappointment and a relief. It was Gaines' office; the call was coming from about twenty feet down the hall.

"Thorton Grovely," he answered the phone.

"I know who it is," Gaines said, "and you know who this is. I think the question is, where are you?"

Gaines still didn't know he was in the office. That could work to Grovely's advantage.

"I'm on my way to a meeting," Grovely said, aligning his phone messages and placing them on the corner of his desk, one inch from the left edge, and one inch from the front edge.

"I hope it's the meeting in my office with Van Brauten and Associates," Gaines said.

Van Brauten was one of Global's best clients, but Grovely didn't have much choice. Right now, with the call about to come in via satellite, he had to get out of there. He just had to keep Gaines talking until he could make his getaway. He walked briskly past Lily, giving her a shush sign with his index finger in front of his lips. She shook her head in a reprimanding way and pointed to her watch to question when he'd be back.

"No, actually, I'm still working on the Taimyr problem," Grovely said into the phone. He signaled to Lily that he would be back at five o'clock. She nodded. He shrugged.

"I need some reassurance that you have a handle on that one," Gaines said.

"Absolutely," Grovely said. He looked out through the glass entrance of the office to the elevator door, which was just starting to open. He ran to the elevator. The cleaning lady pressed the door-open button for him, and he walked inside. "Actually, it's just about resolved," Grovely said. The cleaning lady was about to speak, but Grovely rudely dismissed her and pointed to the phone. He covered the mouthpiece with his thumb.

"I want an update when you get here," Gaines said.

"I'll see you at five," Grovely said, hanging up the phone.

The elevator stopped at the ninth floor. The cleaning lady got out. He checked his watch. Fifteen minutes until the call arrived.

Two men in three-piece suits got on the elevator. Grovely forced a smile and watched one of the men press the button for the eleventh floor. They were going to Global Investors. He was going *back* to Global Investors. He had forgotten to press the lobby button. He pressed the tenth-floor button as quickly as possible, but it was too late.

24

RESEARCH STATION, SIBERIA

The plunger sunk down into the syringe.

Drew supported the bedridden man's distorted left arm as Yurov injected morphine into the intravenous line. Drew watched the faint cloud of the solution swirl into the saline solution running down the line. As the solution reached the intravenous insertion into the man's arm, his flailing subsided almost simultaneously. First the arms and legs relaxed. Then the angry crazed expression on his face. And then his eyes drifted out of focus as his lids collapsed shut.

Drew was still holding the injured arm, trying not to displace the fracture any worse than it already was. Despite his gentle support, he could feel several crunches along the distorted area of the forearm as the broken bone edges rubbed against each other. Audible crunches accompanied several of the abnormal motions. He rested the arm back down on the bed, where it marked a sharp zigzag shape across the white sheet. Even Drew was disturbed by the fracture, less by the sight itself than by the fact that the injury was caused by such minimal impact.

The man in the bed was younger than his unshaven face and unkempt hair would suggest. He might have been forty years old at most. Something bizarre was occurring in this man's body to allow such an injury. Something bizarre was happening with all of these people. The pictures in the plane were bad enough, but to actually witness one of these fractures in person was disturbing.

Drew cradled the man's arm and examined the extent of the injury. He walked his fingers up the forearm, first along the radius and then along the ulna, feeling for contour irregularities. He was used to seeing x-rays of fractures, which facilitated the three-dimensional perception of the underlying injury. In the research station he would have to rely solely on his examination, and let his fingers record the abnormalities. He already missed having all of his usual tools available.

Both bones were broken along their mid-shaft. Even the lightest manipulation of the forearm caused the entire region to shift with a wet crackling sound. The radius seemed to be two main segments, but the ulna rattled as though he was running his hand across a pile of wooden matchsticks.

The others looked on as he felt the wrist with his non-frostbitten fingers.

"I don't feel a pulse," he said. The others nodded with the understanding that the blood supply was no longer passing through the injured area into the hand. This might be due to pressure on the arteries by the swelling and abnormal position of the arm. More worrisome, however, was the possibility that the arteries might be cut by a shard of bone.

Drew would have to improve the alignment of the bone and hope that the circulation would improve. He wondered what he could do if the arteries were cut. Surgical repair was impossible in the research station, and the man would probably lose his arm.

"The radius is badly displaced and angulated," Drew said. "The ulna feels like it's comminuted. I think it's best to try to reduce the fractures now while he's still sedated and before the swelling sets in. Do you have any local anesthetics? The morphine is helping, but I'm going to have to block the fracture site."

Drew looked up at Yurov and Bonacci. “I’ll probably need the two of you to help hold him while I reduce the fracture. If I can get the radius alignment better, it might be okay.” The ulna’s a crap shoot without any fixation hardware, he thought to himself, but if he could get the radius to lock back into better alignment, he would have a chance at restoring circulation to the hand.

A young woman entered the room, reached behind a stack of boxes, and took out a bottle of clear fluid. She acknowledged Drew with a nod, and he returned the greeting.

“Here is some one percent lidocaine with epinephrine,” Yurov said, taking the bottle and handing it to Drew.

Bonacci spoke to the woman in Italian. She nodded and hurried toward the supply cabinet. Within moments she returned with plaster, padding, and a large bowl of water.

“Is she a nurse?” Drew asked Bonacci.

“No, she’s not,” the woman said. Drew was surprised to hear her speak English. Her dark eyes shot toward him. “But she’s learning quickly,” she added, smiling.

“This is Maria Pelligrino,” Bonacci said.

“The molecular biologist?” Drew asked. He looked more closely at her face, the smooth skin, the energetic animation. She seemed far too young to be The Maria Pelligrino.

“Yes, that’s me,” Maria said. Her smile acknowledged her awareness that Drew was impressed. Few people wrote so extensively and become so established in the medical community during their lifetime, let alone by the age of thirty. She stuck out her hand, shook a reminder of the frostbite back into Drew’s hand, and said, “It’s nice to meet you, Doctor Chambers.”

Drew smiled and nodded awkwardly, and then refocused his attention on the fractured forearm. He reexamined the broken forearm, feeling again for the fracture line in the radius. The pressure he was applying suddenly caused a shift along the bone as his fingertip sunk down a few millimeters into a soft depression. He pressed harder with his fingertip, denting the skin to mark the spot.

Maria wiped the area with alcohol and handed Drew a syringe with lidocaine. Drew then plunged the needle through the skin and soft tissue until meeting resistance against the bone. He then gradually advanced the needle along the edge of the bone until it sunk through the broken outer cortex and into the damaged marrow. He withdrew the plunger enough to see some blood travel back into the syringe. He was right where he wanted to be. He injected half of the syringe solution directly into the fracture line to anesthetize the area. A similar but less precise injection into the broken ulna completed the anesthetic block.

"Could you please hold his arm right here and give more counter traction," Drew said to Maria. He demonstrated by interlocking his hands around the man's upper arm, and then switched positions with Maria.

Yurov placed the syringe of morphine in his pocket and assisted Bonacci in restraining the man's shoulders and hips against the bed. "We're down to the last few vials," he said.

Drew grasped the upper forearm with his left hand and the lower forearm and wrist with his right. He gradually pulled his hands in opposite directions, gently rocking them as he pulled. Maria held constant tension on the upper arm, leaning her whole body backwards. They both felt the bones start to shift as the spastic muscle and other soft tissues loosened their hold.

"Hang on," he said to Maria.

They held traction on the arm for several minutes. Occasional crackles accompanied the release of the bones from their abnormal position.

Once the soft tissues seemed adequately stretched, Drew pressed the forearm in a way that temporarily accentuated the angulated deformity, and then quickly snapped the bones back into position. The arm was again straight. Bonacci and Yurov winced at the sound of the bones during the maneuver. Drew smiled and looked up at Maria, who seemed surprised to still be holding onto the arm.

“You can let go now,” Drew said.

Drew felt the forearm again. The radius was back in good position, and that the ulna, despite its multiple fragments, was in much better alignment. He could feel the pulse surging back through the arteries in the wrist.

“The blood flow is back,” Drew said. “Let’s get him in a splint before he wakes up.

The four of them then worked quickly to wrap the arm in soft cotton sheets and a plaster splint. As they finished the moaning and writhing resumed. The morphine was starting to wear off.

25

APARTMENT, RUSSIA

Dmitri Petrov's clothes for the day were arranged in the shape of a little man along the chair.

He laughed. Sasha was going to make a great mother.

In the dim predawn light of their fifth floor one-bedroom apartment, Dmitri watched his reflection in the mirror above the dresser. Alternating reflections bounced between his eyeglasses and the mirror, creating a series of progressively smaller images of him. He tilted his head slightly to maximize the effect, watching himself wind down into an infinitesimally small particle of light.

He knotted his tie, noticing that the lower corner of the gray fabric was starting to fray. He used three ties during his seven years as a postgraduate student at the university – a red one, a blue one, and a gray one. Entering the business world called for some new clothes. For the first time in his life, he could buy a tie without checking his bank account. A thin strip of fabric. Accepting a private research company job had opened the door to many opportunities, starting with these simple pleasures.

Dmitri looked in the mirror, imagining himself in a new tailored suit and a tie without frayed edges.

"Who's that handsome man in my bedroom?" Sasha's voice came from behind him. She was lying in bed.

Dmitri leaned down to kiss her. She pulled his tie, holding the kiss just a moment longer. Then she released her grip and closed her eyes, draping lazily back across the bed.

He watched her for a moment. She was just starting to show. Pregnancy accentuated her beauty. She deserved so much – from him, from life. His PhD had come with a price. Sasha had withstood the limitations that Dmitri's education had imposed upon both of them. She had watched friends of theirs gaining financial independence through other paths – careers that were less demanding and required far less intelligence than Dmitri's. There was no immunity to such emotions. All she wanted was similar opportunities, some relief of her worries. She must have wondered if they would ever reach such a point in their own lives. He could provide that now.

"You need a new tie, Dmitri," she said.

"Because my wife is always hanging from my tie," he said, readjusting the knot.

"Anything to stay close to you," she said, puckering her lips and kissing the air.

He held her by the shoulders and kissed her on the forehead. "I'm sorry to disappoint you," he said, "but I must go to work, or else there will no longer be any work. No work means no ties, and no new apartment, and no new furniture. NuCure expects me to work for my salary."

Dmitri crossed the apartment in fewer than ten steps, scooping up his lunch bag as he passed through the kitchen. The buttery batter scent of fresh-cooked ponchikis filled his nose. He opened the bag to sneak a taste.

"Save the ponchikis for lunch," Sasha's voice came from the bedroom.

Dmitri shook his head. He wasn't sure which amazed him more, Sasha's tendency to see through walls, or her ability to read his mind. He pinched a small piece off the center of the ponchiki anyway. He savored the taste of the small prelude to an enjoyable lunch. With the top of the bag closed again, he unlocked the dead bolts on the front door and stepped out to the hallway.

The burned-out light bulb in front of the doorway still needed replacement. The only dim light came from a single bare bulb at the end of the apartment building hallway. Dmitri knew the building by feel. His feet instinctively hopped over the board with the loose nails that had lifted away from the others in front of the stairs. His hand released the banister in the rough sections where wooden shards protruded. He wove along the 44 stairs to the first floor, avoiding sections that creaked the loudest. He was outside.

A southerly breeze delivered the stale and familiar smell of the brewery. The gray and unwelcome silhouette of the beast rose up out of a nondescript collection of smaller urban outlines. A few people shuffled by with a mission, intent on getting to work or back to bed without interaction, without incident. Dmitri stepped down into the street, beside them, not among them. He faded in and out of the sparse light of the streetlamps and past the occasional lit windows of the factories. Workers were swallowed up and belch out through clanging metal doors. Dmitri remembered his parents – moving parts, strangers to daylight – as he walked past the factories toward NuCure.

The street descended into rows of what were once community storefronts but became reminders of decay. Windows were broken and lower floors were stripped to the cement, leaving only skeletons behind to hold up the overlying apartments. A black dog limped through a gutted grocery store, lifting the edges of abandoned boxes with a dust-covered snout in search of food.

Despite the obvious need for financial influx, the xenophobic community had resisted several attempts by foreign companies to pursue business ventures there. Before NuCure, all of the largest attempts crashed and burned against the blockade of government bureaucracy awaiting them. Their property was vandalized. Their employees were threatened. The companies all pulled out, only to leave another wave of joblessness and homelessness behind. The Marxist holdouts had won again.

NuCure was not immune to the resistance. Dmitri had little knowledge of such issues as a student because they didn't directly impact him. He was too busy focusing on his studies and research. There was an occasional mention of the company in the news, usually included in a discussion of foreign influence in the local economy. But he had much more to read, much more to be focused on at the time. He tried not to be distracted by such matters.

NuCure had several sources of funding, including some from United States investment firms. It was the first company with foreign influence to adopt an "if you can't beat them join them" philosophy, establishing a foothold in the community before even announcing their arrival.

A ten-million-dollar contribution to an urban beautification project helped convince the city officials. The hard-nosed university administration was eager to partner with NuCure, despite the grumbling of the faculty. The new biochemistry facility helped warm their hearts. The partnership would also provide a spark to admissions in an area generally considered by aspiring students to be unprofitable. The desire for quality students and high-profile research programs would be satisfied. They managed to swallow the capitalistic pill that came with the deal.

Dmitri slipped a hand inside his bag and pinched off the corner of a ponchiki. He couldn't wait to see what type of filling was inside. He pulled his hand out quickly, as though expecting to hear Sasha's voice reprimanding him again for stealing a premature taste of the treat. But he couldn't resist; it was in his hands. He sank his teeth into the chocolate filling. He folded the bag closed again, taking care not to crush the food inside.

NuCure was another gray building sticking up out of the cement city. Despite the company's worth, the facility was camouflaged in the same worn and aged exterior of the surrounding buildings – just another company.

During graduate school Dmitri accepted that he was doing research for research's sake, more out of love for the science than out of a need to fit into someone else's grand scheme. Nevertheless, he frequently found himself convincing his friends that his molecular biology and protein research would eventually be incorporated into therapeutic advances, as though medical applications were all that mattered. With this hypothetical endpoint in mind, the work always seemed more significant to them, more relevant to their lives.

Now they would all be satisfied that this imposed goal had come to fruition.

The name NuCure was etched into the stone façade above the entrance. Beneath the name, etched in Russian, were the words "providing new disease cures, one patient at a time." The letters were small and barely legible, even from a few feet away. To Dmitri, the personality of the company seemed so understated, so humble, so Russian, if saying that was allowed.

He walked into the gray building.

26

RESEARCH STATION, SIBERIA

What happened to the Tower of Babel? He couldn't remember.

Drew was no longer a religious man. In discussions on the topic, he would say that he gave up religion for science. The truth was that Matty's death convinced him without a doubt that there was no God – that there couldn't be. So why was his mind dredging up lessons from the Sunday school days of his childhood? Was it the fear of his own death?

Drew was sitting in the dining area. The room was large compared to the others at the research station, but still too confining. The research team barely fit inside. As more people entered, the eight-foot-high ceiling seemed to sink even lower over Drew's head, to progressively press down on him like a torture chamber in a haunted mansion.

The researchers coalesced into groups of nationalities. The Italians were in one corner, the Swedes in another. Three Germans stood with their backs to the far wall, and a less homogeneous group, most likely the Americans, was standing by the door. Several groups of Russians were scattered through the room. It looked like the UN gone wrong.

The groups spoke among themselves in their native languages, waiting for the meeting to start. Gradually, the natural escalation of volume that occurs with multiple conversations confined to a small area led to a cacophony of conflicting languages and dialects.

The sight and sounds of these mixed nationalities reminded Drew of the biblical story of the Tower of Babel. The people in the story were building a tower to heaven. When God saw them, he came down and made them speak different languages so they could no longer work together to build the tower. The people dispersed into the far corners of the land, and the tower was destroyed. Lack of communication – that's all it took to destroy their project.

The babble in the room increased as the groups tightened into their separate fragments. Drew felt out of place in front with Maria and Yurov. He felt the eyes of the others upon him. Did they pity his shared misfortune? Did they trust him? Did they believe that there was a chance at escaping their demise here? Their faces exuded a sense of futility. They were gathering to plan their future – a future that was shortening with every moment that passed.

Maria was pointing out as many of the people as possible as Drew referred to a written list.

Bonacci entered the room, moving with slow, deliberate steps. He spent a few moments with each group, speaking their language whenever possible, easing their anguish. The groups seemed to drift closer into a more cohesive unit in his wake.

As Bonacci walked closer, Drew saw a grimace on his face. The expression seemed to worsen with each step onto his right leg.

"Can we start?" a voice yelled above the rest of the noise. Heads turned toward the Russian man sitting alone on the floor in the corner. Squinting eyes darted through the crowd past low bushy eyebrows. A hand ran along a patchy black beard.

"Do you have somewhere else to be?" one of the Swedish men called out. He was seated with a splinted leg resting up on a chair. The blonde men flanking him laughed.

"We all have somewhere else to be," Bonacci said. "Let's try to make sure we get there."

The Russian with the patchy beard made a disgusted grunting sound and waved his hand in dismissal. He waved himself further back into the corner and eyed everyone with contempt.

"That's Oleg Larianov," Maria whispered to Drew.

"Remind me to keep my distance," Drew said. Larianov was now specifically eying him intently.

"Don't worry," Maria said. "He'll stay at a distance for you. He doesn't get close to anyone, literally or figuratively."

Bonacci strained to stand up near the center of the room. "We have a lot to get done, so I want to get this meeting started," he said. He then paced the room, occasionally pushing down on backs of chairs and people's shoulders for support as he spoke. "I'm not sure about anyone else here, but I don't plan on lying down and giving up. I called this meeting to provide an update on our situation, and to distribute the projects that we need to accomplish to stay alive."

The murmur in the room was swallowed by an expectant hush.

"Fuel is the most immediate problem," Bonacci continued. "Gunnar, can you give us an update?"

A brick wall of a man with a blonde ponytail stood slowly. He pressed and guarded his ribcage with muscular forearms as he worked to speak. "We're down to the last three gallons of gasoline. At this rate that will only last for two, maybe three days."

Bonacci nodded. "How much of the station is being heated right now?"

"About sixty per cent," the man said.

"We need to partition off a smaller area, then," Bonacci said. "And we need to cut back further on our utilization. Take Trepellier and Cortez to help you."

Gunnar snickered and whispered to the two Swedes, who responded with similar expressions. He put his arms on his countrymen's shoulders and said, "Nils and Ingmar will help me."

Bonacci made his way over to Gunnar and placed his hand on the Swede's empty chair for support. He looked up into the fair skinned face that hovered nearly a foot over his own. The room was silent. The Italians seemed to inch closer toward the Swedes.

Bonacci leaned in close and spoke in a low voice audible only to the Swedes. They seemed to be contemplating their options for replying to the expedition leader as they listened. Bonacci smiled, lifted his hand from the chair, and rested it on Gunnar's shoulder as he finished speaking.

Gunnar reluctantly smiled and nodded to Bonacci, and then to the other men at his sides. He lifted a blueprint of the station off a chair and replaced his forearms against his chest. Then he went to join Trepellier and Cortez, who seemed no more thrilled to work together than Gunnar had been. They placed the blueprint onto a table and began to map out their fuel conservation plan.

Drew wondered how long the fuel could last. And how long the temperature in the station could stay at a level compatible with life. A day? Maybe two days at the most. The temperatures outside were unyielding and deadly. It was just a matter of time before the cold penetrated the station.

The discussion then turned to food rations. There were about two weeks of food and water supplies remaining. This in itself would have posed a more alarming problem if it hadn't been for the overriding issue of the fuel shortage. Two Russian kitchen workers were assigned the task of cataloging the supplies and calculating rations to last six weeks.

What would happen after six weeks? Drew chose to ignore that question for the time being. He hoped to live long enough to face that problem.

"Do we want to freeze to death or starve to death?" Larianov asked.

"I don't plan on doing either," one of the Russian men said. A wedding band on a chain hung down in front of the collar of his long black sleeve shirt. "I propose that we send out a group in search of help. I will lead the group. You can join me if you like, Oleg."

"There's nothing within fifteen hundred kilometers of here," Larianov said.

"And the snow mobiles will burn through the last of our gasoline," Gunnar added.

"It's our only chance," the Russian said.

"It's suicide," Oleg said.

"I'll go." Heads turned toward an Italian man on the other side of the room.

The murmur in the room escalated again. Bonacci walked through the center of the room, kneading his face with open palms. He looked at the two men who were planning on heading out for help. "Where will you go?" he asked.

"East toward the river, and then south," the Russian said. "There are two oil rigs in that area that have been used intermittently over the past several years. There's nobody there now, but there may be some means of communication."

"What about our satellite dish and VLF transmitter?" Bonacci asked.

Drew leaned over to Maria to ask her what a VLF transmitter was. Maria whispered an answer before he could ask the question, "VLF stands for very low frequency. It's a radio transmitter with a wavelength pattern that allows transmissions to hug the earth's curvature over extremely long distances."

"I've been working on it," said a short German man that Maria had identified as Heinrich Bohr. He seemed too young for the bifocals that he was wearing. "I still don't know what happened to them, or how either one could have malfunctioned, let alone both of them." He looked around the room suspiciously.

"That's a good question," Bonacci said. "But we won't be able to answer that one right now. Keep working on it. That satellite dish may be our best chance of escaping from here."

"What about the question we all want to ask?" Larianov asked. "What's happening to us? Why are our bones breaking? Does anyone know what's happened here? Does anyone know why three of our colleagues are dead? Or why the rest of us are falling apart? That's what I'd like to know."

Bonacci navigated the room like a minesweeper through hostile territory, stopping close enough to Larianov to silence him.

"Doctor Chambers has now joined Doctors Yurov and Pellegrino in their efforts to solve that problem," Bonacci looked back toward Drew, gesturing with his eyes for the doctor to address the group.

Drew stood and spoke. "We are trying to figure out what's been going on. We're hoping that we can identify the source of the fractures by examining autopsy specimens, and maybe biopsy specimens if we have to."

"How long will that take?" a voice called out.

"That's hard to say," Drew started.

"More than three days?" another voice asked.

This brought on a series of shouts from different locations in the room.

"If so, then what does it matter?"

"Why are you wasting our time?"

"Time? We don't have much time,"

"When we die from the cold or starvation, will it matter anymore if we know what caused the fractures?" This deadly reality stopped the barrage of outbursts in the room. The last comment came from Larianov, who pushed his lower lip out with his tongue and wiped the twisted hairs on his chin with a dirty sleeve. He narrowed his squint even further and glared menacingly at the others.

Larianov stood, pushing first against the floor and then against the wall behind him for support. His eyes were fixed on Drew like lasers. "I do have to say I'd be quite interested in learning what is destroying us, bone by bone. You say you want to learn what's happening to us?" He was hunched with his upper body twisted, slowly advancing. He looked to Drew like a rattlesnake sizing up its prey.

"Of course," Drew said. "That's..."

"That is what you're here to do. Yes." Larionov's squint dialed in another notch tighter, but he didn't blink. Drew hadn't seen him blink yet.

Bonacci took control of the situation. "Yes, the medical team will be trying to treat the injured," he said, "but they'll need help. Everyone in this room can help in some way. Time is our worst enemy at this point, so let's get to what we have to do. If anyone needs help or has suggestions, please come and speak to me. Our only hope of survival lies in the power of this team as a unit. If we don't cooperate," his words died off, mid-sentence.

The room gradually cleared, nationality by nationality. Larianov remained until the end, unwavering in his penetrating stare.

27

GLOBAL HEADQUARTERS, NEW YORK CITY

Coyotes were known to chew off their own limbs to escape from a trap.

Grovely fidgeted with his wristwatch. He checked his cellular phone again to make sure that it was on. Anything to avoid looking at the two men in the elevator. Did they know who he was? Would they mention him to Gaines? Would the door open up to reveal Gaines there waiting for them, waiting for him? He leaned forward and tilted his head, brushing an invisible errant hair away from his brow, letting his hand linger there in an attempt to partly shield his face from their view.

If there were a way to claw and gnaw his way out of the elevator in time, he would try it.

The two men talked to each other, something about stock options, or the weather. He really couldn't tell, really didn't care. As long as they didn't realize whom he was.

Grovely checked his wristwatch again. Eight minutes until the call. But the watch had stopped. No, it hadn't. The tick of the last second just seemed to take an hour. He had eight minutes to get out of the building and receive the call.

The elevator bell sounded. Grovely tried his best to become invisible – back leaned against the sidewall of the elevator, body contracted into the smallest profile possible, head drawn back like a turtle – all hopefully out of the line of view from the front desk at Global. The men hesitated in an awkward moment, gesturing for him to exit first. Grovely shook his head, keeping his averted gaze somewhere in the vicinity of the man's tie clip. He gestured at the elevator floor buttons and pointed to the floor, shaking his head.

"Mister Van Brauten," Lily's voice sang from just outside the elevator, just out of Grovely's view.

Time skidded to a halt.

Had he taken a breath since getting into the elevator? Could the elevator be any hotter? The door began to close. Grovely let out an exasperated breath, wondering if he could remember how to inhale. He laughed nervously, and then sucked an audible gasp of air like a near-drowning man reaching the surface of the water.

"Wrong floor," he said, the last few words hollow with absent breath to support them. The effort to smile jiggled the beads of sweat pooling on his upper lip. They eyed him strangely and made obvious efforts to exit the elevator without turning their backs to him. The doors closed in on the second man. Grovely reached for the door-open button, only to slap against the door-close button. The man's shoulders were pinched multiple times between the shuttering doors before he got clear of their path.

"Sorry, really," Grovely said, tapping the door-close button like a rat in an experiment. Mercifully, the doors shut.

Grovely pressed the lobby button at least four times. His finger left a sweaty smear on the button.

As the elevator descended, the sound of the street became audible. The call awaited him at the other end of the ride, hopefully at some open meadow in Central Park. Why did the elevator feel like a furnace? Was he descending into the depths of hell? One hand pulled a handkerchief from his pocket and pressed it against his face while the other instinctively felt along his beltline for his phone. Still there. Still on. He reached back into the pocket.

Something was wrong.

With the handkerchief still stuck to his face, he patted his pants pockets with both hands. His gasp drew the white cloth of the handkerchief into his mouth. He bit down to block a scream.

The pills.

Where were the pills?

The doors opened as Grovely pulled his pockets inside out. The next set of riders pushed through, their purses and briefcases scraping against him as he shuffled in circles in the doorway. The pills were up in the office. They had to be.

He looked at his watch. Five minutes until the call. Did he have enough time to get up to Global and back out again? Could he get away without Gaines seeing him? The odds were slim. But there was no way he was taking this call without another blue pill. Maybe a purple one too. He needed the pills.

A buzzing sounded and vibrated down his spine. He reflexively reached down for his cellular phone as the elevator doors pinched him in. The display was blank. The buzzing got louder. It was the elevator – impatient, agitated.

He went back inside and started another ascent to Global.

The front desk and waiting area were empty, leaving a clear path to his office. Grovely ran on his toes to minimize the noise along the polished marble floor. He turned the corner. He darted into the office. The pills were in the pharmacy bag on the center of the desk. How could he have left them there? At least he was going to get them in time.

A door opened down the hall.

"How was the cross-town traffic?" It was Gaines' voice. The footsteps were approaching.

"Not too bad. Every now and then things go smoothly," said one of the men who had just ridden in the elevator.

Grovely started for the door. Then he stopped He was trapped. Not even enough time to swing the door shut. He looked for a place to hide. Leather armchairs. Sculptures on narrow pedestals. A mahogany desk with an antique silver ink blotter. He slithered between a lamp and a chair and ducked down beneath the desk as Gaines' voice reached the doorway. He crouched down into a ball, tucked himself into the narrow space, and waited.

He looked at his watch. One minute until the call.

The center drawer of the desk pressed down on his head. The grain of the wood bent his hair, creating the sensation of a thousand dirty little fingers pulling against it. Edges of drawers jabbed him – first in the knees, then in the chest. A tapping sensation against the wood on his left made him jump an infinitesimally small distance to his right. He was uncomfortably contorted now, with his left shoulder nearly touching his right knee. He felt as though he was trapped in a misshapen casket, waiting to die.

How long would they stand at the doorway talking? Did Gaines already know he was there? Was this just part of a sadistic game? How long could he stay crammed beneath the desk?

Grovely reached for his cellular phone – still on his hip. The tapping started again as he leaned back toward the drawers on his left. Rhythmic. Rapid. Like a heartbeat. His heart. The vibration made it seem as though his heart had been removed and placed in one of the drawers, but the tapping was coming from inside his own chest. At least his heart was still beating. Could Gaines hear the tapping from the hallway?

Grovely waited for Gaines' door to close, but the voices lingered. *Go inside – close the door – let me get out of here*, Grovely thought so forcefully that he almost heard the echo of his thoughts inside his wooden trap.

"I'll send out the press release tomorrow," Gaines' voice trailed down the hallway amidst marble-tapping footsteps. He was headed back to his office with Van Brauten and his partner. "Until then we've frozen all assets in our biotech sector."

The announcement? The biotechnology sector? Were they saying what Grovely thought they were saying?

Van Brauten spoke next. "I've been involved in many business deals in my life, but I must admit, this has been the most pain-free process of all of them."

"That's because this is such a good decision for Global and Van Brauten and Associates," Gaines said. "The timing is excellent and it's a win-win venture."

"Well, it's un…" Van Brauten paused. "Is this an African Grey Parrot?" he asked.

"Yes, it is," Gaines said. "They're remarkable animals. They've been known to speak over one thousand words." His footfalls trailed down the hallway.

"So I hear," Van Brauten said.

The bird's beak pecked at the cage. Its' claws scratched through the seeds.

Van Brauten said, "Anyway, as I was about to say, it's unfortunate that Thorton couldn't be here with us. I know how much effort he's put into this area of your business."

"I agree. He has," Gaines said. "But don't worry. I won't be leaving him out in the cold."

Gaines was selling the biotech business to Van Brauten. And he was selling all of Grovely's hard work down the river. Part of him wanted to charge out into the hall and stop the transaction. Part of him wanted to tell Van Brauten that everyone in the Siberian research station was going to die, and that they would bring the entire project down with them. But the rest of him acknowledged that he was trapped beneath a desk in a dimly lit office. What a sight he would have been, crawling out from under his desk like a rat.

The cellular phone vibrated on Grovely's hip, nearly sending him skyrocketing through the mahogany desktop above his head.

He peeked around the corner of the desk toward the open doorway. Should he run for the elevator and take a chance of Gaines seeing him? Should he answer the phone right away and hope nobody would hear him? The doorway seemed so far away, and increasingly narrow.

The second vibration triggered a series of goose bumps throughout his body. He would be taking this call right from where he was. But not without one more pill. He reached out for the bottles of pills with one hand while flipping the phone open with the other.

"Thorton Grovely," he whispered into the mouthpiece cupped between his hand and chest.

Silence at the other end.

Grovely fumbled the lid of the pill bottle with one hand. He listened for Gaines's footsteps. The lid suddenly popped off and several pills ran down across his lap and onto the floor. One rolled out from under his desk and skidded somewhere behind him. Somewhere toward the door.

"Thorton Grovely," he said with a louder whisper into the phone.

He waited, pressing the phone firmly against his ear.

"The only reason you're still alive," the voice started, "is because I enjoy watching you so much." The voice was cold and mechanical. Controlled and compelling. Somehow always in charge.

"I can get what you need," Grovely said, trying to appeal to the calculating machine at the other end. He pressed the phone more firmly against his ear to muffle the sound.

"You should write fiction. I do love listening to your stories." The voice said.

The electronic buzz of the voice scraped against Grovely's eardrum. It seemed to be eroding into his brain.

The Mamba continued. "I'm not happy with your product. It's time to cash in on my money back guarantee."

"I'm fixing the problem," Grovely said. "I sent Doctor Chambers in. That's what you wanted."

"Only part of what I wanted," the Mamba said. "You haven't paid your visit to our good friend, Doctor Atisoy."

"I haven't had a chance," Grovely said. There was silence at the other end. "Are you listening?"

"Yes. But you're not listening." The voice almost expressed emotion. "I have a reputation to uphold. In this line of work, maintaining your good name is everything. The damage control for this will cost me a great deal, so it will cost you a great deal."

It wasn't Grovely's turn to speak. He knew that. He took a blue or a purple pill – he wasn't sure which, he didn't care which – and brought it to his mouth. His vision was blurred. His fingers trembled. The pill stuck against a spot where his upper and lower lips seemed fastened together. With his whole palm, he forced the pill onto the leather surface of his tongue.

"I'm in a generous mood," the Mamba continued. "I'm going to give you a chance to rectify this situation. But it's going to cost you twice the amount that I paid you."

Forty million dollars.

We've frozen all assets in our biotech sector. How was he going to get the money?

The pill that was sticking in the back of Grovely's throat, teetering between being swallowed and being inhaled, leaned a little closer toward his windpipe. The clicking sensation of his heart against the entrails of the desk paused for a few seconds that felt more like minutes.

"That's an outrageous sum," Grovely said, less concerned about someone hearing from the hallway. "I don't have that kind of money lying around." He pulled his right shoulder away from the inner surface of the desk, which was progressively constricting ever tighter around him. "Nobody has that kind of money."

"You should have checked your wallet before you anted up," the voice said.

"But I can fix the problem," Grovely managed to say. He swallowed hard. The small pill lump wedged down his throat.

"From what I've seen so far, you're best at creating problems. Now we're going to let the experts fix the problem," the Mamba said. "But someone has to pay the tab. That's you, Thorton. I'm going to be generous for one last time. You have 48 hours to come up with the money."

"But I'll need more time," Grovely said.

"Then expect what you fear most."

28

NUCURE LABORATORIES, RUSSIA

Green fields. Blue skies. Endless horizons.

A woman was scooping her toddler under the arms and lifting him into the air, triggering a series of smiles and giggles. She held him high over her head and then brought him down so that their noses were almost touching. The sunlight danced around them.

The words "Breast Cancer" appeared in red letters at the lower edge of the screen, almost imperceptibly at first. The sound of laughter faded as the two words increased in size. Suddenly the image ripped down the center of the screen, the woman curling off to the right and the child to the left. Only "Breast Cancer" was left behind – large, bold, and imposing, on an otherwise gray background.

Dmitri was holding a NuCure mug. The logo on the side displayed an outstretched hand cupping a glowing star. Dmitri held most of the star in his own hand as he raised the coffee to his lips.

He was sitting with Andrei Nikitin, the PhD who had recruited him for the job. Nikitin was a professor emeritus at the university. It was his relationship with the university and his pull with the local government had helped pave the way for the NuCure facility to be built. He now headed the board of trustees at the company and had also taken on the role of running public relations.

His new home overlooking the river was evidence that NuCure had repaid him well.

"This is the part where you would speak," Nikitin said. Wide cheeks held up black-rimmed eyeglasses that warped the shape of his eyes and reflected the changing colors on the video screen. His hand was poised in the air as he simultaneously watched and listened for the right moment in the video. The sleeve of his white laboratory coat slid down his arm. The NuCure green embroidery above his breast pocket twisted the letters of his name.

There was more movement on the screen. The word "DEFEATING" appeared and slid into position before the others. "DEFEATING Breast Cancer." The words grew larger as they rose to the center of the screen. NuCure's logo materialized – "NuCure: DEFEATING Breast Cancer." The two ripped edges of the previous image reappeared from the periphery of the screen, reuniting mother and child. The sounds of joy returned.

Nikitin shot his index finger toward the screen as though he was firing a gun. "Right there," he said. "It needs more substance. Something about the cancer vaccines. The human-interest story is fine, but the science is extraordinary." He pulled on the invisible trigger with his middle finger while firing his index finger forward and then back again in recoil. "We don't even have to shoot you. We can just record you speaking for the voice-over."

A door opened. The lights went on. Dmitri spun in his swivel chair to see two men standing at the doorway of Nikitin's office. They were younger than Nikitin, maybe just a few years older than Dmitri. Their suits were well tailored, and their shoes impeccably shined.

Dmitri was immediately aware of his inferior clothing. The fading fabric. The scuffs on his shoes and the partially torn shoelace. He stood up, pulling the lower edges of his suit coat taught. He nodded. He smiled.

Nikitin shook their hands. “Welcome back. How was your trip?”

Eyes flashed toward Dmitri. The question was answered with nods that indicated that the details would follow at a more suitable time.

Nikitin stepped aside and waved a hand in front of the two men and back toward Dmitri. “Gentlemen, this is Dmitri Petrov,” he said. “The one I was telling you about.” He paused to evaluate the next sentence that he was considering. He seemed to nod to himself before smiling proudly. “This is the future of NuCure.”

Dmitri lowered his eyes with humility and lightly shook his head to Nikitin, who turned to introduce his two colleagues. The men’s polite smiles promised that they would wait to make their own judgments.

One of the men, Ilya Lukin, was the subject of a portrait in the front lobby that Dmitri passed every day while entering the building. Lukin was the president of NuCure’s Russian headquarters. Up close the real person looked about half the age of the portrait, but the stately confidence was still there. Pampered blonde hair and a smooth face suggested that he might have been kept indoors and preserved with skin softeners his whole life.

“My name is Ilya Lukin,” he said, reaching out to shake Dmitri’s hand.

“I know,” Dmitri said. “It’s a pleasure to meet you.”

The word “Melanoma” appeared on the screen.

They all glanced momentarily at the video. Lukin was still holding Dmitri’s hand in a prolonged motionless shake. He said, “As I’m sure you have already realized, NuCure is a place of ideas, a place of solutions. We are happy to have you join us. I hope that we can help guide you toward your potential, which may exceed even your own expectations.”

ELIMINATING Melanoma.

"And this is Fyodor Korjev," Lukin said, gesturing to the man beside him.

Korjev's black hair stretched in a slick streak over his head and expanded in rippling waves across his shoulders, high and proud like the mantle of Sampson. His face seemed vertically stretched and was sporadically depressed from several large acne scars. His eyes were opened wide with a perpetually startled expression and set in close to his severely narrow and pointed nose.

"Fyodor runs our immunology laboratory," Lukin said.

Korjev trapped Dmitri's hand in both of his and shook as though trying to pry his entire arm free of its shoulder socket.

"Fyodor knows a few things about research," Lukin said. "He might even be able to teach you something."

Dmitri knew the name well. Working with Korjev had been part of the attraction of joining NuCure, but he still hadn't met the world-renown immunologist. Korjev's work dealt with using tumor cell proteins in "cancer vaccines," a revolutionary advance in oncology. At the most recent meeting of the European Society of Molecular Oncology, Korjev presented his results applying this technique to eliminate breast cancers created in mice. The study complemented his earlier work with melanoma and reconfirmed Korjev's leadership in the field.

"I've read all your papers," Dmitri said. "Your scientific contributions have been remarkable."

"Thank you," Korjev said, his black mane bouncing. "I would like to say that I have read all of your papers, but I have to admit that I simply cannot keep up with the volume. A quest for knowledge burns like a flame inside of you. Few men possess your passion for science. I already have several projects in mind for you."

"Some more pressing than others," Lukin said.

Dmitri waited for Lukin to elaborate.

Bright red light filled the video screen. An animated antibody maneuvered the bloodstream, nudging against red blood cells and weaving among the white blood cells, as though determined to reach its destination. The Y-shaped antibody had two projections at the top that resembled arms, outstretched and undeterred, like the arms of Superman, and the tail glowed like a comet.

The men watched the video screen in silence.

"I hear you have been analyzing the X-ray crystallography studies of the HER-2 protein," Korjev said to Dmitri.

"I have. The model that you've developed for studying breast cancer is fascinating. There's a fourth HER-2 peptide sequence that we should conjugate to the others. Individually the sequence isn't very immunogenic, but when combined with the other three sequences, the response is augmented," Dmitri said.

"Why do you think that is?" Korjev asked.

"I'm not sure yet," Dmitri said. "I've just started looking at the conjugates. I'm glad you're back, though. I can't wait to get your input."

Korjev visibly curbed his enthusiasm and turned to Lukin, waiting for the president to speak.

"We have a new project for you," Lukin said. "A unique puzzle to solve. I think you'll find it more exciting than the breast cancer vaccine."

The vaccine-induced antibody in the video stormed through countless numbers of other antibodies that aimlessly bounced around the outside of a cancer cell. Arm-like projections latched onto brightly colored receptor proteins on the surface of the cell, enabling the antibody to get inside. Others followed. Their glowing tails were swinging through the inside of the cancer cell, destroying it with the ferocity of a baseball bat in a china shop.

"This new project is a perfect fit for someone with your background," Lukin said. "Maybe we can discuss it over lunch today. Why don't you come down to my office at noon?"

Dmitri glanced toward the corner counter, spotting the brown paper bag that he had carried to work. Sasha stayed up late again the night before making ponchikis for him.

The cell in the video exploded, shooting debris across the screen. The words "New Ideas" arched across the screen. "New Solutions" followed. And then "NuCure." The company name and logo rose to the top of the screen.

Providing new disease cures, one patient at a time.

"Sounds great," Dmitri said. "I can't wait to hear about it."

Everyone smiled.

The screen went black.

29

PIZZERIA, ATLANTA

The trigger didn't feel right in his finger. The metal was a little too cold. The edge was a little too sharp.

He cocked his shoulder and looked through the sight. Nothing yet. He hadn't blinked in over a minute. The next gunman was close. There was no telling when he would appear. How many of them had he killed? Seven? Eight? He'd lost count. But there had to be at least two of them left.

His sense of hearing was heightened, and every little sound was deafening for a moment. Footsteps were coming from around the corner. Cobblestone under boots. Military boots. Then a cartridge being loaded into a rifle.

This was it.

He steadied the M-16 in his arms and waited. One second. Another footstep. Two seconds. A swatch of brown fabric came into view along the edge of the doorway.

It happened within a fraction of a second. A boot came around the corner. The rifleman swung into view. Less than ten feet away. A Russian AK-47 in one hand. A female hostage – a civilian – in the other. A pull on the trigger. A loud blast.

"Aaaaaaah," Jonathan yelled, slamming his fist down against the front of the video game. "Not again." The hostage on the screen dropped to the ground. Blood squirted out of a gaping wound in her neck. The wound from Jonathan's M-16.

A muscle-rippled man in a dark green military uniform aimed his rifle forward toward Jonathan, leaving a view straight down the muzzle. A shot sounded as a red flash filled the screen.

A paper plate stacked with pizza crusts fell to the floor. Jonathan bent over to pick up the mess, again aware of his surroundings outside of the realm of the video game. The pizzeria. The mid-afternoon after-school crowd. Boys with pimples and girls with belly button rings. They were staring at him – everyone in the pizzeria.

"That's three times in a row, dude," said a voice through a mouthful of pizza. A junior high age boy was waiting behind Jonathan with a handful of quarters. "You're never gonna get to the next level."

"Yeah, you suck, mister," a younger, shorter, pimpleless version of the first boy added for good measure.

Jonathan patted his pockets. No more quarters. He had to get back to the office anyway. Reluctantly, he walked past the kids waiting to play the Death Seeker video game.

Jonathan accelerated through the Atlanta suburbs on his way back to the office. He dialed Ester Mayfield's number on his car phone. Was there any way that she could have found anything on her database search?

"Bout time," Ester answered the phone.

"You mean you've got something already?" he asked.

"Nothing at all," Ester said. "Whole pile of information about osteoporosis. Osteoporosis: the bone epidemic of the elderly. Osteoporosis: the hip fracture epidemic. Osteoporosis: the postmenopausal fracture epidemic. Even male menopause: the unseen epidemic. Nothing like what's going on with your friends in Siberia."

"You mean you didn't find anything called the Siberian Fracture Epidemic?" Jonathan asked. "Is it time to give up on this one?"

"Not yet, honey," she said. "I still haven't heard back from some of the people who are helping out."

Ester went through the list of resources that she had used for the search. Nearly every medical database imaginable, and all of the CDC file databases. She called friends at the National Institute of Health, the World Health Organization, and USAMRIID, the infectious disease unit of the military.

"You're kidding me, right?" Jonathan said.

"About what?" she asked.

"You called USAMRIID?" Jonathan asked. "McIntyre would have my head if he knew we got them involved."

"I wouldn't say they're involved," Ester said. "I just asked a friend of mine up there if she ever came across anything like this. We've been helping each other since you were still knee high to a duck. USAMRIID doesn't like sharing information any more than the CDC does, but this is just between us girls."

"I don't like involving them on any level," Jonathan said.

"Cool your britches," she said. "She's already called me back. They ain't got diddly squat, as expected. That part of the search is a done deal."

Jonathan pulled up to a parking spot at the CDC. He reached down blindly and grabbed two Circus Peanuts from between the seats. One of them fit perfectly between his cheek and gums like a wad of tobacco. The other went into his pocket for later.

"It sounds like this Bonacci guy is going to get the CDC 'dear john' letter," Jonathan said, walking into the building.

"Give me until the end of the day," Ester said.

"Don't worry," Jonathan said, "I don't think Chip will be able to track him down any time soon."

"You're telling me," Ester said. "Do you know how big Siberia is?"

"Four thousand three hundred forty by two thousand one hundred and seventy miles," Jonathan said.

"You know, sometimes I wonder if you're serious or just making this stuff up," Ester said. "I don't know what the square footage is, but I read on the Internet that you could take the United States and plop it right down in the center of Siberia and not have it touch any of the borders. And then you could take Alaska and every European country except Russia in the corners and still have a little Siberia left over."

"But you'd probably get a hernia the size of Wisconsin," Jonathan said.

He walked along the front hall of the building that housed the special pathogens unit offices. Framed photographs of the original CDC buildings and portraits of founders and past directors lined the walls.

"And it's cold," Ester said.

"You southerners are always cold," Jonathan said.

He swiped his ID card through a wall-mounted checkpoint. The lock on the door in front of him released, and he stepped down two stairs into a long dim corridor. There were no more decorations or photographs. He would soon pass McIntyre's office, and then Susan's office. His own office was at the end of the corridor, the cul-de-sac, as he liked to call it.

"I mean in Siberia," Ester said. "The temperature gets down to negative thirty-five degrees in the winter, that's Celsius by the way, and that's in the southern part of Siberia."

"That's not so bad," Jonathan said. "It gets down to negative thirty-five Kelvin in Chicago. Oh, and that's just the south side of Chicago."

"Then you'd be happy as a hog in slop there," Ester said.

"I wouldn't say that," Jonathan said. "In fact, I don't think I'd ever say anything even remotely like that. Anyway, I have no intentions of going up to Siberia any time soon."

Jonathan arrived at his office at the forgotten corner of the building. As he reached into his pocket for his keys, he noticed a streak of light slipping out from the doorway and slicing through the dim hallway dust. The door was ajar. The light was on inside. What was going on?

Still holding the keys, he swung the door completely open with the back of his hand.

He stepped back again. His arm dropped to his side. The phone almost fell. He looked around the small room, counting the faces.

"Jonathan?" a voice was saying.

Who were they?

"Jonathan?"

More importantly, why were they there?

"Jonathan?" It was Ester's voice coming out of the phone. "Jonathan, are you still there?"

Jonathan slowly lifted the phone to speak, his eyes fixed on the men in the room.

"Sorry, Ester," he said. "I'll talk to you later. I have a meeting."

30

TAIMYR PENINSULA, SIBERIA

It was difficult to pry the bodies apart.

Drew had visions of old black and white Frankenstein movies, of mad scientists sneaking out in the stealth of night, lanterns and pickaxes in hand, to dig up the bodies of the dead. Although ghastly, the task at hand was also necessary.

He was accompanied by Thor Lundgren, a scrawny five-foot-five Norwegian more closely resembling a gnome than his namesake, the wielder of the thunder hammer. Short one snow mobile due to the Russian search for help and another due to the dwindling fuel situation, they traveled by cross-country skis. The skis were more than adequate for traversing the short distance from the station to the encased gravesite of the researchers' cadavers. Skiing back while dragging Brozine's frozen corpse on a toboggan would be more difficult.

Penetrating the layer of ice overlying the wooden lean-to took nearly an hour. After breaking the first shovel futilely against the solid barrier, they began melting the larger ice patches with welding torches. The wooden cover finally released its grip, revealed the underlying corpses encased in icy debris. They scraped and picked at the debris with their tools. Seeing the plastic sheeting that was used to wrap the group of bodies, they were at first relieved to be nearing the end of the battle. But as they exposed the top edge of the plastic, they soon learned that each body and wrapping was still stuck solidly to the surrounding earth. The bodies were as stiff as cement, and reluctant to release their grasp from the earth where they were otherwise destined to lie.

Drew was scraping at the ice on the surface with a pickaxe, trying not to penetrate the bags around the individual bodies. He had no desire to see the contents of the bags. Not out there on the tundra. He stopped to reposition the floodlight resting on the makeshift tombstone that had been erected to mark the spot.

"Which one is Brozine?" Drew asked. He wasn't sure if Thor could hear him. He took a deep breath of frigid air and got ready to repeat the question.

"I can't tell," Thor answered. "He was the tallest of the three, but I can't tell what we're looking at out here." They both stared down at the body shaped mounds of plastic.

Drew made a mental check of his fingers, sequentially wiggling them from thumb to thumb. Ten of them. He could still feel them all. This was supposed to be a quick outing. How long could it take to load a corpse on a sled and drag it a few hundred yards? Everything seemed to take a lot longer at negative forty degrees Celsius. He looked out into the blackness, cursing the ice pellets as they ricocheted against his facemask.

"Maybe we should bring all three bodies back," Drew said. "We could take them one at a time." He had planned to take just Brozine's corpse. Not for any better reason than the fact that the first person to die from fractures seemed like a reasonable enough place to start. Taking all three corpses would require three separate trips. Drew stood and looked back toward the research station. A few hundred yards seemed like miles.

They were on ground slightly higher than the station, allowing a partial view of the building and compound from over the surrounding wall. The U-shape of the station curled away from them, away from the direction of the wind. The lights lining the perimeter of the U seemed less bright than when he first entered the station. From the generator power being conserved? From the power running out?

Somewhere within the U, outside but shielded by the research station and still mostly buried in the ice, was the mammoth.

As though on cue, the wind stopped abruptly. The flying ice particles dropped to the ground, and the iridescent hues of the Northern Lights appeared in the sky. In the compound, capturing the eerie reflections of this celestial demonstration of power, the upper tip of a tusk wound its way skyward like a purple light saber. It was the tusk that originally betrayed the resting place of the beast, the tusk that delivered the mammoth to the twenty first century.

It struck Drew as odd, as he scraped at the frozen corpses, that the people that had come so far to dig up the mammoth would now be lying so close to it in the ice. The mammoth was rising out of the same earth that was consuming the researchers. The mammoth once had to persevere to survive in this desolate place. Now it was persevering in its attempt to remain buried here.

"It was worth it," Thor said, as though reading his mind. He was still working to free the corpses from each other.

Drew looked back toward the corpses.

The bodies were wrapped in individual garbage bags and lined up in a row. Layers of ice had formed over each bag, and in all of the crevasses between the plastic. The underlying corpses were as solid as granite and seemed to have conformed to each other. They had been working on them with spades and pickaxes but continued to make slow progress.

"Coming to get the bodies was worth it?" Drew asked.

"Coming to Siberia," Thor said. "I would do it again."

Drew had decided in his first few seconds on the icy landing strip that coming to Siberia was a mistake. The biggest mistake of his life. Probably the last mistake of his life. Coming to grips with the ramifications of the decision to come to Siberia was something that they all had to deal with somehow. This wasn't the time to question Thor's statement.

Drew quietly swung an axe against an unyielding section of ice between two of the cadavers.

He decided that Thor had probably never had to yield to death, to the senselessness of profound loss. He could still cling to denial without yielding to the reality of their current situation. Unfortunately, Drew was all too familiar with death. He had faced death and lost once; he was stripped of the naïve confidence necessary to defy the undeterred force of death as it barreled down upon you.

But, like Thor, and like the others, something was still driving him forward. Somehow, as long as they were alive, they still had a chance. He bent down again to help Thor with the task at hand.

A crack sounded from within their grasp, an amplified version of the sound of two frozen chicken breast being pulled apart. The first corpse was starting to break free from the others. Drew could now slide his gloves and a chisel under the bag at one end, the end that felt like the head. He pivoted his wrists as best he could within the confined space, whittling away at the ice beneath the head. He followed the contours like a sculptor, delivering a man of ice out of the frozen tundra.

Working from opposite ends of the body, they scraped and chipped circumferentially, freeing the bagged body from the adjacent bag and underlying ice. As they reached the point in the middle where only the torso was still stuck, they each grabbed their end and alternated between rocking the end and striking the underlying area with their axes. At times the frozen corpse felt as though it might snap in half under the force of their pull.

"I think we're almost there," Drew said.

He pulled on the head with one arm while wedging the ice pick between the corpses with the other. He felt the final icy link break and fell backwards into the snow. The frozen corpse followed, lifting into the air and landing along Drew's legs like a white marble statue. Most of the bag crackled into several frozen plastic chips as the corpse came free. It seemed momentarily as though the body had come to life, come back from the dead to attack them for disrupting its eternal sleep.

Thor brushed the snow off of his clothes and knelt next to Drew. He looked down at the corpse and said, "We guessed wrong. This one is – was – Solnorov, not Brozine."

Drew looked down at the lifeless face on his knees – the bald head, the ice plastered beard. Solnorov's mouth was locked open in a frozen scream. Drew waited, wondering momentarily if the corpse was going to speak. It was as though it was still trying to tell him something. Could it, after all this time? He lifted the shoulders and pulled himself out from underneath the corpse.

Drew brought the floodlight in for a closer look at the corpse. He was right. Solnorov was telling him something, practically screaming it. But what did it mean?

"We need to bring Solnorov back too," Drew said.

"But I thought we wanted Brozine," he said

"Solnorov didn't have any fractures?" Drew asked, knowing the answer to the question.

"That's right," Thor said. "He died of…" He stopped short.

Both men shifted to allow their shadows to slide off of Solnorov's corpse, but there was no mistaking the sight. Large openings on both legs of the corpse led down into the depths of the thighs, where foot-long segments of bone were missing.

"Brozine fractured his right tibia, which would mean that this was him," Drew said. He pointed to one of the two corpses that were still frozen together. A similar gaping wound stretched down the lower right leg, from the knee to the ankle, and the tibia was missing.

Thor tilted the shoulders of the fused corpses, and the rest of the rigid forms that once were his colleagues followed. "And three ribs," he added, pointing down at the back.

Drew got up and walked around Thor to get a better vantage for seeing where the Norwegian was pointing. He saw what he expected to see. He just didn't know why.

He helped Thor tilt the corpses further until the backs swung fully into the beam of the spotlight. He reached down as though checking to see if his eyes were recording the sight correctly. There, open directly onto what must have been a frozen lung, was a hole even larger than the ones in the legs.

The broken ribs were missing. Someone had already removed all of the fracture sights from Brozine's corpse.

31

GROVELY'S CONDOMINIUM, NEW YORK CITY

He heard himself make the same sound as the horse in the movie.

Grovely looked down at his naked body, standing there in the middle of the room. How did he get to this point?

He tried to piece it all together.

The tension had been building up inside of him for years. Accepting the position at Global was like getting fitted for thumbscrews, and every day since then, the settings were tightened just a notch. Not enough to make him scream out loud. Just enough to take him to the brink.

The medication slowed the turning of the thumbscrews, eased the sharp edge of the pain. He wasn't sure which pills he had taken tonight, or how many, but he finally achieved the level of numbness that he needed.

He imitated the electronic sound of the Mamba's voice. *Fear what you fear most. Danger Will Robinson.* He laughed for about twenty seconds, or a few hours, or an entire day, laughed until he forgot why he was even laughing. Then the idea of laughing for no reason made him laugh some more.

An instant message must have just appeared on the computer screen. Amazing how the evening could go from being pleasant to being perfect within the timeframe of a computer beep. From numbing to sensual or sensuous or whatever.

Claire was the only person who knew his instant message address. Claire was trying to get in touch with him. He needed Claire. Claire was the only thing going for him right now. Why was he thinking about Claire? The instant message. He had to answer the instant message.

He ran to the computer, limbs flailing like a marionette.

"Are you there?" the screen read.

"Yes," he typed. "I am," he said out loud.

"I've been missing you," the screen said.

Grovely wrote the letter "I" and then was unable to find the apostrophe key on the keyboard. He pressed the equals sign, and a dash, and then a bracket sign. Then he decided to type the apostrophe-less words "I miss you" instead.

He was about to press the "enter" key when the words "What's new?" appeared on the screen.

"Oh, not much," he said out load, laughing.

Then he pressed the enter key.

"That's romantic," Claire's words appeared.

"You make me feel romantic," he typed.

"I wish I could be with you," she typed.

By the time Grovely finished reading the sentence, more words appeared. "But I can't leave here right now," she wrote.

"I can't leave here," he typed, still searching for the apostrophe key.

"Then we need to improvise," she typed.

Improvise? He tried to think of the possible explanations for what she just said but could only think of one. Did she mean what he hoped she meant?

She did.

Grovely stood there, mesmerized by the screen as Claire described every article of clothing that she was wearing and then no longer wearing. She was performing a computerized striptease. Before Grovely knew it, she was in her room, at the other end of the Internet, wearing nothing but her black stockings. At least that's what the computer said/ But that was good enough for him.

"I'm tingling all over," she typed.

"Wait," Grovely typed with one hand, fumbling at his shirt collar with the other.

He had never been this excited. A bead of sweat dripped down from his eyebrows, stinging his eyes and causing him to squint as he watched the computer screen. He removed his tie, folded it gently at the midpoint, and placed it down on the living room table.

His eyes were glued to the computer, where he watched Claire's next sentence appear on the monitor, "You're way overdressed for this party. Maybe I should tear off all of your clothes. First the tie..."

"Ifs ott," he wrote with shaking fingers. He was about to press the "enter" button but noticed his typos. He whacked at the backspace button so hard that he might have drilled his fingertips right through the computer keyboard. "It's off," he typed. "It's off. My tie is off. My tie is off," he said out loud with the repetition of a freight train.

"But we still have a way to go, don't we?" came the answer on the screen.

Grovely whimpered and unbuttoned the top button of his shirt. He wiped the back of his hand with what could have been either sweat or drool. The shirt was off in an instant. He refastened the top button, maintaining the collar crease, and then folded it and placed it next to the tie on the table.

He pictured the symmetry of her lips, the lines of her neck, the angle of her waist. He loved the fact that she wasn't in his home.

He sequentially removed each article of clothing with similar care and placed each on its own space on the table, quickly but neatly. He was standing there, naked, excited beyond control.

Then he heard the grunting sound.

A few weeks earlier, he had watched a Swedish film at the Lincoln Center Theater, and there was a scene in which a young mare was brought in to mate with a large stud. The male, ferocious with animal lust, kicked his front legs high in the air and made sounds that were frighteningly unreal as it performed its task. Grovely was so profoundly repulsed by the scene that he left the theater.

The sound of the horse, Grovely was fairly certain, had just escaped from his own mouth.

The computerized tandem striptease was only the beginning. Claire was typing vivid descriptions of love acts that were almost beyond comprehension. He typed his responses as carefully as he could without delaying too long and losing momentum, but he could hardly keep up with Claire. The words stumbled off his fingers in a bizarre blend of poetic verse and cheap smut. He was still making the noise of the stud from the movie, but the sound seemed more natural, and he no longer cared if it didn't.

Grovely had broken free of the reigns of his normal state of repression. He was petting the top of the computer. He was biting down hard onto his lower lip. He was holding a finger down on the keyboard, causing a string of apostrophes to run across the screen.

Grovely was catching up to Claire's writing, motion for motion. He typed eagerly, lost in love. It was as though she was right there with him, except it was better. He didn't need to be concerned about the cleanliness of what he was doing. He felt unfettered, free to explore his passion through this unique medium.

He typed a message that he could never imagine saying out loud, let alone acting out in person. No response from Claire. He expounded upon the details and resent the message. Then the screen remained silent for a few moments. Was she still there? Had he offended her?

"I'm coming over," appeared on the screen.

Everything in the room seemed to crash to the floor simultaneously.

Grovely stood there, panting like a dog in heat, sweating, drooling. She couldn't really mean it, could she? Would she really come over? Did she even know where he lived? Of course, she did. But did she really mean it?

The large wall mirror partially reflected a hideous form, hunched and crazed. It had to be him, but it looked more like a wild beast, a monster.

"I'll be there in twenty minutes," Claire typed.

Grovely typed "No," and then erased it. He typed "But," and erased that too. The instant message view box blinked and indicated that Claire was no longer online.

She must really be coming over.

Here. To his home.

32

HOUSE, RUSSIA

Sasha Petrov leaned in against the living room window as a burst of sunshine shot her in the face.

"It really is a wonderful view," she said. "So picturesque." She looked over the bushes strewn with purple flowers that wedged up against the house. A field led up to a wooded park that stretched over a hill, a series of hills, before diving down toward the city limits at some unseen distance. She let her cheek brush against the soft fabric of the drapes, imagining Dmitri at her side and their child in her arms.

"My husband and I fell in love with the view the moment we came into this house, nearly forty years ago now," said the woman with straight white hair and crooked yellowing teeth. She leaned diagonally against a faded wooden cane that was several inches too short. "Your daughter will be very happy here, Mrs. Vasilev, and this is a wonderful place for children."

"Please don't misunderstand, Mrs. Eberov. This is a beautiful home," Anna Vasilev said. "But Sasha has a lot of issues to consider. I still don't see how they could afford such an extravagant home, or why they would want to take the chance."

Sasha turned from her dreams in the window. Her mother shot a reprimanding glare that penetrated deeper whenever she was right. Sasha shared her concern about the cost of the house. Her parents had passed the lessons of the deprived conditions of their youth to her. Nothing was free. No matter how you wished or prayed. Buying a first home was an intimidating venture, even when NuCure was making the down payment. Nevertheless, Sasha had to continue pushing against her mother's pessimism, for fear of losing ground in their perpetual battle for control.

"The money isn't an issue," Sasha said. "Dmitri and I just have to decide where we'll be most happy."

"What time will Dmitri be joining us?" Mrs. Eberov asked.

"Any moment now, I'm sure," Sasha said.

"He's late," Anna said with a sneer. "We apologize for keeping you, Mrs. Eberov."

"Oh, that's quite all right," Mrs. Eberov said. "Do you want to wait for him before continuing, or should I show you the rooms upstairs?" She was slowly moving toward the curved banister that ran along the stairs to the second floor.

Anna tapped a knuckle against a wall, listening to the pitch. Whenever the noise sounded hollow, she tapped again and nodded.

Sasha tried to ignore her mother's antics, answering Mrs. Eberov. "Let's wait for Dmitri another minute or two, if you don't mind. He wants to be with me when I see the house the first time."

"He loved the rooms upstairs," Mrs. Eberov said. "Wait until you see the master bedroom."

Anna stopped tapping her knuckles along the wall and turned. "He loves the bedroom? Now that is a surprise, isn't it?"

Mrs. Eberov's face reddened. She averted her eyes from Anna and tilted her head awkwardly. A smile broke through Sasha's attempt at anger as she mouthed the word "Mother."

There was a knock on the front door.

"He must have heard the word 'bedroom,'" Anna said, concealing the side of her mouth that was closest to the direction of the knock with a cupped hand.

"Be right there," Mrs. Eberov yelled, disappearing around the corner in a fading sequence of cane strikes.

Sasha seized this private moment with her mother. "You promised not to mention money."

"Someone has to mention money," Anna said. "You're buying a home. Your first house. Money is an issue. Maybe not in the fantasy world where the two of you live, but in the real world."

"Your definition of the real world no longer exists," Sasha said. "Everything moves a lot faster. We can't sit by and watch the world run past us. We're tired of being spectators to life."

Anna waved both arms at Sasha in dismissal. "You're lucky your father isn't here," she said.

"Yes, we are," Sasha said. "He has been tormenting Dmitri since he took the job at NuCure, and he's been relentless since we mentioned that we were considering buying a home. I didn't want him to spoil this for us."

"Your father is concerned for your well-being," Anna said.

"Then he should congratulate us on our success," Sasha said. "Dmitri has worked hard for this. He deserves all the praise in the world, not all of your skepticism and criticism."

"He deserves some more common sense," Anna said. "Both of you do."

The tapping of the cane made them turn around. Mrs. Eberov was standing in the doorway. Dmitri bounded past her into the room. "Was I right? Isn't it beautiful?" he asked.

"It's even more beautiful than you described," Sasha said. In two steps she met him in the center of the room with an embrace. Over his shoulder Sasha saw her mother roll her eyes.

"There's a room for the baby," Dmitri said, backing away and placing a hand over Sasha's abdomen.

"There's a guest room," Sasha said, winking to her mother.

"That leaves enough room for both sets of grandparents to take turns," Dmitri said, eliciting an acquiescent nod from his mother-in-law. "Until the second baby is born, of course."

"Promising more grandchildren will only get you so far," Anna said.

"Mother's concerned about the price," Sasha whispered to Dmitri, intentionally loud enough for her mother to hear.

"Then it's a good thing she doesn't have to pay for the house," he whispered back at similar volume. He raised his voice again, "Anna, come look outside." He wrapped an arm around his mother-in-law and led her to the window. "No factory smoke. No broken glass on the ground. We're won't regret moving."

"Come see the upstairs," Mrs. Eberov said, tapping her way up the wooden staircase.

Anna slipped from Dmitri's grasp, following Mrs. Eberov. Dmitri held Sasha to his side. They were silent, sharing the view. Their apartment living room window view was partly concealed by a storm drain and looked ten feet over to the next building. It was rare to look outside and not see someone else looking back.

The house was hard for Sasha to believe. "We really can't afford this," she said and asked at the same time.

"We can," Dmitri said. "It's already been arranged. All we have to do is say yes."

"It all seems too easy," she said.

"You worry too much," Dmitri said. "This is how things are going to be. This is what it's like to have your plans work out."

Sasha smiled. She tilted her head to rest on Dmitri's chest as she hugged him and looked out the window. She saw her future – green fields, flowers, and sunshine.

"Hurry up," Mrs. Eberov's voice rang out from upstairs. "There's a lot more to see."

33

CDC, ATLANTA

They didn't sweat, not even in their charcoal suits during an Indian summer in Atlanta. Who were they? What were they?

"Make yourselves at home," Jonathan said. He waved an arm to the three men sitting silently in his office.

There were no smiles. The uninvited company hadn't smiled since Jonathan entered. They probably hadn't smiled in a lot longer time than that. Jonathan made an almost unprecedented decision to keep quiet and wait for them to explain their presence.

Who were they? Not police. FBI? Maybe military. They weren't in uniform, but they met all of the other requirements. They all had the same ultraconservative cloned appearance – little to no hair, the clean shaves, the narrow set eyes. They ate right. They exercised hourly. They never drank.

Jonathan walked around the back of his desk. A man who appeared to be the leader of the group was in his chair.

"Cage," one of the other men said, and questioningly motioned to the door with his head. The man at the desk nodded, and the silent order to close the door was followed immediately.

Cage? Shorthand for initials? Maybe KG? Short for Cajun? Maybe just Cage, not short for anything.

Cage was a forty-something sculpture of steel, with a shaved head that proudly displayed an assortment of scars. Pistol whip scars? He remained still as Jonathan walked behind him, as though assured that nothing that Jonathan could do, even unseen from behind his back, could make him flinch, let alone truly threaten him in any way. The back of his head was smoother than the front, suggesting that a bald spot might have been the impetus behind shaving the rest of his head.

Jonathan reached to the windowsill, lifting a brown-stained glass pot with a sharp pealing sound. The brown fluid lapped at the bottom as he gestured to the men with the pot in the air. They shook their heads succinctly and in unison. Jonathan sat down on the brown circle on the windowsill where the pot had been. He pulled a cardboard box closer and rested his feet on top of it. He filled a Chicago Cubs coffee mug and then cradled it in both hands and inhaled deeply, as though refreshed during a morning hike in the mountains. The aroma of the flat root beer filled his head.

They must have had an interesting reason for dropping in on him like this. He acted as though he had been expecting them, or maybe as though he hadn't noticed them. He would let them initiate the conversation.

Jonathan leaned over to get an issue of Wired magazine, which he opened on his lap. He pretended to leaf through the pages nonchalantly, but his mind was racing. Was he about to be arrested? Interrogated? He ran through the list of people that he had offended in some way during the last few weeks but couldn't figure out what was going on. The list was long, but the offenses all seemed too mild.

One of the men nodded back to Cage in acknowledgement of a signal imperceptible to Jonathan. He leaned over, closed the door, and drew the blind. Jonathan could see the muscles along the man's temples flex as his jaw tightened. The man to his side had an equally animated Mount Rushmore expression. Their jaw muscles now flexed simultaneously, muscles that matched the size of Jonathan's biceps.

"Jonathan Abrams," the sawdust raspy voice of Cage said with sadness, as though starting a eulogy. There was a hint of accent in his voice. Southern? Definitely not Georgian. Cajun?

Jonathan wanted to say, "Abrams? You're looking for that guy too? Wait till I get my hands on him," but he held back. He watched Cage, waiting for him to explain what he was doing in his office with Thing One and Thing Two.

"I've been looking forward to meeting you," Cage said without turning around. "You're going to be very helpful to us."

Jonathan took a sip of the flat root beer. "Us, meaning?" He hoped that he was about to find out who they were.

"Us just being…us, for now," Cage said. Jonathan could see the muscles along the man's temples flex, similar to the others, from his vantage point directly behind his head. He rubbed his own temples, wondering how that could be possible.

"Let's get right to the point," Cage said.

"Please do," Jonathan heard himself say.

Cage spun halfway around on his chair, a four-legged furniture dinosaur from before swiveling roller office chairs. He grimaced and then lifted the chair by the seat to make the rest of the turn. His intensity nearly knocked Jonathan backwards.

"You're sitting on a time bomb in Siberia, and you don't even know it," he said. "Instead, you're sitting here playing games while lives are at stake."

Siberia? This was all about Siberia? Jonathan's mind raced. Ester mentioned that she had contacted someone at the US Army Medical Research Institute of Infectious Diseases, but these guys weren't USAMRIID. Even USAMRIID didn't behave like this. Then the realization of what the man had just said sunk in. There was a time bomb ticking in Siberia. Something real was going on up there. Something bizarre, but something real. At least these three guys thought so.

"We're on top of the Siberia situation," Jonathan said. He flipped a page of the magazine on his lap, trying to look unimpressed, but mostly stalling for time. And then he decided to bluff. "I should say situations, though, shouldn't I? Something tells me you only know about the research center."

They looked at each other, visibly shocked that there would be three such situations simultaneously. "You have no idea what you're dealing with," Cage said. He must have decided to let Jonathan's comment slide for now. "Otherwise, you'd be working on getting a team up there."

A shrill electronic tone began playing "Yankee Doodle Dandy." Jonathan pulled his cell phone from his pocket, causing the volume of the song to rise. He flipped the phone open and saw Chip Williams name on the display panel before pressing the phone tightly to his ear.

"Hello," he said, gesturing to the men in the room with his index finger that he would just be a minute.

"Hey. What's up? Just wanted to get back to you on this Siberia thing," Chip said. "You're not going to believe this."

"I bet I will," Jonathan said, smiling to his guests.

"The transmission came from a seriously high latitude," Chip said. "One of the satellites used to relay the transmission is in an orbit that's way up there. Hardly anyone would bounce off of it unless they were above the Arctic Circle. Mainly adventurers and oilrigs and an occasional military excursion."

"And in this case?" Jonathan asked, carefully limiting his words to avoid alerting his guests to the nature of the conversation.

"Not a clue," Chip said. Jonathan visibly feigned satisfaction at learning this information, as Chip continued speaking. "At least not yet. The source of the transmission's lost.

All I can tell right now is that it seems to have been legit, at least as far as the location goes."

"It sounds like that seals the deal," Jonathan said.

"Hardly. I still have a way to go," Chip said, sounding a bit confused. "But at least there's something to this."

"I completely agree," Jonathan said.

"I'll let you know how it goes," Chip said.

"Sounds good," Jonathan said. "Thanks."

Jonathan closed the phone and stuffed it back into his pocket. He clenched his jaw and looked at each man in turn. "How do I know you've got anything on Siberia?" he asked.

Cage must have given another signal, because Thing Two reached into his suit jacket. He had to be reaching for a gun.

Jonathan wondered if he should charge and dive for the gun? It might have been his only chance. But what good would it do? He was outnumbered three to one. Though he was sitting in his own office, somehow he was playing on their turf. He watched for the gun to appear from behind the black fabric.

Thing Two pulled out a folded manila folder and placed it down on the desk in front of his boss. Then he leaned back again to his post near the door. Jonathan was sure that he heard a rush of relief blow out through his own mouth, but if the other men heard the sound, they showed no signs of it.

Cage removed the contents of the folder, a single sheet of paper. There was no official seal or heading, just several typewritten paragraphs. Jonathan put his mug and magazine down on the windowsill and tried unsuccessfully to read the sheet from where he was sitting.

"I'm sure you know that you're dealing with round two of this fracture disease," Cage said. His tone said that he was certain that Jonathan had no idea that that was the case, and he was right.

Jonathan knew better than to respond with a wisecrack. If he did, he might never see the information that was laid out on the table. As it was, he wasn't so sure he would actually see it. It might just be lying there to tease him. He waited for the man to continue.

"Last year," Cage said. "Along the Russian-Chinese border, about a hundred miles east of a Siberian town called Sretensk."

Cage motioned for Jonathan to come over and read the sheet over his shoulder. He still had his back to Jonathan but seemed to sense when he had moved closer. When Jonathan was close enough to read the paper, Cage draped his large hand across the sheet. The entire back of Cage's hand had been replaced by a wide mat of scar that extended at least as far up as the edge of his sleeve. Jonathan tried to read the sheet between the fingers, which were partially webbed from the scar damage.

Cage continued, "Five Russians in a remote military outpost developed a bizarre, previously unheard-of bone disintegrating disease. By the time they realized what was happening and a rescue team was sent in, it was too late."

"They died," Jonathan said, half as a question.

What disease destroyed someone's bones that fast? What bone disease killed so many people in one place? Cage was right. Nothing that anyone had seen before.

"The records are sketchy, at best," Cage said. "The Russians have a tendency for that, you know." He made a snorting sound. Things One and Two echoed the noise. "According to our information, four men were found dead, the other reported missing. We suspect that the fifth victim was taken in for experimentation so that the Russian authorities could get the scientific information that was needed."

"And the same thing is happening again," Jonathan said.

Cage had obviously told all he intended on telling. He lifted his hand away from the paper in order to allow Jonathan to read its contents. The first two paragraphs recounted the story that was just told. What followed made Jonathan lean closer, no longer able to pretend that he was being bored with old news.

The transmission from the outpost to Novosibirsk, Siberia was translated into English and typed in quotes below the original Russian. "Send medical unit and military replacements. Bone disease worsens quickly. Two are dead. The others can't walk and will not survive long. Proceed with all haste."

"Within two days they were dead," Cage said.

Jonathan read the transmission three or four times, but each time he got down to the bottom, he imagined the name of Aniello Bonacci. How long had it been since the email was sent to the CDC from Siberia? Maybe too long.

"We need to move quickly this time," Cage said. "The CDC has no way to get on site fast enough to intercept the disease."

"But the contacts for assistance came in to us," Jonathan said. "So, the CDC is still in charge of this one. And besides, you might have the ability to get in, but you don't even know where you're going."

"It seems to me that you need to inform us where the expedition is located," Cage said. "Otherwise, everyone there is going to die."

"Actually, it seems more like we need each other on this one," Jonathan said.

"You would need to be able to leave with us immediately," Cage said.

"Consider me gone," Jonathan said.

34

RESEARCH STATION, SIBERIA

It took almost 24 hours to thaw the bodies enough to cut through them.

Drew, Yurov, and Maria spent the morning assembling the supplies needed for the autopsies. They collected anything that would suffice as surgical supplies – scalpels, scissors, clamps. Heinrich Bohr took a break from trying to fix the satellite dish in order to search the maintenance storage room with their itemized list. He returned with arms full of equipment – saws, pliers, wire cutters, even a vice that they modified with silverware and a blowtorch to make a large retractor. They found protective facial visors with the welding equipment, then gathered the few remaining surgical masks, gloves, and gowns in the clinic.

They stacked the equipment on the counter doubling as an autopsy table. Between the stacks of supplies, lying beneath mounds of electric blankets used for the thawing, were the bodies of Victor Solnorov and Mark Brozine.

"I hope that whatever killed them has been inactivated by freezing," Drew said as he pulled on a pair of gloves.

"There's no reason to take chances," Yurov said. "We still don't know what we're dealing with, and it may be infectious. Viruses can survive deep freezing. Prions may be more durable."

Drew pulled back the first electric blanket, exposing Solnorov's body. The corpse looked even more intimidating now than when they first chiseled him off the tundra in the darkness.

Drew took in a deep breath. Yurov stared and frowned. Maria backed a few feet away from the counter. Her cheeks were flushed and her steps uneasy.

"Are you all right to help with this?" Drew asked Maria.

"Of course," she said. "I just. It's so strange to see him like this, someone I've worked with. A colleague."

Drew and Maria began the autopsy on Solnorov while Yurov began working on Brozine.

Drew pointed to the large holes in the legs. "Why do you think someone in the research station would have wanted to remove his femurs?"

"I have no idea," Maria said. "He died from a heart attack."

"That's what I've been told," Drew said. He wondered if they were about to find bone disease in Solnorov's body. If so, who knew that he had the disease? How did they know? Most importantly, what else did they know?

"I want to resist the urge to go right to the bones," he continued, "for fear of missing other findings that could be crucial to making the right diagnosis. We need to start with a thorough external examination before we even make an incision."

Maria nodded silently.

They systematically examined the entire surface of the body, looking for anything unusual. The skin was damaged in several areas by a combination of typical postmortem changes and freezing damage, leaving irregular darkened blotches. Most of these changes were along the back due to the postmortem distribution of blood pooling as the body was left face-up.

"Normal postmortem changes," Yurov said, looking over Maria's shoulder.

"Yes," Drew said. "I don't see anything else externally. I think we can move on to the internal organs. Then we'll come back to those legs."

Maria handed Drew a scalpel. He made a Y-shaped incision down the entire length of the chest and abdomen. He opened the abdomen to expose its internal organs. In the chest he continued his incision straight down to the unyielding ribs. He took out a saw that Heinrich found in the maintenance closet, lined the blade against the lower edge of the ribcage, and cut diagonally upward. The saw wasn't used to cutting human bone, or much of anything for that matter, and it whined its disapproval and spat out small splinters of bone mixed with an occasional puff of smoke. After finishing the cut, he sawed a matching line up the opposite ribcage.

Drew looked up to ask Maria for their homemade vice retractor, but she was gone. Yurov was wearing a surgical gown and donning gloves by the side table. "Your assistant had to leave unexpectedly. I think it had to do with your bedside manner. Would you mind if I assisted you in her place?"

"Of course; I could use your help," Drew answered.

They secured the modified metal appendages of the vice against the edges of the ribcage, and then Yurov turned the crank. The entire chest and abdomen were visible. They removed the entire contents of both cavities with a few swift cuts with the scalpel. They took the organs, en bloc, to a side table.

After examining the major blood vessels, they removed the heart and cut open each of its chambers. Drew ran a gloved finger along the inner surface of the heart, feeling the thickness and consistency of the walls and the elastic resilience of the valves, all of which appeared to be normal.

"There's no evidence of coronary disease," Drew said.

"Not at all," Yurov said. "If it was a heart attack, it may have been his first. Maybe it was caused by an electrolyte abnormality, something we wouldn't be able to see in the anatomy."

Maria reentered the room. Her color looked better, but she still eyed the cadaver with a terrified expression. "Sorry I had to leave. I can help with the specimens." She weighed the heart on the scale – 330 grams. She marked down the result in a lab book.

Drew and Yurov encountered at least two large rock-like masses in the right side of the central chest – the mediastinum.

"I think we've got some mediastinal nodes here," Drew said, squeezing the masses between his fingers. "Infection or cancer, I suspect, although I have to admit they're a surprise."

Drew saw Yurov's eyes tighten. Was he confused or disappointed?

"What do you think?" Drew asked, releasing his grip.

Yurov reached over to feel the masses. "I agree," he said. "These are impressive nodes. I'm as surprised as you are." He backed away to allow Drew to continue.

Drew used the forceps and scissors to cut the masses away from the surrounding tissues. They removed three white egg-shaped masses – two nearly four centimeters in size, and a third about half the size of the others. Maria placed them in bags labeled "lymph nodes, right mediastinum."

The lung surfaces were covered with black splotches.

"Anthracosis. I'm glad to see that you have your share of smoke and air pollution in Russia," Drew said. "I thought New York had the market on that."

"He was a smoker," Yurov said.

"Well, that'll also do it," Drew said, "although I don't remember reading anything in his records about him smoking."

They removed the left lung and sliced it open in segments like a loaf of bread. They examined the sponge-like air pockets of the alveoli; everything looked normal.

As he grasped the right lung, Drew immediately felt a large mass in the lower lobe. The mass was larger than his fist and took up most of the volume of the lobe. "What the hell is this?" he thought out loud.

He looked up at Yurov, whose mouth was gaping so far open that it was visible through his surgical mask.

"I'm not so sure we're only looking at bone disease here," Drew said.

"This looks like a primary lung cancer," Yurov agreed.

Drew hadn't spent much time during his career examining lungs, but he remembered that cancer that's spread to the lungs from other sites generally didn't produce large aggressive masses like this. If they hadn't been dealing with a bone disease, Drew would have sworn that this was a primary lung cancer, and that the cancer had spread to the mediastinal lymph nodes from the lung.

They sliced open the right lung, exposing a cross section of the tumor. The pale gray mass extended from one of the larger airways and extended in irregular strands toward the edge of the lung. There were several reddish, purple blotches where small hemorrhages must have occurred at some point. They handed the right lower lung specimen to Maria who labeled it and placed it into a bag.

The examination of the abdominal organs proceeded in similar fashion, one organ at a time. The most notable findings were in the liver, which contained multiple firm tan masses. The liver, because of its role as a filter for the body, is a common site for the spread of many types of tumors, and this appeared to be what had happened in Solnorov's case. Maria filled a bag with the masses from the liver.

Drew was increasingly eager to move on to the legs, but he stuck to his prearranged protocol. It was time to examine the brain. He cut a ring around the head that penetrated down to the skull.

Maria plugged in the circular saw, which Yurov handed to Drew. Cutting through the cranium went much faster than he had imagined, and within a few minutes, he was able to lift the top of the head off like a lid to expose the brain.

Drew slipped his fingers down between the brain and its encasing dural sheath. He divided the optic nerves coursing forward toward the eyes and the other major nerve branches from the brainstem where they penetrated the bone. Soon the brain was connected only by the brainstem to the spinal cord below. With one hand holding the brain up and forward, he sliced the top of the spinal cord. The brain rolled back into his hand.

Drew rotated the brain to examine its surface. He hadn't held a human brain in his hand since medical school. There was something both captivating and taboo about it, even now. The undulations of the gray matter were glistening and smooth. Drew placed the brain on the side table and sliced down its center with a large bread knife. He then made slices a centimeter apart, dividing the brain into segments like a meat loaf.

Multiple tan round tumors appeared within the cerebral cortex with every slice. Drew ran his fingertips along the surface of one of the slices. The abnormal tan area was coarse and firm, suggestive more of tumor than infection. "It's no wonder he died," Drew said. "He was loaded with tumor. His liver and brain were packed full of mets."

"We need to dissect the legs soon," Yurov said. He sniffed twice. "The benefits of cold preservation are starting to wear off."

"I think you're right," Drew said. "Why don't we each start on one of the legs? Maria, maybe you can get started preparing the tumor specimens for the microscope."

Drew inserted the vice retractor into the left thigh and turned the crank. The quadriceps muscles were pulled to the side with a slurp, exposing the foot-long segment where the femur was missing. Drew examined the free upper and lower edges of bone. Even transections had been made with an electric saw.

Drew looked at the saw on the counter, wondering who had removed the bone, and why anyone would secretly remove it.

Along the base of the hole, a white film was visible. Bone dust left behind from the electric saw? No. There was too much. Drew rubbed a gloved finger along the area, which seemed like the remnants of molten bone. Like hardened lava fields. This was the result of what had occurred to the bone before Solnorov died, not from the bone excision later. He picked at the substance with a mallet and chisel. It extended into the surrounding muscle. One of the hardest substances in the body had liquefied.

Drew rinsed the bone edges. Even along these cut margins, the outer cortex was paper-thin. None of the bone was normal. Solnorov had been walking on a leg made up of muscle wrapped around water balloon bones ready to pop.

Victor Solnorov was the first person to develop the bone disease – the "index case."

"If the disease was this bad in both femurs," Drew said, "then I'm sure we can find something in the other bones."

It didn't take long before he was proven correct. Drew and Yurov exposed as many of the bones as possible, finding disease at almost every turn. There were liquefied regions in each humerus, the left radius, both sides of the pelvis, multiple bones in the feet and hands, and in six vertebrae. The findings in these bones were consistent with what had obviously occurred in the thighs.

Solnorov's body was a disease factory. The bone disease, as impressive as it was, was less of a surprise than the findings in the chest, liver, and brain, which were quite different and were almost certainly cancer.

"We are looking at several parts of the puzzle," Yurov said.

"Yes," Drew said, "But none of them seem to fit together."

35

HIGHWAY, CONNECTICUT

The rain ran like blood down the car taillights ahead.

Grovely shifted uncomfortably in the back seat. He was exhausted, terrified, and uncomfortable, a combination that didn't go well with the pills he was taking. At least it wasn't the train, he reassured himself. The passengers swaying to the starts and stops. Sweaty hands wiping running noses and then grabbing metal hanging straps. God-knows-what coating the floors and seats. And the rain turning the putrid filth into putrid filth soup.

"How much further?" he asked.

"Still thirty miles," the driver said. "That's about 2 hours in I-95 years."

I-95 had been under construction since the dawn of man. But the potholes were still there. The median barrier was still crumbling. Strips of blown out tires from 1979 were still in the middle of lanes like an obstacle course. But the construction went on, and a sign guaranteed that the state of Connecticut tax dollars were hard at work. Another sign blinking up ahead for the past ten minutes now clearly read "Fines doubled in work zone."

"What kind of construction could they possibly be doing," Grovely counted the seconds ticking on his Rolex. "At 4:45 AM?"

The Mamba had given him 48 hours.

Someone has to pay the tab. That's you, Thorton.

He had 36 hours left to get the money to the Mamba, a man who stuck to timelines and kept his promises.

Then expect what you fear most.

He pulled a folded index card out of his wallet. He was tired of looking at the list of names. They invaded his thoughts. They haunted his nightmares. He looked at the top telephone number, wondering whether he should call Doctor Atisoy. At this rate, he might actually get there too late to catch the doctor on his way into the university molecular genetics laboratory. But calling was a mistake. He had to take Atisoy by surprise. That was the only way he could get the upper hand in the situation. He wondered what it would feel like to have the upper hand again.

Then he would go to Philadelphia. And then to Durham.

He wasn't sure if all of the men listed on his index card were responsible for the mess he was in, but he had to find out. That was his only hope to get back the money he paid for the so-called technology. He had no idea how he was going to do it. But his time was running out.

He speed-dialed the number to access his own voice mail. Still no messages. Why hadn't Claire called? Did she really go to his apartment last night? He certainly hadn't stayed around long enough to find out. What if she actually showed up after he left? How would she have reacted?

She couldn't have come over. Was she even capable of leaving her home? For him? Was she actually in love with him?

Traffic was starting to move. Maybe he would make it to University Hospital in time to see Atisoy. He had never been so eager to make it there. The city made his skin crawl. He tried not to touch anything when he went there.

They drove by a billboard advertising a casino on a Native American reservation. A slot machine poured out coins. An elderly couple jumped for joy. A woman in lingerie stood with a tray of drinks. The wind was blowing a tree branch against her knees.

Four more miles. The green highway sign was visible through the wipers screeching across the windshield. The rain slowed. The clenching of his jaw eased slightly. The autumn rain was cold, and he had forgotten to grab his raincoat as he fled from his apartment. No prepackaged meal and no raincoat. It hadn't been a good start to the day, or a good end to the evening. But the rain might stop just in time. Things were looking up.

"Business up there?" the driver asked.

Grovely stared into the rearview mirror at his driver's big round nose and shrub of a moustache. If there were black glasses above, he would have bet that the man was wearing one of those plastic disguises for sale in the Five and Ten when he was growing up. The eyes took turns filling the confines of the mirror like a reflective Cyclops, alternating as Grovely shifted uncomfortably. One of the eyes was looking back at him, but the other seemed to be slightly off center. He tilted his head slightly to the right to direct his comment toward the correct eye.

"I'm meeting a friend," Grovely said, in a way that he expected would end the conversation. Why was this driver prying into his personal business? He wasn't getting paid to ask questions. He was supposed to drive, and he hadn't been doing enough of that.

"Lady friend?" the driver asked. He winked with the eye that was looking somewhere to Grovely's right.

This guy seemed more like an idiot than a threat. Grovely thought about Claire, and the night they had just spent naked in front of their computers. "The lady friend is back in New York," he said.

"Lots of ladies back in New York," the driver said. "You go to clubs?"

Grovely waited as long as possible before answering in the hope that the driver would get the message. He didn't. The eye was still staring at the same spot to Grovely's right.

"What type of clubs?" Grovely asked.

"Strip clubs," he said. "New York's got the best strip clubs."

"Oh, I, no, I never go to strip clubs," Grovely said. The car service was usually more selective with their drivers. Being in the car with this guy was making him squirm. He lifted his hands and secured them in his lap, making sure that none of his skin came into contact with the leather seats. He made a mental note to call the car service when he returned home.

The car slowed down in front of a black iron fence. A red and white sign, wet and glistening, one of the few sources of light on in the street, signaled the location of an emergency room about fifty yards ahead. They parked near a looming black entrance gate beneath a leafless tree somehow surviving from roots that pushed up the sidewalk squares. A gray stone walkway ran up toward two revolving doors. Roman numerals and Latin etchings in the stone above confirmed the significance of this beaten old building. The entrance was dark and gloomy. To Grovely, it always looked like a place where patients checked in but never checked out.

"Here it is," the driver said. "University Hospital. Do you want me to wait here?"

Grovely didn't want to spend any more time with the driver, but he had even worse feelings about what he was about to do, partly because he wasn't totally sure what he was going to do. Coming here was a mistake, a futile attempt at resolving a hopeless situation. But here he was. He wasn't about to tell the porn king that he changed his mind and wanted to go home. He looked at his watch again, stalling, and saw the time change to 5:30 AM.

"Why don't you get some breakfast," Grovely said. "I'll give you a call when I'm ready, probably about eight or so."

Grovely stepped out into the rain and watched the red taillights of the sedan fade into the early morning gray of the city. It was dark, cold, and wet. *Par for the course*, he thought.

He looked across the dark stone walkway toward the entrance. Something moved along the grass. A cat. Maybe a dog. It rustled as Grovely's shoes tapped along the stone. His eyes hadn't adjusted to the darkness. A cold breeze entered his coat sleeves.

Grovely heard a low grunting noise, and then saw the silhouette of a human form rise up out of the place where he thought the dog had been.

It was a homeless man, a mosaic of gray and black clothes with no visible face. He shuffled into the walkway just a few feet ahead. By the time Grovely realized what was happening, he was within an arm's distance of the man. A frayed glove with curled filthy fingernails protruding from cut out finger holes reached out from beneath a ragged black coat and grabbed Grovely's sleeve.

"I need to tell you something," the man said with a thick phlegm-filled smoker's voice.

A moldy smell resembling a urine-soaked rug made Grovely gag. He tried to pull away, but the gloved grasp remained surprisingly strong for a weary old vagrant. Grovely's shoes slipped along the wet stones as he struggled to break free.

"I need to tell you something," the man said again. He was reaching into his pocket. Was it a knife or a gun? "I need to."

"You need to let go of me," Grovely said, yanking his arm away. He felt the searing pain of fingernails ripping into the back of his hand like daggers, and looked down to see drops of blood, flowing in black lines along his fingers.

The man grasped Grovely's bloody hand in both of his. Something pressed against Grovely's palm.

"I need to tell you something," the man said again. "This is from a friend of yours."

The momentum of Grovely's pull caused him to fall backwards as the man released his grip. He tried to catch his balance, only to become locked in a sequence of staggers and slips, eventually landing along the sidewalk just outside the front gate. He looked up just in time to see the shadowy form of the man disappear around the corner of the building, moving with the speed of a nocturnal serpent retreating from a lethal attack.

The simultaneous crackling sound and stabbing sensation in Grovely's palm registered in his head after a moment's delay. What cracked? Something plastic. He had fallen on whatever the man had placed in his hand.

His right hand was still supporting some of his weight. He looked down at the blood streaks along the stone, blood streaks that all led to his hand.

He lifted his hand and looked down at a broken petri dish, a microbiology laboratory container used to grow bacteria. In the dim red glow stretching out from the emergency room sign, he could see the thin opaque layer of bacteria at the bottom of the petri dish. Most of the bacteria was still there. The rest was somewhere inside his palm with the shards of plastic.

He scrambled to his feet and backed away from the dish, pulling pieces of the plastic from the puncture wounds in his palm with his other hand.

A passing ambulance shot streaks of red and blue light past him. It was only then that he noticed the magic marker writing on the bottom of the dish. He leaned in closer and squinted to decipher the words. And then another red flash of light from the ambulance illuminated the words: 36 MORE HOURS.

And then Grovely wondered how he was going to die.

36

NUCURE LABORATORIES, RUSSIA

The smell of dead fish was making Dmitri nauseous.

Ilya Lukin placed the plastic zip-lock bag on his desk. “We need your help with a special project,” he said.

Dmitri waited for Lukin to continue. The smell was getting worse. He looked around the room, trying not to focus on the plastic bag.

Lukin’ s office, despite being located on the underground floor at NuCure and being devoid of windows, exuded the company’s wealth. The mahogany desk was almost the size of Dmitri’s bedroom at home. Lukin sat at a high-backed wooden chair with intricate etching and decorative stone inserts that resembled a throne. The walls were lined with tall bookshelves and paintings.

Two large aquariums filled the wall behind Lukin. A terrarium on the desk contained a collection of brightly colored frogs resting on plants and clinging to the glass. The entire room seemed to be alive.

Dmitri sank into the seat of a large leather chair with embroidered armrests like a child visiting his father’s office. Lukin was now eyeing him strangely. Was he sizing him up, or waiting for a response?

“I’ll help in any way I can,” Dmitri said.

"I appreciate your enthusiasm," Lukin said. He looked back down into the plastic bag as he spoke. His nose twitched. "But this is something you'll have to think about."

Dmitri wondered if he was ready to make another big decision. "Then I suppose I need to hear more," he said. He tried to stretch his feet down to the level of the ornate Oriental rug, the only rug that he'd seen in the entire building, but he couldn't reach. The position of his knees was too far back, and his legs stuck out in front of him. He prepared to listen to what Lukin had in mind, and he prepared himself to say "yes." NuCure had already changed his life, and the lives of his family. He couldn't imagine turning down any request that they made.

"You're familiar with VECTOR, of course," Lukin started. He lifted the plastic bag with both hands and spilled some of the contents onto a plate.

Fish heads. Five small but particularly pungent fish heads.

"Yes," Dmitri nodded. The Russian State Research Center for Virology and Biotechnology, or VECTOR as it was more commonly known, was the only biosafety Level 4 laboratory in Asia, and had been the nation's leading source of infectious disease and biotechnology information for decades. Some of the research work from inside was made public, but some of it was not.

"And the plans for ICERID?" Lukin asked.

Dmitri had heard of the plans to convert VECTOR into the International Center for the Study of Emerging and Reemerging Diseases, but only what was common knowledge. The Russian press, which had improved greatly since the days of the Soviet Union, still underwent heavy filtering and biased slanting before reaching the public. Lukin probably knew a lot more true information about ICERID than he did.

"I know that there have been discussions with the United States about creating an international center out of the facility," Dmitri said.

"They've had more than discussions," Lukin said. He paused between each sentence, obviously choosing his words carefully. "The United States National Institute of Health and the World Health Organization are both involved, as well as several high-profile investors. They're planning on pouring in 25 million dollars for renovations and twelve million dollars a year for maintenance," Lukin said.

Dmitri was perplexed by the direction of the conversation and had no idea where Lukin was heading. But there was no question that he was intrigued. His tried to keep his facial expression neutral, but his expression must have belied his thoughts. Lukin paused, as though reading this expression, and then seemed to make a conscious decision to continue.

"The combination of the United States and Russia working under one roof has significant implications for the future of Russian research in this area, as well as for Russian security." Lukin looked angry for a moment. He took a breath and continued. "The influx of the United States brings the open window of their media, through which the world will line up as spectators to watch what was once Russian research at VECTOR."

"How does this affect NuCure?" Dmitri asked.

Lukin's gaze flashed toward the door and then back. Dmitri followed his gaze. He could see the lock across the door.

Lukin stood up. When he lifted the plate of fish heads, Dmitri was worried that he would be asked to eat one. Lukin smiled, perhaps aware of Dmitri's concern. "The problem with pets," he said, turning toward the aquariums, "is that you have to remember to feed them."

The aquarium directly behind the desk contained flat purple and yellow fish that flickered and bubbled along a bright coral display. Lukin crouched to get a better look at the tank. He leaned his nose against the glass, and one of the purple fish swam up to meet him.

"VECTOR has been an important part of our national security for many years," Lukin said. "Other laboratories will now have to take on some of this responsibility." He walked to the front of the other aquarium. The red, pink, and orange palette of coral lit up the inside of the aquarium, but nothing seemed to be moving inside.

"Have we been asked to do some of the research?" Dmitri asked. He was leaning forward on his seat now, to the point where he felt his toes tap down against the Oriental rug.

"It isn't a matter of being asked," Lukin said. He lifted a flap of metal at the top of the aquarium and poured the fish heads into the water. A bloody mist spread out from the tumbling cascade of eyeballs and gaping mouths. "It's a matter of seeing what needs to be done and stepping forward."

Dmitri watched the aquarium, waiting for whatever was hiding inside to come out for dinner. Some of the fish heads were hung up on branches of coral. Others were coming to rest on the gravel at the bottom. As Lukin returned to his chair, Dmitri made out the faint reflection of his own face in the glass of the aquarium.

Lukin continued, "This is the point where you have to decide whether or not you want to hear more. Our conversation here will have to remain between the two of us. And anything else you hear, and anything else you do, will only be between the two of us and a few specific individuals." Lukin leaned across the desk for emphasis. "That means no discussions at home, and no mention to the others in this company. When you leave your workbench, you carry its secrets with you. This work is not for everyone, but you're a unique individual, someone that I can trust."

A snake darted through the water and bit directly into the eyeball of one of the fish heads. The snake pulled the head toward the back of its mouth and glided to its original hiding place. The heads of other snakes were now visible within openings in the coral.

The sight stunned Dmitri. "They're fast," he said.

"They used to be a lot faster," Lukin said. "In the ocean they eat live fish, but the fish heads are much easier to feed them here. Unfortunately, they've gotten lazy."

"Are they poisonous?" Dmitri asked.

"Five times as poisonous as a cobra," Lukin said. "Almost as poisonous as these guys." He tapped the terrarium glass lightly. The suction cupped feet of the yellow frog on the glass held fast. The frog was about the size of a quarter – small but deadly. "The snakes have a gentle bite, sometimes even imperceptible by the victim, but the results are usually catastrophic."

One of the fish heads disappeared in a puff of scales and gravel. Another sea snake had struck.

"Do you want an answer right now?" Dmitri asked. If his desire to learn more about the research project won out, he would say yes. But there was much more to the decision. What type of research were they doing? Could he become involved in work that he couldn't discuss with anyone else? And then he thought of the down payment that they had just placed on the house. He thought of their plans to visit the furniture store on the weekend. His mind ran in circles as he tried to decide what to do.

Another fish head disappeared.

"Take a day," Lukin said. "I understand that this is a big decision. And it's a decision that you'll have to make on your own. I would normally give you more time than a day for something like this, but this project has to move forward. We have others already working on this project, but the addition of your expertise would be invaluable. You would be able to make an enormous contribution."

"Thank you," Dmitri said. He stood when Lukin came over to shake his hand.

Lukin held his hand for a few seconds longer than usual. "And one other thing – and don't be mistaken about this – your additional contributions to NuCure will not go unnoticed."

"I'm sure that's the case," Dmitri said.

Lukin walked over and unlocked the door. Dmitri took one last look at the aquarium. The snakes were no longer visible, and all of the fish heads were gone.

37

CDC, ATLANTA

Seventy rats, eighty-seven birds, twenty-two lizards, three snakes, three thousand mosquitoes, sixty beetles, and two hundred ants.

Susan Mitchell's Jeep Cherokee was backed against the loading dock of the Special Pathogens Branch at the CDC. Boxes were stacked up in the tailgate and separated by towels stuffed in to cushion the ride. The contents couldn't be spilled. The boxes containing the blood, urine, and tissue samples from the Ebola victims in Gabon. Twelve victims. Twelve deaths. So far.

Most of the other boxes contained the species collected in a defined radius around the village in Gabon where the epidemic was occurring. They had been trapped, sedated, or shot. The smaller animals were wrapped, vacuum packed, packed in dry ice, and boxed. Most of these boxes were now inside the CDC. The boxes filled with blood, urine, and tissue samples from the animals that were too large to send as airfreight were still inside the Jeep.

The process for getting samples from the outside of the building to the central biosafety Level Four laboratory was time-consuming but necessary. Each box was first cross-referenced against a master list. Entry into the facility required a series of clothing changes and cleansings. Containment was crucial.

Every specimen in every box had to be treated as threats to mankind. The researchers inside the laboratory wore one-piece positive pressure suits ventilated by a life support system. Any slip of the hand – a needle stick, a broken pipette or centrifuge tube – could be fatal. Researchers at the CDC were highly trained, but such disasters had occurred at some of the top centers around the world.

Protocols for contamination included treatment during isolation within the facility – in cases in which a known treatment was available. In the case of Ebola Zaire, a viral strain with no known treatment and a mere 10 per cent chance of survival, isolation to prevent spread of an epidemic was one of the few options available. Prevention of such contamination with strict adherence to protocol was essential.

Susan put her foot up against the back bumper and leaned against her knee. She arched her back and lifted a wave of blonde hair away from her shoulders with both hands to cool her neck. She closed her eyes to enjoy the soothing afternoon breeze.

Jonathan saw her profile against the blue-sky background. Did she know what her pose was doing to him right now? She was so attractive.

But she was such torture.

"McIntyre's going to have your ass in a sling when he hears that you've gone AWOL in the middle of an Ebola investigation," Susan said. Her eyes were still closed. She didn't have to see the victims of her verbal assaults.

"He doesn't have to find out for a couple of days," Jonathan said. He pretended to lean against one of the boxes of specimens in order to elicit a response.

Susan's eyes widened. "He'll find out as soon as he asks about you," she said. She reached across Jonathan into the back of the Jeep, causing him to move away from the boxes.

He smiled. She shook her head.

"There's no way I'm covering for you on this one," she said. "Not on a project this big."

"Ebola's Ebola," Jonathan said. "This epidemic is almost burned out already, just like the rest. This disease in Siberia is on the verge of exploding." He wasn't sure if "exploding" was the best description of the bone disease situation, but it was his best chance to justify stranding Susan with several thousand potential Ebola specimens.

"Siberia is an unknown," he added. "It's the kind of opportunity we're always talking about. If I hesitate now, these guys are going to scoop this thing out from under our noses. They certainly have the means. Besides, McIntyre is the one who put me on this Siberia case in the first place. If he was in my shoes, he'd go."

"He put you on it to make it go away," she said. "You know that."

"But it's not going away. It sounds like the real thing," Jonathan said. "The only thing to do is get up there and investigate what's going on."

Bret Riggs, a maintenance worker helping Susan carry the boxes, jumped off the cement landing and nearly stepped on Jonathan's foot. "Sorry, doc," he said, grabbing Jonathan's shoulder with an unassuming iron grip. The grasp caused a nerve in Jonathan's arm to fire, and his hand twitched to the side. "Almost stepped on you."

"No problem," Jonathan said, twisting his shoulder free and trying to find a subtle way to shake the tingling out of his hand.

"Just four more?" Bret asked Susan. He wiped the sweat from his brow with the back of his hand. A large vein curved over a mound of biceps muscle.

"Twelve down, four to go," Susan said. Her smile for Bret was more enthusiastic than any she gave to Jonathan. "You're lucky some of the samples went to the lab in Johannesburg."

Bret looked puzzled.

"You can wait until tomorrow to move those," Jonathan said. He looked at Susan in time to catch her scowl.

"No problem," Bret said, wrapping his muscles around the next box with a level of care that surprised Jonathan.

"Thanks, Bret," Susan said, smiling again. She patted – almost caressed – his shoulder twice. The show of affection made Jonathan wince.

Bret walked the box along the loading dock. Susan pivoted her back toward Jonathan to watch Bret disappear into the building.

Susan turned back to Jonathan and asked, "So who are your friends?" She was looking over his shoulder.

Jonathan followed her gaze toward the far end of the parking lot. Cage and his team were standing like granite statues beneath a weeping willow tree. There was a momentary glare in front of Cage's face. Glasses? Jonathan didn't remember any glasses. He didn't remember any flaws. Maybe sunglasses.

"They're from USAMRIID," Jonathan said, testing her.

"Interesting," she said.

"What?" he asked.

"They don't look like USAMRIID," she said without hesitation.

She stared at him. Her mouth twisted. Her lips pursed. Moist pouting lips. He watched her come to the conclusion that he was lying.

"They're military, though, that's for sure," she said.

"What's the difference?" Jonathan asked with a shrug.

"No difference," Susan said. "McIntyre's going to string you up regardless. You're abandoning the Ebola project. And you're losing this Siberian project to another agency. If I were you, I'd carry my resume on the plane."

Susan got under his skin like tetanus. Every time.

"Listen," Jonathan said. "I'm sorry I can't sit around and help you count mosquitoes. That's all you're going to be doing, and you know it. Nobody's ever identified a vector for Ebola. There's no reason to think you'll be the first. And I'm not turning the Siberia project over to anybody. These guys are way ahead of us on this one, and they've got the go-ahead to do something about it. If I didn't take some initiative, they'd leave the CDC in the dust if it weren't for me."

"And if it's a false alarm?" Susan asked.

"Then I'm sure you'll still have enough samples left over when I get back," he said. He patted the top of a specimen box.

"Your friends are waiting for you to come play," she said.

Jonathan turned around and looked beneath the willow tree. The men hadn't moved. The small reflection flashed again, just long enough to register as something familiar in Jonathan's head. They weren't glasses. They were binoculars.

A cool breeze slipped inside Jonathan's shirt and crawled up his back.

"I'll stay in touch," Jonathan said, walking across the parking lot.

Susan gave an exaggerated shrug.

38

RESEARCH STATION, SIBERIA

"You're not going to believe the histology slides."

Drew and Yurov were up to their elbows in the Brozine autopsy when Maria walked in.

"What do you see?" Drew asked her.

"You have to see them for yourself," she said. "I can hardly describe them to you. I've never seen anything like them."

"At this point nothing would surprise me," Drew said. He looked across to Yurov, who was scooping out disintegrated left tibia from just below the knee. What was once bone looked like curdled milk.

"We can finish the autopsy afterwards," Yurov said.

Drew backed away from the hollow torso of Mark Brozine's corpse. He removed his gloves and untied the stained towel from his waist.

"We took ten specimens from Mark's bones for you to make slides," Yurov said to Maria.

"What did you find?" she asked, looking at the liquefied samples in small jars on the tray next to the instruments.

"Brozine's bones looked a lot like Solnorov's," Drew said. "Just about every bone that we encountered was damaged to some extent, and several were completely liquefied."

"Anything in the lungs?" Maria asked.

"No," Drew said. "Brozine's lungs looked normal. What did the mass from Solnorov's lungs look like?"

"Interesting," Maria said. She motioned for them to follow her.

They walked in single file down the hall toward the microbiology laboratory where Maria had prepared the histology slides. To Drew, the barren hallway seemed even more confining in its energy-restricted dimness. The walls seemed closer together. The ceiling was more noticeable immediately over his head.

The cause of the bone disease was waiting beneath the microscope.

Maria opened the door to the laboratory. A noticeable wave of warm air, the first that Drew had felt since he left the plane in Oslo, escaped from the room.

Drew was stopped short by his first view of the room. The collection of research equipment was extensive and state of the art. Three DNA sequencers, large white boxes inconspicuously resembling refrigerators, filled the center of the room. Laboratory benches around the periphery were covered with microscopes, centrifuges, pipettes, and racks of test tubes. Incubators lined the far wall, well-lit and fully stocked with petri dishes.

Jon Karlssen, one of the cellular biologists, was pressing his face against a microscope. Maria leaned in and tapped him on the shoulder. "Jon, they would like to view the slides."

Karlssen pushed back from the microscope, placed his elbow on the countertop, and leaned his head down into his index finger and thumb. Shaking his head, he stood up from the chair and turned to face the other three. The hair along his forehead was twisted up into odd angles, and there were rings left around his eyelids from the eyepieces of the microscope.

"It doesn't make sense to me," he said. "It has to be..."

"Wait," Maria said, holding up her hand. "I want everyone to look first, and then we can discuss what's there. I don't want to bias anyone's opinion as to what we're seeing. Doctor Yurov, see what you think."

Yurov repositioned the chair and sat. He checked the light and the power magnification, and then adjusted the width of the eyepieces. He cleared his throat and viewed the slide. He lifted his head momentarily, squinted as though questioning his vision, and then leaned forward again. He was silent for several minutes while repositioning the slide with the dials along the slide platform. Finally, he rose from the microscope as though prying himself from the view. The furrows deepened in his forehead.

"That was from the left lung mass," Maria said. "Jon, show Dr. Yurov the lymph node from the mediastinum."

Karlssen switched the slides on the viewing platform.

Yurov repositioned himself at the microscope. He leaned in, viewed the slide, and nodded, remaining deep in thought. "The same," he said.

Maria nodded. "Here's the next slide. It's a bone specimen from the right tibia. It's representative of all the bone specimens."

Drew watched Karlssen change the slide. As the stain passed by, he leaned forward with anticipation, as though he could decipher the blue and red stain with his naked eye. He gave Yurov a "here we go" lift of his eyebrows.

Yurov looked into the microscope. He removed the slide and tilted it in the light a few inches above his eyes. He picked up a spray can with a plastic straw attachment and blew air across glass cover slip. He looked at the slide in the light again before placing it back into position on the microscope. "They all look like this?" he asked, incredulously.

"The bone specimens are almost identical." Maria said. "It's not an artifact,"

"It's real then?" Yurov asked. He looked back at the slide. He opened his mouth to speak several times, only to stop and reposition the slide. "How could it be?" he finally asked. He stood up and gestured for Drew to take his place at the microscope.

Drew made the necessary adjustments to the microscope settings and looked into the eyepieces. He immediately leaned back and did a double take, much like Yurov had done.

The field in the microscopic view was packed with very large purple cells, each with clusters of darker purple circles in their center. "They're multinucleated," he said, thinking aloud.

Out of the corner of his eye, he saw Maria and Yurov nod.

"But," Drew started.

"But there are so many," Maria finished his thought.

Drew adjusted the position of the slide several times. Every field was filled with the large osteoclasts, the cells that normally resorb damaged bone. A few were attached to splintered bone remnants, still clinging to the ruffled, chewed away edges. Others floated in pulverized bone soup. He had never seen so many osteoclasts together on one slide. Nothing even close. There wasn't a single osteoblast. Without osteoblasts to make new bone, the leg didn't stand a chance. It was no wonder the bone melted away.

"There's no question that they're osteoclasts," he said. "Which leads to one of two possibilities. Either the bone destruction has led to a massive increase in osteoclast formation, similar to what's seen after a fracture, only to an extreme extent."

"Or the osteoclasts are what caused the destruction in the first place," Yurov said.

Drew was still looking at the slide. He spotted what Yurov had thought was an artifact – a substance resembling pepper sprinkled over the slide and centered mainly within pockets inside the cells themselves. "What are the black spots?" he asked.

"They're inclusion bodies," Maria said.

"That rings a bell from medical school," Drew said.

"Inclusion bodies are formed when heavy protein deposits accumulate inside cells," Maria said. "When the deposits are large enough, they can be visible through the microscope."

"What type of protein is involved?" he asked.

"Really any type of protein, usually one that is overproduced because the normal regulatory system has broken down," Maria said. "Viruses can also form inclusion bodies."

"I've seen them in Herpes infections," Yurov said.

"But this is in the bone," Drew said. He almost couldn't believe that he was looking at bone, but he was. "There aren't any viruses that attack the bone," Drew said. He thought about the debate on whether Paget's disease, an imbalance in bone production and resorption, was associated with chronic parvovirus infection. But what was happening here was altogether different. "At least no acute, rapidly destructive diseases like this," he added.

Drew continued to look at the slide. He couldn't stop looking at it. "Did you see anything that suggested a viral lung infection?" he finally asked, sliding his chair from the microscope.

"The lung makes less sense than the bone," Yurov said.

"Yes," Maria said, handing Drew the lung specimen slide.

The microscopic lung findings were very different from the bone. Drew was looking down into a sea of small dark purple cells in sheets and rows. "What type of cancer is this?" he asked.

"It's small-cell lung carcinoma," Yurov said. "There's no question about it."

"And it's in the lymph nodes, liver, and brain," Maria said.

Did lightning strike twice?

"Do you think the lung cancer is related to the bone disease?" Drew asked.

"I don't see how they could both be caused by the same process, if that's what you mean," Yurov said. "But small-cell lung cancer can cause paraneoplastic syndromes, resulting in parathyroid hormone abnormalities and elevated calcium levels."

"Those changes can affect the bone," Drew said, "maybe even lead to a fracture in rare cases, but nothing like this. I'm a lumper, not a splitter. I don't believe that lightning strikes twice. But in this case, I'm at a loss. I don't see any way that these findings are related. Plus, we haven't seen anything like this in Brozine's lungs. The lung cancer has to be a red herring."

"And what do you think killed him?" Maria asked.

"It may have been a heart attack in the end," Drew said. "If so, it might have been brought on by hypercalcemia caused by the lung cancer and the bone disease. That could explain the normal looking heart. But that's something we may never know for sure."

"I agree with you," Yurov said. "Perhaps Mark Brozine will tell us more. We need to finish the other autopsy."

Drew put the bone specimen slide back under the microscope. He looked down at the osteoclasts, the destructive monsters that filled the space where Victor Solnorov's bone used to be. He knew how difficult osteoclasts were to grow in the laboratory. They required delicate technique, special media, and often special growth factors.

But Solnorov's body was an osteoclast factory.

Lung cancer and bone disease. A sea of inclusion bodies. Was there a viral infection? There had to be an explanation. Drew just didn't see it yet. And they were running out of time.

"We need a fresh biopsy," Drew said. "Living cells."

"But we're out of anesthetics," Yurov said.

"And pain medication," Maria said.

"Then it's going to be difficult," Drew said.

39

UNIVERSITY HOSPITAL, CONNECTICUT

Blood was dripping on the floor.

"Hello, I need a bandage," Grovely said to the large man resembling Java the Hut filling in the space behind the reception desk of University Hospital. The man's hospital name badge said 'Jerry.' The room smelled of vomit and pus and cleaning fluid.

"What happened to you?" Jerry asked in an effeminate voice. Grovely looked up, wondering how such a voice could emerge from such a mountain of a man. They stared at each other for a moment, both of them displaying their common desire to be anywhere else.

"I cut myself," Grovely said, using a tone that said, 'as though that wasn't obvious enough to you.' He held his hand up to illustrate the point, allowing more drops of blood to trickle to the floor.

"Ooh, you did. Didn't you?" Jerry said. He pivoted to position himself squarely against a computer. He held his fingers poised over the keyboard. "Name?"

Grovely had no intention of giving his name to anyone there. He didn't want medical care. He just wanted to wash his hand, just for a few hours or so, maybe until the end of time. That might not be very long anyway.

"Listen," Grovely said. "I don't need to be seen by a doctor or anything. I just need a place to wash my hand and a bandage to wrap it up."

"I'm sorry, we can't just do that. You have to be registered and evaluated first," Jerry said. "Did you bring your insurance card with you?"

Grovely looked down at his palm, where a few small pieces of plastic were still clinging to congealed blood. He could feel the bacterial contents of the petri dish running inside of him, pulsing through his arteries in warm, deadly spurts. Should he wrap the arm in a tourniquet to prevent whatever had entered his hand to spread to the rest of his body? That was what was done for snakebites, wasn't it? He was sure that it was too late. It was probably too late as soon as he hit the ground. He had been bitten by the Mamba, whose venom was invariably deadly.

"Sir," Jerry said loudly, somehow inserting an extra syllable into the word. "Your insurance card?"

Grovely secured a constricting grasp around the wrist of the bleeding hand with the other hand. The bleeding increased as the hand turned a mottled shade of blue.

"I don't have an insurance card. I just," Grovely started.

Jerry looked up and down at Grovely's suit, increasingly smirking as he did. "We treat a lot of people here who don't have insurance. But you have to be the best dressed of any of the ones I've seen.

"That's not what I meant," Grovely said. "Do you have a men's room? I just need to use the men's room."

Grovely looked through the waiting room as he asked the question. The floor looked like it hadn't been cleaned in a month. Empty seats were speckled with flattened gum wads on some of the empty seats. A young woman was vomiting into a bucket while a man was trying to keep her hair from falling inside. The only other person within a 10-foot radius of her was an old man curled up on a chair with his bloody gauze-wrapped head lying across the armrest. The other patients were pressed as far away from the vomiting woman as possible and were turning their heads from her with nauseated expressions.

"The men's room is being serviced," Jerry said. He leaned closer and whispered, "We've had some problems. You wouldn't want to use it anyway."

Grovely spotted the bright yellow triangular signs in the corner of the waiting room. A stick figure was taking a neck-breaking slip on a wet floor.

"Is that the only bathroom? I just need a paper towel," Grovely said.

"There's another one inside," Jerry pointed to the door on his left.

"Great, thanks," Grovely said. He started moving toward the door.

"I'm sorry sir, but that bathroom is only for patients," Jerry said. He raised his hands to indicate that he didn't make the rule.

"I am a patient," Grovely said, again holding his hand up to demonstrate the entry wounds of whatever was going to kill him. Was it a poison? Was it an infection? Was it just a warning? It seemed like far too much effort to just be a warning. His heart started to flutter in his chest, and he fought to get air through the sensation of being strangled.

Grovely's vision flickered as he heard Jerry say, "Not until you give me your insurance information."

"Sir, you don't look so good," Jerry said. "Did you lose a lot of blood?" He feigned an attempt at standing up, but obviously didn't really want to put in the effort.

Grovely's instincts momentarily overrode his panic. He pushed through the door and entered the main corridor of the emergency room.

He was still light-headed, aware of only glimpses around him as he gripped his wrist tightly and looked for the rest rooms. Eyes squinting from the lights. Voices calling 'excuse me, excuse me' and then 'hey, hey," each time louder, but each time farther behind him. Carts covered with needles and syringes and glass tubes. Twisted moaning figures on stretchers. Bags of fluid dripping, drop after drop, a metronome matching the second after second ticking in his head. Squeezing tighter on the wrist. Death searing the inner surfaces of his veins.

Need to wash my hand. Need to wash my hand. He thought it. He said it. He yelled it. Squeezing as tightly as he could. His numb blue hand. Pieces of plastic sticking to the blood. *Need to wash my hand.*

The men's room door was closed. He cupped his injured hand and used just his fingertips to grasp the doorknob. He couldn't feel the knob but watched his effort as he tried to turn. It was locked.

The women's room door was open. He looked around quickly to see if anyone was looking. Everyone seemed to be looking. A Hispanic woman was approaching the bathroom with a young girl who was walking knock-kneed while tugging at the crotch of her pants. Grovely looked back at the men's room doorknob, and then at the women's room, and then at the little girl. He dodged inside the women's room, pushed the door closed with his elbow, and flipped the lock with a free knuckle.

The sound of angry Spanish exploded outside as Grovely turned the water on. And then he placed his hand under the water, too hot at first, and then too cold. Red streams and flakes of plastic spiraled around the basin and then down the drain. He released his grip and picked at the surface until exposing the wounds. Lots of them. Not very deep. But deep enough to bleed. Deep enough to be lethal?

Grovely let the water run for several minutes. The bleeding increased as his hand turned pink again, and then gradually slowed. He threw the first few paper towels down from the dispenser into the garbage, and then grabbed the next stack, which he used to apply pressure to the wounds.

After a few rounds of paper towels, the bleeding appeared to be stopping. He pressed another stack on the wound, placed a backup supply in his pocket, and listened at the door. The yelling had stopped. He turned the doorknob quietly and peeked outside. A pale-yellow puddle was on the floor where the woman and child had been. They were now at the nurses' station looking for assistance. Grovely looked in the other direction and saw a sign that read 'hospital personnel only beyond this point.' An ID badge sensor was on the wall. There was no way to get through, but there were now too many reasons not to go in the opposite direction.

As if answering Grovely's prayers, the electronic door swung open and a young man dressed in surgical scrubs shuffled through, his hair matted from lying in bed, his eyes still nearly shut. In four quick steps, Grovely was through the door leading into the hospital.

40

NUCURE LABORATORIES, RUSSIA

Fingerprint Analysis Processed. Door Open.

The bright red letters blinked on the monitor display. The door lock mechanism clicked and emitted a soft high-pitched beep.

Dmitri followed Ilya Lukin past the security checkpoint. Their shoes clicked against white tile. Echoes of their footsteps bounced back along the long white corridor, giving the false impression of an invisible army approaching. Butterflies stirring in Dmitri's stomach gave way to a burning sensation.

The door made a definitive locking sound behind them.

They were two, maybe three floors below the basement, the lowest level of NuCure known and accessible to other employees. A series of security checks led to where they were now.

"How many people have access to this floor?" Dmitri asked. He looked forward, trying to decide whether he was avoiding eye contact with Lukin or eager to reach the end of the hall. The special research facility couldn't be much further ahead.

"Six," Lukin said. "Now we have six." He placed a hand on Dmitri's shoulder as they walked.

Dmitri felt privileged to be offered a role in this new research project, but his involvement also carried new responsibilities. The research would be similar, as far as the techniques and processes. And he was intellectually and physically able to do the new research. But that wasn't the point. The applications would be different. The ramifications. He was now keeping a secret from Sasha. That weighed heavily upon him.

The hallway smelled of disinfectant, burning his nostrils. The glare of bright lights reflected off the polished tile walls.

Sasha fell asleep after dinner the night before, looking like all the burdens of life had lifted from her. Dmitri had watched her, contemplating the decision that he had to make alone. Would the first secret lead to others? He shouldn't think about that now. There was no way to predict or control the future. No matter how many times he analyzed the situation, he saw the new opportunity at NuCure as the fastest way to get them where they wanted to be. A normal life, that's all. She deserved it. And he wasn't ashamed to think that he deserved it. Sasha would have agreed with his decision. He convinced himself of that.

"The journey is almost over," Lukin said. His upper lip rose into a smile that revealed only the jagged tip of his canine tooth.

Dmitri smiled but continued thinking of Sasha – draped across the established contours of their fading couch, her belly peaking past the edge of his old T-shirt. She was carrying their child. He was carrying the burden of the secret that would provide for them. Each would do what was necessary for their family.

His acceptance of the new position wasn't purely for the money. Or the new house. Or the new neighborhood. The work would be for more than just him. The benefits would extend beyond his family. The research would influence national security, according to Lukin, whose reputation was impressive. He trusted Lukin. If he didn't, he wouldn't be walking this hall with him.

They entered a small room filled with green surgical scrub suits. A tall stack of shirts. Another of pants. After having his vision dulled by the whitewashed palette of the entrance corridors, Dmitri perceived the color of the material as the brightest possible.

Lukin removed his clothes, saying, "There are two change points. The protocol must be followed carefully to minimize the amount of bacteria entering the central core from outside."

Dmitri spotted a locker with the initials DP. He looked at Lukin, about to ask if NuCure already prepared a personal locker for him. Before the words came out, Lukin nodded a response. Dmitri stripped down to his underwear, feeling a bit awkward. His knees and elbows looked like knotted rope along his pale and thin extremities. He quickly pulled on a green scrub shirt and pants.

Dmitri followed Lukin out the door along the far wall. Another white hallway. Another security checkpoint. They entered a room filled with shower heads.

"This first wash is soap and water," Lukin said. "The next is Lysol." He dropped his scrubs in a hamper and began to shower.

Dmitri undressed and took his position under a showerhead. "It takes a while to get inside the facility," he said as the first jets of water splashed against his face.

"Getting inside is the easy part," Lukin said. "Getting out is more involved. Carrying a little *Staph aureus* in might be problematic, but what you could carry out would be catastrophic."

What was inside? What was he going to be researching?

They dried off, got into fresh sets of surgical scrubs, and entered the next room. Rows of full-length pale blue biosafety containment suits hung on hooks like hollow specters.

"The one on the right should be your size," Lukin said. "Every time you come in here, you will need to check your suit for any defects. The smallest gap in the lining or tear in the material could be fatal. I'm sure I don't need to tell you that."

Dmitri nodded. He saw a suit with his initials. He lifted it off the rack. It was surprisingly heavy. He raised the suit above his head, looking for any penetration of light through it. He ran his fingers along the smooth material, taking more care near the seams. Satisfied with the integrity of the suit, he started to slide a leg into the lower half.

"Wait. First put on a pair of gloves," Lukin said, holding a box in his direction. "Then clean your visor. Then when you're ready to put on the suit, be careful of the air and cooling system along the lining." He took Dmitri's suit and pointed to the thin tubes that coiled along the torso and ran along the extremities. "The filtered air passing through these tubes will be your only source of uncontaminated oxygen," he said.

They zipped up the suits, leaving just a small opening at the neck. Lukin grabbed two cylindrical tanks in customized backpacks and handed one to Dmitri. "You'll need one of these breathing-air transfer units."

They helped each other strap the units to their backs.

Dmitri sensed the weight of his gear. Fatigue had to be a factor over the course of the day when working under such conditions. He made a mental note to assess his level of concentration periodically during the day. He couldn't make any mistakes. Just one slip…he didn't want to think about it.

They took large gulps of air, zipped the remaining sections of the suits closed, and pressed the airtight seals securely shut. Dmitri was now completely encased within the isolated world of the biological containment suit. He felt the distinct cool touch of the air tubes coiling around him. He smelled his own breath bouncing back into his face. Coffee. Tuna fish. He switched to breathing only through his mouth. Sounds were muffled. He peered out through the visor in the hood.

The Lysol shower was next. They stood under the spray, allowing the disinfectant to spread along the entire surface of their suits and gear. A thin mist filled the room. Dmitri worried at first that a fog was accumulating inside his visor, causing a brief spasm of panic. He felt Lukin hold his arm and lead him out of the room.

As the mist cleared, Dmitri saw red air hoses hanging over his head. Lukin turned the knobs beneath two of the tubes, causing them to hiss and writhe like coral snakes. He grabbed a hose with each hand and passed one to Dmitri, all with swift, efficient, and surprisingly dexterous movements. Lukin passed the tip of the hose over the entire surface of his suit. The pressure caused the material to indent as though being pressed by an invisible hand. The remaining drops of Lysol spread and then evaporated.

They donned boots and taped the upper edges to the pant legs of the suit to avoid leaving any exposed openings. They used similar tape lining to secure the edges of a second pair of gloves to the shirtsleeves. When they were finished, Dmitri turned toward an imposing black metal door marked "Level Four Entrance."

"The entire area beyond this door is set up as a laminar flow system," Lukin said, speaking loudly to be heard across layers of protective garments between them. "Inward suction minimizes the chance of leakage of the agents into the surrounding area."

Dmitri's mind lingered on the word "agents."

He couldn't wait to get inside the Level Four facility, to see the research that was going on inside. The scientist in him was taking over, and he was fascinated by the prospect of working with pathogens so terrifying that they required this type of precaution.

Dmitri was on the verge of crossing the threshold from the outside world to this new world. This secret world.

Lukin opened the door to the other side.

A free thread on the shoulder seam of Dmitri's suit stirred as the door opened. The suction effect was slight but noticeable.

To minimize the chance of leakage of the agents.

What kind of agents were inside? Something dangerous enough to justify building this expensive and elaborate biosafety facility. Something requiring this level of security precautions.

His research project waited inside.

41

AIRSTRIP, VIRGINIA

Latitude 76° 15' North. Longitude 106° 10' East. He knew the destination coordinates, and not a moment too soon.

The jet had a corporate look, not at all what Jonathan had expected. And from what he could tell, there were no signs of the nature of their mission. Each of the six men had gotten onto the plane carrying no more than a small duffle bag. They hardly seemed prepared for an Arctic mission abroad.

Cage was there with Thing One and Thing Two. The two pilots looked as though they were carved out of the same material as the others. Jonathan felt like an unwanted outsider, and with good reason.

But this was everything Jonathan wanted. The field visit to end all field visits. An exciting end to his drought.

They were headed halfway around the world.

Latitude 76° 15' North. Longitude 106° 10' East.

The coordinates where the research center was located were burned into Jonathan's mind. Chip Williams had been a savior once again, coming up with the location just in time. The numbers were Jonathan's ticket to Siberia. He didn't ask how Chip came up with the location. He didn't want to know. As long as there was no doubt about their accuracy. The last thing he wanted was to lead

Cage on a wild goose chase through foreign air space. Somehow that seemed as though it wouldn't go over well with his hosts.

Jonathan's bluff of knowing the location of the research station had gone further than he expected. Luckily, he now had a set of coordinates to deliver. They would have to bring him along until he provided the long-awaited information.

Hopefully they would find the research station waiting at the other end of their flight, sitting right in the middle of the promised coordinates. But then what? In the old movies, they would discard him in the snow to die. He pictured himself lying face down on the snow, full of bullet holes, bleeding to death.

Jonathan shivered.

"Cold already?" Cage asked. He looked up and down at Jonathan and gave an "I thought so" smirk, almost certainly wondering how long he would stick it out. "Wait until we hit Siberia. It's a nice crisp negative twenty outside." He waited long enough for the desired effect, and then he added, "That's without the wind chill."

"Have you been up there before?" Jonathan asked.

"I've been almost everywhere," he said.

"Have you been with this unit for a long time?" Jonathan asked.

Cage responded with a stone expression. He didn't look like someone who spent much time on the answering end of questions.

The stairway clanked away from the plane and one of the pilots shut the door.

"You could give us the coordinates now and get yourself out of this," Cage said. "You have no idea what you're getting into."

Jonathan shook his head. “I want to work with you on this one. I was given this assignment in Atlanta, and I want to follow it through. I’m sure you can appreciate that.”

“I can,” Cage said with what might have actually been a genuine smile.

The plane rolled into motion. The mission was starting. Jonathan did his best to contain his excitement. McIntyre would kill him when he returned. He might even lose his job. But this kind of experience might never pass his way again. This was worth the gamble.

Cage rubbed an index finger along one of the many scars on his scalp. “I’ve been in this type of work for about fifteen years.”

“Which branch of the military are you in?” Jonathan asked.

Cage smiled again. “You think we’re military?”

“Requesting permission to laugh, sir?” one of the pilots called out. The others suppressed smiles. The man who had spoken was probably the youngest in the group. Gum rhythmically squeezed out through his smile as the muscles along his typical team temples bulged in synchrony. The motion made a short cropped blonde cowlick bob on his forehead.

Cage shot the smile away with a fiery glare. The chewing stopped. The lights dimmed in the cabin.

Cage turned back to Jonathan. “We’re not military,” he said. “Not in the traditional sense.”

Jonathan seized the opportunity to ask more questions, realizing that it wouldn’t last very long.

“You’re part of a government agency, then?” Jonathan asked.

The plane accelerated down the runway.

“Do you think a government agency could have arranged this little excursion on such short notice?” Cage asked.

Jonathan shook his head. The CDC probably never could have arranged a field visit beyond Russian borders.

Cage's expression changed, signaling to Jonathan that his time for asking questions was over.

The force of the plane's liftoff pushed them back squarely against their seats. The pilots extinguished the lights, and silence followed the darkness. It was only about 10PM, but none of them knew when they would get another chance to rest.

Jonathan closed his eyes and wondered for one of countless moments that day whether he was making a mistake. What was he doing on a mission with this group? Was he ready to face whatever awaited them on the ground in Siberia? Each time he closed his eyes, he saw patterns of blood spreading out to saturate the freshly fallen snow. By the time he fell asleep, he was no longer wondering whether he had made a mistake. He was trying to determine how big of a mistake he had made.

Jonathan awoke to the sound of metal hitting metal.

Where was he? Darkness surrounded him. He tried to get up, but something held him back. A seatbelt. He was still in the plane, and they were back on the ground somewhere. He illuminated his watch and checked the time. 1AM. Only three hours had passed. Where could they be?

A cold wind crashed in through the open door. Everyone else was exiting onto the pitch-black runway below. Even the runway was pitch black. As Jonathan reached the door, he could hear the men below, relaying supplies from a truck to another plane.

In the fading illumination from his watch, he saw a box labeled "biological containment suits" go by. Coats, boots, and other clothes followed, some white and reflective and others black and essentially invisible in the night, all sealed in plastic wrap and organized in stacks.

Then he saw the source of the sounds that had awoken him. Stacks of firearms and duffle bags containing what must have been ammunition were passed from man to man and up into the plane. Jonathan recognized AK47s from the third level of Death Seeker. Some of the other guns were even larger.

Jonathan tapped the shoulder of one of the pilots as they made their way toward the stairs. "Where are we?" he asked.

The pilot hesitated. "Iceland," he replied.

"I always wanted to see Iceland," Jonathan said, purveying the darkness.

"Yup, sure is beautiful," the pilot said, waving a shadow of an arm between them. "Here," he said. When Jonathan didn't respond he repeated, "Here."

A hard object pressed against Jonathan's abdomen. The pilot had handed him something. It was a facial visor.

"Put it on," the pilot said. He put his own visor on. "It's infrared."

Jonathan strapped the visor on his head and acquired night vision. The technology before his eyes was amazing. Everything came into view – the men, the supplies, the other plane – in varying shades of green. He watched each of them in turn, looking at the sky, the ground, anything he could in between. The new plane was a lot smaller than the one they just left. Sleeker. Probably faster. Probably easier to maneuver.

He looked past the plane onto the infrared horizon. Not much there. Not much at all. Were they really in Iceland? He had no way to tell. He'd probably never know for sure.

"How can I help?" Jonathan asked one of the men.

"By getting to your seat," he said. "We're almost done down here."

Someone called out a warning. Jonathan ducked away from a crate passing by his head. The crate was the type seen in the supermarket loaded with oranges, except this one contained endless rows of artillery shells.

"Medicine with muscle," a familiar voice said. Jonathan turned to see Cage.

"That's the understatement of the year," Jonathan said, taking another look into the crate.

There was a lot of firepower going into a plane designed for a medical rescue mission. So far, the closest things to medical equipment on the plane were the biological containment suits.

"I see the muscle," Jonathan said. "I just don't see much medical."

The two men walked together up the stairs into the plane as the last of the boxes was taken inside.

"We have everything we need," Cage said. "You're nervous because you know very little about the mission, and you doubt that you're prepared. You're not used to working under such conditions. Our team functions quite differently from the CDC. Only two men on this mission know much more than you at this point. The first is me, and the second is someone designated to take over my command should the need arise. The only difference between you and the others is that they are trained for this type of work. They know without any doubt that they're ready for anything we can encounter out there."

"All I really know is the coordinates of where we're heading," Jonathan said.

Cage removed his night vision visor off with both hands. Jonathan saw his scars, bright green etchings on his head. The sight was more intimidating through the distorting view of the visor. Jonathan removed his visor, but the green jagged lines still glowed in his vision.

They sat down across a narrow aisle from each other. Jonathan adjusted his position along the worn leather seat and pulled a shoulder harness around his chest.

The harness buckles clicked shut.

Cage leaned in close to Jonathan and said, "I know the coordinates."

Jonathan stared through the dark cabin toward Cage. He wasn't sure what to believe at first. Cage had to be bluffing. One final attempt to convince Jonathan to back out. One final attempt to wash his hands of the CDC's involvement in this case.

"Latitude seven six degrees one five minutes north. Longitude one zero six degrees one zero minutes east," Cage said.

The sound of Jonathan's jaw dropping must have been audible, or else Cage had infrared vision without the visor, because a satisfied grunt arose from his direction.

"You have knowledge and guts, a rare combination," Cage said. "More importantly, you look more like a researcher than a member of my unit. You will be an integral part of my plans if my predictions are correct."

"What predictions?" Jonathan asked.

"In due time, professor," Cage said. "You're part of plan B, not plan A. Premature knowledge is knowledge wasted."

Everyone was now on the plane.

"I'll be briefing the unit in phases, starting as soon as we get into the air," Cage said to Jonathan.

The plane accelerated rapidly along the black runway. The force pushed them back into their seats.

"And that should be in just a few seconds," Cage said.

42

RESEARCH STATION, SIBERIA

The pain of a scalpel slicing through the skin is unbearable.

Drew was watching from the other side of the room with Maria as they scrubbed their hands for the biopsy. Under normal conditions a bone biopsy was a straightforward procedure. But with no more anesthetics or pain medications, a massive obstacle was lying in an otherwise straightforward path.

When Yurov first recommended using hypnosis for anesthesia, Drew declined in a manner that was as politically correct as possible. Most of the reports of hypnosis in the western anesthesia literature dealt with the treatment of chronic pain, and the results were marginal at best. The descriptions of hypnosis for surgical anesthesia were even sketchier and were almost always in the context of an adjunct to traditional medications, not in place of them. In the few cases in which hypnosis had been used alone, the procedures were extremely minor, hardly the extent of cutting into bone.

Yurov had written sections on hypnosis and acupuncture in the anesthesia chapter of his wilderness medicine textbook. His enthusiasm encouraged Maria, but Drew was no closer to being convinced of the merits of the technique. He did, however, allow Yurov to attempt hypnosis with the understanding that any painful response would terminate the procedure immediately.

As Drew washed his hands, he was certain that he wouldn't even be able to complete the skin incision.

"You still don't believe that he can do it?" Maria whispered.

"No," Drew said.

Luigi Mincini's grotesque left arm extended out from the blanket covering the rest of his body and rested along a small table.

Yurov was leaning over Mincini, murmuring at a low volume that was imperceptible to the others. He rested a hand on Mincini's forehead, rhythmically rubbing the side of his thumb against the area between the eyebrows. Yurov assessed his patient's response to the hypnosis. He gauged the pulse in the non-injured wrist. He leaned his head down low to feel the breaths with his cheek. He watched for the movement of the chest.

"His breathing has slowed during the last few minutes," Maria said.

Drew nodded. "You're right. He was in a lot of pain from having to move his arm. He was at 24 breaths per minute when Yurov started, but now he's down to about 10."

"Not bad for crazy Russian folk medicine." Maria said.

Drew turned quickly to respond, but then caught himself.

"There are more things in heaven and earth than are dreamt of in your philosophy," Maria added.

Being assaulted with a Shakespearean quote by an Italian woman in Siberia came as a surprise to Drew. He wondered if he had deserved such a comment. "Slow breathing and complete anesthesia are two very different things," he said. "But don't get me wrong. I certainly hope he can do what he swore he could."

Yurov checked Mincini's pulse again. He closed his eyes and gave a satisfied nod.

"He almost looks as though he is hypnotizing himself," Drew said.

"He is, in a way," Maria said. "A physician's mental state has to be altered before any change can be achieved in the patient."

Mincini's bare arm was bruised and swollen, and visibly fractured along the bony mid-shaft of the forearm, where the contour bent outward at an unnatural angle. Drew watched the arm from across the room, making a mental image of where he would make his incision. He would have to minimize the distance down to the bone in order to reduce the pain.

While Drew watched the arm, he realized that it hadn't moved in several minutes. Not even the fingers. They hadn't so much as flickered. They were resting on the table in the natural fingertip cascade configuration of a completely motionless hand.

"I'm starting to believe we can do this," Drew said. "If we get a biopsy that resembles what we saw in the autopsies, how long will it take you to figure out what's in those inclusion bodies?"

"Normally I'd say it would take a week, but those osteoclasts were loaded with inclusion bodies," Maria said. "And I've never seen such a high osteoclast count. We may have our answer on the inclusion bodies within days. We may also be able to grow the osteoclasts. You know how difficult they normally are to grow. But with the way those cells looked in the autopsy specimens, anything is possible."

Drew nodded, but he was still stuck on the words 'within days." Normally having an answer regarding an unknown disease within a few days would have been a pleasant surprise. In this case they might not be alive in a few days.

"Will we be able to keep a laboratory room warm?" Drew asked.

"It's been a battle with Gunnar from the beginning," Maria said. "If those incubators get too cold, everything we have will be lost. The room must stay warm"

"What's in there so far?" Drew asked.

"We have nearly eighty per cent of the mammoth genome cloned and sequenced," Maria said. "That's a lot further than anybody's ever gotten with mammoth DNA. Usually, the cells are far too damaged to provide useful DNA. The amount of preserved tissue in our mammoth is unprecedented. We can learn more from this mammoth than any before."

Drew was impressed with Maria's persevering enthusiasm for the research. Most of the team members would have scrapped the bacteria in petri dishes long ago in exchange for an increased chance of survival. After all, the laboratory equipment burned up fuel at an impressive rate. But to Drew, and apparently to Maria, the laboratory remained a key factor in their struggle to survive.

"Maybe we can convince Gunnar to re-designate the sectors of the station that will remain warmed and include the laboratory," Maria said. "We could even move some of the injured people in there to maximize utilization of the space."

From across the room, there was a brief but loud noise resembling a stifled snore. Yurov signaled with an index finger that he was almost ready. He gently tilted Mincini's head back to facilitate his breathing and again felt for the next exhalation with his cheek. He nodded and waved them over to begin.

Drew gave Yurov an impressed nod, although he remained skeptical that the hypnosis would be adequate. The Russian doctor either didn't notice or didn't acknowledge the gesture. He rolled the blanket back a few inches to allow better exposure to the arm.

Maria coated the arm with alcohol. The cold touch of the alcohol normally elicited movement in a conscious patient, but there was no response.

Drew donned one of the pairs of gloves that they had made from bed sheets and sterilized in the autoclave. He spotted the scalpel blade and a pair forceps lying at the edge of the instrument table. How much pain would he cause? How deep would the scalpel go before he had to stop?

Drew lifted the damaged arm and waited for most of the blood to drain from its veins up toward the shoulder. Yurov inflated the blood pressure cuff on the upper arm, creating a tourniquet effect on the arteries that would minimize the bleeding. Assuming, of course, that Mincini didn't jump off the table when the sharp blade jabbed through his skin.

"Hold the arm," Drew said softly, positioning Maria's hands over Mincini's wrist and elbow. "The blade can do a lot of damage in a small amount of time if he moves during the incision.

Yurov rolled his eyes and shook his head.

Maria held the arm. Drew lifted the scalpel. Light reflected off the tapered tip of the blade as it approached the skin. Drew stretched the skin in opposite directions with his free thumb and index finger and lined the stainless steel along the area in between.

He thought of his last operation back in New York. He looked around the room, waiting to see the broken Picasso form of Matty. There was no sight of him yet.

Drew held his breath as he plunged the blade through the skin.

The arm remained motionless. Yurov nodded. Maria smiled. Drew took an audible breath.

They would have the biopsy specimen that they needed.

43

UNIVERSITY HOSPITAL, CONNECTICUT

For once things were going his way.

The triage nurse at the emergency room entrance proved to be the biggest obstacle between Grovely and the University Hospital genetics research laboratory. He walked the rest of the way, through the halls, up the elevator, as though he had tenure at the university, as though he owned it.

The well-polished and streamlined look of the newer wings was in sharp contrast to the dingy halls of the emergency room and original hospital building. Dusty portraits of the frowning fathers of medicine yielded to high tech photos of chemical structures and modern art designs. Ahead, after a series of turns, toward the end of the technological history depicted in the hallway artwork, was one of the most advanced genetics research facilities in the world.

Grovely knew the hallways by heart. He had spent many afternoons there, long before Dr. Atisoy rose to greatness in the genetics world, long before the Atisoy wing, as Grovely called it, was added to the hospital. He met Atisoy when he received his Rockefeller Award from the Museum of Natural History. Grovely serendipitously overheard the young geneticist speak while he was trying to meet James Watson, the day's keynote speaker.

Grovely didn't know much about genetics then. In fact, he knew only a little less than he did now. But something about

Atisoy made a lasting impression. It wasn't the science, per se, or the presentation itself, though both were delivered in typical Atisoy precision and flare. What impressed Grovely most about the young doctor was his ability to tactfully but unmistakably dismantle a reporter who stood up to criticize his interest in cloning research. To Grovely, anyone who could take such a publicized and controversial topic and make it seem as essential and American as baseball and apple pie was someone worth watching closely.

Atisoy was brilliant and charismatic. More importantly, he was lucky. He had the Midas touch in genetics. He was the first and the best at all he did. Grovely met him for only a few minutes at the museum that day, but he followed his progress thereafter, and their paths crossed several times. As Grovely became involved in medical research ventures, he watched Atisoy with a keener eye.

During the last ten years, Grovely funneled Global funds into several of Atisoy's projects, which proved lucrative for both men. Atisoy inspired the medical technology sector at Global, and Global was a major contributor toward the Atisoy wing.

Up until O-168, everything seemed to be going well.

Now, as Grovely crossed the threshold of the Atisoy wing of University Hospital, he tried to convince himself not to kill Atisoy. which would only add another problem to the growing list.

Grovely still needed to figure out exactly what he was going to do when he saw the geneticist. Atisoy was the most likely source of the O-168 failure, the sabotage, as the Mamba had put it. And Atisoy was probably the only man still alive who could fix the problem. But he also knew that he'd never be able to convince him. Nobody had ever been able to convince Atisoy of anything, and Grovely was no exception. So why was he sneaking through University Hospital on his way to speak to the doctor?

Nobody would be in the laboratory yet. The students and postdocs were science fanatics, but even they stopped for a while to sleep. If anyone was going to be there before 8AM it was Atisoy, but that still left Grovely with a little time to spare. At least enough time to tend to his hand. Then maybe he could find a place to wait for the doctor. He would have to catch Atisoy off guard.

But then what?

He once again encouraged himself not to kill Atisoy.

Where to hide? Where to hide? There was now nothing but a straight hallway leading up to the doors of Atisoy's office and the main laboratory area adjacent to it. No matter where Grovely waited, Atisoy would easily see him.

Grovely walked the hall, trying to turn the knobs with a paper towel. He shouldn't leave any fingerprints, just in case things got out of control. In case he failed to heed his own advice and killed Atisoy. All the laboratory doors were locked, as anticipated.

Where to hide? He would have to find a good spot. He would come up behind Atisoy to startle him, to get the upper hand in the conversation. That's all.

Grovely reached Atisoy's office. The lights were off. He'd try the doorknob, but it would be locked. He was right. But as he leaned against the knob, the door surprised him by swinging open.

It was that easy.

He looked down the hall to make sure that nobody was looking, and then he slid through the doorway into the dark office. He closed the door behind him, making sure that the lock clicked. Now what? This was almost too good to be true. He had time to go through Atisoy's records. What were the odds of finding information on O-168? There was only one way to find out.

Grovely shuffled through the room with the lights off and blinds closed. A computer screensaver provided the only light. Where was the best place to start? Bookshelves filled with rows of papers? Cabinets? Desk drawers? Computer files?

Grovely looked at the computer screensaver, two growing chains of colorful circles, intertwining as they stretched across the screen. Strands of DNA. The screen emitted an ever-changing series of hues across the room.

He pulled a dry paper towel from his palm, which glowed red, then blue, then green. He made sure not to let any blood drops fall. He was just going to speak to Atisoy, but he didn't want to take any chances. The last place he wanted to leave behind DNA evidence of his presence was in the university genetics laboratory.

He would start searching desk drawers, then try to access the computer files. As he walked around the desk, he stumbled, almost falling into the window. He looked down into the darkness beneath the desk, expecting to see an upturned edge of a rug.

He didn't see an upturned edge of a rug.

There was no question that the body lying beneath the desk was dead, and there was no question that it was Atisoy. Grovely recognized him despite the gruesome distortion of the face. The purple color of the skin. The bulging, bloodshot appearance of the eyes. And the tongue. He had never seen anything like the tongue.

Grovely tried to look at the rest of the body, the rest of the room, anything except Atisoy's mouth, but he couldn't. The tongue was swollen and half chewed off, and there was a stream of frothy pinkish white foam pouring from the mouth onto the floor.

It looked as though Atisoy died during a seizure.

It looked as though an unfortunate illness caused Atisoy's untimely death, taking the famous geneticist from the world.

But there was no doubt in Grovely's mind that Atisoy had been murdered. He didn't believe in coincidences. What would cause a seizure? A nerve toxin in his bloodstream? A toxin that would never be detected? A toxin too new to even have a name. There was a new terror at every turn.

There was a new reason not to touch anything. Whatever killed Atisoy might still be in the room somewhere. Maybe just a few dust particles. On something he touched? On something he ate? Something so small and so deadly could be anywhere.

Grovely used a paper towel to tap the computer mouse, causing the DNA to fade away. A login box appeared on the screen. A dead end. He pulled open the desk drawers and looked inside. Nothing but typical generic desk items – pens, paper clips, a ruler, a stapler. They would have already gone through his desk. There would be nothing left of any value to Grovely.

He had to get out of the office before anyone saw him. He had made quite an entrance through the emergency room. Did he mention his name back there? Did he mention Atisoy's name? He was certain that he hadn't, but the morning was a blur. He had to get the limo driver back to the hospital so he could escape this mess. The driver. Had he said anything to the driver?

He started to leave, and then something made him stop.

The telephone was tilted on the receiver. Had Atisoy been on the phone shortly before dying, or had someone else made a call? He took a fresh paper towel from his pocket and lifted the phone. He listened. No dial tone. After tapping the receiver, a dial tone sounded. Then he spotted the "repeat dial" button.

Should he press the button? Was there anything to lose?

As he pressed the button, the rapid sequence of tones sounded, and the number being dialed appeared on the phone display screen. He recognized the number immediately. He shook his head. He blinked at least three times. The number was still there. But it didn't make any sense. Why would Atisoy or his killer dial that number? How would they know that number?

He hung up as soon as he heard the voice at the other end of the line.

He had to get out of there fast.

44

APARTMENT, RUSSIA

He spent the day with the most notorious killers in history.

Smallpox virus was there.

Smallpox spreads easily through contaminated clothing and bed linens, or even through the air. Entering the mouth or lungs, it spreads through the bloodstream. A rash appears. Pus-filled lumps form. Death often occurs by the second week. The fortunate survive with scars all over their body.

Smallpox was once a worldwide killer, causing hundreds of millions of deaths. A worldwide vaccination program initiated in 1967 completely eliminated smallpox from the earth by 1977. The World Health Organization restricted storage of smallpox to two locations – the Institute of Virus Preparations in Moscow, and the Centers for Disease Control in Atlanta. All other sites were to destroy their stores of the invisible killer. They didn't all listen.

Yersinia pestis bacterium was there.

Yersinia pestis, the bacteria causing plague, lurks in fleas on rats between epidemics. If an infected flea bites a person, up to ten thousand bacteria are injected into the bloodstream. The bacteria trick the immune system, take over the body, and drain its nutrients. Enlarged lymph nodes called buboes form in the armpits, groin, and neck, becoming so painful that they prevent movement.

Gangrene forming in the extremities led to the term "black death" associated with plague. Sepsis leads to coma, which leads to death.

The first recorded plague epidemic spread from Egypt in the 6th century, wiping out 50-60% of North Africa, Europe, and central and southern Asia. The second major epidemic began in 1346, lasted nearly 100 years, and killed 20-30 million Europeans, approximately one third of the continent's population. Today, the form of *Yersinia pestis* that caused these epidemics is generally controlled with sanitation and hygiene in industrialized nations.

The subsequent generations of research-generated *Yersinia pestis* that were there, however, growing inconspicuously in petri dishes, might not be controllable.

Ebola virus was there.

Ebola is the world's most deadly virus, killing between 60-90% of victims. Human to human spread can occur through close contact. The virus invades every type of cell in the body, except bone and muscle. Fever, chills, headaches, muscle aches, and loss of appetite progress to vomiting, diarrhea, abdominal pain, sore throat, and chest pain. Up to 100 million virus particles can be present in a single drop of blood. The resulting hemorrhagic fever is a ghastly horror. The blood fails to clot, causing bleeding from the gastrointestinal tract, skin, and internal organs. The victims bleed to death internally and externally. The "reservoir" where Ebola hides between outbreaks is still unknown.

But there it was being grown in abundance.

Bacillus anthracis bacterium was there.

Inhaled anthrax bacteria grow in the lungs and release toxins causing internal bleeding, swelling, and tissue death. Black skin lesions form, providing the rationale for the name *Bacillus anthracis*, derived from the Greek word for coal. Oxygen, electrolyte, and nutrient levels in the blood become abnormal. The blood pressure may plummet. Half the victims who die bleed into the lining of their brain or spinal cord. One quarter bleed into their lungs. Swelling inside the chest can become so pronounced that the victims suffocate to death. Once enough toxin is released, the infection becomes fatal even if the bacteria can be completely eliminated with antibiotics. Death can occur in hours.

An entire room was designated for anthrax.

Clostridium botulinum bacterium was there.

Botulinum toxin is the most poisonous substance known. A single gram of pure crystalline toxin, evenly dispersed and inhaled, could kill more than a million people. Once absorbed, the toxin travels through the bloodstream to nerve endings, causing paralysis. Vision, speech, and swallowing are often affected first. When the diaphragm and chest muscles fail, breathing is impossible. Victims who survive may be left comatose, in need of a mechanical ventilator for months. If treatment is not initiated in time, death often occurs. The brain is completely spared, leaving victims alert within paralyzed bodies, totally aware of their demise.

Three types of naturally occurring human botulism exist. A fourth, the most feared inhalation type, has been created by man. Several generations of refined inhalation botulism were there.

NuCure had them all.

Dmitri had seen them in the freezers and incubators of the subbasement laboratory earlier that day.

Other deadly viruses were there – Marburg, the world's third most deadly virus, with its predilection for the eyeballs and testicles; HIV, which took more than 3 million lives and infected 5 million more during 2002 alone; Hanta; Lassa; Rift Valley fever; Venezuelan equine encephalitis; West Nile; dengue fever. Enough to wipe out the entire population of the world several times over. And there were countless others, some names familiar, some not.

Many of the killers were considered Level Four, because there were no vaccines to prevent them and no treatments to stop them. Victims could only pray for their lives at the beginning of their infections and pray for death toward the end.

Access to the Level Four facility was through fingerprint analysis and a personal code, restricted to six NuCure employees. Level Four viruses known to the outside world were only the beginning. In the back corner, filled with the company's highest concentration of expensive equipment, was a maximum-security sector designated for "novel agents." Three simultaneous fingerprint recordings were required to release the security mechanism leading to this area, and one of them had to be Lukin's. This was where Dmitri would be doing his research.

Nothing at NuCure frightened Dmitri as much as the virus upon which he would begin working. Nothing anywhere in the world or within his imagination had ever frightened him as much.

O-168.

A virus too new to have a name. O-168 was a "novel agent," a killer of undetermined capacity. Hearing the description of what the virus could do left Dmitri nauseous. Could it be true? All that destruction. All that pain. He didn't want it to be true.

Lukin knew how it worked, this novel agent. Not in rats or hamsters. Not in monkeys. He knew what O-168 did in human beings. The horror that he described occurred in human beings.

The others were testing vaccines to prevent infection from the virus. Dmitri would lead the development of treatments for those who became infected.

The work would be an enormous challenge. His own health would be in jeopardy. But someone had to do the research necessary to protect families like his own from these deadly agents, and he was as qualified as any.

Dmitri's research was about to begin. According to Lukin, O-168 virus victims were arriving at NuCure the following day.

45

AIRPLANE, OVER ARCTIC OCEAN

The skin is cold and may be blue in color. The pupils become dilated. Weakness is profound and is accompanied by a lack of coordination and slurred speech. There is a gradual loss of consciousness. Breathing may be imperceptible. The body becomes rigid.

Jonathan closed the military manual, "Survival at Extreme Temperatures," resting in his lap. He had a white-knuckle grip on the manual, and every muscle from his fingers up to his neck was locked in a rigid contraction. He made a conscious effort to lower his shoulders and extend his elbows – motions that seemed to take minutes and make audible creaks.

His index finger remained wedged in the section on hypothermia, marking his page. Submersion injury and frostbite were next.

The dim cabin light of the plane stretched diagonally across Jonathan's shoulder and painted a sheen across the upper left-hand-corner of the manual.

He leaned across the aisle. "Cage," he whispered.

Cage was writing on a diagram in a notebook. For the last two hours, the scratching of pen against paper was the only sound in the cabin. He scribbled, scowled, scribbled some more. An arm of stone rose high into the air and then bounced a forearm across the top of his head. A wandering index finger rubbed at one of the scars on the back of his scalp as though trying to lift it off. The pen in his right hand squeaked under the pressure of his grip as though the ink was about to shoot out, and then drew a diagonal line across the diagram and turned the page.

"Cage."

The next diagram was underway. Cage was oblivious to everything else happening in the plane.

Jonathan reopened the manual.

The heart slows and the blood pressure deteriorates. It may be impossible to determine if the individual is still alive or dead.

Maybe I ought to start at the beginning, Jonathan thought to himself. He flipped the pages back to the beginning of the chapter on hypothermia. He squinted at the pages through the dim light.

Human beings are a tropical warm-blooded species and, as a result, are prone to hypothermia. Any body temperature below 98.6 degrees should be considered abnormal. Hypothermia can occur at mild temperatures, and most cases are reported in the spring and summer.

What did Ester say? The temperature gets down to negative thirty-five degrees in the winter, and that's in the southern part of Siberia.

So, what about Siberia? How long would it take to become hypothermic at negative thirty-five degrees?

He kept reading.

As the core body temperature drops from 98 to 95 degrees Fahrenheit, the victim feels cold. The skin becomes numb. Muscle function is mildly impaired, most notably in the hands. Shivering begins as a compensation mechanism to generate heat internally.

Between 95 and 93 degrees, more obvious weakness and loss of muscle coordination occur, forcing the victim to move at a slow stumbling pace. Shivering becomes more pronounced. Mild confusion begins and the victim may become withdrawn and apathetic toward the cold. The skin becomes pale and cold to the touch.

Between 93 and 90 degrees, gross loss of muscle coordination occurs with frequent stumbling and falling and inability to use the hands. Mental sluggishness occurs, resulting in slowed thought and speech. Retrograde amnesia occurs.

Between 90 and 86 degrees, shivering stops as the normal compensatory mechanisms become derailed. Severe loss of muscular coordination is associated with stiffness and inability to walk or stand. The victim becomes incoherent, confused, and irrational.

Between 86 and 82 degrees severe muscular rigidity develops. The victim can barely be aroused, even with sharp painful stimuli. The pupils dilate. The heartbeat and pulse become imperceptible. The skin becomes ice cold.

Core temperatures below 82 degrees result in unconsciousness, coma, slow breathing, heart arrhythmias, and death.

"Cage," Jonathan said, this time loud enough to be heard by everyone awake on the plane, and to wake a few who weren't. He heard his own voice as though it was crossing back from the dead.

Cage looked up, his pen still pressed against the notepad.

"Why am I on this flight?" Jonathan asked, his voice even louder than before and wavering mid-sentence.

"Because you missed your connection in Iceland?" Cage said.

"I mean, what's my role on this mission?" Jonathan asked.

"Your role," Cage said, "is to listen to what I say and stay alive. And to avoid interfering with the rest of us staying alive. That's it. That's your only assignment. But you'd better not screw it up. If I feel at any point that someone here is jeopardizing this mission, it's my responsibility to take them out of the picture."

He leaned across and tapped his finger on the manual in Jonathan's lap. "Reading that is a good start toward staying alive."

"I always love the in-flight magazines," Jonathan said.

"Have you ever seen someone die from hypothermia?" Cage asked.

Jonathan shook his head. His finger slipped out of the manual.

"Have you ever seen *anyone* with hypothermia?" Cage asked.

Jonathan shook his head again. He tried to wiggle his shoulders loose from the muscles contracting around them.

Cage exhaled audibly.

"It's impressive," he said. "Actually, it's more humbling than anything else. The entire body shuts down. Every organ. Every regulatory mechanism. Every metabolic function. Every cell."

"You've seen severe hypothermia?" Jonathan asked.

"I lived through it," Cage said. "On a training mission in Alaska." Even through the darkness, Cage's expression was unmistakable; he hated the fact that he had been weak, hated the fact that he had been unprepared, and hated the fact that he had to admit these failures to Jonathan.

"The shivering gets bad. You feel like your whole body's going to lock up," Cage said. "Then the shivering stops. You're relieved. You think you're coming out of it at that point, and your head isn't working right, so the cold no longer gets to you. But inside you're a mess. You piss out half of your body fluid while the other half is pooling in your lungs. Your secretions thicken, and your cough reflex freezes away, and you start drowning from the inside out. Your blood sludges from the dehydration and the cold. Your stomach ulcerates. Your kidneys dry up like baked beans. Your spleen contracts into a ball."

Cage paused long enough to allow Jonathan a full mental image of a spleen contracted into a ball.

"The tissues cry out for oxygen," Cage continued. "Acid levels increase. Carbon dioxide follows. The brain damage becomes irreversible. The seizures start. You slip into a coma."

A shiver crept through Jonathan's subconscious and worked its way up to the surface. Hopefully Cage's description was over.

A voice sounded behind them. "The electrical impulses in the heart are blocked by the cold. The rate slows, forty beats a minute, twenty beats a minute. The contractions weaken. The rhythm becomes erratic. Ventricular fibrillation leads to cardiac arrest."

Jonathan pivoted in his seat and looked behind him. Thing One or Thing Two was sitting in the darkness. "Thanks for the bedtime story," Jonathan said.

"No problem," he said.

"Naptime is almost over," Cage said. "I'm going to brief the team in a few minutes."

46

RESEARCH STATION, SIBERIA

“It’s a virus,” Maria said.

Drew was still standing with Yurov in the doorway of the laboratory, about to enter. Behind them was the low steady whistle of the wind, in front of them the hum of laboratory equipment.

“But like nothing you’ve seen before,” Jon Karlssen added. He raised his head from a microscope and stood to greet them.

Maria was seated at the sterile hood, an encased metal workstation that minimized contamination from its surroundings. The laminar flow air system created the sound heard in a conch shell along the beach. Her breath fogged intermittent streaks on the outside of the hood’s sliding glass window. Her arms curled under the edge of the window as her gloved hands nimbly sorted through the petri dishes inside.

“Show them the bacteria cultures plates,” Karlssen said.

Maria’s face tightened momentarily. She held two of the petri dishes closer to the window.

Drew leaned in closer, expecting to see the “halos” of dead bacteria resulting from spreading circles of viral infection. There was nothing there. No bacteria at all.

“What are we looking at?” Drew asked.

“Dead bacteria,” Maria said.

But an entire plate of bacteria couldn't disappear that quickly.

"Eight hours," Karlssen said, as though reading Drew's mind.

Maria slid the petri dishes to the back corner of the hood and brought two others closer toward the glass. Now Drew saw thin layers of pale yellowish-green bacteria interrupted by clear circles. The circles were large, resembling the typical findings seen after about 24 hours of culture. A high-power electron microscope would reveal seas of virus and decimated fragments of dead bacteria inside the clear circles.

"Three hours," Karlssen said, tapping against the glass. "Three hours."

Maria nodded. "This virus is replicating extremely fast."

"Show them the bone plate," Karlssen said. He tapped on the glass again to draw Maria's attention to the back corner of the hood.

Maria looked up at Karlssen with an expression that depicted her distaste for following commands. She silently conceded and reached toward the back of the hood. She moved a small stack of petri dishes to the side to reveal one that was familiar to Drew – the dish where he had placed the bone biopsy specimen. The glass fogged again, but it was obvious that the entire inch-long section of honeycomb-textured bone from Mincini's diseased forearm was gone.

"I cut slivers of the specimen for my analysis," Maria said. "Then I left the rest of the bone in this petri dish and put it in the back of the hood."

The glass window cleared again, giving Drew a better view of the plate. The chunk bone was gone, but the plate wasn't empty. A grayish yellow film lined the bottom and rose to an apex toward the center. Bone debris?

"I took some of this gray substance and did an H and E stain on a slide," Karlssen said. "Take a look under the scope." He eagerly waved them over.

Drew followed him to the microscope, where the slide was in position on the platform. Before his face even reached the eyepieces, he could make out the full field of large multinucleated cells.

Osteoclasts.

The petri dish in the hood was now filled with osteoclasts where there had recently been a piece of bone. The osteoclasts from Mincini's arm had disintegrated the entire biopsy specimen within a few hours. How quickly were they eating away at the bone inside Mincini's body?

Karlssen walked to a counter in the back of the room where centrifuge tubes were standing in racks. He removed two of the tubes. "I've been drawing off the fluid from the halos and spinning it down in a sucrose gel to isolate the viral contents. It's an RNA virus. Do you see this band?"

He held one of the tubes up into the light, revealing the striped pattern of layers in the gel. He pointed to a thick line near the lower third of the tube. "This band is the viral RNA."

Karlssen now held the other tube up to the light so that the two gel patterns were visible side by side. The thick line matched in both tubes.

"It's the only band that's present in both the infected bacteria and the infected osteoclasts, so we knew it was the virus," Karlssen said. "We've been purifying and sequencing the band. I didn't think we'd have a prayer at getting enough RNA to analyze the sequence, but this virus grows so fast that we're running all three machines simultaneously."

Drew turned to see the humming sequencing machines churning out data behind them. "How fast can you have the virus sequenced?" he asked.

"To have every base pair mapped out would take weeks, maybe months," Maria said.

"But I think we can have enough information on portions of the sequence to get a rough estimate of homology by tomorrow," Karlssen said.

"Do you mean you can tell what type of virus it is?" Drew asked.

Karlssen nodded.

"What type or what types," Maria said. "Whatever this is, it might be homologous to multiple types of virus. Keep in mind that this preliminary testing is suboptimal, at best."

"But it's something," Karlssen said. "If we can get a rough estimate of what type of virus we're dealing with, we may be able to figure out a treatment."

Drew turned to Yurov. "What type of virus do you think it is?" he asked.

Yurov contorted his face in thought. "It's like none that I've ever seen," he said. "Or that anyone has ever seen, I would have to assume."

"How can a new virus just materialize like this?" Drew asked.

"It happens far more often that we'd like to think," Maria said. "Look at HIV. Before 1983 nobody had ever heard of HIV. Today over 40 million people are infected. And Ebola wasn't reported until 1976."

"The deadliest virus known to man, and it's only been around for 26 years," Drew said.

"Ebola has probably been around for many years," Yurov said. "RNA viruses are some of the oldest entities on the planet."

"Where was Ebola waiting all these years, then?" Drew asked.

"Some unknown reservoir," Yurov said. "Like rat fleas carrying bubonic plague. The flea and rat go unscathed. But the next thing you know, 20% of Europe is gone. The threat is always there."

"Viruses have a way of persevering," Maria said. She turned back toward the hood.

"And adapting," Yurov said. "Nothing changes faster than an RNA virus. They're so vulnerable to mutation. That's why our medications can't keep up with viruses like HIV. What would appear to be a design flaw has actually kept them one step ahead."

"This bone disease virus had to come from somewhere," Karlssen said. "I don't think we can rule out the mammoth as a possibility."

Drew spoke rapidly, "I've been wondering about that for the past few days, but I thought it would sound foolish. Do you think that it's possible that the bone disease virus was released from the mammoth?"

"We shouldn't jump to such conclusions," Maria said over her shoulder. She was shaking her head.

"It's not foolish at all," Karlssen said. "In fact, it is one of the only possibilities at this point. Imagine a virus that's been dormant, preserved inside a woolly mammoth for thousands of years, and then released into a previously unexposed population. The results could be devastating. Like what we have here."

"A time-traveling Trojan Horse," Drew said. "Maybe the mammoth curse isn't so crazy after all. But what are the odds that a large mammal could be a reservoir for such a virus?"

"There's no reason to assume that the mammoth was just a reservoir," Karlssen said. "It may have been infected as well. Such a virus could even support the disease theory of mammoth extinction."

"Now we've proven MacPhee's disease theory," Maria said, waving a hand in dismissal.

Karlssen wasn't dissuaded. "A mammoth could also be an unaffected reservoir. It's happened with elephants. African elephants are silent carriers for a strain of Herpes that's lethal to Asian elephants. The normal habitats of these elephants don't overlap. But when they are housed together in zoos, the Asian elephants can become infected. Their hearts fail and their blood vessels rupture."

Drew nodded. "All because they're brought together due to unnatural circumstances."

"That's right," Karlssen said, "and there's no reason why the same process can't occur between mammoths and humans. We could be exposed to a virus that was eliminated with the reservoir thousands of years ago."

"Not eliminated." Drew added. "Just hidden away."

"Until now," Karlssen said.

"It seems as though everyone who is sick contracted the virus all of a sudden." Yurov said. "After being here for months, we start breaking like china dolls. Why now? Why did it take so long? This is what's been confusing me the most."

"That's a good question," Karlssen said. "The virus may have a long incubation period, weeks or even months. Or else the virus is capable of spreading quickly, but we weren't exposed until the past few weeks, perhaps as the virus was released from the environment, or from the mammoth."

It was difficult to imagine anything surviving in this harsh environment. But the virus wasn't alive. It never was. Viruses don't ever "survive," they "persist," as Maria had said. They persist, they infect, they replicate, and then they do it all over again. Drew had avoided the threats of exposure to killers such as hepatitis and HIV while working in New York City. But this was something altogether new, something more terrifying.

"Is there any way to tell who has been infected?" Drew asked. He visualized the tiny protein filled packages surging through his bloodstream, the osteoclasts chewing through his bones.

"Not at this point," Karlssen said. "I have been assuming that we are all infected."

"What are our chances of developing a cure?" Drew asked.

The question hung in the air.

The front door of the laboratory squeaked. Drew turned around. Oleg Larianov had been peeking in through the open crack in the doorway, but now turned and disappeared into the hall. Drew ran to the door, but Larianov was gone. How much did he overhear? How much did he know already?

"I don't trust him," Maria said.

"I don't either," Yurov said.

"We need to talk to Larianov," Drew said.

47

1ST AVENUE, NEW YORK CITY

Why Claire?

The question kept playing through his head. The answers were still unacceptable, still intolerable. What did she have to do with this?

Atisoy was dead, and Grovely had left a clear trail to him, practically signed "Thorton Grovely" on his dead body. The police would track him down. He would be accused of the murder. It was inevitable now. He had to keep moving.

But none of that matters, he kept telling himself, *it doesn't matter at all, because of the stranger with the petri dish. I'm next. I am going to die. The killer is already at work in my bloodstream.* He was sure of it.

His mind had been reeling since he staggered out of Atisoy's office. He had lost sense of time altogether. He wasn't living in years and months and days anymore. He was counting the hours, living from minute to minute. His world was changing that fast, probably ending that fast.

Why Claire?

Why did Claire's phone number show up on the screen when he pressed the redial number in Atisoy's office? Did Atisoy call her right before he died? Or was Atisoy's killer the one who made the call? Either way it didn't make sense. He was still suppressing the plausible explanations. He didn't want it to make sense.

He was back in Manhattan, walking up 1st Avenue in the east 80's. Cars honked and jockeyed for position through the street. Brake lights and streetlights swirled through the overcast afternoon.

A man in a gray overcoat brushed up against his shoulder while blurring by. Grovely retracted from the contact as though he'd been stabbed. His upper body pivoted, and his arms swung backwards. The overcoat vaporized around the corner at 84th street. Just another faceless form fluttering through the nightmare that he was living.

Pedestrians coalesced and scattered around him. Countless pairs of eyes. Countless potential attackers. He zigzagged to minimize his chance of contact, minimized his chance of any interaction. He had never walked through this area of Manhattan before, never had to. Who would live up here? Of all people, why would Claire live up here?

Again, he looked at the sheet of paper with Claire's address. Four more blocks. Just a few more minutes. She'd be home. She was always home. What was he going to say? Was he making a mistake by heading to her apartment? He was making a habit of making mistakes. Lately it was what he did best.

His hands were trembling. They might have even twitched, once, maybe twice. Was his throat tightening? Was it just his nerves? He was too tired to decide. Too tired and too confused. He wondered how Atisoy was inoculated with whatever killed him. Injection? Ingestion? A substance on his skin? What symptoms struck first? Did he even notice? Maybe his hands were trembling. They were probably twitching.

Maybe Atisoy died immediately. Just a deep breath and then a seizure. Not even enough time to get away from his desk.

He remembered Atisoy's body, lying in a heap at the foot of the desk. Most of the image was a blur, but the tongue...The sight of the tongue was so revolting. It didn't look like part of a human being. He could still see it clearly. It was as though it was following him through the streets of Manhattan, chasing him toward Claire's apartment.

His right hand twitched. Definitely a twitch this time, wasn't it? The entire hand jerked back at the wrist, as though an electrical shock had just passed through it.

He crossed 92nd street. He looked at the sheet of paper again. His vision was a little blurry and the sheet was shaking, but the address was the same. There had to be a mistake. Otherwise, her apartment was coming up soon on his left. He walked closer to the street and looked further uptown. The condition of the buildings was progressively deteriorating up ahead. He yearned for gold-buttoned doormen, monogrammed awnings, and etched marble facades, only to find graffiti-coated stone, rusted black bars, and broken windows.

A man in a gray overcoat was waiting to cross the street from the opposite side. The same man as before? He didn't look likc he belonged here anymore than Grovely did.

A burning vibration rushed through Grovely's neck. His tongue felt swollen. Is that the way it started for Atisoy? He saw Atisoy's crumpled body again. He felt Atisoy's purple chewed up slab of beef of a tongue in his mouth. These sensations passed, but the fear lingered.

The man across the street was gone. Where did he go? Grovely spun almost completely around. No sign of him.

Grovely walked faster.

The sheet with the address was twirled into a mangled wad in his hand. It was wet, as though it had been through the wash. He opened it and flattened it as much as possible on his palm. He wanted the address to be something else, but he was standing in front of Claire's building.

It was time to go inside.

He took out his pills, which were now combined in a single bottle. There was no way he was going in there without at least one pill. The lid rattled in his trembling hands.

A series of shots rang out across the street.

Grovely's whole body tensed at once, waiting for the jolt of the bullets. He inadvertently fell into a crouching position and looked at the direction of the sound. Somewhere children were laughing. Small children, maybe ten years old. Not joyous laughter. It was devious laughter. A flash rose up from the edge of the building on the corner. An orange whizzing streak struck the building over Grovely's head. Another cracking sound brought shreds of paper down around him.

Bottle rockets and firecrackers.

The second noise startled the pill bottle out of his hand. As though trapped in slow motion, he watched the bottle bounce high off the sidewalk, spin into forward motion, and skid over a sewer grating. Before he could react, the bottle fell down into the sewer.

While Grovely was assessing the various sources of shock assaulting his body, a window opened on the third floor above him, and a gray-haired lady leaned out. She waved a chubby fist and yelled in Spanish across at the invisible children.

Grovely crept along the sidewalk and looked down through the sewer grating. He knelt down on the granules of broken glass coating the sidewalk in order to get a better look. The pill bottle had to be somewhere in the pile of assorted garbage resting down at the bottom, but he couldn't see it, and there was no way to get it out. His psychological defense had fallen into the garbage; he would need some form of physical defense.

As though some god had reconsidered and taken pity on him, Grovely spotted a broken handle of a baseball bat lying next to the grating. It wasn't much, but it was better than nothing. He grabbed it, stood up, and looked at the front door. More graffiti. Mostly Spanish. He could make out some profanity and interracial slurs.

How did Claire live here?

The front door of the apartment building flew open and clanked against the cement façade. The recoil sent the door crashing back against the tall toothpick of a man in a Mets jacket emerging at the top of the staircase. The heavy wood drew a groan and a series of smoker's coughs. The man staggered down the stairs in a cloud of stale alcohol. He mumbled something that sounded like "better go up." Then he snarled, or maybe smiled. Neither interpretation seemed particularly reassuring.

Holding his breath, Grovely maneuvered past the man and grabbed the closing door just in time. The bat handle seemed smaller than before, but he held it tightly as the dark hallway gradually came into focus. With the sharp end pointed in front of him, he started down the hall. Then he realized what the man had just said. "Batter up." He was pretty sure of it.

The hallway had looked better out of focus. Patches of wallpaper with curled edges were intermingled with partially crusted, partially painted shapes of wall, creating the effect of an incomplete jigsaw puzzle. Paint chips and dust balls were scattered along the warped wooden floor.

When the door clicked shut, Grovely sensed that someone else was in the hallway. He spun quickly toward the door, but nobody was there – just the words "G MAN" written in dark red paint, maybe blood, on the inner surface of the wood. His left eyelid began to twitch rapidly. He rubbed the lid with the back of his index finger, but the movement wouldn't stop. His feet felt heavy. Acid was boring a hole through his chest.

Grovely's feet made a sticky peeling sound as he walked. One step. Then another. Aged floorboards creaked. One cracked. The stairs were a few feet ahead. 2C. Just one flight up. Was anyone up there? If so, they would certainly hear him coming.

How could Claire live here? It didn't make any sense. Nothing seemed to make sense anymore.

He crept up the stairs, turned at the landing. Another crack of a bottle rocket sounded outside. His breathing stopped, mid-inhalation, and then a peeping sigh escaped. The acid splashed along the inside of his chest. The eyelid flickered wildly. Would it ever stop?

The second floor was even darker than the first. An old carpet ran down the hall, the central fibers worn down to the brown mat base. The doorway to apartment 2A was just a few feet ahead. An argument was occurring somewhere ahead. A man and a woman. Maybe several women. The anger was unmistakable, but the individual words were undecipherable.

Grovely walked down the hall. The bat was swimming in his sweaty hands. He wiped his palms against his pants and then restored his grip on the weapon. He clutched it with both hands like a desperate villager on a vampire hunt.

The front door creaked below and then slammed shut. No footsteps. Not yet. Was someone sneaking up? He ran on his toes past the yelling in 2B. 2C was around the corner ahead. The stairs creaked somewhere behind him.

Grovely turned the corner. There was no door on 2C. At the far end of the empty studio apartment, sunlight penetrated the two narrow gaps on either side of a roller blind and sliced dusty stripes through the air. There was no furniture. Nothing on the walls. A few torn shreds of newspaper were scattered along the floor.

Empty beer bottles and chocolate bar wrappers were piled in the far corner. Nobody's lived here for a long time, Grovely thought.

The footsteps left the wooden stairs and shuffled along the rug.

Grovely ducked behind the wall along the doorway and listened. He raised the broken bat above his head and waited for his vampire.

The footsteps stopped. A man cleared his throat and spat. Keys rattled. The sound of yelling got louder. Yelling, laughter, applause. A television talk show. The door closed and muffled the sound again.

Grovely lowered the bat and closed his eyes with relief. Both eyelids were flickering against his eyeballs.

A new smell broke through the foulness of the building. A smell that didn't belong there.

Flowers – roses – perfume.

Grovely opened his eyes and saw Claire standing in the doorway.

The bat fell from his hands and rattled along the floor.

"I knew you'd come back for me," she said.

She was beautiful, just like he remembered her. She was pointing a gun at his face.

48

NUCURE LABORATORIES, RUSSIA

Dmitri knew just about everything about O-168.

It was an RNA virus, a new relative of one of the oldest entities on the planet. It was about the size of HIV, and it contained a sequence of RNA that was identical to part of the HIV sequence. Other segments matched those of influenza, Human T Cell Leukemia Virus, and Ebola. Interspersed with these naturally formed virus sequences were several man-made regulator sequences that maximized the speed and efficiency with which the virus caused infection, found its cellular target, and replicated.

O-168 was a hand-made killing machine. It could withstand dry conditions and varying temperatures. It could enter the body in several ways, but most importantly, it spread easily through the air to the lungs, making it highly contagious.

The transmission rate was nearly 100% in laboratory animals. Infection invariably led caused bone destruction, leading to progressive pain and debilitation and eventually causing death.

Dmitri knew all this information about the virus. He just didn't know how to destroy it.

There had been a flurry of activity behind the closed doors of the patient isolation facility all morning as preparations were made for the arrival of the first victims. First Lukin went in by himself. Then he returned with a short white-haired man introduced as Doctor Boris. Then a young woman joined them. Dmitri had watched her pass, seeing only dark eyes within the small window of exposure allowed by the containment suit visor.

Lukin left the two visitors alone in the patient facility for about two hours, which struck Dmitri as uncharacteristic for the regimented NuCure supervisor. Dmitri glanced periodically at the door, wondering if he would ever be allowed inside.

Lukin passed by several times, wheeling carts of supplies into the patient facility. Dmitri tried to watch discreetly but found it difficult to see what was in the carts. He eventually found himself standing on his toes and craning his neck for a better vantage. When Lukin passed by with what appeared to be bags of intravenous fluid, he stopped suddenly.

Dmitri's gaze passed from the bags of clear fluid, along the white cart, and up Lukin's containment suit until reaching the Plexiglas visor. Lukin was looking back at him. Their eyes locked momentarily.

Lukin stood up from the cart and approached as Dmitri looked down at the protein blot gels on the counter in front of him.

"This is taking longer than I anticipated," Lukin said. "We have a small window of time with which to prepare the facility. I'm going to need your help."

Dmitri had been a bit embarrassed and more than a little nervous about being spotted watching the preparations. He was relieved to be included in Lukin's plans. He placed the gels back on their rack and looked up at his boss. "I can help," he said.

He followed Lukin toward the entrance to the patient facility. He noticed Rozalina and Kazimir watching them from across the laboratory.

Lukin pressed the access code next to the door.

"How do you know it's O-168?" Dmitri asked.

Lukin had to turn around completely to look face to face at Dmitri through the visors of their containment suits. "We know."

The door beeped, and they entered the facility.

They were standing along one side of a hexagonal room. A round countertop surrounded file cabinets and computer stations at the center of the room. Doctor Boris and the dark eyed woman were working at two of the computers. Each side of the hexagon room had a Plexiglas wall with a door leading into a patient room. The rooms more closely resembled high tech jail cells than hospital rooms.

Each of the six rooms contained a specialized isolation stretcher encased in a clear plastic tent. Blue, red, and yellow hoses extended from the bases of the tents. Similarly colored nozzles lined the walls. Small strips of paper fluttered in front of vents along the base of the walls, and larger vents hummed along the ceilings.

Lukin led Dmitri toward the counter in the central core where the others were seated. They passed a "crash cart" for cardiac resuscitation and supply carts filled with different colored blood tubes, intravenous fluids, and other supplies. Cardiac monitors were wired to each room.

Doctor Boris stepped away from the computer. Black typing attachments on his gloves gave the impression of alien fingers.

Lukin said, "Dmitri will be helping to transport the patients when they arrive, so that the two of you can remain in here."

The woman at the computer spoke without looking up. "Nothing should interfere with our primary objectives here."

"Paulina is correct," Doctor Boris said. "Once the patients are inside, Dmitri will have two tasks. First, he must try and determine a cure for this virus." He spoke as though Dmitri wasn't there.

Dmitri said, "We should probably treat them with tetracycline first, since the virus contains several tetracycline off switches."

"We'll need him to identify an alternative treatment," Dr. Boris said, still acknowledging only Lukin. "We need to be able to treat the variation of O-168 that has had the tetracycline switch deleted."

"But to save these infected people..." Dmitri started.

"Of course," Lukin said quickly before Dr. Boris could respond. "You may start with tetracycline. But the tetracycline won't eliminate the virus – only neutralize it by stopping replication. We need to be able to eradicate the virus from the body."

Doctor Boris was glaring at Lukin.

"Your second task," Lukin continued, "is to determine why these individuals have reacted differently to the virus. They have all been exposed, but their responses range from a complete lack of symptoms to severe disease. One of them was on tetracycline, but the others seem immune without any explanation."

"The one on tetracycline was lucky," Dmitri said.

"Yes, lucky," Dr. Boris said.

"Where were they exposed?" Dmitri asked.

"In a closed area far from here," Lukin said. "They're being flown in."

Dmitri repeated his question. "But where were..."

"We don't want to befuddle your analysis with extraneous information," Dr. Boris said, directly acknowledging Dmitri for the first time.

"Six people were exposed?" Dmitri asked.

"Six people are coming here," Lukin said. "We are expecting them by midday tomorrow."

"You will achieve your two objectives," Dr. Boris said.

"I'll do everything I can," Dmitri said. The answer seemed inadequate. He wondered if the small rectangular snapshot visible through his visor conveyed his fear to the other men.

Lukin walked into one of the patient rooms. "It's the ones who weren't infected that I'm most interested in," he said. "They are the..." As he pulled the Plexiglas door shut, the sound of his voice came to an abrupt halt. There was no door handle on the inside. Lukin pushed against the door with his shoulder, but it didn't budge. He ran his fingers along the edge of the door, trying to pry it open. He nodded with satisfaction and then gestured out to them.

Dr. Boris unleashed a menacing smile at Lukin, as though considering whether or not to release him. Lukin's face flashed a momentary belief that he might actually remain locked inside. Then Dr. Boris walked to a box on the wall and pressed button number four. The door to room four clicked open, and Lukin stepped out.

"We need to know why they weren't infected," Lukin said. He nodded at the clear door as he closed it behind him. He seemed to notice something in Dmitri's expression and said, "Because that information may benefit our vaccine development."

"The transmission and transvection rates were nearly 100% in our laboratory research," Dr. Boris said. "The fact that anyone would be exposed and not get infected comes as a shock."

Lukin's eyes darted at Dr. Boris. Dmitri wondered where the white-haired doctor had worked on O-168.

"Do you think one of the off switches has been activated?" Dmitri asked.

"Not without tetracycline," Lukin said.

"The virus mutated," Dr. Boris said.

"It shouldn't have," Dmitri said. "It contains a proofreading stabilizer sequence."

"You're right," Lukin said. "The proofreading stabilizer should have reduced the mutability of the virus to almost nil. At least that's what the in vitro studies have shown. But once the virus infects humans..."

"It mutated," Dr. Boris said again. "It's breaking down like the original virus. Atisoy's proofreader is innovative, but it's far less impressive than his ego."

"What was the original virus?" Dmitri asked.

Dr. Boris looked at Lukin, whose face was a red rectangle on the other side of his visor.

"They haven't told you much here, have they?" Dr. Boris asked. He smirked at Lukin again, and then turned back to Dmitri. "Ilya and I have different views on running a research facility. But I'm in charge of this project, and now that I'm here, the rules are going to change."

Dmitri wanted to ask who had originally engineered the virus. He had wanted to ask the question since he first encountered O-168, but this was the first time that he might have a chance to hear the correct answer. The question now consumed his thoughts. It waited at the tip of his tongue. He could almost hear it being spoken, or maybe thought, out loud.

But he let the moment pass. He didn't want to get between Lukin and Dr. Boris. Maybe he didn't want to know anyway. Maybe it was better not to know.

I don't want to befuddle your analysis with extraneous information.

Dmitri would be treating infected people. He could still assure himself that he was doing the right thing, making the right decision.

The victims would be there in twenty-four hours.

49

AIRPLANE, OVER SIBERIA

"We're going in."

Jonathan closed his manual and shifted upright to listen. He heard simultaneous movement throughout the cabin – a waking stretch or two, some shifting, then uncontained anticipation.

"We're ten kilometers from the touchdown point," Cage continued. He stood in the cabin, the dim light bouncing off his shoulders "Our surveillance loops will take about twenty minutes."

Lights in the plane suddenly illuminated. The brightness forced Jonathan's eyes closed, but he fought to reopen them to a narrow squint. Cage was holding a topographical map. Something red was at the center. Maybe a star. Vast white emptiness spanned the remainder of the map. A strip of blue at the top came into focus as the Arctic Ocean. It had to be more than 100 kilometers north of the red star in the center. A thin blue line of a river ran down from the ocean along the eastern end of the map, never less than 150 kilometers from the star. A long white expanse with few topographic elevation lines – a flat, vast frozen wasteland.

"Our primary assignment is to evacuate the researchers at the woolly mammoth research station," Cage said. He pointed at what was now definitely a red star. "The station is isolated in the middle of the Arctic, over 1,000 kilometers from the nearest town, 1,400 from the nearest airport." He pointed to a spot due west from the station. "There's a short flat stretch used as an airstrip nearly ten miles from the station; that's our first-choice touchdown point."

Their first choice didn't sound very appealing to Jonathan. He wondered what the second choice was.

"The researchers make up an international team financed by Global Investors, a U.S.-based company," Cage said. "They've developed a rapidly destructive bone disease. Global funneled piles of money into the project early on, but they're out of the picture now. They pulled out when the reports of the bone disease were confirmed. No more supplies. No fuel. No food. Satellite communication went down."

Cage distributed sheets of paper to the team. "We know that there were originally twenty-six researchers at the station. Here is the list of names. Most of them speak some English."

Jonathan looked down at the list. The names were grouped into seven nationalities, and several were marked with asterisks.

"The seven marked with an asterisk are dead," Cage said in a tone he might have used for ordering a loaf of bread at the deli.

Jonathan looked at the six names – Bohr, Brozine, Crinley, Juneau, Larsen, Skolnick, and Solnorov. Seven names. Seven asterisks. Seven dead bodies in the snow. For some reason, the sight of the names gave substance to the threat waiting ahead.

"The seven deaths were associated with the bone disease," Cage said. "We suspect that Solnorov was the index case. The nature of the disease is not fully determined, but we have reason to suspect that the cause is an unknown virus. You should assume that every person there has this disease, regardless of their apparent condition. Full isolation precautions must be used at all times."

Full isolation precautions. Standard procedure for an epidemic. But what kind of epidemic? What was happening there?

Abrams looked out his window into the darkness below. Somewhere down there was a team of researchers, some of the most intelligent scientists from around the world, gathered to evaluate a giant beast that was unearthed from the tundra after fifteen thousand years. Could any of them still be alive? Could this rescue team unravel the mystery of the illness in time to make a difference?

A mission in Siberia would turn CDC protocol inside out. What could they actually accomplish when they got to the research station? They could take specimens from the victims, if there were any left alive. They could document whether there was a true epidemic occurring. They could delineate the disease process, hopefully limiting future outbreaks, but could they have an impact on those currently suffering from the illness? What would he tell them when they arrived? He didn't feel much like a savior today. He felt more like a stranger visiting a frozen graveyard.

"We have help on the inside," Cage said. "He goes under the name Jon Karlssen. We are to protect his identity and use him as a last resort. But he will be integral to our success."

The plane leaned hard to the port side, driving Abrams' right shoulder against the window. "What's happening?" he called out. He looked outside. There was still only blackness below them. There was nothing down there. Where were they going?

Cage swayed through a second turn without losing his balance. He spoke more quickly. "Our first task is to secure the station. Then we'll begin to triage the survivors. The three primary targets will be removed immediately, along with others determined by triage priority."

Something about "securing the station" caught Jonathan's attention. He continued to lean against the window, staring out into the blackness with no sense of their altitude. A bright orange glow stretched out from what must have been the ground. He cleared his throat to ask what he had just seen, only to feel a thunderous jolt rock the plane.

Jonathan felt the seatbelt dig into his thighs as the plane dropped from the sky. Cage was tossed against the ceiling. He was pinned there, as though defying gravity. His eyes were wide. His arms swung for something to hold. The plane seemed to roll end over end, throwing him back to the floor. He was still alive, scrambling for his seat.

"We've been hit," yelled one of the pilots.

Hit? By what?

"Ground to air missile," Cage yelled back to the front. "They're firing at us."

Who was firing at them?

Jonathan saw the fire in Cage's eyes through the flickering lights of the cabin. He had to be thinking what Jonathan was thinking – that they were facing imminent death. Jonathan was terrified. Cage seemed thrilled.

A second orange streak of light pierced the sky, and then a third. The source of the lights now seemed to be directly in front of them. That could only mean one thing – the plane was heading straight toward the ground.

The two flashes burned by the right side of the plane, one of them close enough to touch. The plane spun to the left, pinning Jonathan's face against the window. Blood was no longer reaching his brain. Green and gold and white flashes filled his vision. Flashes from inside his head.

Jonathan was about to pass out. He was pretty certain that he would die shortly after that. Death seemed a preferable alternative to experiencing the frigid darkness of Siberia.

50

RESEARCH STATION, SIBERIA

Within just four hours, the temperature in the kitchen dropped from 50 degrees to 26 degrees Fahrenheit. By eight hours, the temperature was down to negative 10 degrees.

Everyone in the research station was now crowded into the cellular biology laboratory, trying to focus on anything but the fact that the fuel had run out and the battery-operated generator had already exceeded its expectations.

They had sequentially sealed themselves into smaller areas of the facility, allowing the rest to freeze. The laboratory, which was centrally located and built with the strictest temperature control, was selected as the final sanctuary from the cold.

Temperature sensors distributed throughout the station led to a monitoring panel located between the sterile hoods. Everyone watched with a combination of morbid fascination and horror as the temperatures throughout the station plummeted. Despite the craftsmanship used to construct the facility, despite all of their attempts at insulation, the non-heated portion of the station succumbed to the cold at an alarming speed.

The kitchen, located at the end of the building, froze the fastest. The centrally positioned rooms took a bit longer, but each had reached sub-freezing temperatures within eight hours. The temperature monitors had a lower limit of negative ten degrees; most of them were no longer registering.

The small auxiliary heater running off the generator in the laboratory wasn't prepared for the task. The room was getting cold.

Some of the researchers were sitting on the floor. Most of them were limited to lying on the floor due to the extent of their disease. The room was dim, lit only by the laptop computer in the corner where Karlssen was finishing his sequencing analysis.

Drew tended to the injuries as well as he could. There were no more medications, no more supplies. They would all be dead from hypothermia by the end of the day. He wondered why he was still playing doctor. Maybe to keep his mind from straying toward the inevitable. Maybe just to keep warm.

Everyone in the room was reflecting on someone – people in another place, another time – families, friends, maybe lovers. Drew read it in their faces. He heard occasional mentions of home that slipped out, the memories of people and places and events that stung too severely to bear for longer durations. They made obvious efforts to avoid such discussions, but there was no resisting such topics that occur when the proximity of death becomes a certainty.

Every period of silence in the room turned Drew's thoughts to Matty. He hoped that he was wrong for all these years. He hoped there was some omniscient force looking over the world. He wanted an afterlife to exist more than he could remember wanting anything since Matty died. It was the only way to get the only thing he wanted. It was the only way to see Matty again.

Thankfully, someone always steered the conversation back to the mammoth research. The topic was shared by all, and one that prevented the painful solitude of each of their personal memories.

Yuri Kosmonolov and Luigi Mincini were the most talkative. Kosmonolov was the Chairman of the Department of Comparative Zoology at the Russian Imperial Academy of

Sciences and had worked with Bonacci's projects over a decade. Before that, he had spent most of his career working with the National Geographic Society. The severity of his injuries could have easily killed him already. Every extremity was secured with splints. Several vertebrae were broken. He sat against the wall, next to the others, struggling to maintain his balance as he spoke.

Luigi Mincini, the man whose bone had undergone the bone biopsy, was an entomologist from Rome. During the past few months, he isolated hundreds of species of insects that had been frozen and preserved along the hair of the mammoth and in the surrounding sediments. He used an assortment of hair dryers to systematically melt this way down to the mammoth, layer by layer.

The mammoth, Drew learned, was initially found by Arctic Petroleum International, an oil company exploring the area for drilling. Global Investors, a capital investor for API, took over immediately, but kept the mammoth discovery under wraps. They brought the first members of the research team to the site in order to decide how best to study the mammoth. Bonacci wanted to take the creature and its surroundings en bloc to another site such as an ice cave, similar to what the French did with the Jarkov mammoth.

"We would have measured the ice cave first," said Mincini.

Kosmonolov said, "The French used a helicopter to haul their twenty-three-ton ice block nearly 200 miles from the Taimyr Peninsula to an ice cave near Katanga, only to learn that their mammoth wouldn't fit through the entrance. They wasted time and money widening the cave entrance while the ice block sat outside. When they finally started working, they discovered that their highly publicized intact preserved mammoth was little more than a couple of tusks and some strips of mammoth bacon."

Mincini smiled. In the dim light of the room, his tobacco-stained teeth carried deeper shadows.

"We've come a long way since Herz and Pfizenmayer," Kosmonolov said. "In 1901 they took a frozen mammoth from a cliff along the Beresovka River and traveled nearly a year by train, boat, sleigh, and horseback."

"They cut the mammoth into pieces and brought it back to St. Petersburg, where they reassembled the body," Mincini added. "The exhibit was the hottest ticket in Europe."

"They should have stripped out all of the organs," Mincini said. "They weigh a lot, and they decompose the fastest."

"I noticed that the organs had been removed from the mammoth outside" Drew said.

"We removed each organ, storing them individually for research," Mincini said. "So far we've only finished working with the stomach. It had over 500 pounds of plant material and debris packed inside. We studied the contents. The stomach was like a time capsule. We're learning a lot about the mammoth's diet."

Kosmonolov added, "The food preserved in the stomach was loaded with bacteria and parasites. Many have been extinct for thousands of years, and some are newly identified species."

A time capsule. A time-traveling Trojan Horse?

Jon Karlssen walked over from his computer and took Drew aside. "I've run the homology programs on the sequencing that we did. It looks like we're dealing with at least several well-known sequences linked together in this one virus."

"Which viruses do the sequences resemble?" Drew asked.

"It's not that they resemble them," Karlssen said. "These RNA sequences are identical to known viral sequences. Parts of this virus are straight out of influenza and Ebola. The influenza sequences might explain how the virus has been so contagious."

"You mentioned earlier that DNA generated from the virus is probably incorporating itself into the osteoclast DNA in order to stimulate the cells to destroy bone," Drew said. "Is that coming from any of the RNA sequences you've identified?"

"No," Karlssen said. "RNA transvection rates are usually low, mainly because the RNA is so unstable to new mutations. We've been seeing transvection rates approaching 100%, which is unheard of. So essentially, exposure to this virus guarantees infection, and infection guarantees bone destruction."

Drew looked around. Fractures had reduced a hearty group of individuals to a human wasteland. "That doesn't surprise me."

"Several of the sequences also matched known genetic laboratory tool sequences," Karlssen said. "There are at least two commonly used promoter sequences."

"But that means…" Drew started.

Karlssen nodded. His voice lowered. "That means part of the virus is man-made."

"Are the man-made sequences ones that you have here in the laboratory?" Drew asked.

"A few of them," Karlssen said. "The ones that are pretty standard laboratory tools."

"So, it may have been released from the mammoth after all," Drew said.

"No," Karlssen said. "There's no homology to the mammoth sequences, so I don't see how that could be the case."

"But then there's only one other possibility," Drew said.

"That's right," Karlssen said. "The only possibility is that this is a biologic weapon. Someone's taken parts of the deadliest viruses known to man and constructed a new virus, a Frankenstein monster of sorts."

The possibility of a biologic weapon had occurred to Drew, but he continued to turn to other possibilities. He hadn't wanted to believe that someone might have created such a virus with the intention to destroy. He still didn't want to believe it.

"There were several other laboratory sequences in the virus," Karlssen said.

"I found tetracycline switches," Karlssen said. "We use these often in the laboratory to control gene function. These particular ones are off switches, so when the virus is exposed to tetracycline, the adjacent gene is turned off. The virus has several of these switches."

"That means we could treat them with tetracycline if we had it" Drew said. He pointed toward the corner where Yuri Kosmonolov was seated with his back against the wall for support.

"It might," Karlssen said. "We use tetracycline in the laboratory. I doubted we had enough for everyone, so I checked the cabinet as soon as I saw the homology results."

"How much is there," Drew asked.

"None," Karlssen said. "It's missing. Someone took it."

Suddenly, Larianov grabbed both men by the arm. His hunched appearance created an illusion of weakness, but his grasp was firm. He licked a patch of beard along his lower lip.

"Who has the tetracycline?" Larianov asked. "Is it one of you? Is it the lady doctor?"

Karlssen pulled his arm away indignantly. He looked as though he was about to strike Larianov, who released his grip on Drew in order to shield his face.

"You seem to know a lot about what's going on," Karlssen said. "You may even be responsible for what's happening."

"What's happening here," Larianov said, "is that we're part of an experiment. Isn't that obvious? We're rats trapped in a cage. But who is running the experiment?" He held up a crooked finger to emphasize the point. "Who's running the experiment?" He lowered his finger, pointing at Drew and Karlssen, and then pivoting to everyone else. "Evil isn't where you expect it. That's what makes it truly evil. That's why evil always wins."

Larianov shuffled back to the far corner by himself. The computer light splashed color across his face, and then he faded into the darkness.

There was something bothering Drew about what Karlssen had told him. Something about the switches, but as he watched the oddity of Larianov, the thought slipped by.

Instead, Drew asked another question that had been puzzling him. Another uneasy feeling. Something else that seemed wrong. "Why osteoclasts?" he asked. "How does the virus know where to go?"

Karlssen tapped his temple as though disappointed he had forgotten to mention this. "One of the virus' genetic sequences is known to produce an osteoclast surface receptor binding protein."

The information hit Drew with a jolt. A binding protein that attaches to an osteoclast surface receptor? Only one gene for such a protein had been sequenced. He was well aware of that fact. The sequencing had been done in his laboratory. He had named the protein, named the gene.

"It's called…" Karlssen looked down at a sheet of paper.

"SRBP-168," Drew said.

"You've heard of it?" Karlssen asked.

Drew's mind was racing. Why SRBP-168? How?

Then it occurred to him why Global Investors sent him to Siberia in the first place. It wasn't so that he could save the researchers. He was sent there to die.

But he also knew why he hadn't succumbed to the virus, and why he probably never would.

"I've heard of it," Drew said.

Karlssen said, "So because this protein is part of the capsid, the virus selectively binds to..."

"Osteoclasts," Drew said. "It's the key to the virus reaching their target."

PART 3.
HUNTER THEORY

"Man hunted the mammoth to extinction. Throughout time man's thirst for destruction has remained unparalleled by any other species on earth and will eventually lead to the extinction of our own species."

– Oleg Larianov, PhD

51

FDR DRIVE, NEW YORK CITY

She's smooth as velvet, Grovely thought.

Sunlight splashed across Claire's face as she stepped out from the shadow beneath the FDR Drive. Her hair was down, released from the bun that Grovely so fondly remembered. At times it was difficult to believe that he was looking at the same person. But then the breeze angling off the East River would lift her hair away from her neck, or her black brushed-leather coat would ride a little higher above a flicker of muscle definition in her calf. In those brief moments, there was no mistaking her perfectly oriented muscle lines, symmetrical and proportioned, like those of da Vinci's anatomic studies.

Such thoughts kept invading Grovely's head. But each time, he tried to refocus on her right hand, sleek and slender, perfectly manicured, tucked into her Coach handbag, and carrying the gun that was the impetus for their walk along the river.

She was in charge here. There was no mistaking that.

"Where are we going?" Grovely asked.

The traffic on the Harlem River Drive perpetually accelerated on their left as they walked uptown. Grovely looked out across the East River, Manhattan's "other river." The South Bronx rose up from the opposite bank, with its scattered warehouses and weathered docks, and the constant flow of traffic on the Major Deegan Expressway.

"Uptown," she said. Her cheek drew taught and her lips puckered slightly. Her chin tilted upward as she judged their progress toward some unseen target in the distance.

Grovely stared at the outlines of her face, her silver lining. Then he thought of Atisoy, lying twisted on the floor. "How did you kill Atisoy?" he asked.

Genuine surprise broke through her otherwise composed demeanor. But she had to know that Atisoy was dead. Was she just surprised that he knew about it? Grovely felt as though he had snuck in a jab, interrupting an otherwise thorough beating.

"I know he's dead," Grovely said. "I saw him."

"Then how do I know you didn't kill him?" she asked.

"Because the killer called you from Atisoy's office," Grovely said. "You know who killed him." Another jab, maybe his last.

Claire looked stunned at first. She seemed to stop, mid-stride, and then resumed her pace. "You had the same motive that we did, that I did, to kill Atisoy. He sold you that piece of garbage, the proofreading stabilizer sequence, and you sold it to me. When it didn't hold up to its promise, the backlash was inevitable. He died for the same reason that you're dying."

She was gaining momentum now. "It's just a matter of time before you're linked to Atisoy's death," she said. "When they find your body, they'll call off the search."

The death flowing through Grovely's veins made him bold. "The Mamba killed Atisoy himself, then," he said.

"The Mamba doesn't kill anyone," she said. "He has everything figured out. He keeps his hands clean. You can appreciate that, can't you – keeping your hands clean."

"Do you know who he is?" Grovely asked.

A heavy black man was fishing from the walkway. He lifted his hat slightly and looked at them. He squinted and tilted his head, as though trying to decide what they were doing in his neighborhood.

Grovely wondered what Claire would do if he made a run for it right in front of this man. Would she chase him? Shoot him? In broad daylight, right along the highway? He noticed her hand sink deeper into the purse. The leather tented out toward him.

Claire allowed Grovely to pass by first. He stepped around the empty white bucket for the day's catch. This was his best chance to run. He could push the man into Claire, hit her with the bucket, whatever it took to knock her off balance, and then run. He'd make it several steps before she could react, and then she'd have to decide what to do. Would she really shoot him right there?

The man nodded as they passed. Grovely nodded back. Claire smiled at the man, and then gave Grovely the slightest shake of her head that said, "If you try it, you'll be dead within seconds."

The opportunity passed.

Claire took several steps past the man, and then answered Grovely's question from earlier, as though the fact that she almost had to kill him moments earlier was of no consequence to her. "Nobody knows who the Mamba is."

Grovely's heart was still racing. "You know what he looks like?" he asked.

"No. Nobody sees the Mamba," she said. "It's better for everyone involved. None of the scientists have seen him. None of the buyers have seen him. I've never seen him. If the money didn't keep showing up in my accounts, I'd say he didn't really exist."

"It must be difficult accessing your accounts, given the severity of your agoraphobia," Grovely said. "You put on a nice act."

"It had to be agoraphobia for you, Thorton," she said. "You needed someone even more disturbed than yourself. Atisoy's interests were a little more creative. I am whatever I need to be."

"Your apartment?" Grovely said. He was thinking out loud, asking the series of questions that was running through his head.

"That lice infested crack house?" she said. "I never saw the place until I followed you there today. My real home is less than a block from yours. I knew you'd never venture to the outskirts of the Upper East Side, so that's where I said I lived. You surprised me today, though. I guess true love can overcome anything."

Grovely approached a broken bottle. A long shard extended from the neck, reflecting the sunlight. How long would it take to grab the bottle and slice her with it? One quick jab in the throat.

"That night on the computer?" Grovely said. He was stepping over the bottle. There was no way. He'd never make it in time. He'd be shot before he even got it in his hand.

"I was actually at Karl Van Brauten's apartment that night," Claire said.

Van Brauten? Why Van Brauten? He looked at her through a cloud of confusion. She knew she was stunning him, landing uppercut after uppercut in verbal blows. She smiled, waited for him to recover, and then delivered a low blow.

"He even typed some of the messages to you," she said. "Some of the steamier ones. He seemed to enjoy it too much."

"Why Van Brauten?" Grovely thought out loud.

"He owns the mammoth project now," Claire said.

Grovely stared at her.

"Gaines thought he was dumping a financial disaster on Van Brauten," she said. "He threw the mammoth research station into a multimillion-dollar deal involving several other scientific projects, presumably as icing on the cake. But relieving the burden of the mammoth project was his sole incentive for initiating the deal with Van Brauten. *Caveat emptor*, right? But what he didn't know was that I had informed Van Brauten about the bone disease. He knew far more than Gaines."

Grovely listened but disagreed. The research project was a disaster. A medical disaster and a financial disaster. Gaines was savvy to get rid of it. Claire had no idea what she was talking about. Van Brauten had just wrapped an albatross around his neck.

"What Van Brauten knew," she said, "was that every person at that center had been infected with a viral agent. The holy grail of biologic warfare. 100% transmission. 100% transvection. Extensive bone destruction. Incapacitating pain, massive economic impact, and no treatment. And all you need is one infected person, a human viral bomb, to get it started."

Grovely stared at her.

"Aren't you proud?" she asked. "It's what you helped to build. Some of the key components of the virus came from our transactions with you. You knew what you were doing. You were turning medical technology inside out, selling it for biologic warfare. I bet you never believed it would amount to anything."

She paused to see if she had peeked Grovely's interest. She did. "When the virus was ready for testing, the remote station run by the very weasel who sold the faulty component seemed ideal. The experiment was impressive. You should see what it did to their bones. The virus is just a few adjustments away from perfection. Every national government, every military faction, every terrorist group in the world wants a piece of it. They're emptying their wallets for it."

Grovely remained speechless. She had him on the ropes now. "Van Brauten could care less about the mammoth. He was buying the virus. Every person at the research station is like a walking viral culture, and they're all up for auction. They're going to the highest bidder."

She had been right. When Grovely originally sold the technology to the Mamba it was easy. Unseen buyer. Unseen victims. It hadn't seemed real at all. He didn't even believe that the research secrets would amount to anything. It was like free money. Even if the merchandise was flawed. The mammoth station epidemic came as a shock to him at first, but a shock that he could handle. The idea that all the victims were now being sold for the virus inside them was mind-boggling. "Van Brauten doesn't deal in biologic weapons," was all he could say.

"He doesn't have to," she said. She patted him on the shoulder. "You never dealt in biologic weapons before this project, and look at you. A murder suspect. Injected with the contents of a mysterious petri dish."

Grovely looked at his palm. The wounds were still partially open. The edges were getting red, maybe infected. They suddenly felt as though they were on fire. His fingers were trembling.

Claire feigned a concerned "poor boo-boo" expression and then laughed.

"All Van Brauten had to do was want the money," she said, "and the rest of the transactions were made for him. He never has to go to Siberia. Or see the bodies. He never has to meet with the other parties involved. The Mamba takes care of that for him."

"But if the proofreading stabilizer sequence isn't working," Grovely started.

"It's close enough," Claire said. "The first people to become infected at the station were destroyed by the virus. They contain the most powerful strain. They're going for the most money, some alive, some dead. The group that originally bought the technology isn't happy about it, but if they didn't want to share, they shouldn't have released it in Sretensk last year."

"Who is that?" he asked.

"Where are your business ethics, Thorton?" she asked. "I don't want to breech client confidentiality."

"And the rest of the researchers?" he asked.

"They're going to other buyers," she said, as though she was talking about beef cattle. "Thanks to your decision to cut off their supplies, they'll be dead within a day or two. Then the corpses go out."

The river angled to the left. Grovely looked across the traffic and saw a large painted mural with the title "Crack is Wack" painted across the top. Black and white skeletons twisted and contorted across the mural, their vacant eye sockets haunting him as he walked along. Pushers and addicts. Ruined minds.

Grovely wished that he hadn't dropped his pills into the sewer drain.

He turned to Claire. "Where are we going?" he asked again.

She jabbed her purse forward with her gun, indicating that he should keep walking. The hum of the traffic was louder now.

"What are you going to do with me?" he asked.

"Oh, the fun's just starting," she said. "We're going to play a little game."

52

GROUNDED PLANE, SIBERIA

Orange flashes.

Falling. Tumbling. An incredible jolt. Metal crunching. And then silence.

Cold. So cold.

Jonathan opened his eyes to complete darkness. Blindness? Something pulling across his chest – the shoulder harness. Still in the plane. Had he been unconscious? Pain in his head. A lot of pain. Yes, probably unconscious. For how long? A tilted world. Everything getting fuzzy again.

Colder.

Howling wind. Gusts across his face. Something being draped across him. Someone covering his face. A shroud? But he wasn't dead. Not yet. He should tell them.

Too tired to speak? Just a dream? But his eyes were open. No ability to concentrate. No idea where he was. He drifted closed.

Jonathan's own shivering woke him up. Still dark. What time was it? He'd check his watch. Fingers shaking inside of gloves. Where did the gloves come from? The Gore-Tex rattled against the buttons. Several more attempts. About to give up. The watch finally illuminated. He could see it. Not blindness, just darkness. Relief. But it hurt to focus on the numbers.

A hand grabbed his wrist and covered the light. Jonathan turned to see who was there. He still had a yellow glow remnant in the center of his vision.

"Don't do that again," said a recognizable voice. Cage.

"What happened?" Jonathan asked. His voice crackled.

Cage gave an emphatic "shush." "We were shot down."

A moaning sound came from one of the seats behind them.

"Why? Who did it?" Jonathan asked.

"Whoever they are, they're sophisticated enough to be carrying an RPG-7. Keep your voice down," Cage said. He was whispering directly into Jonathan's ear now.

A metallic click and scrape sounded. Cage was loading a gun.

"Can you move?" Cage asked.

"I don't know," Jonathan said. He wiggled his fingers and feet through the rigors of his shivering. Bent his knees. Lifted his legs a little. He was amazed that nothing else hurt. Amazed and relieved. Somehow, he had survived the crash. "Yes, I think I can move. But I feel like a tractor trailer ran over my head."

The wind howled through the broken windshield of the plane. Jonathan heard Cage load another rifle and then place it on the floor. Then the seats creaked in succession toward the cockpit. Because the plane was tilted at an angle, Cage was forced to use the seats for support as he walked through the plane.

When the howling faded, Jonathan heard something dripping in the cockpit.

Cage crept back to Jonathan's side. "Podunk is still alive, but he's in bad shape," he said. "Everyone else is dead."

Jonathan was silent. A prolonged shudder spread throughout his body.

"Get these on," Cage said, handing Jonathan his night vision goggles.

Jonathan raised the goggles while trying to mentally prepare for the carnage in the plane. He closed his eyes while securing the strap along the back of his head.

The dripping sound had opened into a steady splatter on the cockpit floor.

Jonathan saw more than he wanted to through the goggles, everything in varying shades of green. The plane was compressed and twisted in the center like a used aluminum soda can. Most of the windows had blown out. The free edges of shattered glass fluctuated with the strength of the wind.

The pilot was lying across the control panel. A lever penetrated his face and suspended his head. Blood ran down the lever, across the panel, and in a stream onto the floor. Green blood, bright from the heat at the center of the puddle and fading into the cold surroundings at the periphery. The flow matched the sound that Jonathan had noticed earlier.

Cage was looking out through one of the windows, his rifle poised. Jonathan looked past Cage's shoulder, out to where the wing used to be.

"We need to block the open windows," Jonathan said.

"Not yet," Cage said over his shoulder. "It has to look like nobody survived."

"But the cold," Jonathan started.

"The cold won't be the first thing to kill us," Cage said. "We have to get ready. They're going to be here soon."

"Who?" Jonathan asked. He also mouthed the word "Why?" but the wind pushed his breath back down his throat.

"Here, take this," Cage said. He handed Jonathan one of the rifles. "Have you ever shot one of these before?"

Jonathan held the rifle. It was heavier than it looked. He wrapped his Gore-Tex gloves around the front and back ends, making sure not to go near the trigger.

"Have you ever shot any gun before?" Cage asked.

Jonathan's silence answered the question.

"Great," Cage mumbled.

Jonathan heard the faint sound of a motor in the darkness.

"Company's coming," Cage said.

"What if we turn ourselves in?" Jonathan asked. He moved his hand closer to the trigger to see if his gloved finger would fit. He pointed the rifle an exaggerated angle away from Cage.

Cage loaded a third rifle. "Not an option," he said. Then he loaded a fourth.

The sound of the motor was now more distinct. Both men leaned in to one of the broken windows toward the source of the noise. A small speck of a snow mobile was approaching from the horizon. No, two specks. Three specks. Three snowmobiles. They were headed for the plane.

"Change in plans," Cage said. "They'll see us if we go out there now." He pulled the rifle out of Jonathan's hands and placed it with the other two in the back of the plane. Then he started unbuckling the shoulder harnesses of one of the men in the back row. "They're going to come in through the front. We have to be in the back. And we have to play possum. Get those other straps off."

Jonathan held onto the seat as he navigated the sloped aisle toward the back. Podunk was lying across the seat behind his. His entire face had been smashed by the impact, and his nose had caved in. His breaths were shallow. Jonathan rested his hand on Podunk's shoulder, and then continued further toward the back of the plane.

The man sitting in the last seat was unquestionably dead. It was Thing One or Thing Two. Jonathan couldn't tell anymore. A wave of nausea spread through him, but he suppressed it as best he could. He wedged his foot at the junction of the seat leg and the floor and undid the man's shoulder harness. With the tension released from the harness, the body fell across the seats and slammed into the window.

Jonathan struggled with the body, trying to lift it away from the lower edge of the plane. His head throbbed. Through the window he could see the snowmobiles approaching in halos of ice and steam.

Cage reached across Jonathan and helped him drag the body out of the seat. Together they made their way toward the front of the plane with the dead weight. They placed the body in Jonathan's original seat and refastened the shoulder harness.

Jonathan walked back to the seat in the rear of the plane. Green blood was everywhere – on the seats, on the ceiling. He heard the blood squish under his footsteps. He prepared to play dead. If the plan didn't work, he wouldn't be pretending.

"Get your strap on fast," Cage said. He secured his own harness. He allowed his body to fall to the right and then tucked two rifles along the edge of the seat.

"Stash your goggles under your seat," Cage said.

Jonathan obeyed. He returned to complete darkness. He was still shivering. From the cold? From the fear of death? It didn't matter. Either way the shivering was involuntary. How could he keep still when their attackers arrived? Somehow, he would have to. The snowmobiles were getting louder, getting closer.

"I need my rifle," Jonathan said.

"You don't get a rifle," Cage said. "Not this time. Maybe next time."

Next time?

"Your job is to play possum," Cage said. "They're going to come through here and make sure we're all dead. There's going to be gunfire. Lots of gunfire. Just stay still. I'll take care of the rest. If we're lucky they'll all come inside. That's the plan. No more talking from this point."

The sound of the snowmobiles was sawing through the darkness. They had to be within a hundred yards now. Another gust of frigid air blew through the broken glass portals of the plane. Atlanta never seemed so desirable.

Jonathan leaned forward and to his right, trying to reproduce the position in which Podunk was lying in the seat in front of him. He felt for the sensation in his fingers and toes. He wiggled them lightly. Some of them seemed to be missing.

The snowmobile engines idled next to the plane. Men spoke what sounded like Russian. Metal clanked. At least three voices spread out around the plane, circling. One of them laughed.

The main entry latch sounded, but the door didn't open. Jonathan shivered. Relaxing his muscles seemed to make the shivering worse. He tried tightening them, and the shivering subsided. He braced himself for gunfire.

The voices resumed circling.

Glass shattered. They were banging out the rest of the front windshield. The voices entered the cockpit. First one. Then two.

Bursts of machine gun fire thudded against the pilots' bodies. A flash of light came like a brief shutter release on a camera. Jonathan saw a snapshot of two gunmen. His ears were ringing. Everything was muffled, as though he was lying under water. The two Russians sounded so far away, but he had seen them right there a moment earlier. When was Cage going to shoot? How could he tell where they were? Was he waiting for them to get closer? Was he waiting for the third man to enter the plane?

A burst of gunfire into the right front seat. Snapshot: dead body propelled against the window. Then another burst to the left. Snapshot: blood spray. Muffled Russian spoken. Muffled laughter.

Boots wedging, occasionally slipping, along the legs of the seats. Nothing from Cage. How long was he going to wait?

“Noge otpechatok,” one of the men said. The voice was louder, more rapid. The tone was different. He was concerned.

Cage unleashed the weapons. Gunfire streamed out of the back of the plane. Thudding, slapping, and splattering sounds ripped through the two Russians. They fell to the floor almost immediately. Moans became gurgles and then faded away.

Outside, boots slid along the nose of the plane. Cage clanked toward the cockpit, somehow maneuvering along the bloody slope and over the dead Russians. Jonathan pulled on his night vision goggles in time to see Cage leaning out through the windshield, rifle in hand. He fired down at the third assailant. There was no mistaking the sound of the direct hit.

Cage rested his rifle by his side, looking out into the snow.

Jonathan looked around the cabin. There were green blotches everywhere. “What was he saying?” he thought out loud.

“What?” Cage asked.

“I wonder what they said right before you shot them,” Jonathan said.

“He said ‘noge otpechatok’” Cage said. “It’s Russian for ‘footprints.’ He saw our bloody footprints on the floor.”

Jonathan shivered for the first time in several minutes.

Cage turned around “You ever ride a snowmobile?”

53

RESEARCH STATION, SIBERIA

Global never wanted SRBP-168. That's what they told him.

They didn't see the value of a protein that could preferentially and predictably bind to osteoclasts. The protein might have some long-range potential in bone disease treatment, Thorton Grovely had told him, but there just wasn't enough immediate market potential. Private funding was all about market potential.

The bone disease virus carried the SRBP-168 sequence. It made the binding protein. *His binding protein.*

SRBP-168 was supposed to modulate bone turnover. When linked to the right inhibitor, it could limit bone resorption. It was supposed to be part of the treatment for osteoporosis, metastatic cancer, and other diseases leading to bone destruction. It was supposed to help children like Matty, whose bone disease led to frequent fractures and unbearable pain.

It wasn't supposed to kill people.

Global must have stolen the genetic sequence for SRBP-168. There was nothing to stop them. They had signed the appropriate legal documents, of course, but what did that mean? Proprietary and confidentiality agreements were safety nets in Drew's world, but they had no value in the underground weapons market.

There was no immediate market potential for a bone modulator used to cure diseases, but there was apparently a huge market for a bone destruction weapon. That's what he had unknowingly created. A weapon. The key component to the osteoclast virus.

Drew sat on the floor of the research station laboratory, huddled together in the darkness with the others, wrapped in whatever blankets and extra clothing they could assemble.

It had gotten much colder in the six hours since the generator shut down.

Maria paced between the incubators and the temperature monitors, illuminating her watch every few minutes. She periodically gave an unwanted report on the temperature. "It's been two hours. It's forty-eight degrees," she said the first time, and the room became silent. "It's been four hours. It's thirty-six degrees," she said later. The announcement was punctuated by a low groan. The temperature was the first item on everyone else's mind, but the last thing they wanted to think about or discuss.

Maria's watch illuminated directly in front of one of the incubators. Drew could see his breath freezing in the greenish yellow glow. "It's been six hours. It's twenty-five degrees," she said, as though in disbelief that it was continuing to get colder in the room. She held her palm against the top of an incubator.

Drew was thinking about Matty.

The Picasso boy from the operating room emerged from the darkness. Crooked arms were outstretched to either side in casts, and both legs were wrapped together in a single splint. The broken limbs were unmistakable, but the face was a hollow swirl of vapor. Matty was splints and casts and broken bones.

Drew couldn't remember the rest, couldn't even piece together a face. "I'm sorry," he whispered. "I tried so hard, and this is where it led."

"You're sorry for what?" a voice whispered next to him. It was no longer Bonacci next to him. The accent was Russian.

The dropping temperature was starting to affect Drew's mind. He could no longer distinguish reality from hallucination. He looked in the direction where he had just seen Matty, hoping that his son would stay with him until the end, but he was gone. Drew turned toward the voice that had spoken next to him but saw nothing there. His eyes would probably never adjust to this degree of darkness. The room was completely devoid of light.

"Who said that?" Drew whispered.

There was no answer.

Drew leaned quickly to his right with his arms outstretched. He collided with someone's face, a bearded face.

"What are you doing?" the man asked. It was Larianov.

"I couldn't see you," Drew said. "I wasn't sure if there was really anyone there."

"I'm here," he said. "I'm just waiting."

"For what?" Drew asked.

"For whatever she's waiting for," Larianov said in an echoing whisper that must have passed through cupped hands.

Drew slid a few inches away from Larianov's voice. It made him uncomfortable to be sitting so close to his paranoia in the dark, even though death was waiting right around the corner anyway. He thought back to what Larianov had said a few hours before. *We're part of an experiment.*

Drew's mind kept replaying the words. *We're part of an experiment. We're rats trapped in a cage here.* The words rewound and played again. Something about the tetracycline switches. Something that wasn't right. Why would an off switch be in a virus used as a biologic weapon? *We use these often in the laboratory to control gene function.* That's what Karlssen had said. *We use these often in the laboratory.* That's why an off switch would be in a biologic weapon – if you were using it in an experiment. *We're part of an experiment.* Larianov was right.

But who was running the experiment? *Evil isn't where you expect it.*

"It should have happened a while ago," Larianov whispered.

"What?" Drew asked.

That's what makes it truly evil.

"Whatever she's waiting for," Larianov said.

"What?" Drew asked again.

That's why evil always wins.

Drew was too weak to concentrate now. He needed a nap. Just for a short time. He remembered telling himself not to nap several times earlier, but now he couldn't remember why. He closed his eyes and tried to bring Matty back.

"Do you have the stomach for this?" Larianov asked.

A nightmare seemed preferable to the reality of Larianov, the reality of the situation. If he just kept his eyes closed, he'd be asleep soon. Larianov would disappear.

The Matty with the broken bones was not waiting for Drew when he closed his eyes. Instead, he saw a mammoth striding toward him, tusks twisting toward the sky, legs like sequoia trunks.

"I have the stomach for it," Larianov said, but his voice seemed to be from a distant dream, a world Drew had already left.

The mammoth became reality, only now he saw a herd of mammoths. Orange-brown strands of wire-like hair twisted across the heads and backs of the giant beasts, swayed like reeds below their bellies and along their legs. They were circling around him, stalking, hunting.

"I want you to remember that, in case we never see each other again," a Russian voice said from the other world.

"I'll remember," Drew murmured.

"It shocks me to hear you say so," the Russian voice said.

Drew tried to see who was talking, but he was surrounded by men with spears. Not savages in loincloths. Businessmen using briefcases as shields. Thorton Grovely was there. The boy with the broken bones was gone. They were circling where the mammoths were just a few moments ago. There was no doubt that they were about to kill him. It was what they came there to do.

An aircraft batted through the sky as the men circled closer.

When the door swung open and the glare of the floodlight filled the room, Drew assumed that he had died and reached the afterworld. He had been wrong for so many years. The warmth of a smile rushed up into his face.

"We found help," someone behind the light was saying.

It was cold. Where was he? How long had he been asleep?

"It's Tarasov and Torelli," Bonacci said from a few feet to Drew's right. "They've made it back."

Drew squinted through the glare of the floodlights and saw the silhouettes of two men breathing smoke in the doorway.

It seemed too good to be true.

Tarasov walked through the room, shining the lights at each one of them in turn. Torelli was calling out names. It was the Russian and Italian who had driven out on the snowmobiles for help. Bonacci was right – they had made it back.

"Luigi Mincini," Torelli called out.

"I'm here," Mincini said with relief.

"Come with us," Tarasov said, pulling Mincini to his feet.

"Vladimir Yurov," Torelli called out

"I'm here, but I'm one of the healthiest," Yurov said. "Maybe you should take one of the others first."

"You're coming first," Tarasov said, sending Yurov toward the door with more of a push than a guiding hand.

"Oleg Larianov," Torelli called out.

The room was silent. The floodlight scanned the piles of blankets until falling on Larianov, who was lying with his eyes shut and his mouth open.

"Whether you're dead or alive, you're coming with us, Oleg," Tarasov said.

Larianov opened his eyes slowly and scratched his beard. He reluctantly stretched his legs and stood. He watched Drew over his shoulder as he made his way toward the others.

"Maria Pellegrino," Torelli called out. "Drew Chambers."

Maria was already standing with the others near the door.

Drew struggled to his feet. His legs seemed to be vibrating, and he wasn't sure if he could walk. He was confused, as Yurov was, as to why they were taking some of the healthiest people first.

"Where is Jon Karlssen?" Torelli asked.

"He's dead," Maria said. "He died a few hours ago."

Drew looked along the course of the floodlight and saw Karlssen lying face down along the wall. Thor Lundgren rotated the body, which was already in a state of rigor mortis. The floodlight beam caught Karlssen's wide-open and motionless eyes. His tongue was jutting out of his mouth, swollen and bloody. He was obviously dead. What had happened to him?

Drew started toward Karlssen, but Tarasov held him back. Drew was too weak to force his way past the young Russian.

"We need Solnorov's body," Torelli said. "And his left femur. It's frozen in the antrum of the mammoth's stomach where Larianov hid them. But first let's get everything from the main incubator out to the helicopter."

"But that will take up space for at least two other people," Yurov said.

"That's the way it has to be," Tarasov said. Everyone we just named has to get out to the helicopter immediately. They're flying us out of here. But we have to move quickly. There isn't much time. We're going to have to come back for the others."

Drew walked past the researchers – Bonacci, Lundgren, Kosmonolov, the others – wondering if he'd see them alive again. A guilty sensation worsened as he reached the others in the first group to be rescued. They exited the door in front of Tarasov and Torelli and shuffled, single file, through the frozen station.

The floodlight beam arched off the walls as they walked through the hallway. The sound of the generators was notably absent. The station was dead quiet.

How had they found help? Maybe miracles happened every now and then. They were about to get out of the station, escape from their frozen tomb. As he stepped through the front doorway of the station, Drew could hear the batting of the helicopter through the wind.

Four more men met them at the door, two Italians and two Russians.

"Thank you," Drew said, ducking his head from the wind.

He noticed their gear, which had a military quality.

Then he noticed their rifles.

54

EAST RIVER, NEW YORK CITY

"They smote each other not alone with hands, but with the head and with the breast and feet, tearing each other piecemeal with their teeth."

Smoke bellowed from Claire's mouth as she spoke.

"I thought you considered yourself a student of the classics," she said with a laugh.

Grovely was silent. He tightened his grip on the side of the small motorboat, a collection of faded planks, and spread his legs to better brace himself.

"The River Styx," Claire said. She held the outboard motor handle with one hand and waved the gun with the other. Her eyes disappeared in the shadows, leaving two empty sockets. "Dante's Inferno. Imagine the fury needed to smite someone with your breasts, or tear at their flesh with your teeth. It's so perfectly violent, don't you think?"

Still no response. The motor puttered, threatening to stall.

"You're so quiet," Claire said. "Do you still love me? Penny for your thoughts."

The first penny would have bought his fears of what was lying ahead at the other end of the evening boat ride along the Harlem River. The second penny would have bought his desire to kill Claire, to tear at her with his teeth, as uncleanly as that sounded, anything to make her suffer for what she was doing to him. If she had a third penny, it would buy his wish that he had learned how to swim, so that he could dive off the boat and escape.

"Don't you wish you could swim?" Claire asked. "Then you could jump off this boat, instead of joining me across this murky river to Hades."

Something brushed against Grovely's nose. Snow. It was unseasonably early for snow in New York City. He looked up into the sky in disbelief. The flurries resembled falling ashes. Small pale ashes – thousands of them. They were hovering more than falling. They fluttered in front of the lights of the city skyline, barely moving. Another flake brushed against his face.

"I love the first snow of the season," Claire said. "It's so, I don't know, romantic. I mean, here we are, all alone in this small boat, floating along the river, the skyline as a backdrop. It's a beautiful setting. If the torture that awaits you wasn't hanging over your head, I bet you'd see the romance in it all."

The tram from Manhattan to Roosevelt Island hummed over their heads. Another pack load of commuters was headed home. Another collection of lawyers and businessmen escaping the daily chaos of the city. Grovely looked to his left, to the center of Roosevelt Island, the most developed section. The lights petered out toward the southern tip. Where were they headed? What did Claire have planned?

"Almost there," Claire said. She seemed to be reading his mind, or else programming his thoughts. It had been that way since they met, hadn't it. She always seemed one step ahead of him. He followed the direction of her gun as she pointed it somewhere ahead, somewhere into the darkness along the shore to their left.

Grovely tried to focus on the invisible target point as the boat sputtered forward. There was nothing but blackness for the first few minutes. Then, as Claire started to angle the boat toward the shore, a glowing collection of floodlights appeared. A gray stone edifice sprung up from the wooded area near the southern end of the island. Was this where they were headed? If so, why?

Claire ran the boat up onto a sandy bank. A dense odor of motor oil pressed against Grovely's face as the light breeze with which they had been drifting slid past them. The boat tilted to and fro as the current pushed in from the left.

Claire wrapped both hands around the gun end poked it in the air in Grovely's direction. "Get out."

Grovely stretched his legs into an upright position, but he was reticent to release his grip on the edge of the boat. Instead, he tilted at a severe angle at the waist. Another sudden lurch of the boat convinced him that he had made the correct decision.

"Where are we?" he asked, feeling the muscles along the base of his thumb quivering.

"At our destination," Claire said. "Welcome to Hades. Get out now." She lifted the gun from a chest level target to his face.

Grovely stepped out onto what he thought was solid ground, only to have his shoe sink several inches into soft mud. Beads of broken Styrofoam swirled around his leg until sticking to his pants. The smell of dead fish was nauseating.

Claire continued to force Grovely forward, up the bank and through a stretch of tall grass. His ankles twisted over unseen mounds of dirt and clumps of grass. He looked down in an attempt to monitor his steps, only to walk up against a chain link fence.

"Look out," Claire said, pushing him aside. She went straight up to an area of the fence completely hidden by shadow. After some rattling, a large rectangle of the fence broke away and fell to the ground. "Go through here, she said."

Grovely bent over and tucked his arms in by his sides to avoid getting punctured by the free edges of the cut fence as he slithered through. He took several steps up a small hill, crouching and walking on all fours like a dog. When he reached the top and stood up straight, he saw the building up ahead.

The stone façade, with its large granite stones, resembled a deserted castle. The building was three stories, with sharp squared off edges and turrets. A Gothic tower sprung from the top. Floodlights cast an eerie glow on the surface. Empty window holes revealed the blackness inside. Grovely squinted toward the unusual triangular shaped arches on the third floor, wondering what used to be inside and, more importantly, what was inside now.

"It's a treasure, isn't it," Claire said. "It's seen better days, but it's still a stunning piece of work. It was designed by James Renwick, Jr., the man who designed St. Patrick's Cathedral. I know you had some difficulty at St. Patrick's recently, but I'm sure you can still appreciate the quality of the architecture."

"What is this?" Grovely said. He contracted and spread his toes, trying to expel the river water from his shoes. The movement caused his pants to shift, pasting itself to his shin.

"This is the Smallpox Hospital," Claire said. "It was built in 1856 using the stone from this island. It was the first hospital in the country devoted to the treatment of smallpox and plague."

"Thanks for the history lesson," Grovely said. He regretted the words as they escaped from his mouth.

"That's the easiest lesson you'll learn here," Claire said. "So, enjoy it."

They were approaching the entrance, a large stone porch bordered by a two-story protrusion of pillars and arches. Knotted vines of ivy tugged at the stone, boring holes through the interstices and wearing grooves into the surface. The vines curled along the base of the building, as though tightening to drag the entire edifice to the ground, but the evil palace resisted.

They pushed aside the gangly branches of a bush and stepped through the man entrance. The darkness in front of them was in stark contrast to the floodlights outside. An assortment of foul smells – rotting flesh, feces, and overripe fruit – slowed Grovely's steps, but a gun from behind pushed him forward.

Grovely turned to Claire just as her flashlight illuminated, causing a sharp pain behind his eyes. He turned and followed the course of the beam, his footsteps slapping beneath him. The beam revealed little more than stone, a uniform blending of gray shades that created the sensation of being deep underwater. The labor required to breath contributed to Grovely's sensation of drowning.

The smell, whatever it was, was increasing as they walked.

Claire continued to push Grovely forward. She navigated through the darkness better than him, dealing with the smell better than him. There was no question that she had been here before.

"The first floor was used for the smallpox victims," Claire said. "But between epidemics, the upper two floors were used for patients with other diseases." She laughed. "Imagine that, taking the risk of being exposed to something as lethal as smallpox. It makes your skin crawl, doesn't it?"

They turned the corner and entered a large room with no windows. The smell was horrible now. Grovely's eyes were tearing and his nose was running. He swallowed against a lump forming in his throat. He looked around the room but didn't see the source of the smell, only a large wooden chair in the center of the room. The large wooden and metal contraption was a cross between an antique dental chair and an electrocution chair. Wooden armrests were lined with leather straps, and similar straps were dangling down from the sides of the seat. A metal crank was at the base.

Then he heard the rustling sound for the first time.

"It's been a long trip," Claire said. "Have a seat. I'm going to tell you a story, and then I have a few questions for you."

55

RESEARCH STATION, SIBERIA

It didn't look like anyone was alive inside.

Jonathan and Cage had ridden their snowmobiles for about two hours before locating the research station. Cage had Solnorov strapped onto the back of his snowmobile, and Jonathan had the gasoline from the third snowmobile, two of the isolation suits and oxygen tanks, two of the rifles, and as much ammunition as they could fit on his.

The night vision goggles revealed pale green shades of tundra in every direction. Nothing moving, nothing warm. After the first few turns, everything looked the same to Jonathan. He sensed that they were circling through the same area repeatedly, but he really wasn't sure. There were no landmarks. No trees, no sources of light. Even the wind seemed to change direction on a second's notice, occasionally driving so fiercely that he had to angle the snowmobile against the force.

The station would be significantly warmer than the surrounding tundra, making it light up like a Christmas tree through the goggles. He waited for the bright light, but there wasn't any. Instead, he was surprised to follow Cage's sudden signal to the right and see, perhaps just two hundred yards away, the unmistakable but relatively dim outline of the station.

A mound of earth, an inverted moat of sorts, surrounded the area. The station itself must have been elevated several feet, because it rose up higher than the mound. With no windows, the structure looked like a giant icebox. There were no lights on, and nothing was moving in the compound.

They drove around the mound to a flatter area where a tall fence was visible, and then stopped the snowmobiles in front of the gate. Jonathan walked to the gate, expecting Cage to be right behind him. Instead, he turned to see Cage crouched in the snow, brushing his glove along the ground. He walked to Cage's side, sensing the additional crunch below his steps as he approached. The area appeared to have been swept clean of the soft layer of snow and ice pellets covering the surrounding area. The underlying surface was more solid and contained two parallel impressions.

"Helicopter," Cage said, rushing back toward the snowmobiles. He grabbed two of the loaded AK-47s and tossed one to Jonathan.

Jonathan caught the rifle with a bear hug, unable to resist a blink and a flinch as the thought of the rifle discharging gripped him. He lifted the rifle into his hands. It still seemed heavy. Cage was already passing through the gate, which had previously been sheared open along its latch.

A layer of ice sealed the front entrance to the station shut. They took turns striking the ice until the door finally yielded. Before going in, they helped each other into their isolation suits. Jonathan found maneuvering into the suit while wearing so much gear to be difficult, but Cage moved deftly, donning most of his gear without assistance, including his oxygen tank. When they were ready, Cage led the way through the entrance.

The inside of the station looked like a frozen tomb. There were no sounds except the soft fizz of oxygen running through the suit. The smaller items had been stripped from the first few rooms, leaving behind an occasional chair or desk, the skeletal reminders of human inhabitance. The wind was gone now, but the temperature otherwise seemed comparable to outside. They flicked the light switches, but the power was out. It must have been out for some time now. In each room, after using the night vision goggles to confirm that nobody was inside, Cage would shine a flashlight. A glimpse of detail would appear, followed by the return of the green shadows of the goggles.

Cage crept through the hallways, rifle in hand, ready to shoot through whomever they encountered. Jonathan would have had a lot of questions about this behavior, given the fact that they were there on a rescue mission, but having had their plane shot down several hours earlier had taught him that there would be a lot on this mission that wouldn't make sense to him, and if he wanted to survive, he should follow Cage's lead without asking too many questions.

As they passed further into the station, there were additional reminders of life. With the flashlight on, they saw posters of mountains and fields, shorelines and sunsets, and photographs of people waiting back at home. These objects conveyed the hopes that were still alive when the researchers left the rooms behind them but were abandoned when the time came to move to the next part of the station. They were getting closer to them now. If the researchers were still here, they would be together in one room somewhere ahead.

Back in the hallway, the station ahead was still silent.

Cage continued cautiously but walked a little faster. He spent less time in each room, less time looking with the flashlight. This was a relief to Jonathan, who preferred not to see any more reminders of the lives that were lost in the station and was waiting to see if they found anyone alive, or if they needed to use their rifles. They passed through one of the laboratories, where millions of dollars of equipment were now covered with thin films of frost.

Jonathan walked toward the back of the room, turning his head to look through the rectangle of the world permitted by the isolation suit visor. Several glass containers along a counter had shattered as their liquid contents froze, leaving ice sculpture casts standing amidst the broken shards. He made a conscious effort not to touch anything, for fear that he might puncture his suit. Without a plane, he wasn't sure how he was ever going to get out of the station alive, but he wanted to be careful with the aspects of his future that he could control to some degree.

As Cage's flashlight and Jonathan's path crossed, Jonathan stopped dead in his tracks. Did he see what he thought he saw, or was he losing his mind? He wasn't sure anymore. The light was gone now, and his vision flipped back to the green shades of the night vision goggles.

He waited.

"Cage," he said, low enough to avoid detection, possibly so low that Cage couldn't hear him.

The flashlight was still pointed to some other part of the room.

"Cage," he said again, a little louder this time.

The flashlight turned toward Jonathan's direction. He followed the beam back toward where he was looking earlier.

He was right. In the back of the room, lying across a table, was a dead body.

Cage must have seen it also, because the flashlight beam centered on the body and brightened as it advanced toward the target. Jonathan gagged inside his suit, wondering what would happen if he actually vomited inside. He took several deep breaths to fight off the nausea. Condensation formed on his visor.

Cage rushed past him and was the first one to the body. Jonathan followed. The corpse had been filleted open along the chest and abdomen. All of the internal organs were missing, and large sections of the limbs had been removed. All of the open areas were lined with frost like a freezer-burnt steak.

"This must be one of the first victims," Cage said. "It looks like someone's done an autopsy.

Jonathan turned and nodded to Cage. It was more of an excuse to stop looking at the frozen gore than to demonstrate agreement, since Cage's words had hardly registered through Jonathan's other thoughts.

"We should keep moving," Cage said, still staring down toward the corpse's legs.

"I agree," Jonathan said. He locked his view on Cage, only to see the frozen gaping wound in the reflection of the visor.

They returned to the hall and walked toward what must have been the far corner of the station. The hallway ended at a doorway. Both men stopped and raised their guns.

Cage held the door latch. He turned, slowly. The door made a smacking sound as it peeled away from the frame. At the first suggestion of sound, Cage yanked the door completely open and stepped in, rifle first.

The room seemed warmer than the rest of the station, but still must have been below zero degrees Fahrenheit. Now for the first time, there were other bright green images besides that of the two men themselves. Bodies were lying throughout the room, at least fifteen of them. They were warm enough to be detected by the night vision goggles, but none of them were moving.

Cage forced the door closed with his hip, and then crept through the room, aiming his rifle at each glowing green form and pushing at them with his boot. An occasional moan or garbled speech revealed that at least some of them were still alive.

Jonathan followed Cage's lead, circling in the opposite direction to check the status of the men. Only a few responded. When the two of them reunited at the far end of the room, Cage was crouched over one of the men, turning him by the shoulders.

"Most of them look dead," Jonathan said.

"Only one of them is definitely dead. There's a saying about hypothermia that nobody is declared dead until they're warm and dead," Cage said. "When they're still cold, it's just too hard to tell. Hypothermia can fool you, and the human body can show incredible resiliency."

The man that Cage was holding was more difficult to see than the others. For the first time since they entered the room, Cage turned on the flashlight, exposing the man's dark blue face. The light panned lower, exposing a long slash along the front of his neck.

"This was Karlssen," he said. "He was our contact working on the inside here. They killed him. And if I'm correct, they've already taken several of the researchers from the station."

"Who's taken them?" Jonathan asked. "Who or what are we dealing with?"

He was answered by the rumbling of a motor from somewhere outside.

"Hopefully that's the reinforcements in our contingency plan," Cage said, "If not, we're about to see what we're dealing with up close."

56

NUCURE LABORATORIES, RUSSIA

They seemed so peaceful when they were wheeled in. They were so still, almost dead.

Dmitri was helping to wheel in the last victim, the Russian doctor, the oldest in the group. Like the others, the Russian doctor was lying, sedated, inside the isolation stretcher. The clear plastic encased him, warping his dimensions in random segments like the view in the warped mirrors of a traveling carnival funhouse. Oxygen hissed in through a tube in the back, and a second tube led out to a containment canister beneath the stretcher.

They brought him inside the isolation room to the far left, closed the door, and then opened the clear plastic, as though exhuming his body from a coffin. It took all four of them to lift him onto the new bed. They moved quickly now, attaching his cardiac monitors and changing his intravenous fluid lines in a coordinated fashion practiced with the first few patients.

They drew blood samples. They had learned earlier that the sedative wouldn't last long enough or be profound enough to obtain bone specimens. That would take some rethinking.

The man in the center room was getting agitated again. They had already had to sedate him twice since he got there. "If there's one that absolutely has to remain alive," Lukin had said, "it's this one." He was the orthopedist from the United States.

"This one doesn't learn." Doctor Boris said, opening the lid of a bottle of yellow liquid while walking toward the center room.

Lukin pressed the code to open the door to the center room. Doctor Boris entered, followed by Lukin and Paulina. Dmitri secured the door to the Russian doctor's door, and then walked to the doorway where the others were, waiting to see if he was also needed inside the small room.

Lukin and Paulina held the man's arms as he flailed in an attempt to get loose. In their white isolation suits, they resembled aliens abducting an unsuspecting earthling in an old movie.

Doctor Boris poured the yellow fluid onto a gauze pad. He placed the bottle on a counter and moved in, holding the gauze pad with both hands. As he reached the American's face, a flailing arm slapped the gauze free from his grasp.

"Someone get it," Doctor Boris said. He looked at Lukin and Paulina, who were struggling too much to hold onto the American to provide any other assistance. Then he spotted Dmitri in the doorway. "Quick, before he tears a hole in our suits."

Dmitri stepped inside and grabbed the gauze off the floor. He raised it between his index finger and thumb.

"Quick," Doctor Boris said. "What are you waiting for?"

Dmitri grasped the gauze in both hands as Doctor Boris had moments earlier and forced it against the American's mouth. He felt the facial muscles and the lips contorting beneath the gauze.

"Watch your fingers," Lukin said. "If he bites through your suit, you're dead."

The thought of being millimeters away from being infected with O-168 sent a shiver through Dmitri. He slid his fingers back a little but maintained his force on the gauze. Within seconds, he felt the facial motion slow, and the man's entire body went limp.

Dr. Boris reached across and smacked the sedated man across the face with a gloved hand.

57

NUCURE LABORATORIES, RUSSIA

There was no way to open the door from the inside.

Drew ran his hands along the Plexiglas of the front wall of his cage. The entire surface was smooth. Not a single edge where he could secure a finger, or even a fingernail.

His mind was clearing. The mammoth station already seemed like a bad dream, but one that had extended directly into whatever nightmare he was living now. The rescue team had met them outside at gunpoint, herding them all into the refurbished military medical helicopter. They were sedated with something forced against their faces. He remembered the bitter smell, but not much else. They must have been sedated until reaching this place, wherever they were.

Back at the station he had feared that he would die. Now he was more afraid that he wouldn't.

His arms stung from the lines of needle holes coursing along his veins. Intravenous fluid was running from clear bags down through the tubes connected to his arms. He wouldn't pull the lines out again. Getting forced to the ground, cattle prodded, and shot up with sedatives three times, maybe four or five times, was more than enough. He had learned his lesson.

Rats in experiments would learn not to hit the button that caused electrical shock.

They were letting him wake up now. Why? What were they doing with him? Where was he? Where were the others?

He ran a hand up under his shirt to scratch an itch, only to catch his fingers along the cardiac monitor pads along his chest.

There was no way out. Nothing he could even throw at the Plexiglas. He pulled at the bed, which was more like an operating table, but it wouldn't budge. Not even the cushions. There was hardly anything in the room, and what little was there was indestructible. There were no accidents or coincidences here. He was a prisoner.

He pressed his face against the Plexiglas, trying to see what was next to his cage. All he could see was the central station, a counter backed by stacks of monitors and supplies. The same four people passed through, all in white isolation suits. He could now distinguish them through the glimpses provided by their facial visors. There was the white haired ghoulish looking man who seemed to be running the show, and another man who could have passed as a Russian Thorton Grovely. They seemed to be enjoying this the most. Their expressions beamed through their visors. Then there was a black-haired woman who hadn't left the computer station long enough to offer a clear view.

A fourth man occasionally passed by. There was something different about him. He never looked directly at Drew when he passed by. Why? Was he afraid that he would be recognized? Did he recognize Drew? Neither explanation made sense. Maybe he didn't want to be there at all. Was he the only one ashamed about what they were doing? His face had been visible a few times when he was speaking to one of the other three. There were beads of sweat on his upper lip. He seemed to be fighting back nausea.

What was that man's role in all of this?

Before he could answer any of those questions, he had to determine why they were taken here in the first place. The possible explanations running through Drew's mind began to make more sense as his ability to concentrate returned.

The bone virus made the osteoclast binding protein SRBP-168. Global had the genetic sequence and the technology to produce the protein. When the epidemic broke out in the research station, it was Global that decided to send Drew in. Now he was taken to this place. Why? He wasn't sick. He probably wouldn't ever get sick.

They weren't in a hospital. It was a laboratory. Once again, Larianov's words seemed most accurate. They were rats in a cage.

His thoughts turned back to his early days at Manhattan Memorial. He hadn't gotten any NIH funding yet, just some loose change from the hospital, enough to get the lab started. He spent the first several months identifying the appropriate surface proteins on osteoclasts and osteoblasts, only to go back to the drawing board after full funding was available. The antibodies that he had created bound perfectly to the initial cells used to create them, but not to any others.

He had been so baffled by the results. He had been so foolish, in retrospect.

SRBP-alpha, the product of the first generation of experiments, didn't attach to anyone else's cells. They only attached to the original cells – and the original cells were from his own body. And his bone cells, because he was a genetic carrier for a rare bone disease, had abnormal surface receptors. He didn't know that until he started doing the research. There was no way to know that his genetic flaw contributed to Matty's disease, to Matty's death.

Normal osteoclasts were used to make SRBP-168, a later version of SRBP-alpha. SRBP-168 attached strongly to the normal cells. It entered osteoclasts through their specialized receptor proteins. For some strange reason, it could attach equally well to osteoclasts from Drew's bone, but it couldn't enter his cells. SRBP-168 just stuck to the surface of his cells like crazy glue.

Since SRBP-168 couldn't get into his osteoclasts, the bone virus couldn't get in either. The disease that had killed his son was now protecting him from the virus.

It was no coincidence that Drew was sent to the research station. Was he just a test? Were they trying to determine if he could contract the disease? Was he brought to this dungeon laboratory to identify a cure?

There was a knock on the Plexiglas.

Drew turned to see the man with the sweat on his upper lip standing in the doorway. He considered forcing his way past the man and run for the exit, but he had no idea where the exit was, and he was certain that he was outnumbered and would be punished for his actions.

He wasn't going to press the button that led to electrical shock. At least not yet. There was too much he needed to learn first.

Drew peered through the man's visor. The Russian was about his age, maybe a little younger. What was he doing with these people? Why did he decide to do this with his life?

"I'm not going to hurt you," the man said with a thick Russian accent. His facial expression was one of forgiveness, or maybe embarrassment. "But we need to talk. The people I work with need to talk to you."

58

RENWICK RUIN, NEW YORK CITY

"They're one of the fastest and deadliest in the world."

The leather straps were digging into Grovely's wrists. Sweat ran down his arms, and blood oozed from the wounds on his hand. He was no longer struggling. He gave up on any chance of escaping several hours earlier. He was completely immobilized against the electrocution chair.

A needle pierced Grovely's right shoulder, and then the warm pain of fluid filled the muscle below.

Claire appeared from behind the chair, an empty syringe in her hand. She walked over toward the hissing sound and crouched down in front of a glass cage that contained endless coils of black snake. She shined a flashlight into the snake's eyes, reflecting a bright green glow from their depths. The snake coiled tighter and flicked its tongue toward the beam. Claire put her face down against the glass and licked her tongue back at the snake, making a hissing sound that sent shudders up Grovely's spine.

"I love snakes," she said. "They're untrustworthy and unpredictable." She tapped on the glass suddenly, eliciting a flash of fangs from inside the cage. "Take this one for example. I've fed him rats and rabbits for months. Plump tasty rabbits. Without me he would have died in his cage. Died. But if he got out of there, he wouldn't hesitate to bite me, not for an instant."

She spun around at Grovely. His instinct was to recoil from her, but the strap across his forehead held him secure. An attempt at blinking simply pulled on the strips of tape pulling his lower eyelids down. Tears that had accumulated along the lower edges of his eyeballs raced down his cheeks.

"Can you relate to that?" she asked. "All the cash the Mamba fed you, and you had to get together with Atisoy and bite him. You're full of venom, Thorton."

"I don't know what you're talking about," Grovely said. Every word tugged on his eyelids. His heart ricocheted in his chest.

"Maybe this will refresh your memory," she said, pressing a small device in her hand.

A photograph projected against the wall. The sudden light was startling enough, but the photograph's subject was horrifying.

"I didn't kill him," Grovely said.

Doctor Atisoy's face filled the screen. Not the Atisoy that Grovely wanted to remember. Not the esteemed professor of genetics. It was the face of the phantasm that Grovely tripped over in the office at University Hospital. The cheeks were blown up and the eyes were bulging, almost hanging out of their sockets. The tongue was a gigantic bloody mess. Two dark spots were visible on the surface toward the tip where the blood seemed to be wiped away. What were they?

"I know you didn't kill him," Claire said. "But you plotted with him, and it was that plot that led to the doctor's premature demise."

Grovely's right cheek twitched three times, each time pulling his eyelid, maybe his eyeball with the strip of tape.

"I didn't know about the stabilizer until months after I gave it to you," he said.

"It wouldn't have been as much of a problem if you had given it to us," Claire said. "But you sold it at a premium price, and you knew the stabilizer was flawed."

The snake hissed in its cage.

Grovely tried not to think about the snake, and not to think about whatever Claire planned for him. He stared at the photograph projection of Dr. Atisoy on the wall – the two marks on the tongue. The focus faded momentarily. Was it the projector, or was his vision failing? What did she inject in his shoulder?

"The stabilizer was Atisoy's project," Grovely said. "He was working on the sequence for HIV treatment, to stop the high mutation rates seen with the virus, to slow it down so medications would have time to work. His data looked authentic. There was no reason to think that it wouldn't work in O-168."

"Oh, it was authentic," Claire said. "And there's no question that the stabilizer worked. But what the two of you didn't tell us was that the sequence also contained a segment that made the stabilizer the target for one of the other HIV medications that Atisoy was working on."

"He never told me that," Grovely said. "You have to believe me."

"I would believe you," Claire said, "except that the other HIV medication was Retroverse, and the financial support for Retroverse research comes from..."

"Global," Grovely said. The words leaked out of his mouth and seemed to take several seconds to reach his ears, warped and stretched out, as though pushing their way through water.

He didn't feel the straps holding him down anymore; it was as though they had fallen off. But he had less urge to break free, to run and escape. He didn't know where he'd go anyway.

"That's right," Claire said. "What a coincidence. The stabilizer goes into O-168. 0-168 becomes an international threat, and nobody but Thorton Grovely and Atisoy have the treatment. It's all built into the stabilizer that you sold us, just one small strand of DNA, and a secret worth so much money."

"Is that why you're doing this to me?" Grovely asked.

"I haven't started doing anything to you yet," she said, reaching behind the snake's cage. "But I'm not doing this for me. No. This is a request from the Mamba."

She pulled something out of a second smaller cage. It looked like a string at first. A black string attached to something. He tried to see what it was, but his eyes were still out of focus. They felt like they might crack from the dryness.

Grovely heard the sound of a rodent squeaking.

"Rats are amazing creatures," she said. "I read that there are more than ten rats for every person living in Manhattan. But we don't see them that often, so, where are they? Some are probably running in the subway tunnels. Others are swimming in the rivers. But imagine how many are down in the sewers and rolling around in the garbage? Maybe millions of rats. What do you think?"

As Claire crossed the light projecting Atisoy's tongue onto the wall, Grovely could see the rat hanging upside down from her grasp. It was flexing and twisting at the torso, trying to pull itself high enough to bite her hand. Its claws scratched at the air. Grovely could feel the claws scratching along his neck, even though the rat was several feet away.

"Don't you find it amazing that a creature could live in garbage, in sewage?" she asked. "You, of all people, must find that mind-boggling."

She was right in front of him now, holding the rat by the tail in front of her. The creature had its back arched, its limbs outstretched, and its mouth stretched wide open.

Grovely's attention alternated between Claire and the rat. The images were passing before him now like an old movie strip getting caught in the projector, flickering, changing position, changing subjects. First Claire, then the rat, then Claire again. At times it appeared as though the rat's face was on Claire's body, and Claire's face on the rat's body.

"It's just a rat," Grovely tried to tell himself, but may have said out loud instead. He tried to swallow against a wave of nausea, but his throat was too dry.

"I know it's just a rat," she said. "A rat from the sewer. How much damage could it do?"

She pressed a button on the remote control in her hand, and Atisoy's tongue finally went away. In its place was a new projection – a list. The only word Grovely could read was the first, which was thicker and larger than the others. "BACTERIA."

"You wouldn't believe how many bacteria this little guy can carry," Claire said, dangling the rat over Grovely's injured hand. "You can't read the list, can you? The ketamine is kicking in. Let me help you. *Bacillus piliformis, Bordetella bronchiseptica, Campylobacter species, Cilia-Associated Respiratory Bacillus, Corynebacterium kutscheri, Erysipelas rusiopathiae.* I hope I'm pronouncing that right. Then there's *Hemophilus* species, *Klebsiella pneumoniae, Leptospira icterohemorrhagiae, Mycoplasma* species, *Pasteurella pneumotropica, Pseudomonas aeruginosa, Salmonella enteritidis, Spirillum minus, Staphylococcus aureus, Streptobacillus moniliformis, Streptococcus pneumoniae*, and *Streptococcus* species."

She lowered the rat down slowly, until its claws almost reached the blood-smeared skin on Grovely's hand. His fingers were twitching through the sedation. The rat reached for the flickering fingers with its claws.

Another flick of the remote control brought a new list on the screen. "The viruses are even worse," Claire said. "There's Adenovirus, Herpesvirus, rat cytomegalovirus, Papovavirus,

Parvovirus, rat virus, H-1 virus, rat orphan parvovirus, Poxvirus, cowpox virus, Bunyavirus, hemorrhagic fever with renal syndrome virus, Coronavirus, sialodacryoadenitis virus, Paramyxovirus, pneumonia virus of mice, Sendai virus, Picornavirus, mouse encephalomyelitis virus, Reovirus, infectious diarrhea of infant rats virus, reovirus, Retrovirus, and rat leukemia virus. Ugh, some of those sound downright disgusting."

The rat grabbed onto Grovely's wrist with its front claws and began sniffing at his palm. A stretched-out strip of sandpaper surfaced tongue reached into the depths of one of his wounds.

Claire lifted the animal a little higher by the tail. "I'm sorry about that," she said. "He so hungry he'll eat anything right now."

Grovely was half-sedated and half-terrified. His nervous system was having a tug of war. He could hear his own voice screaming inside his head, but he couldn't get out.

Claire advanced to the next slide. "You probably know about these. The rickettsia, the fungi." Another slide filled with organisms. "Pneumocyctis, protozoa." Another slide of terrors. "Nematodes, cestodes. Ooh, here's one you'll like." Another slide appeared. "These are the different types of fleas and lice and mites that rats carry."

She gave the rat a little shake.

"I don't know about you," she said, "but I can't wait to get onto the fun part."

She bent down out of view and then reappeared. The rat was gone. Grovely felt claws pull their way up his right pant leg and wedge against his thigh. He waited for the bites to start.

Claire walked back toward the snake cage. "Do you know a black mamba can detect its prey from over fifty feet away?"

59

RESEARCH STATION, SIBERIA

There was certainly something to be said for having a backup plan.

Jonathan still didn't know how Cage knew two backcountry pilots in the middle of Siberia. He didn't know how a man with a Russian accent as thick as the Ural Mountains could be named Brendan. But right now, he didn't care.

All that mattered was that this gray-haired couple, AC and Brendan, rumbled over the research station in time to save their hides, as Cage had said earlier.

"I told him to fly in earlier," AC said, whacking Brendan's chest with a swift backhand.

"We were given orders to wait," Brendan said, gesturing to Cage.

"You did the right thing, my friend," Cage said. He patted Brendan on the shoulder. "If you had flown in a day earlier, you probably would have been killed. We got shot out of the sky last night."

Jonathan poured one of the tanks of gasoline into the generator. "How did you know we were here?" Jonathan asked.

"Plan B," Cage said. "They were waiting for our signal that we had reached our destination here. When that signal didn't come at the scheduled time, they took off."

The generator rattled as what would have otherwise been a dim light appeared as a blinding contrast to the darkness that preceded it. Cold air blew from the heater.

"What's the rest of plan B?" Jonathan said, not expecting an answer.

"Brendan stays here to guard the fort," Cage said. "We're flying south with AC."

Jonathan's relief to be leaving the frigid station was tempered for his concern for Brendan. He looked at the pilot, who was more than twice his age, and wondered how he would survive here by himself.

Brendan raised an AK-47 into firing position, aimed it across the room, and made a "pow" sound. "Who do you think will get here first?" he asked. "The good guys, or the bad guys?"

"These researchers are a hot commodity, dead or alive" Cage said. He was pulling the first researcher toward the heater, which was now blowing a less frigid breeze in their direction. "The good guys ought to be here within about two hours. If the welcome we got last night is any indication, there's going to be a race to get here."

They began lifting the other researchers by the arms and dragging them into a tight circle around the heater. Jonathan questioned whether he actually heard the faint sound of breathing coming from the tall Italian-looking man as he pulled him toward the others, or whether optimism was blurring his senses.

"You know what to do?" Cage asked Brendan.

The Russian man nodded.

60

NUCURE LABORATORIES, RUSSIA

"You passed the test."

The white-haired Russian scientist that they called Doctor Boris was staring at Drew.

"I didn't think it was possible," the man said, peering through him. "You were the only person exposed to the virus who didn't succumb to its effects." He looked up and down at Drew, as though wondering what type of kryptonite would bring him to his knees.

Drew looked at Maria, who seemed to be sitting just a little too close to their captors. She was exposed to the virus, just as Drew was, but she didn't get sick. Why not? And then there was Larianov, who was still back in his cell.

"Three of us didn't get infected," Drew finally said.

"That's right," Boris said. "But the other two were protected."

Maria and Larianov? How were they protected? There was only one way that he could think of. The tetracycline off-switch. But how did they know?

Maria was looking away, trying not to make eye contact with Drew.

Doctor Boris snickered. “You were the only one that wasn’t on tetracycline,” he said. “Maria has been taking it, because we knew that the O-168 prototype has a tetracycline switch.”

“And Larianov is working with you?” Drew asked, staring at Maria.

“Larianov isn’t working with anyone,” Boris said. “He’s just lucky enough to have been born paranoid.”

“He saw me taking the tetracycline, and then he must have stolen our supplies from the laboratory,” Maria said. “Then when Victor Solnorov died Oleg started taking his tetracycline.”

“How did he know to take tetracycline?” Drew asked.

“Because he carried the virus into the station,” Boris said.

“He carried the virus for over a year,” Maria said. “He sold it for over a year.”

“I don’t understand,” Drew said. He turned to each of them in succession, waiting for an explanation. He looked at Dmitri, who seemed to have no better understanding than he did.

“Victor Solnorov was exposed to the virus last year in a military outpost near the Chinese border,” Boris said. “He was taking tetracycline for acne at the time. The other four men died, and then their bodies disappeared. Solnorov realized the significance of the virus that he was carrying in his body.

“The virus isn’t just deadly,” Maria said. “It’s the prototype for the perfect biologic warfare agent. It’s highly infectious. It’s relentless, and eventually deadly, but first it’s painful and debilitating.”

“It inflicts its damage on the bone, and then on the economy,” Boris said. “Solnorov was smart enough to realize all of this. He knew that he would become the target of militia groups interested in obtaining the virus for biologic warfare. He went into hiding.”

"But then he got greedy," Maria said. "He sold the virus at least twice. Each time he stopped taking the tetracycline for a few days to allow his blood titers to rise."

"Is that what he was doing in Siberia?" Drew asked.

Maria nodded. "He was going to sell his blood samples to Global Investors. But by this time his body was a time bomb."

"As soon as the tetracycline was out of his system this time," Boris said, "his calcium levels skyrocketed from instantaneous destruction throughout his bones, and he died from a massive heart attack."

"And then the virus was loose," Maria said.

She knew that Solnorov was infected. She knew all those people in the research station were in danger. She knew why they were collapsing from bone disease and dying.

"How fortunate that you were already on tetracycline," Drew said.

Dmitri was looking at Maria.

"But you're not on tetracycline," Boris said. "You're the only one. My little experiment was a success."

"I guess I'm just lucky," Drew said.

"But you're not lucky, are you?" Boris said. He walked closer to where Drew was sitting and rested a hand on his shoulder. "Your son died." He sported an amused smile. "He died because you gave him a rare bone disease. You and your wife. Excuse me, your ex-wife. His bone was so fragile."

A snapping sound pierced the air. Boris walked in front of Drew and tossed a broken pencil into the garbage can.

"Your bone isn't normal, is it?" Boris asked. "Your osteoclast surface receptors are abnormal."

Now everyone else in the room looked surprised. Everyone except Boris and Drew.

"You're still alive because of your surface receptors," Boris said. "You're a freak. The abnormality that you gave to your son, the abnormality that killed him, is now keeping you alive." He made a tsk tsk sound and leaned in closer again. "Doesn't that make you feel guilty?"

"Why did you bring me here?" Drew asked, but he already knew the answer.

"To save your friends," Boris said. He gestured toward the patient cells. "Mincini and Yurov are dying. That concerns me very little, and the world wouldn't miss a stupid old man and a bug collector, but I thought you might want to save them."

Drew was silent.

"You've probably figured it out already, haven't you?" Boris said. "You know how to treat the virus. There's still enough time. Your little boy is dead. You blew it last time. But this is your big chance. The cure for the virus is inside of you. It's in your bones. You can help us, or you can let your friends die."

61

RENWICK RUIN, NEW YORK CITY

He couldn't have been happier.

Money poured into his offshore accounts. The components of O-168 had treated him well. He never imagined that he could have so much wealth, at least not with any legal activity. And soon he would have the finished product, the virus itself, worth an amount that dwarfed the sum of its components, and he didn't have to pay a dime for it. His problems had been resolved or erased. And now he was going to get a little revenge, have a little fun.

The Mamba smiled in the darkness.

He was in control. He liked it that way. Everything in line. Everyone in position. Right where he wanted them.

Soon he would be making a cameo appearance in the show that he was directing.

The Mamba took a step along the stone floor. Silent. Careful. Always careful. The sound from the next room rose as he advanced. All of his senses were heightened. It was always that way when he stalked his prey. He could feel his ears turn like an owl's, his nostrils flare like a wolf's. And his sight – it could almost penetrate the stone wall in front of him.

Moaning and crying were getting louder in the next room.

The cool air stimulated shaved hair follicles on the Mamba's hands and ran up his sleeves. Rubbing his hands along his arms, he savored the sensation. The skin was still perfect from the oil, not greasy, just smooth – smooth as reptilian scales.

He was missing so much of the fun where he was standing. How much longer could he wait? The prey had to be prepared just right. Killing Atisoy had taught him that. He enjoyed injecting the poison into his enemy, loved watching him die, but it all happened so fast. It was all over in less than a minute. Now he knew better. He would enjoy this one. This time he would savor the experience.

"I think the snake is hungrier than the rat."

He could hear Claire's voice clearly now. She was doing a good job, following his instructions perfectly. What an actress.

Thorton was making a bizarre combination of noises. He alternated among babbling, crying, and screaming. The ketamine was just the right ingredient to throw into the torture stew that was brewing. The dose seemed perfect. It knocked him out just enough to keep him down, but not so much that he couldn't enjoy the sensation of the rat digging into his thigh. The rat from the pet store or from the sewer if that's what you chose to think.

Claire was preparing to release the snake, the so-called mamba. The caged reptile was just a ten-dollar rat snake from a pet store. It was the right color for the role, and could deliver a decent bite, but it didn't have a drop of venom in it. Claire knew that, but Thorton didn't. That's all that mattered. Torture was all about mind games. Thorton's psyche was a house of cards. The telephone calls had removed a card here and there. The imaginary bacterial injection in Connecticut wacked out an entire level. Tonight's production was like a hurricane hitting the rest of the cards.

Claire was reaching for the lid to the snake cage. The light from the projector was playing off her back. She was beautiful in the dark. He was going to miss her.

Wait, the Mamba's not in the cage. He's here behind you.

The Mamba entered and cornered his prey.

62

RESEARCH STATION, SIBERIA

There would have to be no trace.

The American in the white biocontainment suit walked through the mammoth research station. His boots echoed up and down the narrow halls as though he were the last human being left, not only in the center, but on the planet. He enjoyed that feeling. He spent consecutive weeks in the darkness while exposed to extremes of temperature and deprived of sleep. He could stay partially submerged in water or adherent to a vertical cliff edge for days. Whatever it took. Whatever the mission required.

He leaned hard against the door marked "biochemistry laboratory," which squealed open. The flashlight reflected against the DNA sequencers, standing silently in a line. The sequencers, bought for over two million dollars less than a year before, were state of the art, and represented just a small fraction of the value of the laboratory equipment within an arm's length. But compared to what was already outside, the sequencers might have just as well been used dorm room refrigerators.

The Russian they called Brendan was packing the last of the frozen petri dishes into a metal box.

They didn't have to speak Russian now, as secluded as they were, but they didn't break protocol.

"What's going to happen to this when it thaws?" Brendan said, holding up a handful of frozen petri plates. He eased the plates down into the metal box with the rest, and then sealed the lid. He patted the lid like a sleeping infant with his oversized puncture-proof glove and then flipped the latch closed.

"Probably nothing," the American said with a Moscow accent that matched that of his Russian counterpart.

"Then why..." Brendan started.

"You'll learn not to ask that question," the shorter man said.

The final check of the laboratory was complete. All of the culture dishes were accounted for. The logbooks and scattered paperwork were outside. They had everything on the list.

The men each grabbed one side of the metal box, and then lifted it as though it might blow to smithereens with the slightest tilt in the wrong direction.

The explosives were set symmetrically within the building, synchronized to detonate simultaneously at the flick of a single remote switch. The goal wasn't to make it look like an accident. The goal was to erase any evidence that a station was ever here. There were at least ten times the amount of explosives needed to make that happen.

"Are all of the researchers conscious now?" Brendan asked.

"Almost," the American said. "They're awake, but they're still groggy."

"Then we have to hurry," Brendan said.

They walked faster with the frozen plates of virus-infected bacteria. Their steps a little softer as they made their way through the dark corridors leading to the main entrance. Brendan slowed down momentarily to get a tighter grip on the box.

The American, who was leading the way with the flashlight in one hand and the box handle in the other, didn't anticipate the change of pace. The box slipped away from him, beginning with a slow slide and progressing to a free fall. He spun around, lunging toward the box while the flashlight bounced along the floor.

Despite being separated from the virus by layers of ice, glass petri dish lids, a metal container, and an impermeable biocontainment suit, Brendan froze, staring in horror, unable to prevent the box from falling. The box was falling in strobe light fashion due to the effect of the bouncing and flickering flashlight.

Crouching and pivoting backwards, the American caught two fingertips beneath the box a fraction of a second before it would have crashed against the ground. The two of them then eased the box to a rest along the floor.

Brendan was staring down at the box in silence.

"They're frozen," the American said.

"And we're wearing the suits," Brendan said.

The two men looked at each other. The American could see his own reflection, pale, slack-jawed, and sweating, in Brendan's visor. Brendan didn't look much better.

The Snow Cat rumbled on the other side of the partly opened entrance to the station just a few feet away, serving as a reminder of the task at hand.

The door swung open, releasing a frenzied wind into the station. Another American in a biocontainment suit, even larger and more formidable than the one inside, stood at the entrance.

"We're running behind schedule," he yelled over the wind. "What are you two doing?"

The other two men lifted the box, watched each other as they began moving, and walked toward the door. The wind and the sound of the Snow Cat almost drove the back inside.

"Are we far enough away?" Brendan asked.

"Almost," one of the Americans said as the other drove the vehicle over the snow.

They drove several hundred yards further, and then the large machine turned around to allow a view of the dim light rising from the research station on the otherwise invisible horizon.

"I'm amazed that they all survived the hypothermia," the smaller American said.

"Me too," the driver said. "Are you ready?"

Brendan took out the radio control and watched the station as he edged his thumb closer to the switch.

"Go ahead," the driver said to Brendan. "Let's do it."

Brendan lifted the small metal control to his chest in order to glance at the switch but not miss the explosion of the station. He eased his thumb down on the switch, wondering if there would be a delay between the switch, the flash, and the sound. He braced himself for the blast.

The red and orange flash rose up into the night. The brightness and the sound that followed, and the realization of the destruction made Brendan fall backwards into his chair.

The station was gone.

A few moments later the rushing sound of the wind mingled with the rumble of the Snow Cat. The darkness took over again, except for a dim smoldering remainder of what was once in front of them.

"Good to know the equipment works," the driver said, turning the large vehicle away from the station again.

"They're coming around," the other American said. "The effects of the hypothermia will be with them for some time yet, but their temperatures are all improving. They're all going to survive."

"From the hypothermia," Brendan said.

"From the hypothermia," the American said.

They looked at the researchers huddled and shivering in blankets at the bottom of the Snow Cat as it rumbled to the airstrip.

63

NUCURE LABORATORIES, RUSSIA

"If you were really here to save people, you'd let us free."

Dmitri looked around to see if anyone was watching before responding to Doctor Chambers. Lukin was trailing too far behind them to listen to their conversation. "You can't be let free," Dmitri said. "Don't you understand? The virus that you are carrying could destroy too many lives. Even if I thought you should be released from an emotional standpoint, I couldn't allow myself from a medical standpoint."

"Why are you here?" Chambers asked. "Why are you involved with these people?"

"We are keeping our country safe," Dmitri said. He no longer believed what he just said, but he was trying to convince himself as much as he was trying to convince the American.

They walked past the patient cell that held Yurov. The Russian doctor was sitting on the stretcher. He looked eagerly at them at first, as though expecting to be released. Then, as they continued walking past, Yurov shook his head, grabbed a markedly swollen leg with both hands, and shifted it to a more comfortable position on the stretcher. A severe grimace wrenched his weary face, and his entire frame sagged with lost hope.

The next room must have held Mincini, but there was little left that Chambers could recognize. He was lying flat on his back with a series of fluid-filled tubes sweeping down from all corners of the room to enter his body. His chest was heaving with labored breaths, and the heart rate monitor was fluctuating rapidly.

"You're responsible for all of those researchers getting sick and dying," Chambers said.

"I had nothing to do with that," Dmitri said with more conviction.

"Your organization was involved," Drew said. "They were there at the station when it happened. Maria Pelligrino, and Tarasov and Torelli. Do you expect me to think that was just a coincidence?"

Chambers' patient cell was several strides ahead. Dmitri could sense his patient, his captive, slowing as they approached.

"I don't know anything about what happened up there," Dmitri said. "I never met any of those people before. All I know is that a deadly virus has been released, and it's my job to find a cure."

"You don't have to keep us captive to find the cure," Chambers said.

Dmitri took the last few steps to the open door to Chambers' cell and waited for the doctor to catch up.

Chambers reached the door and stopped. "Do you have a family?" he asked.

Dmitri thought of Sasha, and their unborn child. What would she think of what he was doing? As soon as the thought came to him, he forced it out of his head angrily. He was doing exactly what the American wanted him to do.

"Go inside," Dmitri said. "We will return later to plan the next steps in fighting the virus."

"I had a family," Chambers said. "If I were you, I would do whatever I could to protect my family. You have to do whatever you can to keep them safe."

“Get inside,” Dmitri said, reaching out to grab Chambers’ arm. He spotted Lukin eyeing him from back down the hall.

“I understand what you’re doing,” Chambers said, “and why you’re doing it. But you’re not one of these people. You’re not a monster.”

Dmitri pushed the door closed, and the beeping of the locking mechanism sounded. Chambers’ last few words dampened significantly behind the glass.

As the two men stared at each other across the glass, Dmitri wondered which one of them was trapped.

64

NUCURE LABORATORIES, RUSSIA

It looked like any other boring gray building.

Surprisingly, some of the most cutting-edge molecular research took place inside the gray walls. The future cures for cancer were emerging. The latest technology in vaccine immunology was being developed. Also inside this stone building in the center of this small, old, crumbling Russian town, was one of the most advanced biologic warfare research facilities in the world.

Jonathan was crouching down in the tall grass along the hill overlooking the city. His face felt as though the night vision goggles were still on, but dawn was arriving. He was tired and frightened, and he had to go to the bathroom. He shifted uncomfortably, wondering if he should just pee in the weeds, wondering if the proper military etiquette was to put your rifle down or somehow hold onto it while he went. He rocked in place, trying to ease the pressure on his lower abdomen.

Jonathan looked over at Cage, wondering if the scar-headed rock of a man could read his mind. Cage was perfectly still, looking down at the NuCure building as though he could see through its walls. He held his rifle low to the ground but kept his finger near the trigger at all times. He hadn't slept, hell he had hardly blinked, all night, but there was no doubt that he was ready for anything that awaited them. The orange rising sun reflected in his pupils.

Four other men flanked them. They appeared during the night, as promised by Cage. Like the other members of Cage's team, they seemed to be his subordinates, and they lacked names and any other items to define their identity. They spoke to Cage only in Russian, and Cage only translated a small fraction of their conversation to Jonathan. They looked identical in the darkness, a quartet of AK47-carrying dark complexioned men with several days of facial hair growth. They could have easily been clones produced for the completion of this task ahead of them. In the rising sunlight, the subtle differences hardly erased the image from Jonathan's imagination.

"They have four people from the research station inside," Cage said to Jonathan, his eyes still fastened to the NuCure building. "I want to save as many of them as possible, but the first half of our mission is to keep Doctor Chambers alive at all costs. We know that at least one of the other three is working with the NuCure unit. That person was planted at the research station to try and get a hold of the virus. There's a good chance that it's one of the Russian men, but don't discount the Italian woman as a possibility. We have to treat them all as a potential threat."

Jonathan thought back to the photographs that he saw during the flight. He had their faces memorized. He wondered how they looked after suffering the effects of the past several weeks.

One of the other men spoke softly to Cage. Jonathan strained to listen, although he couldn't understand any of the Russian.

"Boris may be inside," Cage said to Jonathan. "We've heard reports that he might be involved here. You won't miss him. He's the one with the white hair. You saw him in the photos. He looks like a friendly grandfather, but he's the most dangerous, by far. He's slipped through our fingers several times already. I want to keep him alive if at all possible." He rubbed one of the most pronounced scars on his forehead. "At least for a while."

"What about the others?" Jonathan asked.

"They've confirmed that Illya Lukin is inside," Cage said. "He is the brains behind NuCure. He reports only to Boris. Try to keep them both alive if possible, but do not allow them to escape. Then there are the laboratory worker bees, Dmitri Petrov and the husband and wife, Kazimir and Rozalina. The two from the research station, Tarasov and Torelli, are probably the only ones that are armed, but the others may surprise us. All five are expendable from an intelligence standpoint, so don't hesitate to fire on them."

"How will we get inside?" Jonathan asked.

"Through the front door," Cage said. "We'll be inside before you know it. Just make sure you're ready."

"Are we just blasting our way in?" Jonathan asked.

"We're not blasting anything," Cage said. "As soon as the first shot's fired, we lose the advantage of surprise."

Jonathan nodded.

"The only reason you have a rifle," Cage said, "is so that if you get shot, I won't feel as guilty as I would if you had no weapon."

"I might surprise you," Jonathan said. He walked over toward a small stack of stones and supported his rifle with his forearm while unzipping his pants.

The entrance to the NuCure building opened slightly, and a red laser-thin light flashed three times from the doorway.

"That's Paulina," Cage said. "We're mobile. Move it, CDC."

Within seconds the five men were down near the ground, rocketing down the hillside. Jonathan was on the verge of relieving himself and had to tighten his entire midsection to avoid wetting himself as he tugged at his zipper. He was visually losing track of the others, who were somewhere within the wake of swaying grass and brush rushing down the hill. He tugged one final time on his zipper. Still wouldn't budge. The rifle came loose from his forearm and pivoted toward his head. He released his pants just in time to grab the rifle and prevent it from blowing his head off.

He grabbed the rifle with both hands and crouched as he struggled to catch up to the others. No matter how hard he tried to get his body down, he felt as though he had a flashing neon bullseye on his chest.

The brush ripped at his legs. Roots jumped up to trip him. It wasn't going to take much to send him sprawling, tumbling down the hill with a deadly weapon in his hands. But his greatest fear at this moment, more than the sum of all of the other fears conspiring against him, was his fear of being stranded on the hill, alone, in the middle of nowhere. He had to run faster, oblivious to his surroundings. He had to catch up to the others.

A woman in a white nurse's outfit was standing in the open doorway up ahead. She had to be Paulina, the one that Cage had spoken about. There always seemed to be someone waiting to lend a hand or open the door for Cage. Friends in the right places. Was it all preparation, or was there some luck involved? Jonathan looked up at the woman in the doorway, her long black hair blowing in the morning breeze, and didn't care how or why she was there, as long as she was there.

The others reached the edge of the brush and stopped, giving Jonathan a chance to catch up. Were they waiting for him, or were they just planning their next move? He decided that they wouldn't have stopped just to wait for the slow guy.

Jonathan was gasping for air as he reached the others. He felt a hand on either side drag him closer toward the ground. Cage was motioning with a hand for him to stay low.

Jonathan couldn't hear anything other than the sound of his own breathing. His mouth was gaping wide and his eyeballs seemed like they were bulging out of their sockets. Before Jonathan could catch his breath, Cage lunged forward and signaled for the rest of them to follow.

A short sprint toward the entrance followed. Jonathan was waiting to be spotted, but there was no yelling, no shooting. They just walked in the front door, just as Cage had promised.

So far it seemed easy.

65

RENWICK RUIN, NEW YORK CITY

"What are you doing here?"

Grovely thought the words as Claire spoke them. He shut his eyes forcefully several times, trying to distinguish the nightmare before him from the ketamine-induced hallucinations in his head. After several attempts to make the vision disappear, he accepted the presence of the man in the black overcoat before him.

"What are you doing here?" Claire said again, this time with a panicked realization that she already knew the answer to her own question.

Troy Gaines passed through the hazy light beam from the slide projector and lit up like a poltergeist penetrating a wall. "I'm the one who invited you here," he said. "This is my party. I'm so glad you could make it"

Gaines looked at the leather straps pinning Grovely to the chair and smiled. Gaines walked toward Claire, who took a step backwards for every step that he advanced. The snake slid sideways along the inside of the glass cage, its attention focused on Claire.

"You're the Mamba," Claire said, angling her backward steps to keep the cage between her and Gaines.

Grovely's head was swimming. Gaines was the Mamba? The Wonderboy? The clean-cut preppy businessman? It didn't make any sense. Grovely saw the Wall Street Journal articles and the humanitarian awards spinning around his head, taunting him. He heard the sound of the robotic voice from all the telephone calls. Gaines?

Gaines and Claire were pressed up against either side of the cage now, the snake eagerly swaying from one to the other between its glass boundaries.

"You've been a good girl, Claire," Gaines said. "You've followed all of your instructions well. Every last detail, down to a T."

"I did," Claire said. She looked different now. The sense of control was gone. She tilted side to side in response to Gaines' smallest movements, staring at him with the wide shifting eyes of an undecided squirrel in the approaching headlights of a car. It was just a matter of time, her fear said. "I did everything you said. I tried..."

"You tried," Gaines said, "to screw me out of millions of dollars. You tried to feed information to Van Brauten behind my back. You tried to make an ass out of me. But you made a huge mistake."

The bite hole in Grovely's leg got a little deeper, forcing him to cry out in pain. His hand felt like an over inflated balloon on the verge of exploding. He couldn't think about anything else. As the snake swayed more quickly, he thought of Cleopatra clutching the asp to her breast to bring on death. Now he was trapped, with nothing standing between him and death except for an undetermined amount of pain, and he pictured the mamba, teeth-deep in his chest, bringing on a long-awaited end to this anguish.

"Thorton," Gaines said. "Let this be a lesson to you. Women aren't always what they appear to be. Remember that for the rest of your life." He laughed so loud that even the snake recoiled slightly. "Or for five minutes, whichever comes first. You know, I hate it when people aren't what they appear to be."

Gaines reached into the inner breast pocket of his black overcoat for what was almost certainly a gun. Instead, he withdrew a small shining gold object that resembled a cigarette lighter. Two green jewels adorned the top, two jewels slits forming the eyes of a serpent head.

"I've done what you asked," Claire said to Gaines. She pointed at Grovely. "He's right where you want him – sedated and strapped down. The rat is feeding, and the mamba is ready."

"I see," Gaines said. "Thank you. I don't have anything else for you to do. Your work here is done." He flipped open the metal object, revealing two protruding hypodermic needles.

Claire ran for the doorway, but Gaines was too fast for her. He grabbed one of her arms in one hand and raised the gold snakehead in the other. Claire screamed for help as she kicked and scratched to get free.

Gaines rammed the golden snakehead, hypodermic needles first, into Claire's neck. He held it therefore several seconds, until Claire's movements became more subdued.

Claire turned to Grovely, as though expecting him to break free of his bondage and save her from the poison that was already spreading through her system. Her body stiffened with the abruptness of an electric shock, and her eyes twisted backward until only the white sclera was visible.

Gaines released the snakehead from Claire's neck, causing two red streaks to run down from the puncture marks left behind. He closed the serpent mouth with both hands, taking care not to come near the dripping fangs.

Claire's entire body was gripped with a series of forceful convulsions. She twisted and jerked along the floor, her own muscles conspiring to assault every part of her against the unforgiving stone surface.

Gaines stood up and turned toward Grovely. He slipped the serpent head back into his pocket and brushed some of the gray dust off his coat. He pulled a handkerchief from his shirt pocket and wiped his brow. He was ready for whatever else he had planned.

"She would have been better off cooperating with me," Gaines said. "She had a wicked streak in her, and I liked that, but she was filled with a little too much venom. And now, well..."

A particularly violent convulsion cracked Claire's head against the floor behind Gaines, but he didn't flinch.

"She's got just a little more venom, and she's paying for her greed," Gaines said. "She was a greedy one, Thorton, but she was nothing compared to you."

Grovely's wounds burned a little deeper, and the straps holding him immobile seemed a little tighter.

66

NUCURE LABORATORIES, RUSSIA

The cuts were clean, but the floor was a mess.

Don't look. Don't look.

Jonathan followed the other men closely, determined not to be separated in the building. The inside of NuCure was just as nondescript as the view from the hill outside. A few portraits of businessmen in gray suits hung on eggshell-colored walls. One was definitely Ilya Lukin, the president of NuCure. There was no mistaking the pampered blonde hair and smooth features.

The gray wall-to-wall carpet stretched through the waiting room and extended down the hallway. The blood was still wet.

Don't look. Keep moving.

Two close circuit monitors were on a desk near the front of the hallway. One of the black and white images was the view from a camera over the front entrance. Everything was still, although the view a minute earlier would have shown six gunmen entering. The other monitor showed a closed door somewhere inside.

A newspaper was open on the desk. Red spots of varying sizes were soaking into the fine filament of the paper.

Just keep moving.

The chairs were empty. Their throats must have been slashed simultaneously to leave the bodies so close together.

Jonathan tried not to look at the dead men as they neared the stairwell, but the bodies were impossible to ignore.

They were heaped together on the floor between the chairs. Their skin matched the color of the walls. Their throats were gaping wide open where they had been slashed with swift even strokes. Jonathan had never seen the work of a professional assassin up close, but there was no mistaking the sight.

Paulina was already out the front door. Jonathan spotted her on the monitor. Her white outfit was as pristine as a communion dress. She had penetrated the depths of the NuCure organization and delivered Cage to his target. She was somehow clean of the bloodshed. She escaped untouched. She would remain untouchable. And within seconds she was gone.

Biocontainment suits and oxygen tanks were on the floor next to the security desk, compliments of Paulina.

"Get these on fast," Cage whispered to Jonathan, while slipping his legs inside the oversized pant legs.

Two of the men stood guard as the others got into their suits. Within seconds Cage was completely dressed, with oxygen running, and had taken over one of the guard positions.

Jonathan struggled with his suit while the others stood, one by one, fully sealed off from their surroundings and fully armed. He expected them to abandon him, but they waited as he fumbled to get inside the suit. Each fist banged against the armpits of the suit repeatedly on their way toward the sleeves. By this point, the others helped seal off the remaining openings of his suit. He could only watch his hands rattle together with tremulous futility.

The suit was finally sealed. The oxygen began flowing. Jonathan was sealed off from the rest of the world. He lifted the rifle with gloved hands.

He was terrified.

Cage's men resumed their penetration through the building. Their movements were precise and efficient as they cut through the empty halls and wound down the staircase.

Jonathan alternated between holding his finger on the trigger, and keeping it jutting out forward. He shifted his rifle position between the extreme left and the extreme right, away from the changing location of the others. He made sure that the rifle didn't fire at the wrong time. He didn't want to shoot it at all. He was hoping, beyond all else, that there wasn't really any biologic warfare facility below, that there weren't any researchers infected with a deadly virus, that it was all just a big mistake.

Pulses surged out to his fingertips, and up through his temples. His eyes were darting in every direction, because any direction could bring an attack. Every sound was a startle, every shadow a threat, every turn an unknown.

They descended the stairs toward the depths of the building, as though it was swallowing them whole. Their footsteps were the only sounds, echoing louder. They were probably right over their targets' heads. How could they not hear their approach?

They emerged from the staircase into a hallway. There was no protection here, no cut-out cubby holes, no stacks of barrels, no pillars. Just a wide-open hallway leading to a seemingly impermeable metal door. Cage moved swiftly but silently toward the door, and the rest followed. He must have had the blueprints memorized; he looked as though he had been practicing the mission in this building every day for years.

There was a card key slot and a fingerprint monitor. This was it, Jonathan thought. The end of the line. Then he noticed the LED display reading a zone fault. Thanks, Paulina.

Cage listened against the door. Rifle poised, he signaled one-two-three. His arm muscles tensed while grasping the latch.

He eased the door open.

67

NUCURE LABORATORIES, RUSSIA

Without tetracycline, they were going to die.

The instructions were clear. The solution wasn't. Boris insisted that without tetracycline, they could observe the natural course of the disease, observing its physical and physiological manifestations. Without tetracycline, they could fully assess their attempts at fighting the virus. But without the tetracycline, three of their "patients" were guaranteed to die.

Dmitri sat at the medical station watching the patient monitors. Luigi Mincini's heart rate was irregular, with premature beats and widened complexes. His serum calcium level was rising. His kidneys were failing. The rest of his electrolytes were becoming increasingly abnormal. The effects of the minute virus particles in his bone were working their way out through his system.

Dmitri walked over to the enclosed room and peered through the glass. The young Italian man was lying on the stretcher, unconscious. He was taking deep, rapid breaths and perspiring.

The portable yellow defibrillator was on the shelf above one of the intravenous infusion pumps. Dmitri looked up at the electrode pads, wondering if he would have to apply them to the man's chest before the day was through. The heart rhythm was progressively worsening, and the day was young. He had never defibrillated anyone. He had never treated a heart condition in any way. He was a molecular biologist, a laboratory researcher. What was he doing here?

A defibrillator, applied in the wrong way, or at the wrong time, could stop the heart, rather than correcting its abnormal rhythm. It could kill the person hooked up to the leads, rather than saving their life. What if he was wrong when he made the decision to use it?

It was time to administer the calcitonin injections. Paulina was nowhere to be seen. He might be able to administer the shots, but he wasn't sure if he knew the exact dose. All he really knew was that the calcitonin would help stabilize the calcium levels. Paulina had a good sense of the rest, perhaps even a better sense of medical treatments than Doctor Boris. But where was she?

Doctor Chambers was still standing at the door, where he had spent most of his time since he woke up from the transfer sedation. The doctor would be a big help, even with this relatively minor task. Lukin and Doctor Boris wanted to extract information out of the doctor, but they had no intention of working side by side with him.

Dmitri would never convince Lukin and Boris to let Chambers free. What if he just let him out? What if he let them all out? Maybe he could make it look like they escaped. But then what? They were too weak to escape. They would all just end up in their cells again. Cells. Now he had said it. They weren't patient rooms. What was he doing locking people in cells?

One of the monitors at the station began beeping. Was Mincini going into cardiac arrest? It hadn't taken very long. He walked briskly toward the monitors. He was right. One of the monitor tracings was a flat green. This was it. There was nobody else right here, and Mincini was coding.

No, it wasn't Mincini. Mincini was in room four. The flat line EKG tracing was on monitor two. Who was in room two? Oleg Larianov. One who actually had a chance to survive. Was this how sick they really were? How was he going to keep any of them alive?

Dmitri turned to room two, where Larianov was collapsed across the stretcher, his left arm draping lifelessly toward the floor. Where was everyone else? Dmitri's first response was to call out for help, but he resisted the urge. What if he was mistaken? What if it wasn't an emergency? Doctor Boris didn't seem like the kind of person who took well to false alarms. He had to evaluate the situation first.

He ran to the wall where the release buttons were. He pressed the button for the second room, and the glass door in front of Larianov's room clicked open. Dmitri wheeled an emergency cart filled with medications into the room.

"Are you all right?" Dmitri yelled.

He shook Larianov's shoulder, nearly forcing his body over the edge of the stretcher. There was no movement. He tried awkwardly to wrap his containment suit covered arms around Larianov's shoulders to turn him over. The man's beard scraped against the white material. He tried to feel a pulse but had difficulty through the thick gloves.

Wait.

Did Larianov move? Maybe he was still alive after all.

The monitor was still reading a flat line. But where were the leads?

Larianov moved so quickly that Dmitri hardly saw what happened. He felt his hand pressed down against the stretcher, and then at least two sharp needles penetrated the back of his hand. He watched the blood spreading between the layers of gloves, wondering what happened. Then the first red beads bubbled out through the holes in the latex.

Two needles were sticking out of his hand. Rubber coated wires ran out from the needles. What was happening?

The electrical shock rocked every square inch of his body at the same time. A bright flash filled his vision and blasted through his head. His arms and legs shot in different directions, and the room wouldn't stop moving. Was he seeing smoke coming out of his hand, or was his vision just that distorted?

Larianov was standing over him as he crashed to the floor. The wires attached by one end to the needles in Dmitri's hand were leading into a yellow box held by Larianov. It was the defibrillator, or at least part of it.

Larianov was pressing down on one of the buttons again with his thumb. His beard was sticking out at odd angles as he smiled for the first time that Dmitri could remember.

"No, don't," Dmitri tried to yell, only to hear an unintelligible roar escape his mouth.

He felt as though there were butterflies fluttering in his chest. Dizziness gave way to the sense of an impending black-out.

If the first electrical shock was like a lightning bolt, the second was more like a switch being turned off. All of his strength disappeared. He fell back toward the open glass door.

Then everything went black.

68

RENWICK RUIN, NEW YORK CITY

Death was luring him forward, and that was exactly where he wanted to go.

"Are you," Grovely started. His words seemed to be getting stuck between his brain and his mouth. "I don't." He tried again. "How could?" Everything was disconnected inside him.

"Am I the Mamba?" Gaines mocked him with a crying voice. "But you don't see how. How could I be? How could Troy Gaines be the Mamba?"

He lunged forward and grabbed Grovely by the throat.

"You thought you were so smart, Thorton, didn't you? You siphoned money out of Global for the last five years. You thought you were getting away with it. You thought you had me fooled."

Grovely couldn't breathe. The pressure in his face increased as Gaines' grasp tightened.

"But do you know what you did?" Gaines asked, his face right up against Grovely's. "You dug your grave, one dollar at a time. I saw everything you did. Every single backstabbing move. You're a stupid fool. You stole money from Global, but you gave every penny back to me tenfold, because you were running my second business, a more profitable business, on the side."

The last few words faded away as Grovely nearly lost consciousness. He closed his eyes and waited to die, wanted to die, only to feel the grasp go away. No, finish it now, he thought. I can't take any more of this.

Survival instincts sucked a massive breath into his lungs, a breath restricted only by the pressure of the straps around his chest.

When Grovely opened his eyes, he saw the gaping jaws of the black snake in front of his face. Gaines was holding the snake with both hands and leaning in closer.

"How did it feel to get those calls from me, Thorton?" Gaines asked. "Did they send a chill through your bones? It's amazing what someone will do for money, especially a rat like you." He slapped Grovely's thigh, stirring the rat inside his pants. Pain shot down his entire leg. "I needed someone like you, Thorton. Someone who would sell research technology, knowing that it would be going toward viral warfare. Someone who would stop supply runs to a research station in Siberia, knowing that everyone there would die. Someone who would send a doctor to his death for the sake of saving his own hide."

"I," Grovely said, his throat aching. "I, but."

"You," Gaines said, leaning closer until the snake's mouth snapped shut just beyond the tip of Grovely's nose. "You have no idea how difficult it is to find someone like you."

The snake ran its tongue along Grovely's nose and opened its mouth again. Grovely shuddered. He looked down at Claire's body, which was now twitching in a pool of blood on the floor.

"I've wanted to kill you for so long, Thorton," Gaines said. "But I had to let my desire for revenge yield to my better judgment. I had to kill Atisoy first, and then Claire."

Gaines was squeezing the snake so tightly that its mouth was twisted sideways while its body twirled to get free.

"There won't be any question in anyone's mind that you committed those murders," Gaines said. He shook the snake at Grovely. "I've already notified the authorities that you stole millions of dollars from my company. I told them that you stormed out of the office yelling Atisoy's name a few days ago. I told them that you were under a lot of stress from your girlfriend Claire."

"Now Atisoy and Claire are dead, and all the trails lead to your door. They'll arrest you the moment you return home. Nobody will believe you when you deny the murders."

Something inside the snake cracked, and the scaly body went limp.

"And jail is a scary place, Thorton," Gaines said. "At least from what I've seen on television. It's disgusting in there. They never clean the cells. The floors are covered with cockroaches and the beds with lice. And just think what the other inmates will do with a scrawny pretty boy like you in there? All those filthy disease-ridden men. I don't even want to think about it."

"Kill," Grovely said. He forced the words out. "Kill me."

Gaines laughed so loudly that it hurt Grovely's ears. "You're so much fun, Thorton." He threw the limp snake over his shoulder, and it landed across Claire's dead body. "But killing you would be too easy."

"What are," Grovely said. "What plans?"

"Originally I wanted you to kill yourself, to admit to the two murders in a nice tidy suicide note," Gaines said. "Of course, I would have even been willing to help you out with the suicide, since we go way back. But I didn't want to let you off the hook so easily. I want you to suffer as much as possible, and you have to stay alive to do that. But I want you to spend every day being reminded of how big of a mistake it was to underestimate me, to double cross me."

"I know," Grovely said. "It was."

Gaines looked around the room until he found the syringe with the ketamine that Claire had used earlier. He lifted the syringe into the projector light to check the volume.

"She gave you a heck of a dose," Gaines said. "I'm surprised you're still standing, well, sitting anyway. This can knock you for a loop. I hear it can even give you nightmares and hallucinations. Is that true?"

"True," Grovely said, unable to nod.

"I bet you already had some, didn't you?" Gaines said. "I think we ought to double the dose." With that, he rammed the needle into Grovely's shoulder and forced the medication in.

"Listen to what I'm saying now," Gaines said. "You might have some difficulty concentrating soon." He leaned his face in close and tilted it at distorting angles. "Are you listening in there? Are you listening? This is important, Thorton."

"Important," Grovely said. He looked down at Claire and the snake. They looked peaceful. Their nightmares were over.

"That's good, Thorton," Gaines said. "You think you have no way out of this. But I'm here to help you. There is one way out. Only one way. I'm going to bring you up the river to the psychiatric institute. It's a nice place. Very peaceful. You can be anonymous there. You'll be safe from the police. You'll be safe from me. But only as long as you stay there, and only as long as you don't tell them who you are."

"Safe there," Grovely said. The first wave of medication was flowing through his head.

"We'll go there soon," Gaines said. "No more worries, Thorton."

Somewhere beyond the next few waves of ketamine, the rat along his thigh disappeared, the pus draining from his hand dried up, and the straps binding him began to loosen. Eyes closed, Grovely slipped away from the Smallpox hospital and into the deepest recesses of his brain.

"No worries," Grovely said.

69

NUCURE LABORATORIES, RUSSIA

They didn't have much time.

Chambers could only see part of Larianov through the small window connecting their cells. He couldn't see the Russian at all. He heard the man's agonized cry a few moments earlier, and watched his body fall toward the floor, out of sight. What had happened?

Larianov was out in the hall now, running toward the buttons that would open the rest of the cells. Drew watched his glass partition, waiting for it to open and release him. He wasn't sure what he would do once he escaped. His chances of surviving would be increased, but so would his chance of being killed immediately.

Just as Larianov reached the buttons, Doctor Boris appeared from the right and struck him with a fire extinguisher, ramming him against the wall. Larianov fell off balance, and the white-haired doctor sprayed him with the white jet while kicking him in the chest.

Drew watched from the glass partition, helpless, hoping that Larianov could somehow fight back against his attacker.

Someone began yelling from the area just beyond the entrance to the room. The voice was loud, but the language was unmistakably Russian. Drew's impression that the yelling was a warning was confirmed by Boris' response. His head shot up. He turned toward the opposite hallway and yelled in Russian to his colleagues.

He was gesturing to someone just beyond Drew's visual field. A woman's voice responded. It was Maria. Drew still couldn't see her, but she was yelling back to Boris.

Boris struck Larianov again with the fire extinguisher, causing him to wobble toward the floor. Boris yelled again toward the still unseen Maria, and then hit the button on the far end of the panel. A door slid open to one of the rooms on the right. Drew wedged himself against the window on the right, enough to know that it wasn't Mincini's door that was open. It had to be Yurov.

A single gunshot went off toward the direction of the door that just opened.

Maria's voice sounded again, and Boris signaled to her. He pressed the next button.

They were killing the prisoners.

Drew looked into Mincini's room again. Maria entered her countryman's room with a large handgun.

"No," Drew yelled, banging on the glass. "No, don't."

Maria didn't hear him, or else she didn't care. In either case, she showed no response to Drew's pleas.

There was more yelling from outside, and then the sound of glass breaking. "Hold them. The rest of them are inside." English. Someone was on their way in, but it was going to be too late.

Boris was looking into Mincini's room. Larianov was pulling himself up along the wall, reaching for the switch that would release the entrance to the patient facility.

Maria walked over to Mincini, unquestioning in her intent. She put the gun against Mincini's head as he lay there panting for air.

Drew closed his eyes as the gun went off. The sound was closer now and made his entire body flinch.

When he opened his eyes again, there was no questioning that the extent of the damage from the high caliber gun at close range had killed Mincini. The body was motionless, painless, for the first time in many days.

Maria looked at the splatter with what might have been a small smile, and then walked out of the room.

Boris pressed the next button, and the glass partition of Drew's cell opened.

The first two were the easy ones, the worker bees, as Cage had put it. They were defenseless, but their yelling must have alerted the others, wherever they were.

One of Cage's men was back at the main entrance to the Level IV facility. Another was back at the doorway to the laboratory itself. A third man stood guard in front of the laboratory workers, who were laying face-down on the floor with their hands behind their heads.

Jonathan followed Cage and the other gunman as they ran toward the door in the far corner of the laboratory. This was the only other way out of the room and must have been the way to the prisoners.

The door was locked.

Someone was yelling in Russian on the other side of the door.

A shot rang out from inside.

More yelling. Another shot. A loud buzz sounded along the door.

Cage responded immediately, turning the latch and opening the door. Inside a man in a biocontainment suit was swinging a fire extinguisher at a hunched over bearded Russian with no protective clothing. The bearded man ducked, and the fire extinguisher crashed against the wall, sending its holder tumbling in their direction.

The fire extinguisher skidded past their feet. Cage ran over to the man in the biocontainment suit, pressed the gun against the back of his head, and yelled "Don't move." The man on the floor stopped immediately, and then turned slowly to look at his captor.

Through the visor of the headgear, there was no mistaking the white hair and sharp features of Doctor Boris.

A gun shot rang out from across the room, and then footfalls ran away down the hallway. Jonathan froze, waiting for the pain to rip through him. Instead, Cage fell backwards against the wall, and slid down toward the floor. He clutched his thigh as blood ran down his white suit.

Boris, without getting up from the floor, scrambled through the open glass partition leading to the first patient cell. He ducked behind the stretcher. He had to know that he was trapped.

With a tap of a button, Larianov brought the glass partition to a closed position, locking Boris inside patient cell number one.

The person who shot Cage was gone.

70

NUCURE LABORATORIES, RUSSIA

Jonathan chased the footfalls through the hall, and then into the room in the far corner. He waited at the door. Was he supposed to kick it open, or shoot the handle? He turned to Cage, who was still running, with decreasing speed but increasing determination. The blood now covered the majority of his right pant leg.

There was no sound inside.

Cage motioned for Jonathan to go to the far side of the door, while he positioned himself on the near side. He grabbed the handle and turned, slowly but unimpeded by a lock.

Jonathan raised his gun and slipped a gloved finger along the trigger. He felt more prepared to pull the trigger, now that one of his team had been shot. Now that he had seen the dead bodies of the researchers in the patient cells as they ran by.

The first crack of light slipped out through the opening door. Increasing amounts of a meeting room were exposed. Both men pointed their guns toward the opening. Jonathan held his breath in an attempt to hold the gun motionless.

They could see flipcharts on easels, and then a large table. Cage forced the door fully open and entered the room, gun first. Jonathan followed.

There was nobody inside.

"That's not supposed to be here," Cage said, pointing to an open door in the back of the room. He was furious but kept his voice down to avoid detection.

Footfalls tapped along a staircase somewhere over their heads.

"Did you see who it was?" Jonathan asked.

"No," Cage said. "But it must have been Lukin who shot at us."

The doorway led to a staircase. The last of the footfalls sounded above, and then a door screeched open and shut.

Jonathan led the way up the stairs. He had the mental image of Lukin before him. He was ready to kill him if he had to. He hadn't been so sure a week ago, or a day ago, or even an hour ago. But now he was. If he could capture Lukin alive he would, but if it came down to it, if it was Ilya Lukin or Jonathan Abrams, Lukin would have to die.

Cage was trailing behind, but Jonathan didn't care anymore. He picked up his pace, even taking the steps two at a time for a stretch, despite the obstacles of the clumsy white suit.

The door at the top of the steps was ajar. Jonathan peered through the opening, which led to a dimly lit hallway. A single door was the only way to go, down at the far end of the hall. Jonathan stepped silently now, although he knew that his target was expecting him to arrive any second.

It's just like playing Death Seeker, Jonathan told himself. But somehow the words Death Seeker left him far from settled.

He tightened his grip on the gun and continued forward. When he reached the end of the hall, he spun to press his back against the corner, and then inched along the wall toward the door. The handle was just beyond his fingertips. A little closer. A little closer. He could reach it now.

Sweat had seeped along the narrow space between his hands and the tight gloves surrounding them, forming a generally even layer occasionally interrupted by air bubbles. The bubbles shifted as he wrapped his fingers around the door handle.

He lightly pressed the handle. Locked. Great. Now what?

Cage reached the top of the stairs. He was too far behind to solve the problem. Jonathan would have to decide what to do.

Jonathan lowered the gun down to the area just next to the handle and fired, blowing a baseball sized hole through the door and obliterating the locking mechanism. Pivoting his body and kicking with all his might, he was amazed to see the door fly open.

He stood at the entrance of a plush office. The walls were lined with tall bookshelves and paintings. Decorative high-backed wooden chairs surrounded a massive mahogany desk. He spotted a man in a white biocontainment suit and nearly fired his gun.

But he held back.

The man, who had to be Ilya Lukin, wasn't shooting back at him. Instead, he was standing behind a woman with an arm wrapped around her neck and a gun pointed to her head.

"Don't take another step, or I'll shoot her," the man said. He pressed the gun more firmly against her temple.

The woman was beautiful, with long brown hair and olive-toned skin. She was positioned squarely toward Jonathan, blocking all but Lukin's right elbow and the edge of his face.

"Please don't shoot," she said. "Listen to what he says. He'll kill me." The direction of her attention suggested that she was more afraid of Jonathan than of Lukin.

They stood behind the desk, with their backs to a large aquarium. Bubbles trickled up through the water on either side of them. Endless shadows waved through the bottom of the tank.

Jonathan held his aim at Lukin, alternating between his face and his elbow, depending on which was more exposed to his view.

This had to be Maria Pellegrino. Was she really a prisoner here, or was she working with Lukin? There was no way to tell. But it was Lukin who was holding the weapon. The elbow? The face? There wasn't much of a target.

"Now," Maria screamed, beginning to duck away from Lukin as he released his grip.

Jonathan squeezed the trigger. The aquarium behind Lukin exploded with a shower of glass and water. The fish, or whatever they were inside, poured out onto the floor.

Lukin was still standing. Jonathan had missed completely.

Lukin's gun swung in Jonathan's direction. A second blast went off, this time from just behind Jonathan's right ear. A hole appeared in Lukin's eye as he was thrown back onto the jagged edges of the aquarium.

Cage was standing behind Jonathan, his leg dripping blood onto the floor.

Maria was screaming from her crouched position on the floor. "Get them. Get them off of me."

Jonathan looked over the desk. There were more than a dozen wet snakes fastened to Maria, writhing like Medusan locks as she collapsed to the floor.

"She was the one," Cage said. "The Siberian researcher from NuCure."

"So much for taking them alive," Jonathan said.

The snakes were in a frenzy. Maria was already motionless.

"We still have Boris," Cage said.

He looked too calm.

Drew was standing outside of the patient cells now, looking in at Doctor Boris. This was the man that allowed everyone at the research station to suffer, Drew thought. This is the man who decided to have me go up there. The man who brought us in here like laboratory rats, experimenting on us and killing us slowly.

Boris smiled at him. Drew couldn't smile back. Instead, he alternated glances between the glass partition and the button on the wall.

The two laboratory workers were in the second cell. The Russian that Larianov electrocuted with his modified defibrillator gun was in with them, alive, awake, but still a bit dazed.

Boris walked toward the front of his cell and pressed his gloved palms against the glass partition.

One of the armed rescuers said something in Russian. Larianov laughed.

"What did he say?" Drew asked.

"He said that Boris is trapped like a bug," Larianov said.

Drew smiled. "Thanks to you," he said.

Larianov forced a smile between the large purple lumps on his face. He patted Drew on the shoulder.

Boris tapped on the glass with a knuckle. He shook his head with a frustrated expression.

It was true. The biologic weapon mastermind didn't seem so dangerous to Drew now. So much for home field advantage.

Boris worked his way toward the edge of the glass, tapping his knuckle all the way. Then he followed the wall, tapping in similar fashion. He ran his hand along the top of an empty shelf, and then along the bottom. He stopped, as though finding something. He smiled again, and then held one finger like a mime instructing his audience to wait for something truly entertaining.

"What's he doing?" Drew asked.

Both gunmen were inching closer to Boris' cell.

Boris pressed his finger up against the bottom of the shelf, and a beep sounded along the glass partition of his cell. He gestured with both hands toward the glass. Ta da!

He turned and walked to the back of the room. Pressing his fingers against the back wall, he began to pry one of the white panels loose.

Both gunmen were raising their weapons. They yelled simultaneously to Larianov, who ran back to the button panel on the wall. He pressed the button to room one, but nothing happened. He pressed it again. Still nothing.

Larianov spoke to the others in Russian, and then told Drew, "The release isn't working. He's done something to it."

Boris had the panel completely removed, revealing a narrow corridor. He turned to wave goodbye.

The first gunman fired. The bullet embedded in the glass. Only a short thin crack extended out from the deformed bullet. The rest of the glass was intact.

Boris bowed to them.

The second bullet hit the glass, and then the third. The sound was deafening, but the result was equally disappointing.

Boris blew kisses as bullets struck the glass. The molten metal blobs formed two clusters, but the glass was unyielding.

"He's getting away," Drew yelled.

Doctor Boris slipped into the gap between the white wall panels and disappeared from view.

71

EMPIRE STATE PSYCHIATRIC INSTITUTE

It was time to take the garbage in.

Troy Gaines, the Mamba, was watching through binoculars from behind a tree several hundred feet away. He was lying in the tall grass near the river, imperceptible to anyone looking for him, let alone the unsuspecting night staff working inside the Empire State Psychiatric Institute.

Thorton Grovely was lying in a heap in front of the stone facade of the building. He was still asleep from the ketamine, which was combining with several weeks of escalating pressure and several hours of unbearable torture to produce an unending sequence of night terrors.

"The rats. The rats. The rats are eating me. Get them off of me," Grovely howled, curling his legs into a fetal position and swinging his arms against the stairs.

"That's it, Thorton," Gaines whispered to himself. "That's it. Cry out for help. You're making this so much easier than I expected. And even more fun than I could have ever hoped."

A face appeared in one of the windows near the front door. An old woman with a white nurse's cap was looking outside, trying to determine the source of the commotion. She spotted Grovely on the stairs and turned to call for help. Within a minute, the woman appeared at the doorway with two massive guards.

The guards each grabbed one of Grovely's arms, causing him to flail more urgently, eyes still closed, nightmare still progressing.

"Get the snake," Grovely said. "Get the mamba." He grasped at the air in front of his face, coming up empty each time, and swinging again.

It was time to take the garbage in.

The guards looked across the choppy unattended lawn surrounding the psychiatric institute but saw nothing. There was no explanation for the mess of humanity lying at their feet. Just another diseased brain finding its way to its appropriate home, probably its permanent home. There was no reason to suspect that a Mamba was lying in the grass along the edge of the night.

They lifted Grovely, flailing and screaming, and forced his arms into a straitjacket. In one rapid motion Grovely's arms were wrapped tightly and secured with a lock behind his back.

"Keep your poison away from me," Grovely yelled, kicking at the phantasms haunting his nightmare.

More help came inside, and within minutes they had Grovely loaded onto a stretcher and secured with leather straps. Together, they lifted him up and took him inside.

"I can't get the rat," Grovely yelled as the massive, wooden door crashed closed against the stone frame.

Gaines recoiled from his hiding spot and wound his way through the tall grass for a long distance before standing. That was fun, he thought, but the Mamba will have to have a lower profile for a while.

72

NUCURE LABORATORIES, RUSSIA

The white pills were going to buy them time.

The researchers were wheeled in, one after another, in stretchers covered with clear plastic isolation tents. Yuri Kosmonolov and Thor Lundgren came through first, both smiling up through the plastic at Drew. Aniello Bonacci looked weakened but not beaten. He gave Drew a thumbs-up sign as he passed by. Drew gave him a reassuring nod as he tapped lightly on the top of the isolation tent.

They were taken to the patient rooms. The glass partitions were removed, but the technology remained. They would remain inside the NuCure facility until they had fully recovered from their illness.

One of the nurses was tearing open a cardboard box. She tore open the lid to reveal stacks of white pill bottles.

"Start the tetracycline right away," Drew said.

Drew walked down the hallway toward the meeting room in the back. The murmur in the room stopped when he entered. He spotted Dmitri immediately. The five other researchers were new faces, a collection of experts assembled from around the world.

"Thank you for your help," Drew said. "Today you will see the devastation of this new virus, this weapon that has been released. It is our job to contain this virus, and to save the lives of these victims. We will accomplish this task. You will be safe inside the building. No one," he paused, looking at Dmitri. "No one will leave until the virus has been eradicated."

He walked over to the easel and flipped a large sheet of paper over the top. A diagram of the O-168 virus was underneath.

"Dmitri Petrov knows more about this virus than anyone else alive," Drew said. "I have asked him to lead the research efforts."

Dmitri stood up sheepishly and walked up to Drew with his back to the others. "I don't know how I'll ever repay you for this," he whispered.

"Repay me by saving my friends," Drew said.

They shook hands.

"You have my word," Dmitri said.

"It's time."

Cage was a few feet behind Jonathan. His leg wound was cleaned and wrapped, but still obviously causing him pain that he would never acknowledge.

Down the hill, in the clandestine loading dock backing NuCure Laboratories, the last of the injured researchers were being wheeled inside.

"Time for what?" Jonathan asked over his shoulder into the darkness.

Cage grunted slightly as he struggled to catch up to Jonathan. "Time to tell you why you're here," he said.

Jonathan stopped short, causing Cage to bang into his back. There were so many questions to ask, questions that he'd wanted to ask since the first day Cage appeared in his office. Was he about to have the answers? Did he really want to hear the answers anymore?

"You mean I wasn't here to hunt down Ilya Lukin?" Jonathan asked.

"Oh, you were," Cage said. "In fact, you were meant to be the hero here."

Jonathan remembered the hole that he shot through the aquarium. He was just an inch or two off to the left. That's all. And if Cage hadn't been there, Lukin would have killed him a split second later. His mind was still buzzing from all the excitement. He was proud of what they accomplished as a team. But he wasn't sure if he felt like a hero.

"You saved my life," Jonathan said. "If anyone's a hero, it's you."

"That's not my role," Cage said. He took a few steps and turned around. "I don't get to be the hero. I have to stay anonymous. I don't even exist. Do you understand what I'm saying? I don't exist."

The wind blew a few dry leaves between them. Jonathan listened as they scuttled across the other leaves lying along the hill.

"You sure existed when those men were coming in through the plane," Jonathan said.

"What plane?" Cage asked.

Jonathan hesitated. "And when Lukin was about to blow my head off."

"You were the only one there," Cage said.

"But," Jonathan started. A chill crawled across his neck.

"You did it all," Cage said. "You led the international team of CDC members and local military personnel to break up one of the most dangerous biologic warfare operations in Europe, maybe in the world."

"Who's going to believe that?" Jonathan asked.

"Everyone who listens to your story," Cage said. "That's the advantage of being alive at the end. That was all you had to do. Just stay alive. Now you can tell everyone about it. The press. The

U.S. and Russian governments. Maybe even your friends back at the CDC."

"I'm not going to have a job at the CDC," Jonathan said. He pictured McIntyre chewing him out when he got home. Then he pictured McIntyre beaming in front of a bevy of reporters at an Atlanta press conference, the rolls of fat on his neck red from the sun and moist with perspiration. Jonathan would have to trade away a good chunk of his undeserved glory for the fat man's affection.

"Maybe not the same job you had," Cage said.

Cage was right again. He took a few more steps and turned around. He had crested the hill and was headed down into the darkness of the adjacent valley.

Jonathan stood still along the crest. "What if Doctor Boris comes back?" he asked.

"He won't," Cage said.

"How will we protect the laboratory?" Jonathan asked. "Everyone will want a piece of this place. Every government. Every militia group. How can we keep the researchers safe?"

"It's been arranged," Cage said. He kept walking.

"Are you leaving?" Jonathan asked.

"I was never here," Cage said over his shoulder. He faded in and out of view as he passed under the incandescent streetlights, each time slipping further into the darkness, each time seeming less real. Eventually he fused with the darkness itself.

EPILOGUE

73

RUSSIA

"It was kind of you to come here," Veronika Yurov said in slow deliberate English pronunciation. She had the soft and soothing voice of a Siren.

Drew Chambers dipped a torn off piece of homemade bread into the thick stew. He took a small bite from the corner of the bread, and then wiped his mouth with a white embroidered napkin.

"We both appreciate your visit," she continued, gesturing to the old man next to her at the faded dining room table. The old man nodded and smiled politely.

"Let your grandfather know that I appreciate his hospitality," Drew said. "I expected to stay in a hotel during my visit. You really didn't have to put me up in your home."

Veronika spoke in Russian to the old man. He listened, wrinkling his thick gray eyebrows. He dismissed what must have been the suggestion of a hotel with a wave of his hand and took a sip of vodka from a coffee mug. He was an aged version of what his son Vladimir would have become.

"Grandfather said the only hotel in town is filthy," Veronika said. "He didn't want me to repeat that to you. A friend of his owns the hotel. But it is filthy. Besides, we are happy to have you here."

"You are very kind," Drew said. He held up a spoonful of the stew. "And your cooking is wonderful."

Veronika's cheeks reddened as she fidgeted with the napkin in her lap.

"You are a dedicated friend to travel so far to deliver bad news," Veronika said.

"The bad news preceded me," Drew said. "I bring good news. Your father died in a brave effort to save his friends at the station."

"Is it true that everyone who escaped from the research station alive was cured of the virus?" Veronika asked.

"Thanks to your father," Drew said. "He helped identify the source of the illness and began working toward a cure."

"I just wish he had lived long enough to make it out of the research station," Veronika said. "Then he might still be alive today."

She didn't know. Vladimir Yurov was shot at point blank range, assassinated by a so-called scientific colleague involved in biological warfare research. He survived the virus in Siberia, but he couldn't escape the evil of NuCure. But somehow the stories that emerged from NuCure hardly resembled the truth. Would Veronika be better off knowing the truth?

"That's right," Drew said.

"He was a wonderful man," Veronika said. "His death has created a void in our lives. Grandfather has taken it the worst. He loses sleep at night and remains so quiet during the day."

"He's still grieving," Drew said.

"He has a weak heart," Veronika said. "I fear that he will carry his grief to his grave. I suppose everyone expects to lose their parents. But there is a deeper sense of loss, even a sense of guilt, when you outlive your son or daughter."

Drew gulped against the piece of bread sticking in his throat.

He nodded. "I lost my son."

Veronika looked shocked, and then disappointed, and then ashamed. "I'm so sorry."

They ate in silence for several minutes. Veronika's grandfather, the remaining Doctor Yurov, watched her for a sign of what was happening.

"It was several years ago," Drew said

More silence. Spoons clicked against bowls. An old clock on the mantle ticked.

"He must have been quite young," Veronika said.

"He was eight???" Drew said.

"It must be so difficult for you to speak about it," she said.

"I haven't," Drew said.

Matty was in the room now, not a haunting hallucination of broken bones, but a full memory – a radiant face, a resurrection of hope.

"The pain never completely goes away," Drew said. "That and the sense of loss. But you have to remember everything positive about the person's life. All the good times. And with time, the guilt sometimes fades away."

Veronika glanced up at the wall, and Drew's gaze followed. There was a recent photograph of Vladimir and his father standing in front of their office in white doctors' coats.

"You carry their memory with you," Veronika said.

Drew nodded.

The old man tapped Veronika's arm with the back of his hand, pointed at Drew, and spoke in Russian.

"No grandfather," she said.

"What does he want?" Drew asked.

"Nothing," Veronika said. "Sometimes he's just a foolish old man."

The old man pointed an arthritic and sun damaged index finger at Drew. Veronika avoided eye contact with her grandfather as she stood up and began collecting the dishes from the table. When her arms were full, she disappeared into the kitchen just a few feet away. The floorboards creaked under her steps.

The old man reached back for his wooden cane, which was leaning against the wall behind his chair. He pushed himself away from the table and used the cane to support most of his weight. He motioned with an index finger to Drew that he would be back soon, and then walked in a hunched position along the hallway leading toward the bedrooms.

Veronika returned with a plate of home-made pastries. She looked surprised at her grandfather's absence. Then she shook her head when she looked down the hall.

Drew turned around to see the old man, cane in one hand, and white linen draped over the opposite forearm. The cane tapped a shuffling and erratic beat against the floor as he approached.

Veronika positioned herself between Drew and her grandfather, trying to hold the old man back. In a sudden motion, the cane banged down against her foot, causing her to lurch away just long enough to permit him to pass. He lifted the white linen, now visible as a doctor's coat, and draped it across Drew's right shoulder. Then he patted both coat and shoulder and returned to his seat. He spoke with more authority to his granddaughter.

"Okay," Veronika said.

Drew looked at the coat and then up at the photograph of Vladimir. He smiled at the old man. "Tell him it's very kind of him to give me his son's doctor's coat."

The arthritic finger pointed at Drew again. Veronika frowned.

"The coat isn't for you to have," Veronika said.

Drew gave her a confused look.

"It's for you to use," she said.

The old man was smiling.

"He wants you to help him with his practice," Veronika said. "My father used to see most of the patients. In fact, Grandfather was about to retire when my father went to work at the research station. Grandfather's been taking care of the patients since then, but he's too old to do everything."

"He wants me to work with him," Drew said.

"I told you he's a foolish old man," Veronika said. She grasped the coat, but Drew held onto it.

"Maybe I can stay for just a little bit," Drew said. "I know how hard it can be to come out of retirement."

He reached over and shook the old man's hand.

74

EMPIRE STATE PSYCHIATRIC INSTITUTE

What a perfect day to buy a hospital.

Stella Beady, the hunched director of the chronic patient wing, led the group of nurses and their two guests through the halls of the Empire State Psychiatric Institute. “Unfortunately, some of the patients here may never make it back into society.” She placed an arthritic hand against the door, releasing a burst of sunlight from the next hallway.

Troy Gaines assisted her with the door and gestured for her and the others to proceed. He squinted from the light and looked at the chart in the rack outside the first room on the hall. The unknown patient name “John Doe” was written in bold black magic marker on the spine of the chart.

“The patients down this hall have a variety of disorders,” Mrs. Beady said. She stopped momentarily, and then closed her eyes and shook her head. “We all have to stay optimistic in our line of work. You can’t give up on anyone, you know, and sometimes the smallest sign of improvement makes all of our efforts worth it, but these individuals, well...” Her voice trailed off.

“Everyone here is so dedicated to their work,” Gaines said.

She smiled and tapped him on the shoulder. “I think I’m going to enjoy working for you.”

“How many people are down this hall?” Gaines asked.

"Just six," Mrs. Beady said. "Most of them have already been here for years. But the one in the next room got here just a month ago."

They walked up to the metal door and took turns looking through a small window into the room. There wasn't very much to see. A bed. A dresser. An empty desk. On the floor, easy to miss at first glance, was a man with unevenly cropped blonde hair, sitting with his legs tucked into his chest, staring out the window through a series of black metal bars.

"We literally found this man on our doorstep," Mrs. Beady said. "He hasn't said a word since he got here. There's a flicker of recognition in there at times, as though he's got something to say, but we really haven't made any progress."

"What's his diagnosis?" the white-haired man next to Gaines asked.

"It's post-traumatic stress disorder," she said. "It's difficult to identify what the triggering event was, but when we found him, he was bloody and infected and strung out on drugs. Although there seem to be several layers of pathology that we may never reach because we can't crack the surface.

Troy Gaines looked in through the door at Thorton Grovely. A little higher, in the pale reflection of Grovely's face in the window, he saw the eyes of his beaten enemy flash wide open with sudden horror.

"I've never seen a more beautiful view of Manhattan," Gaines said.

"Oh, isn't it?" Mrs. Beady said. "Anywhere else you'd pay top dollar for that view. But here, well, some people say we waste the best rooms on these people, but it's the ones who will never make it back outside who really deserve the best, don't you think?"

"Absolutely," Gaines said. He picked at a flaking chip of blue paint from the doorframe with a fingernail.

"This hospital has been in need of a face lift for so long now," Mrs. Beady said. "I'm so happy that you're taking such an interest in renovating it. It isn't every day that you run into someone whose heart is really in the right place, and it isn't every day that you run into someone with your financial clout, and the combination, well, it goes without saying how rare that is."

"Well thank you, Mrs. Beady," Gaines said. "That's kind of you."

"And Doctor," she hesitated. "I'm sorry I keep forgetting your last name, but we've heard so many great things about you from Mister Gaines. It sounds as though you will be an excellent addition to the staff."

"His techniques are cutting-edge," Gaines said, "But as you have already noticed, the pronunciation of his name is his biggest problem."

The white-haired man leaned forward with a smile and said, "Most people just call me Doctor Boris."

75

TAIMYR PENINSULA, SIBERIA

When dawn finally tracked down the northern tip of the Taimyr Peninsula, there was nobody there to see it.

A snowdrift covered the ruins of the mammoth research station. Particles of ice jingled in seemingly choreographed swirling plumes along the surface of the snow, reflecting the gold sunlight.

A little higher on the hill, beneath a frozen solid strip of black plastic, was the body of Stuart Crinley, which still hadn't found its resting place beneath the ground. The corpse was progressively fusing with the surroundings, still and glistening.

Deep inside, preserved within the hard outer cortex of the bones, nearly 100 million O-168 virus particles waited.

THE END

MICHAEL J. MCLAUGHLIN, MD, is a writer, entrepreneur, and former surgeon. Born in Brooklyn and raised in New Jersey, he received degrees from Harvard College and Columbia University's College of Physicians and Surgeons. His suspense novels include *The Satin Strangler Blogs* and *Woods*. His nonfiction includes the physician career change book, *Do You Feel Like You Wasted All That Training*. He lives with his family in New Jersey.

Learn more at McLaughlinBooks.com.

Also by Michael J. McLaughlin

FICTION

The Satin Strangler Blogs

Woods

NONFICTION

Do You Feel Like You Wasted All That Training?

Learn more at McLaughlinBooks.com.

Made in the USA
Middletown, DE
29 March 2024

52037249R00209